STAR TREK®

VOLUME 12

Story Consultant:

ROBERTO ORCI

Cover by

TONY SHASTEEN

Collection Edits by

JUSTIN EISINGER and ALONZO SIMON

Collection Design by

CLAUDIA CHONG

Publisher

TED ADAMS

Star Trek created by Gene Roddenberry.
Special thanks to Risa Kessler and John Van Citters of CBS Consumer Products for their invaluable assistance.

For international rights, contact licensing@idwpublishing.com

ISBN: 978-1-63140-664-5

19 18 17 16   1 2 3 4

Ted Adams, CEO & Publisher
Greg Goldstein, President & COO
Robbie Robbins, EVP/Sr. Graphic Artist
Chris Ryall, Chief Creative Officer/Editor-in-Chief
Matthew Ruzicka, CPA, Chief Financial Officer
Dirk Wood, VP of Marketing
Lorelei Bunjes, VP of Digital Services
Jeff Webber, VP of Licensing, Digital and Subsidiary Rights
Jerry Bennington, VP of New Product Development

www.IDWPUBLISHING.com

Facebook: **facebook.com/idwpublishing**
Twitter: **@idwpublishing**
YouTube: **youtube.com/idwpublishing**
Tumblr: **tumblr.idwpublishing.com**
Instagram: **instagram.com/idwpublishing**

STAR TREK®

VOLUME 12

Written by
MIKE JOHNSON

Art by
TONY SHASTEEN

Colors by
DAVIDE MASTROLONARDO

Letters by
NEIL UYETAKE and CHRIS MOWRY

Series Edits by
SARAH GAYDOS

LIVE EVIL

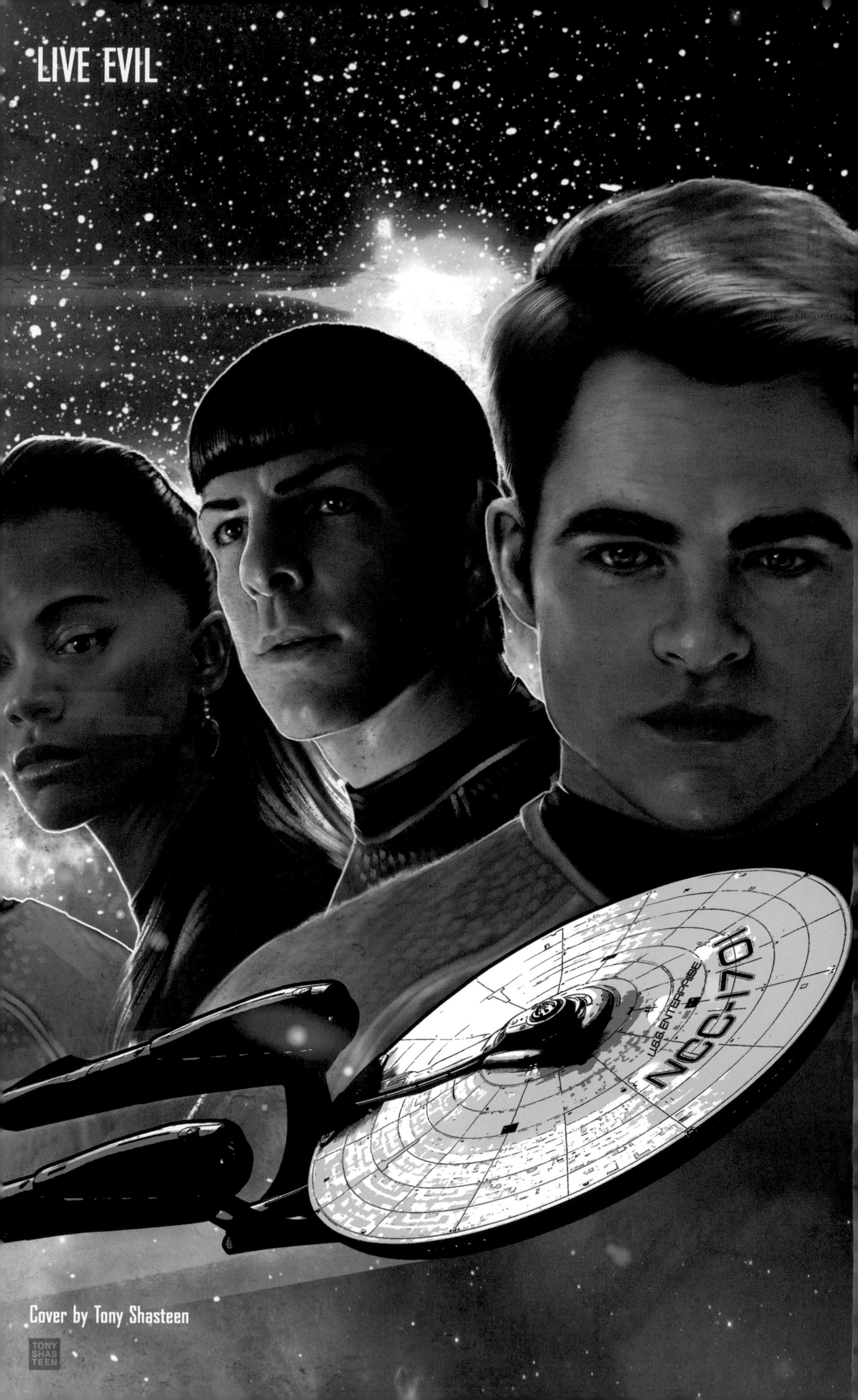
U.S.S. ENTERPRISE
NCC-1701
TONY
SHAS
TEEN

Cover by Tony Shasteen

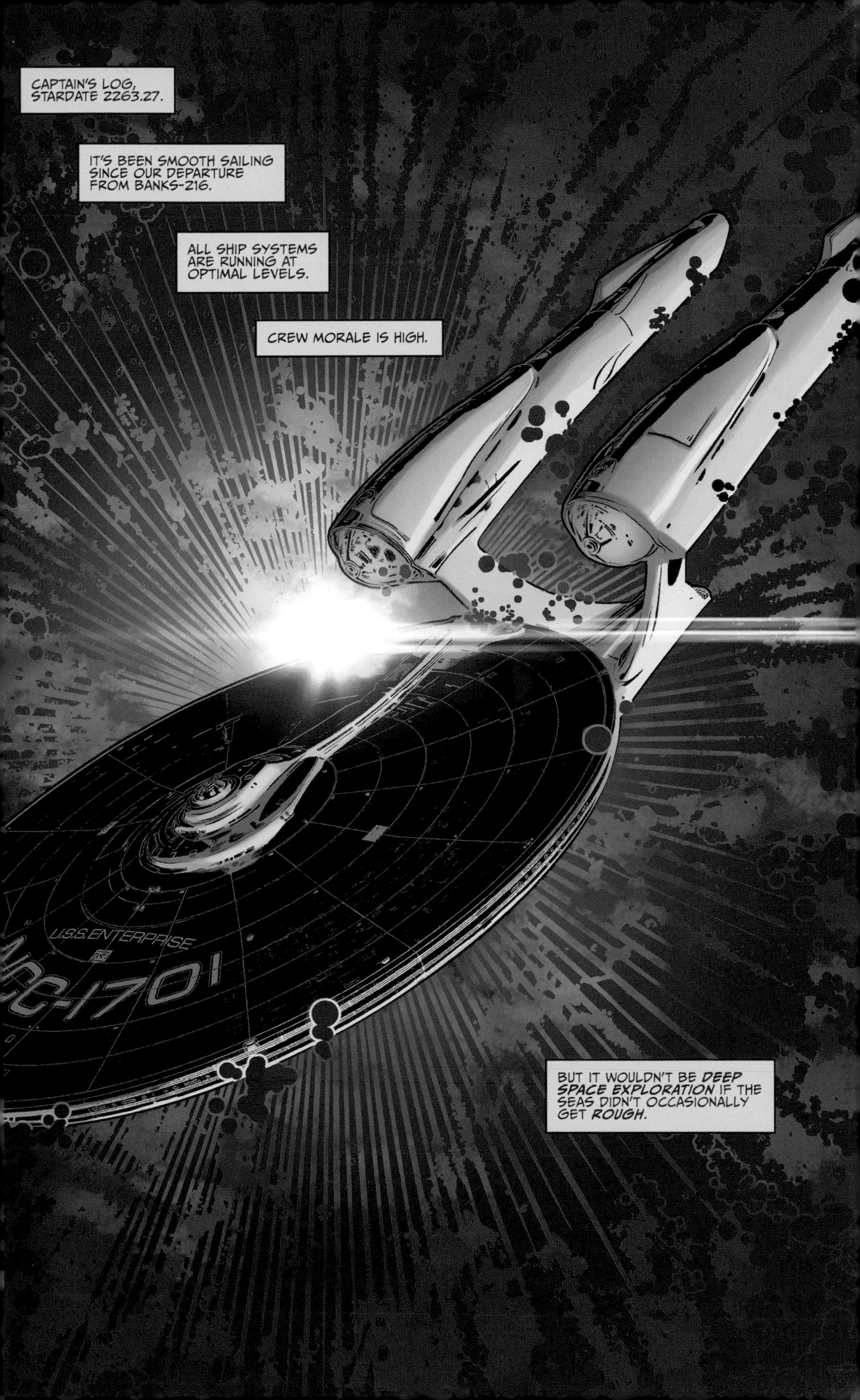
CAPTAIN'S LOG, STARDATE 2263.27.
IT'S BEEN SMOOTH SAILING SINCE OUR DEPARTURE FROM BANKS-216.
ALL SHIP SYSTEMS ARE RUNNING AT OPTIMAL LEVELS.
CREW MORALE IS HIGH.
U.S.S. ENTERPRISE
CC-1701
BUT IT WOULDN'T BE *DEEP SPACE EXPLORATION* IF THE SEAS DIDN'T OCCASIONALLY GET *ROUGH*.

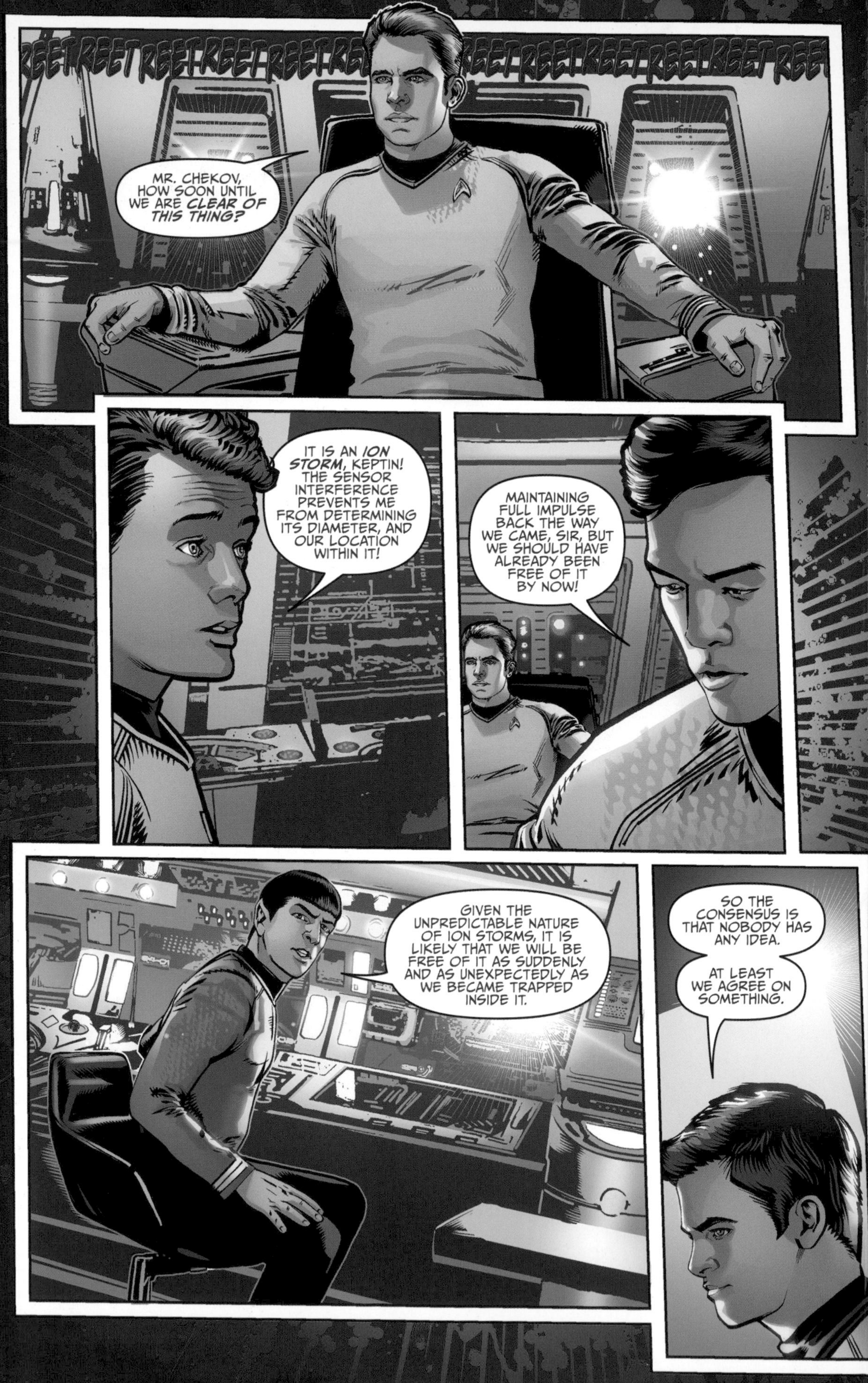
REET REET REET REET REET REET REET REET REET REET REET
MR. CHEKOV, HOW SOON UNTIL WE ARE *CLEAR OF THIS THING?*
IT IS AN *ION STORM*, KEPTIN! THE SENSOR INTERFERENCE PREVENTS ME FROM DETERMINING ITS DIAMETER, AND OUR LOCATION WITHIN IT!
MAINTAINING FULL IMPULSE BACK THE WAY WE CAME, SIR, BUT WE SHOULD HAVE ALREADY BEEN FREE OF IT BY NOW!
GIVEN THE UNPREDICTABLE NATURE OF ION STORMS, IT IS LIKELY THAT WE WILL BE FREE OF IT AS SUDDENLY AND AS UNEXPECTEDLY AS WE BECAME TRAPPED INSIDE IT.
SO THE CONSENSUS IS THAT NOBODY HAS ANY IDEA.
AT LEAST WE AGREE ON SOMETHING.

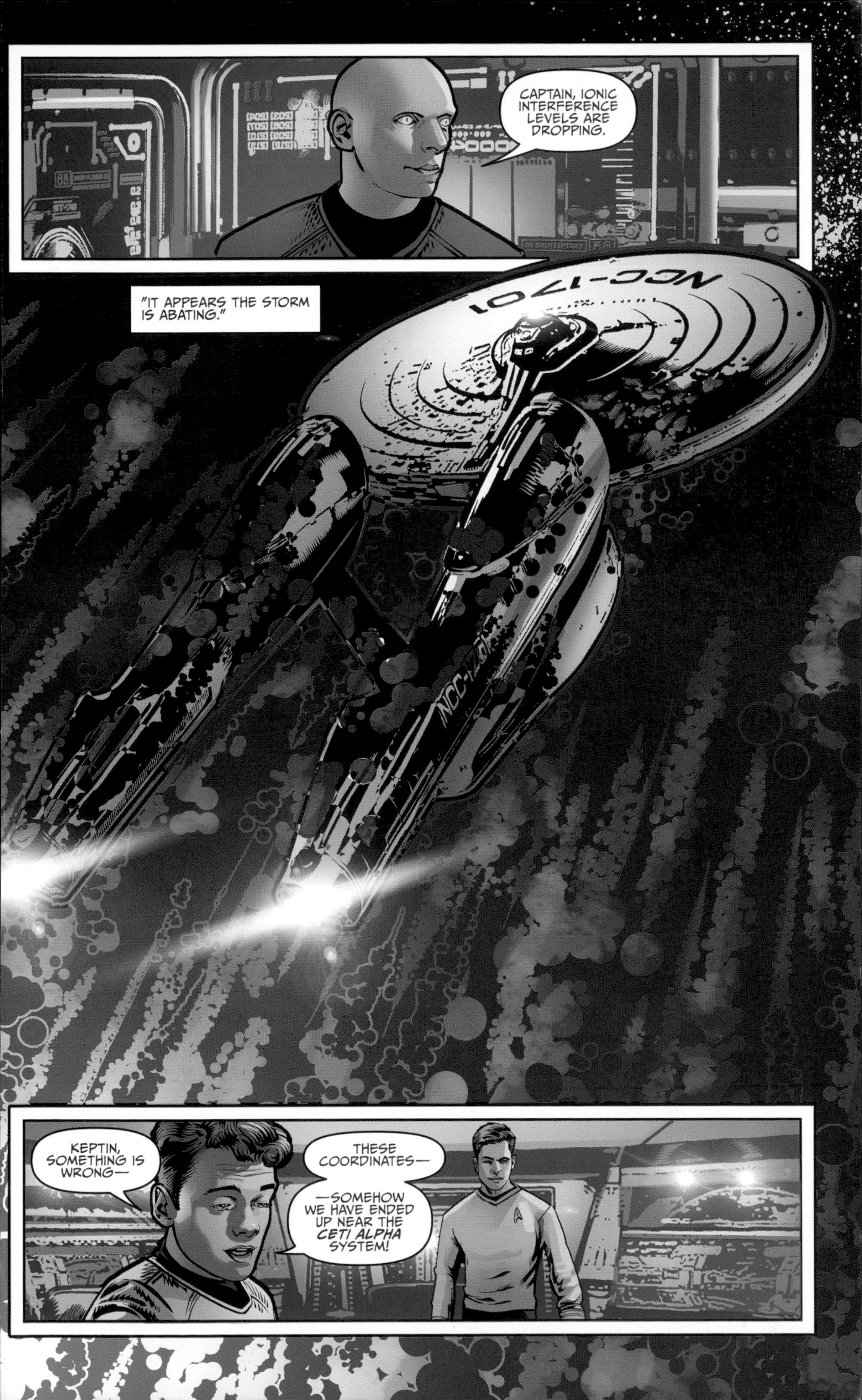

CAPTAIN, IONIC INTERFERENCE LEVELS ARE DROPPING.
"IT APPEARS THE STORM IS ABATING."
NCC-1701
KEPTIN, SOMETHING IS WRONG—
THESE COORDINATES—
—SOMEHOW WE HAVE ENDED UP NEAR THE CETI ALPHA SYSTEM!

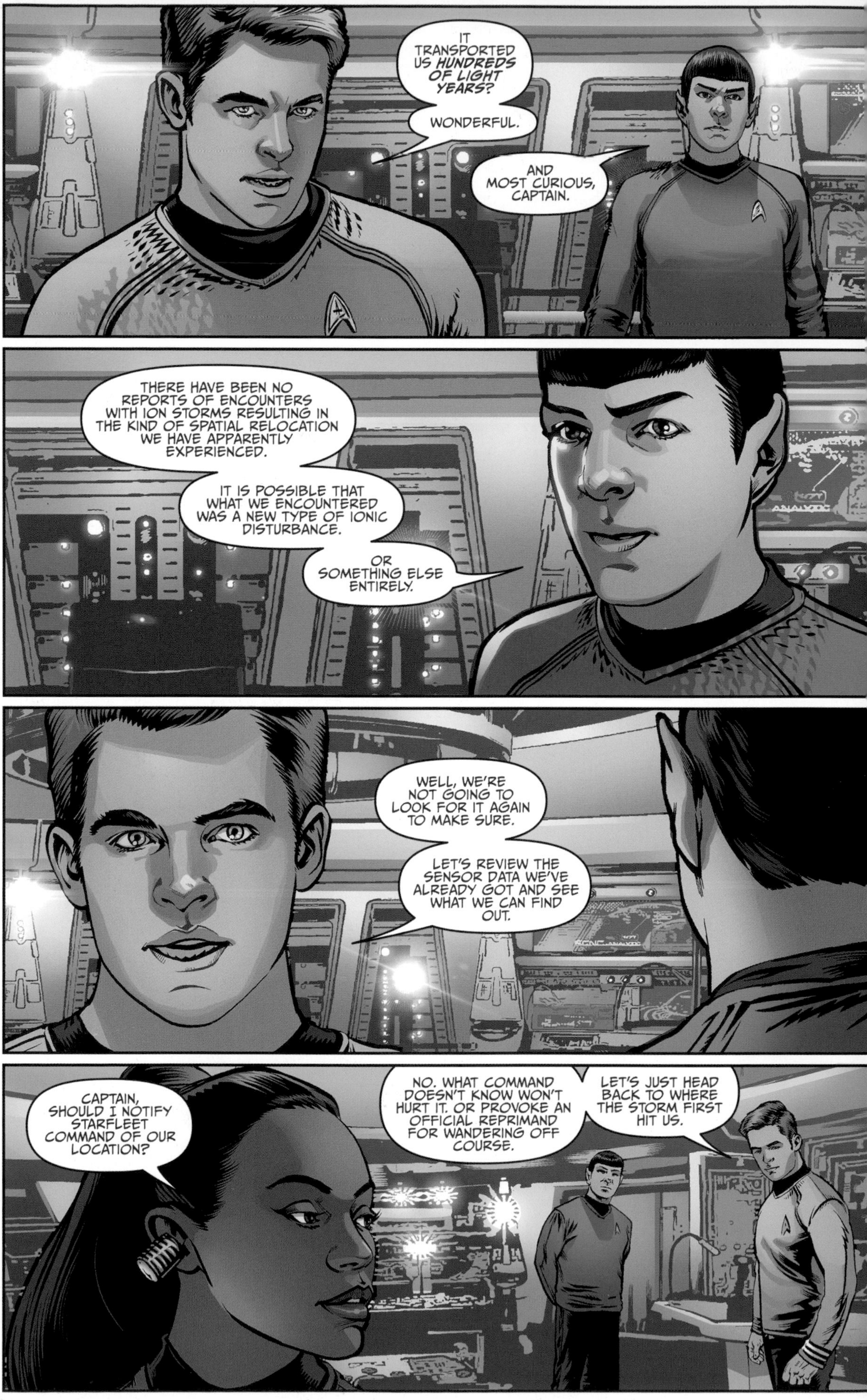
IT TRANSPORTED US HUNDREDS OF LIGHT YEARS?
WONDERFUL.
AND MOST CURIOUS, CAPTAIN.
THERE HAVE BEEN NO REPORTS OF ENCOUNTERS WITH ION STORMS RESULTING IN THE KIND OF SPATIAL RELOCATION WE HAVE APPARENTLY EXPERIENCED.
IT IS POSSIBLE THAT WHAT WE ENCOUNTERED WAS A NEW TYPE OF IONIC DISTURBANCE.
OR SOMETHING ELSE ENTIRELY.
WELL, WE'RE NOT GOING TO LOOK FOR IT AGAIN TO MAKE SURE.
LET'S REVIEW THE SENSOR DATA WE'VE ALREADY GOT AND SEE WHAT WE CAN FIND OUT.
CAPTAIN, SHOULD I NOTIFY STARFLEET COMMAND OF OUR LOCATION?
NO. WHAT COMMAND DOESN'T KNOW WON'T HURT IT. OR PROVOKE AN OFFICIAL REPRIMAND FOR WANDERING OFF COURSE.
LET'S JUST HEAD BACK TO WHERE THE STORM FIRST HIT US.

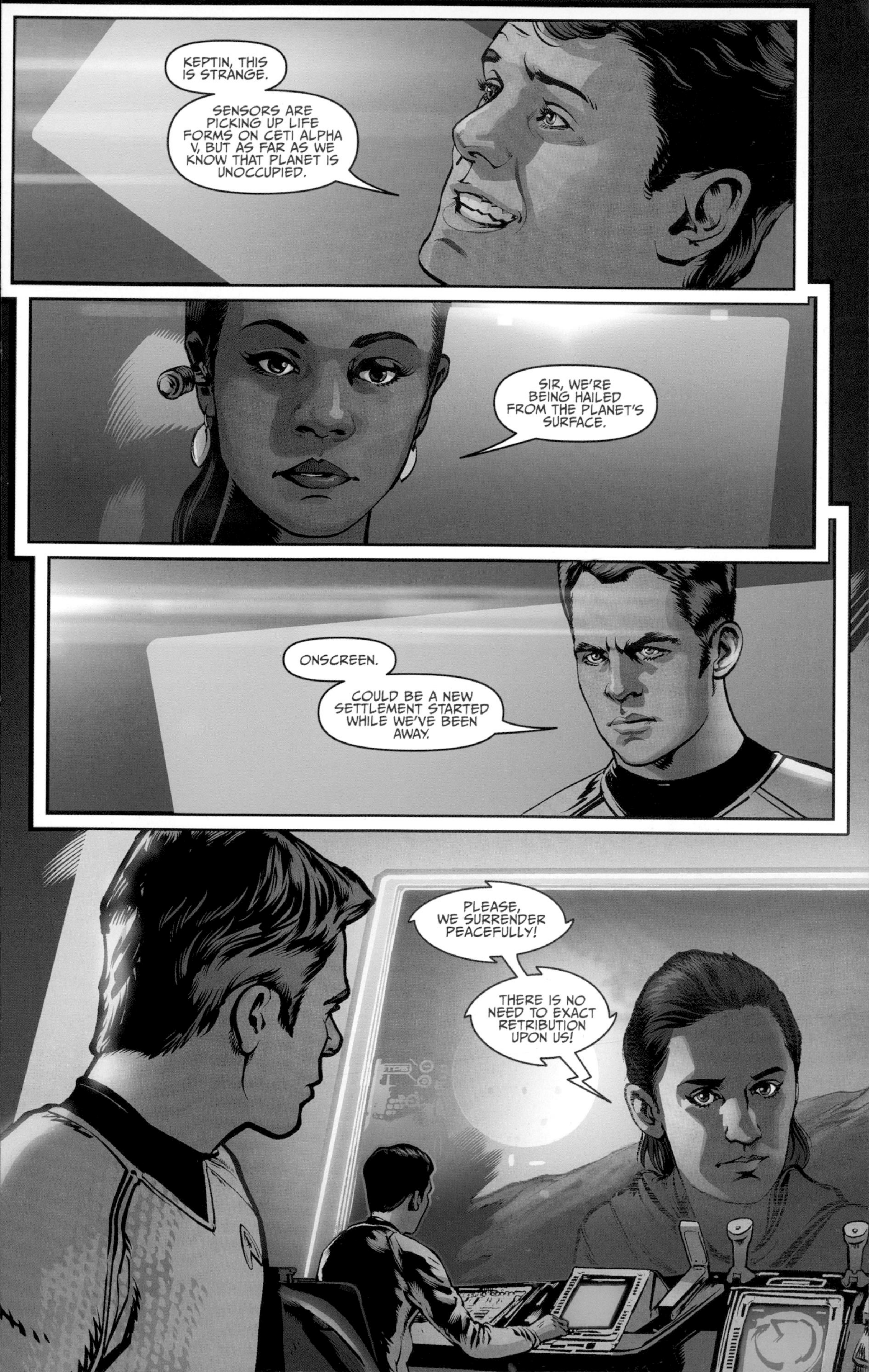
KEPTIN, THIS IS STRANGE.
SENSORS ARE PICKING UP LIFE FORMS ON CETI ALPHA V, BUT AS FAR AS WE KNOW THAT PLANET IS UNOCCUPIED.
SIR, WE'RE BEING HAILED FROM THE PLANET'S SURFACE.
ONSCREEN.
COULD BE A NEW SETTLEMENT STARTED WHILE WE'VE BEEN AWAY.
PLEASE, WE SURRENDER PEACEFULLY!
THERE IS NO NEED TO EXACT RETRIBUTION UPON US!

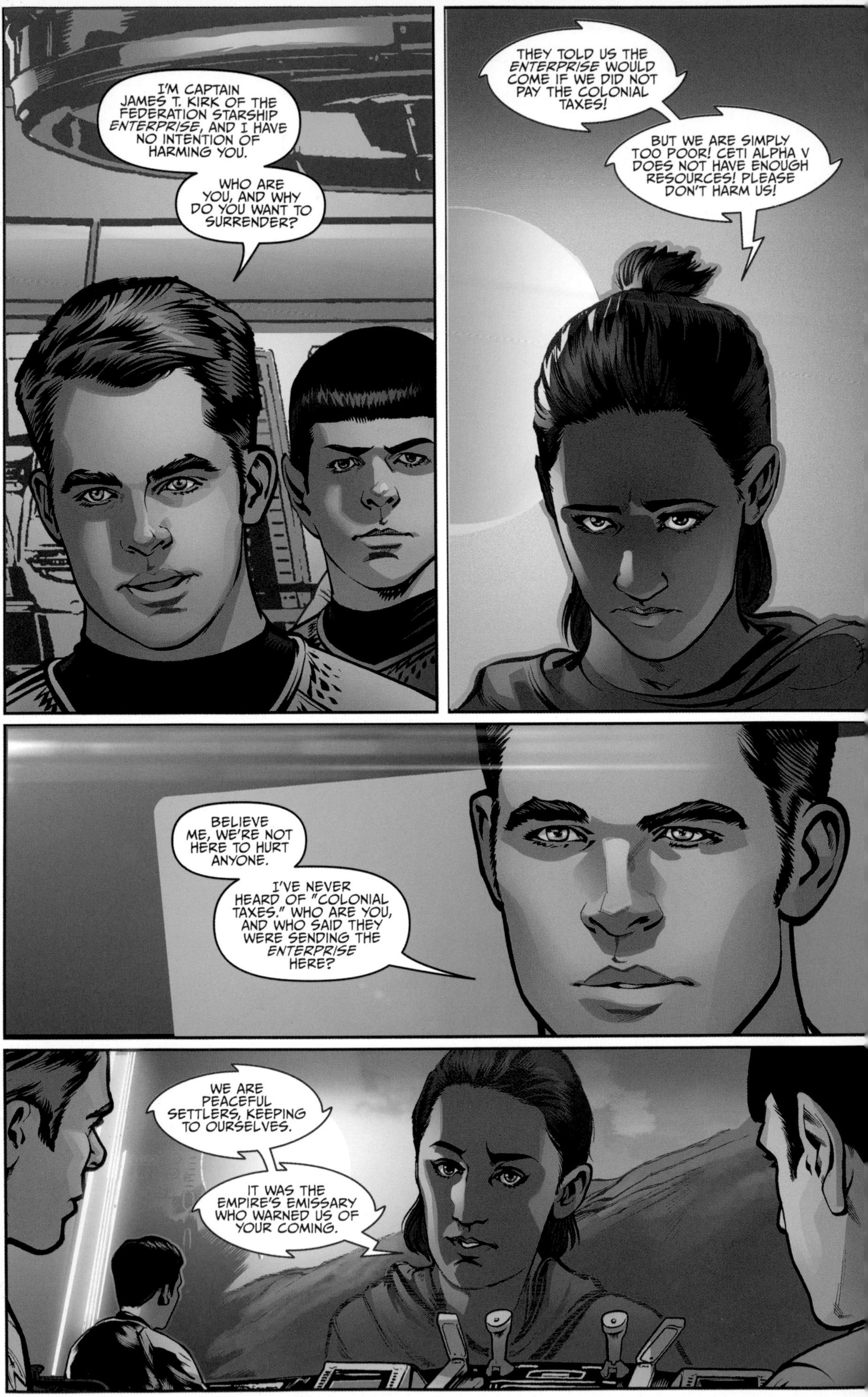
I'M CAPTAIN JAMES T. KIRK OF THE FEDERATION STARSHIP *ENTERPRISE*, AND I HAVE NO INTENTION OF HARMING YOU.
WHO ARE YOU, AND WHY DO YOU WANT TO SURRENDER?
THEY TOLD US THE *ENTERPRISE* WOULD COME IF WE DID NOT PAY THE COLONIAL TAXES!
BUT WE ARE SIMPLY TOO POOR! CETI ALPHA V DOES NOT HAVE ENOUGH RESOURCES! PLEASE DON'T HARM US!
BELIEVE ME, WE'RE NOT HERE TO HURT ANYONE.
I'VE NEVER HEARD OF "COLONIAL TAXES." WHO ARE YOU, AND WHO SAID THEY WERE SENDING THE *ENTERPRISE* HERE?
WE ARE PEACEFUL SETTLERS, KEEPING TO OURSELVES.
IT WAS THE EMPIRE'S EMISSARY WHO WARNED US OF YOUR COMING.

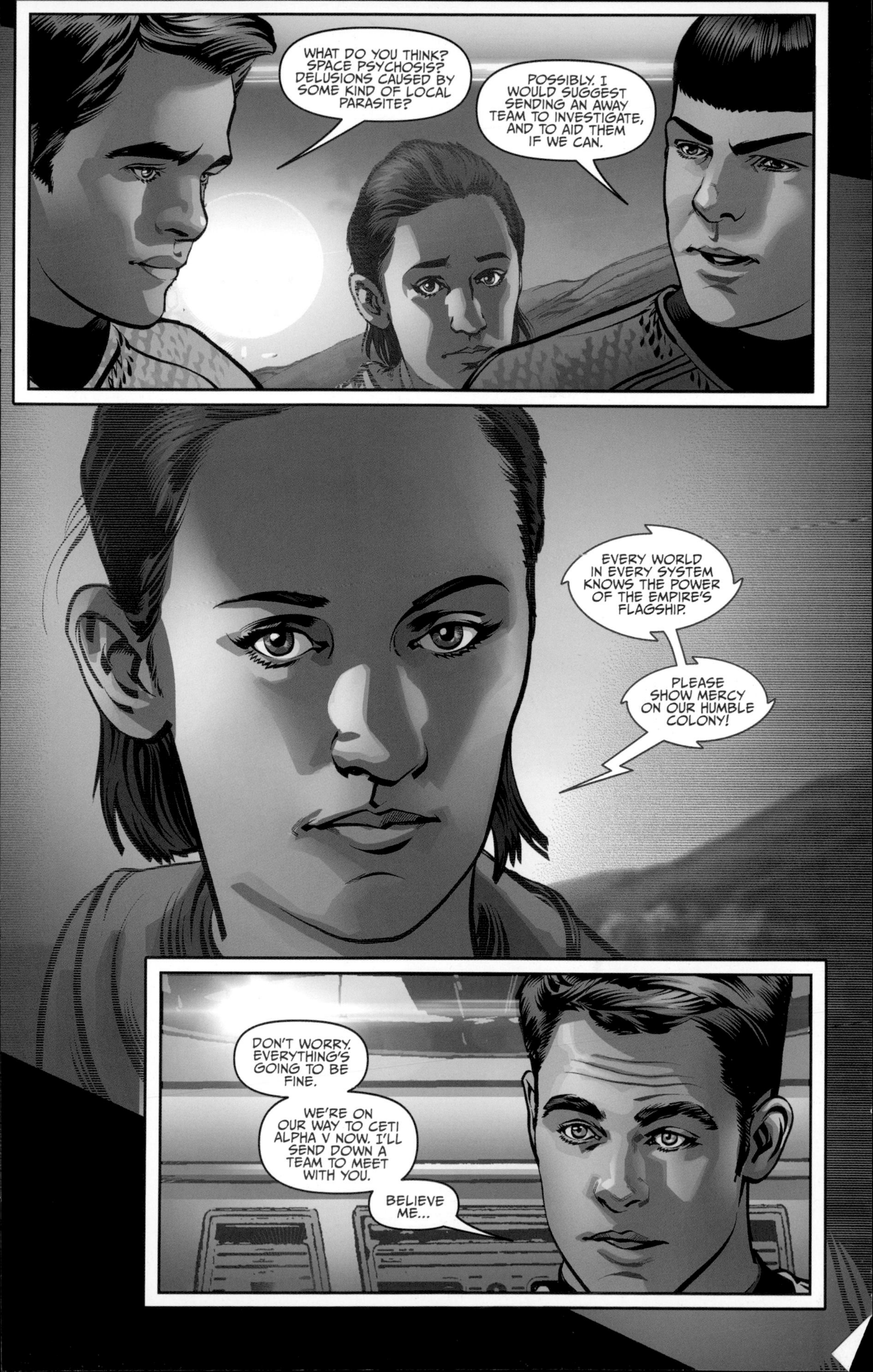
WHAT DO YOU THINK? SPACE PSYCHOSIS? DELUSIONS CAUSED BY SOME KIND OF LOCAL PARASITE?
POSSIBLY. I WOULD SUGGEST SENDING AN AWAY TEAM TO INVESTIGATE, AND TO AID THEM IF WE CAN.
EVERY WORLD IN EVERY SYSTEM KNOWS THE POWER OF THE EMPIRE'S FLAGSHIP.
PLEASE SHOW MERCY ON OUR HUMBLE COLONY!
DON'T WORRY. EVERYTHING'S GOING TO BE FINE.
WE'RE ON OUR WAY TO CETI ALPHA V NOW. I'LL SEND DOWN A TEAM TO MEET WITH YOU.
BELIEVE ME...

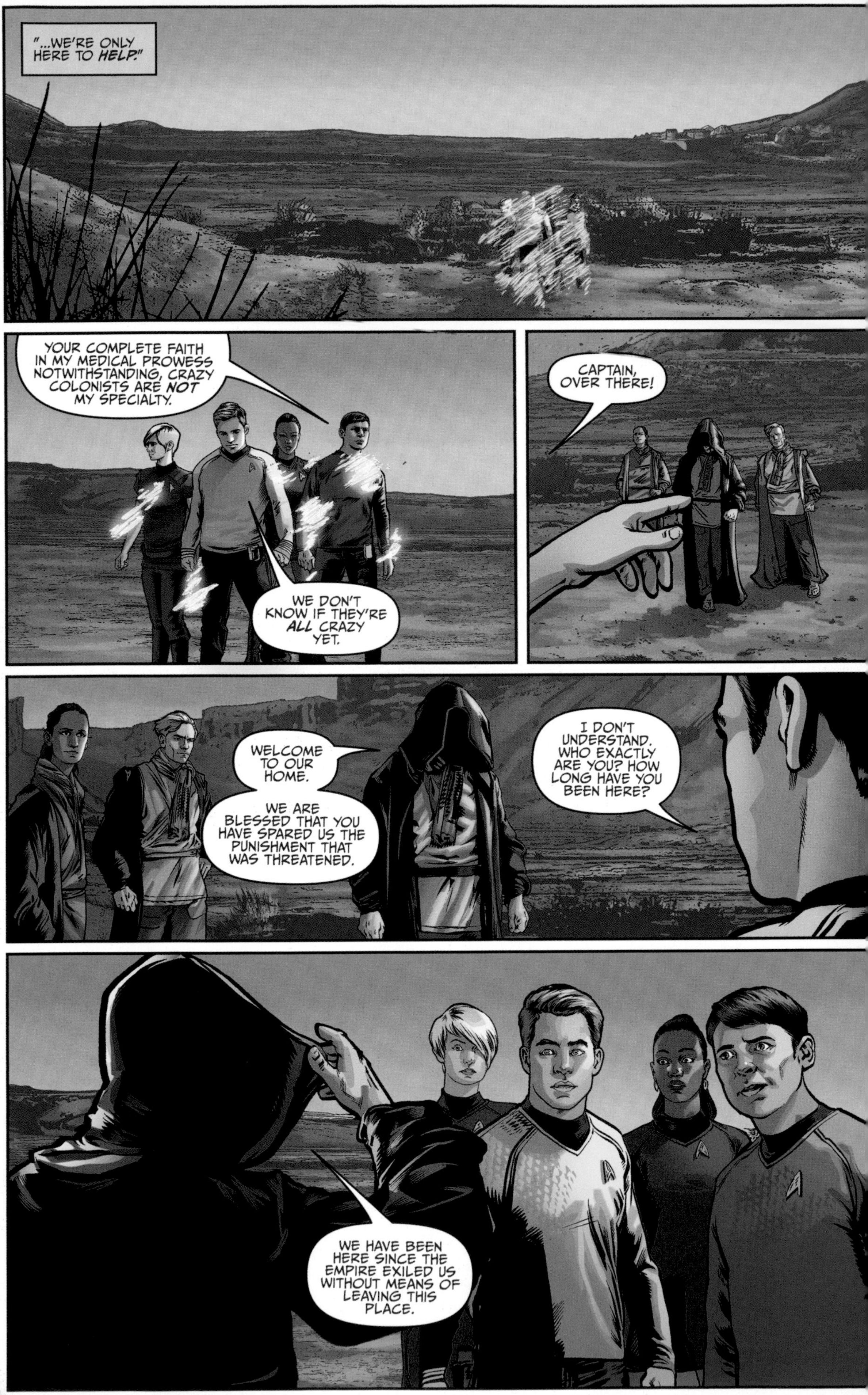
"...WE'RE ONLY HERE TO *HELP*."
YOUR COMPLETE FAITH IN MY MEDICAL PROWESS NOTWITHSTANDING, CRAZY COLONISTS ARE *NOT* MY SPECIALTY.
WE DON'T KNOW IF THEY'RE *ALL* CRAZY YET.
CAPTAIN, OVER THERE!
WELCOME TO OUR HOME.
WE ARE BLESSED THAT YOU HAVE SPARED US THE PUNISHMENT THAT WAS THREATENED.
I DON'T UNDERSTAND. WHO EXACTLY ARE YOU? HOW LONG HAVE YOU BEEN HERE?
WE HAVE BEEN HERE SINCE THE EMPIRE EXILED US WITHOUT MEANS OF LEAVING THIS PLACE.

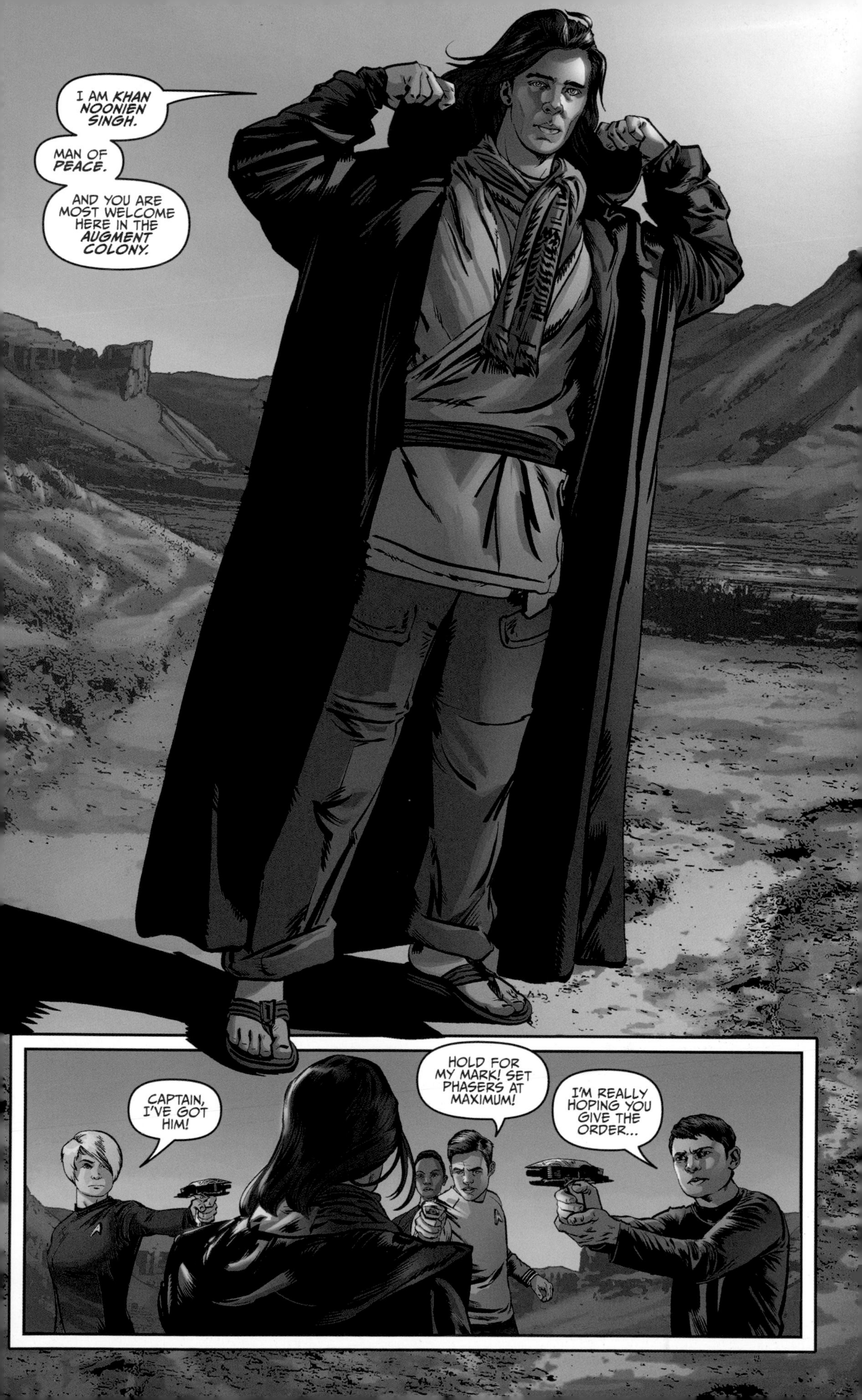
I AM KHAN NOONIEN SINGH.
MAN OF PEACE.
AND YOU ARE MOST WELCOME HERE IN THE AUGMENT COLONY.
CAPTAIN, I'VE GOT HIM!
HOLD FOR MY MARK! SET PHASERS AT MAXIMUM!
I'M REALLY HOPING YOU GIVE THE ORDER...

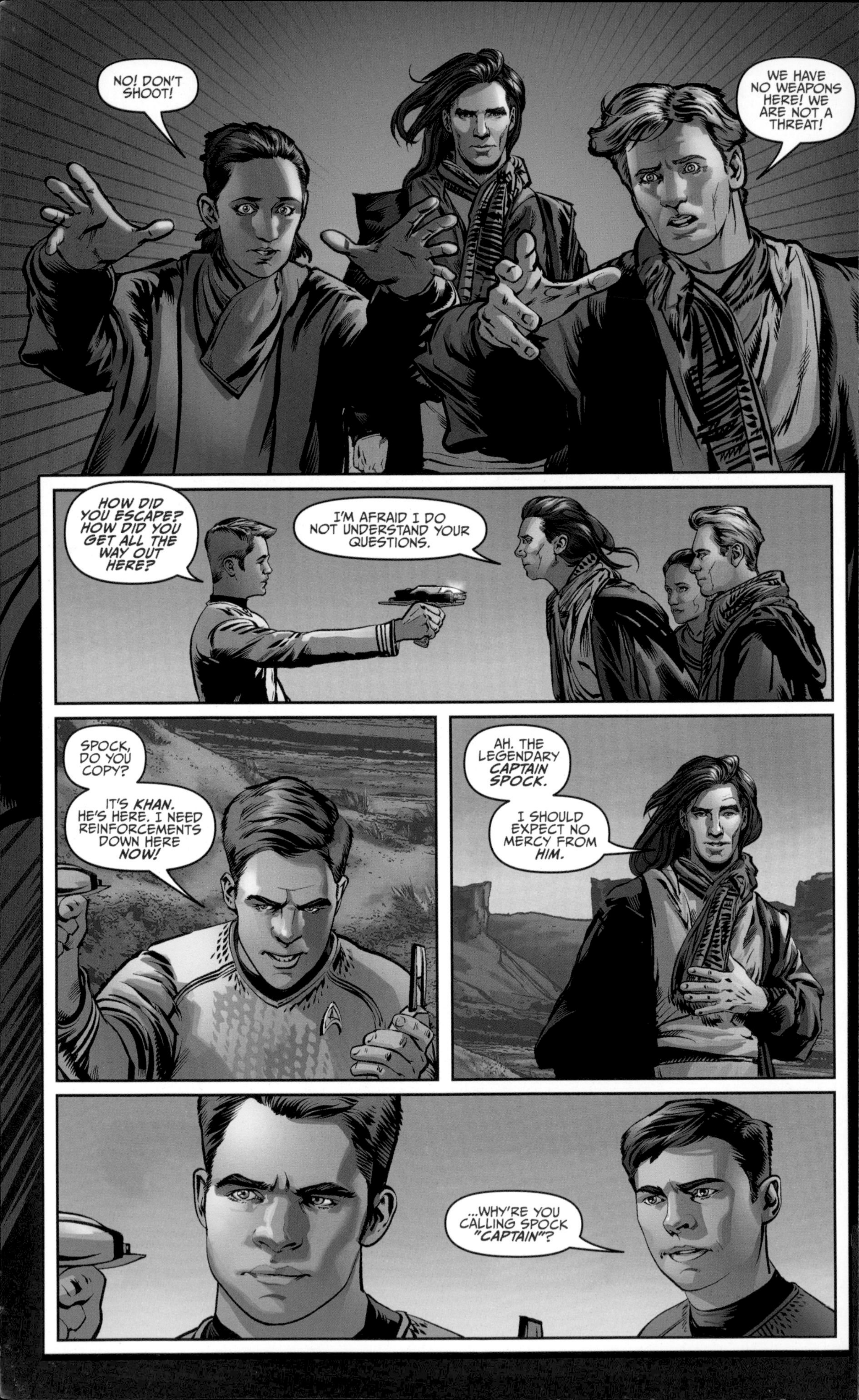
NO! DON'T SHOOT!
WE HAVE NO WEAPONS HERE! WE ARE NOT A THREAT!
HOW DID YOU ESCAPE? HOW DID YOU GET ALL THE WAY OUT HERE?
I'M AFRAID I DO NOT UNDERSTAND YOUR QUESTIONS.
SPOCK, DO YOU COPY?
IT'S KHAN. HE'S HERE. I NEED REINFORCEMENTS DOWN HERE NOW!
AH. THE LEGENDARY CAPTAIN SPOCK.
I SHOULD EXPECT NO MERCY FROM HIM.
...WHY'RE YOU CALLING SPOCK "CAPTAIN"?

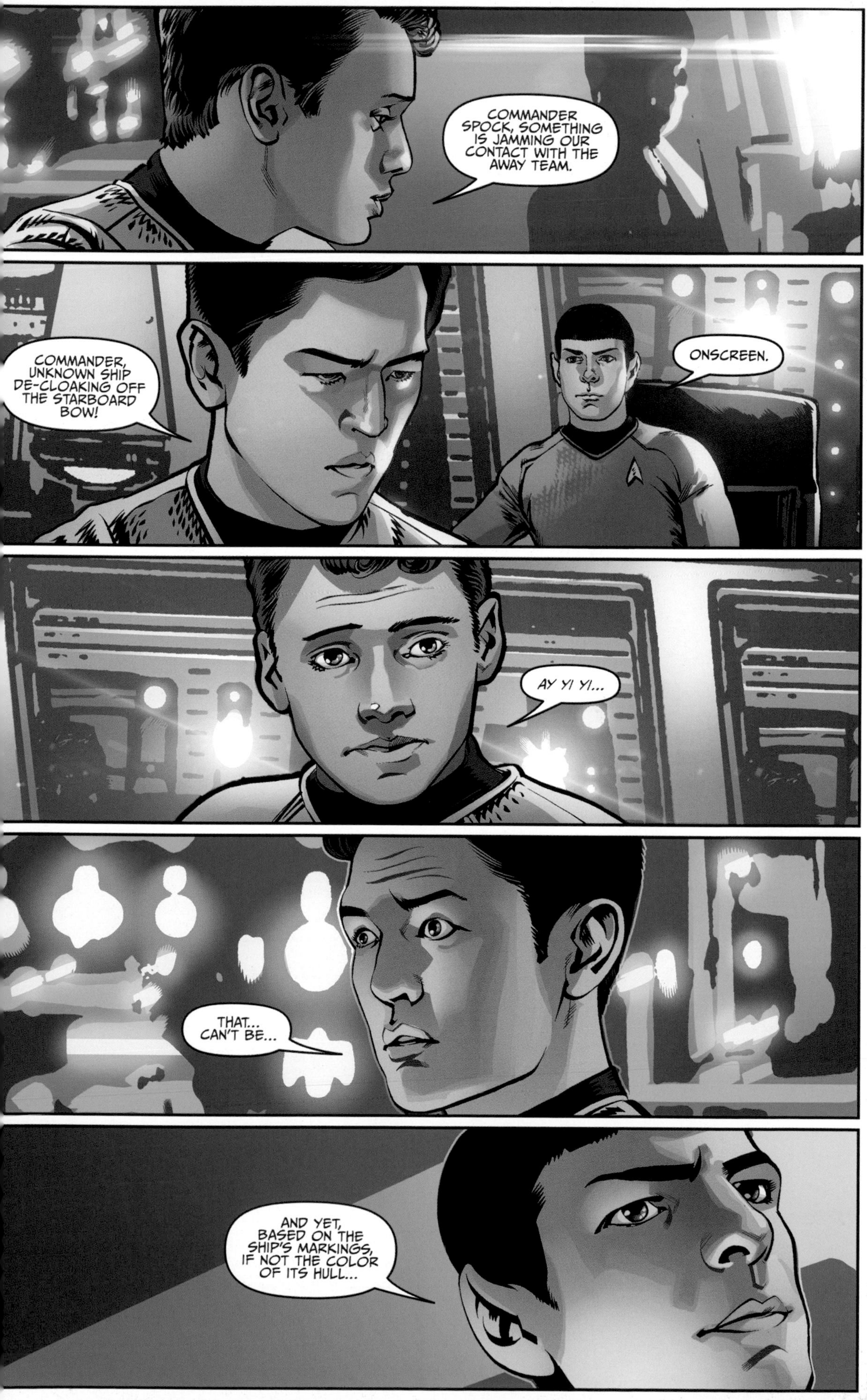
COMMANDER SPOCK, SOMETHING IS JAMMING OUR CONTACT WITH THE AWAY TEAM.
COMMANDER, UNKNOWN SHIP DE-CLOAKING OFF THE STARBOARD BOW!
ONSCREEN.
AY YI YI...
THAT... CAN'T BE...
AND YET, BASED ON THE SHIP'S MARKINGS, IF NOT THE COLOR OF ITS HULL...

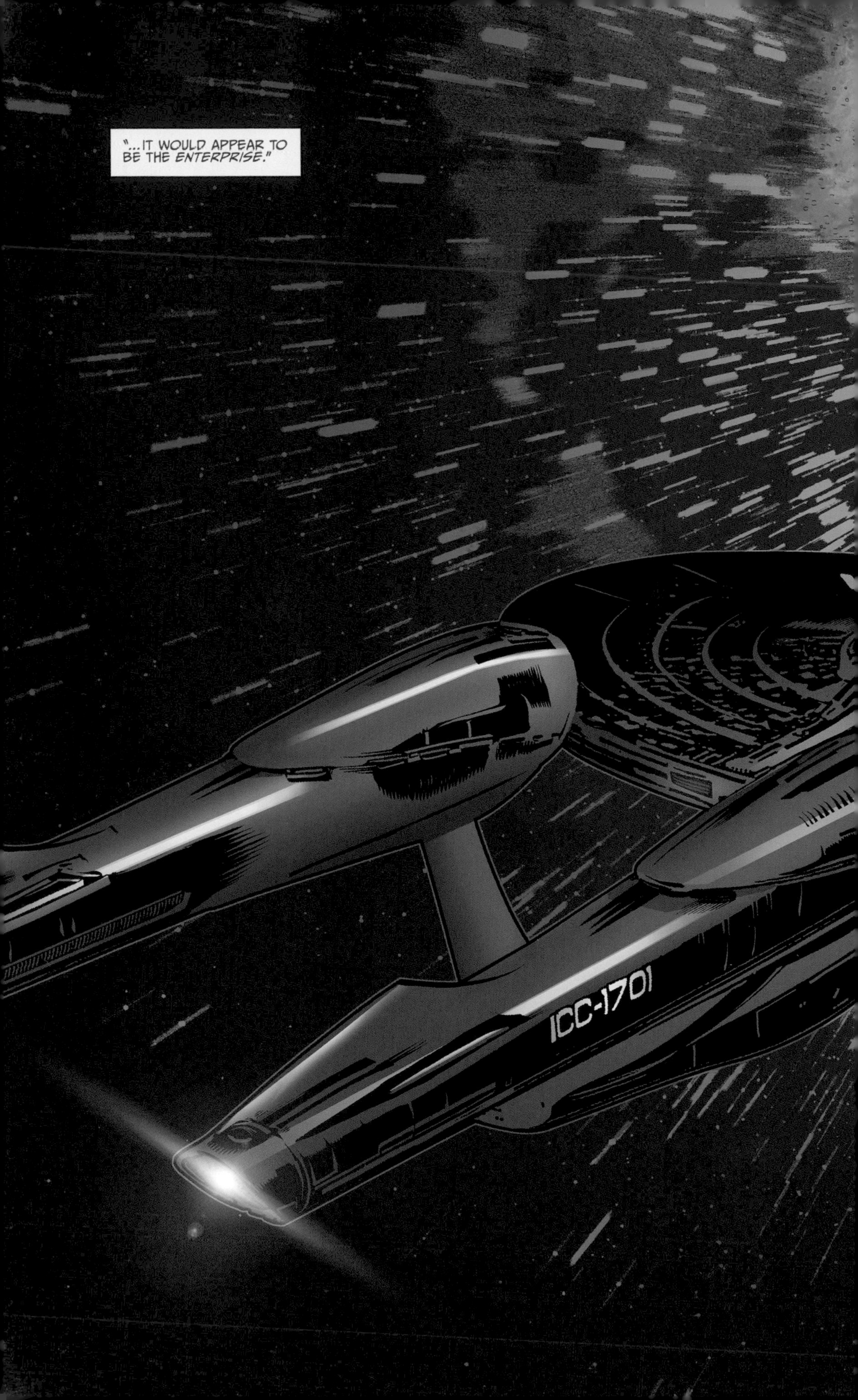
"...IT WOULD APPEAR TO BE THE ENTERPRISE."
ICC-1701

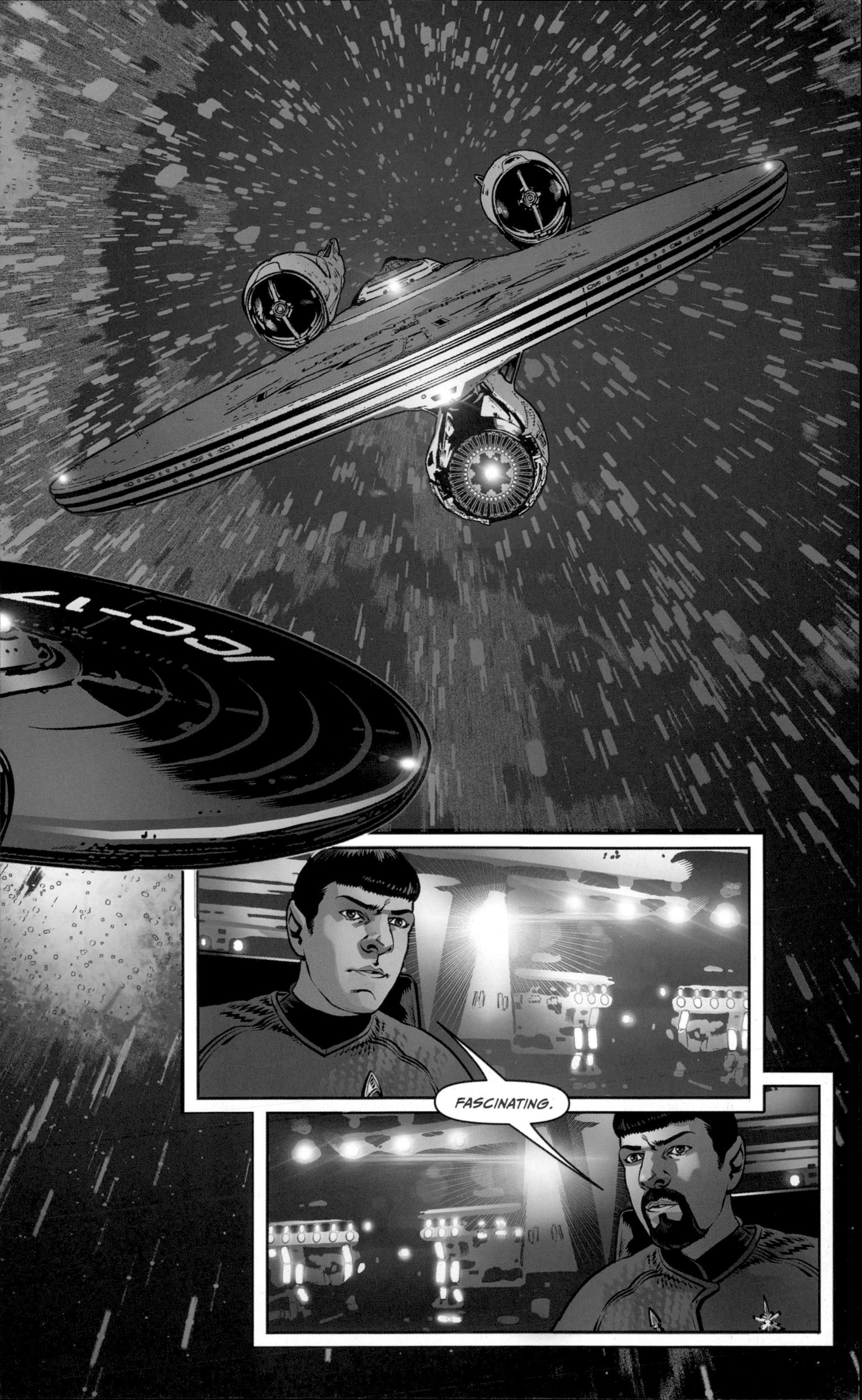
FASCINATING.

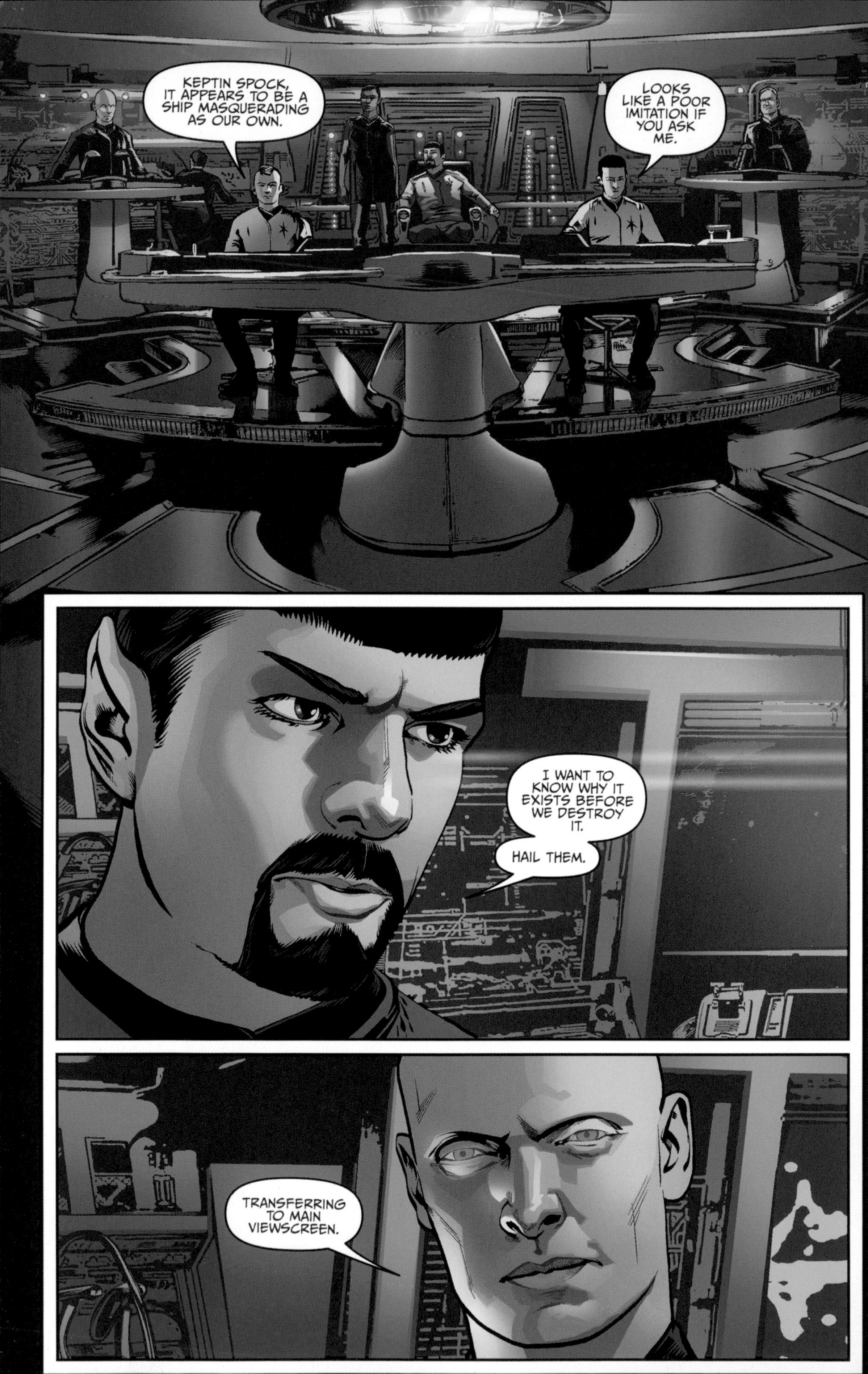
KEPTIN SPOCK, IT APPEARS TO BE A SHIP MASQUERADING AS OUR OWN.
LOOKS LIKE A POOR IMITATION IF YOU ASK ME.
I WANT TO KNOW WHY IT EXISTS BEFORE WE DESTROY IT.
HAIL THEM.
TRANSFERRING TO MAIN VIEWSCREEN.

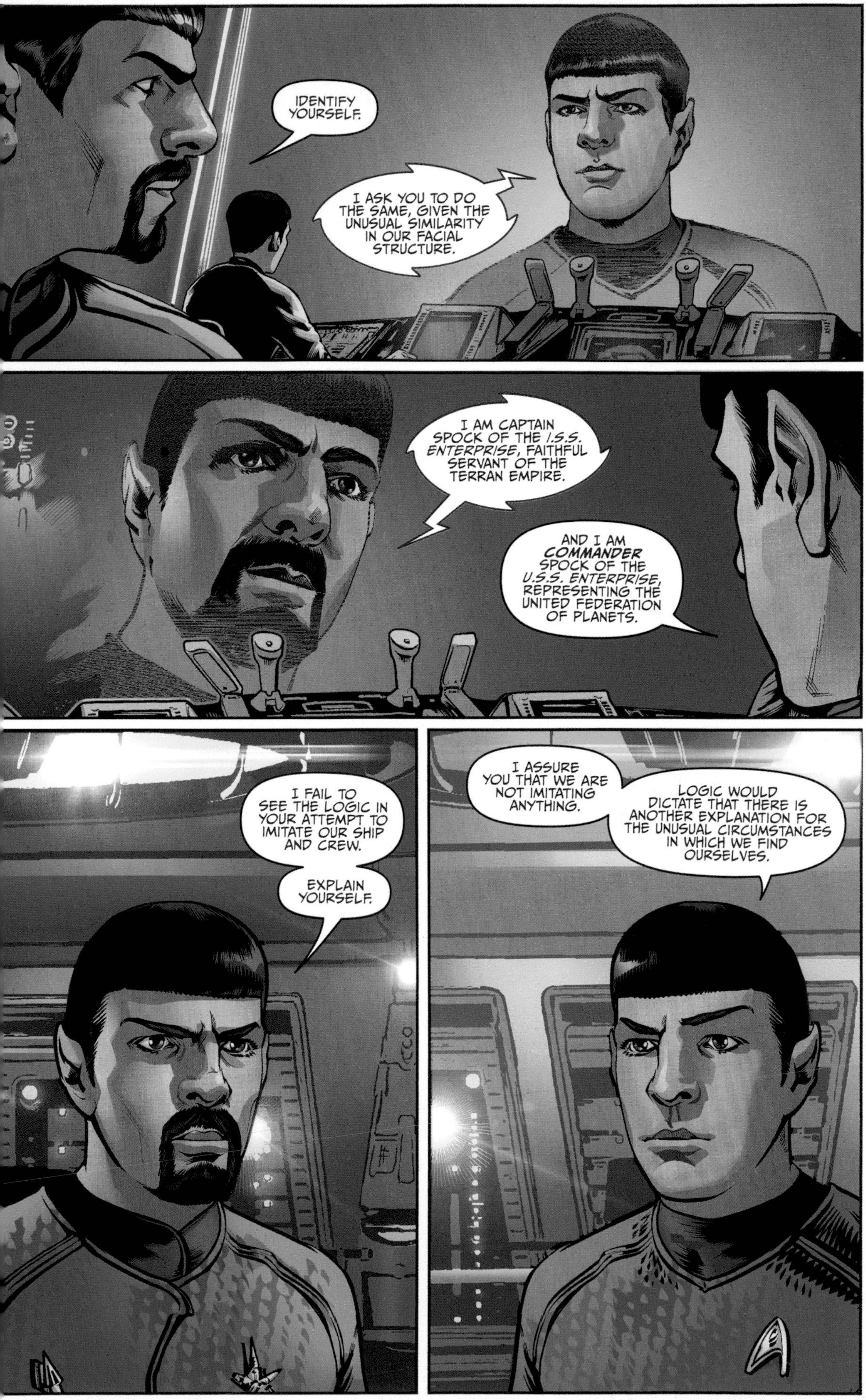
IDENTIFY YOURSELF.
I ASK YOU TO DO THE SAME, GIVEN THE UNUSUAL SIMILARITY IN OUR FACIAL STRUCTURE.
I AM CAPTAIN SPOCK OF THE *I.S.S. ENTERPRISE*, FAITHFUL SERVANT OF THE TERRAN EMPIRE.
AND I AM ***COMMANDER*** SPOCK OF THE *U.S.S. ENTERPRISE*, REPRESENTING THE UNITED FEDERATION OF PLANETS.
I FAIL TO SEE THE LOGIC IN YOUR ATTEMPT TO IMITATE OUR SHIP AND CREW.
EXPLAIN YOURSELF.
I ASSURE YOU THAT WE ARE NOT IMITATING ANYTHING.
LOGIC WOULD DICTATE THAT THERE IS ANOTHER EXPLANATION FOR THE UNUSUAL CIRCUMSTANCES IN WHICH WE FIND OURSELVES.

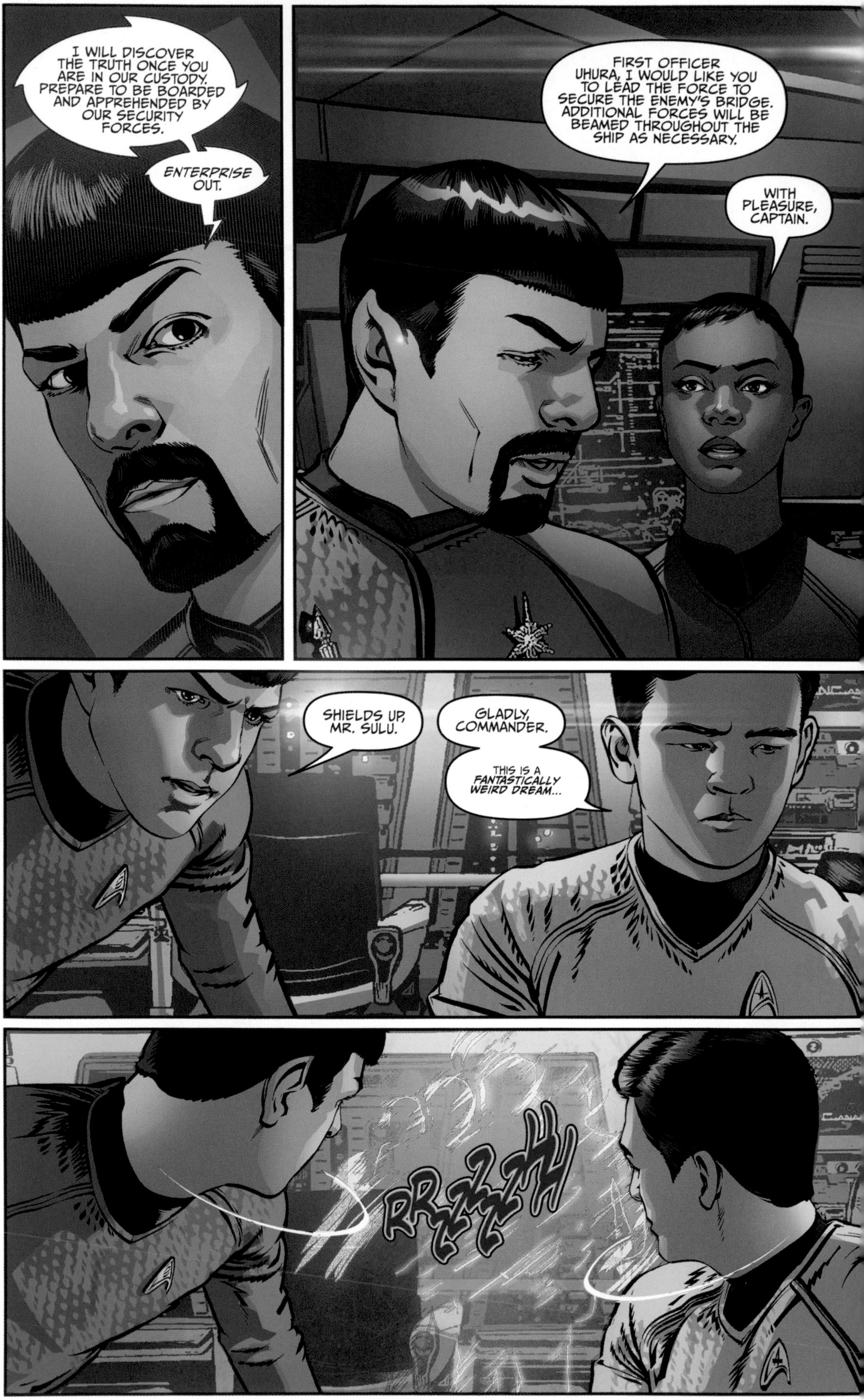
I WILL DISCOVER THE TRUTH ONCE YOU ARE IN OUR CUSTODY. PREPARE TO BE BOARDED AND APPREHENDED BY OUR SECURITY FORCES.
ENTERPRISE OUT.
FIRST OFFICER UHURA, I WOULD LIKE YOU TO LEAD THE FORCE TO SECURE THE ENEMY'S BRIDGE. ADDITIONAL FORCES WILL BE BEAMED THROUGHOUT THE SHIP AS NECESSARY.
WITH PLEASURE, CAPTAIN.
SHIELDS UP, MR. SULU.
GLADLY, COMMANDER.
THIS IS A FANTASTICALLY WEIRD DREAM...
RRZZZZHH

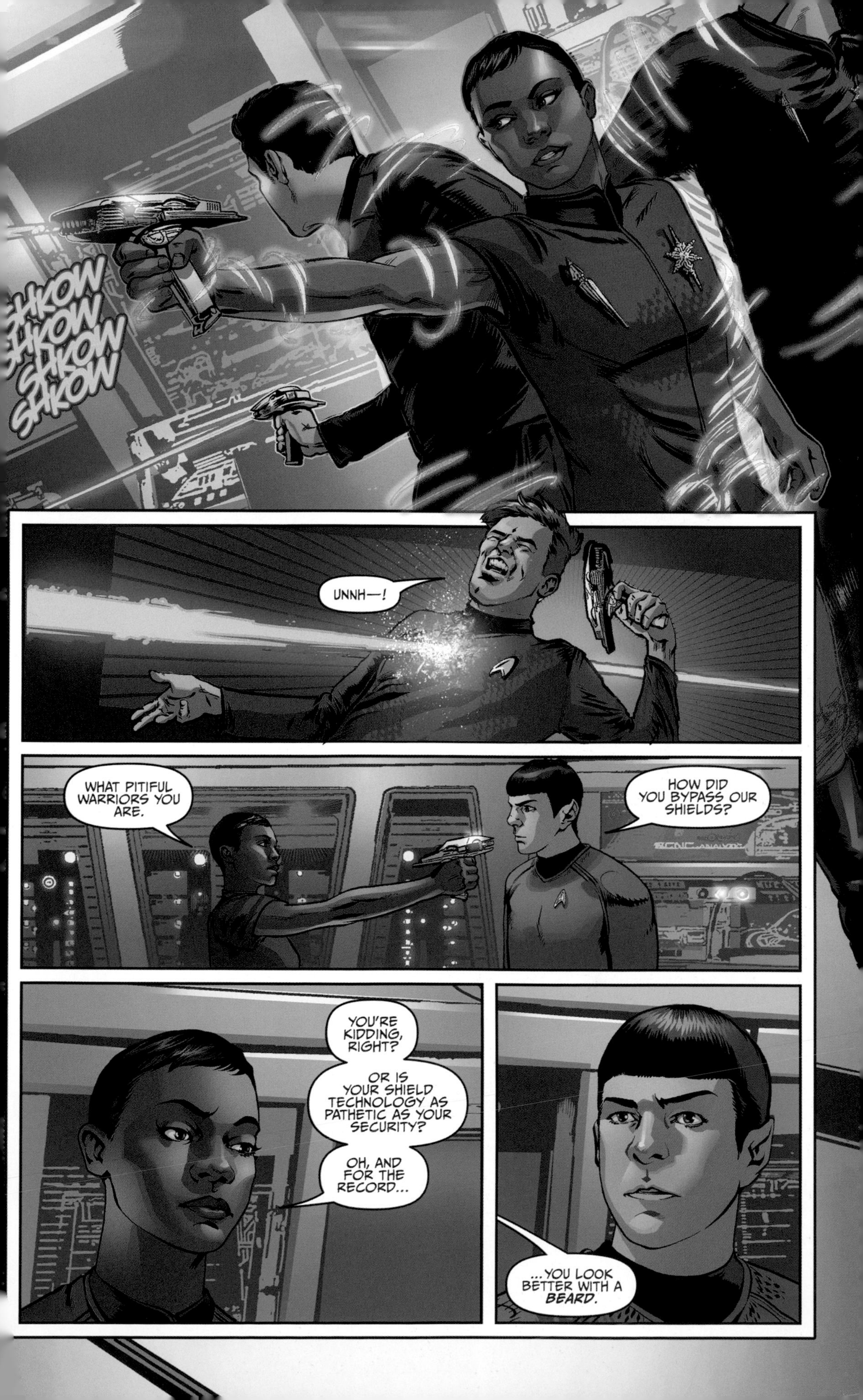
SHKOW SHKOW SHKOW SHKOW
UNNH—!
WHAT PITIFUL WARRIORS YOU ARE.
HOW DID YOU BYPASS OUR SHIELDS?
YOU'RE KIDDING, RIGHT?
OR IS YOUR SHIELD TECHNOLOGY AS PATHETIC AS YOUR SECURITY?
OH, AND FOR THE RECORD...
...YOU LOOK BETTER WITH A BEARD.

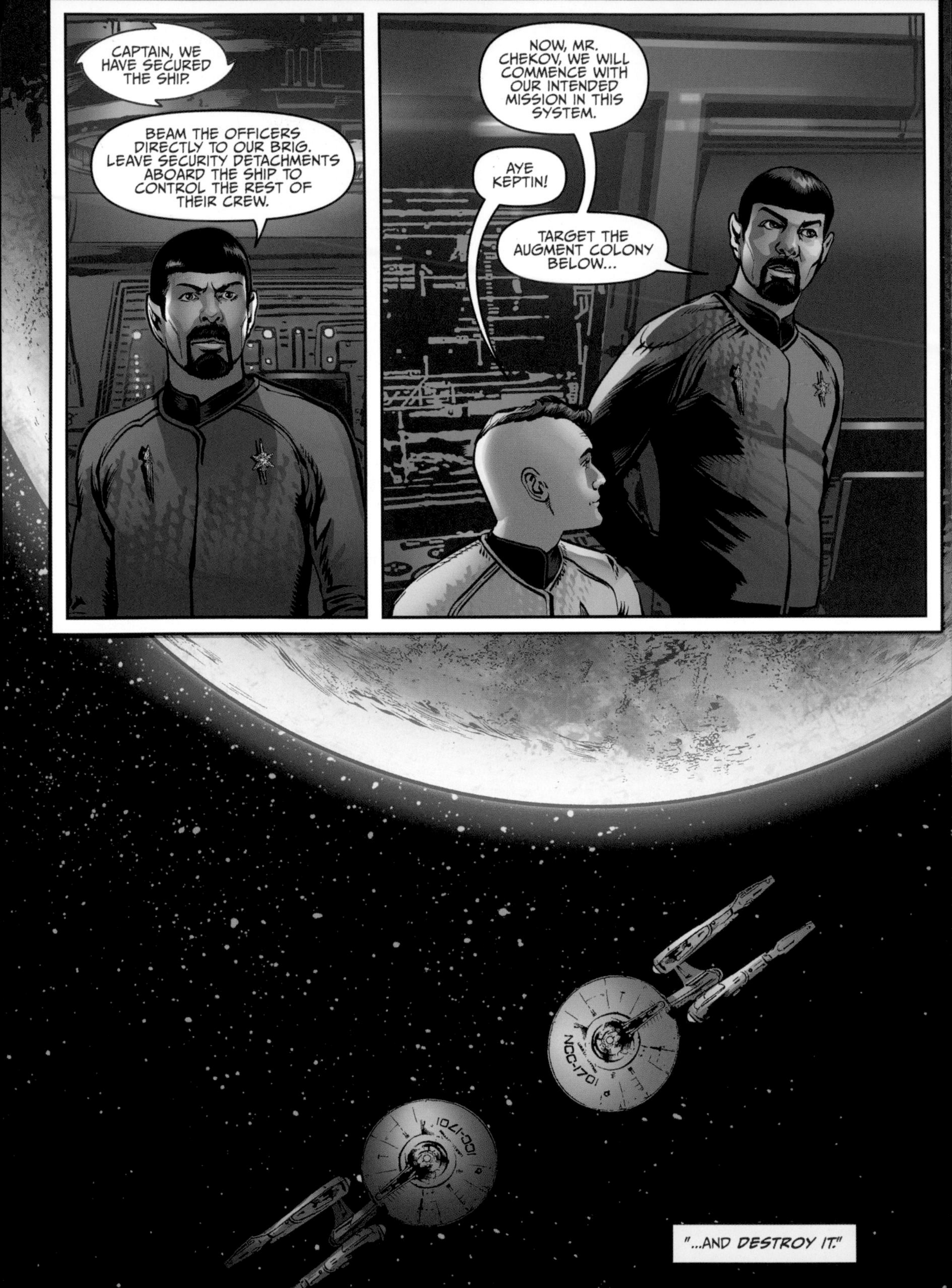
CAPTAIN, WE HAVE SECURED THE SHIP.
BEAM THE OFFICERS DIRECTLY TO OUR BRIG. LEAVE SECURITY DETACHMENTS ABOARD THE SHIP TO CONTROL THE REST OF THEIR CREW.
NOW, MR. CHEKOV, WE WILL COMMENCE WITH OUR INTENDED MISSION IN THIS SYSTEM.
AYE KEPTIN!
TARGET THE AUGMENT COLONY BELOW...
NCC-1701
NCC-1701
"...AND *DESTROY IT.*"

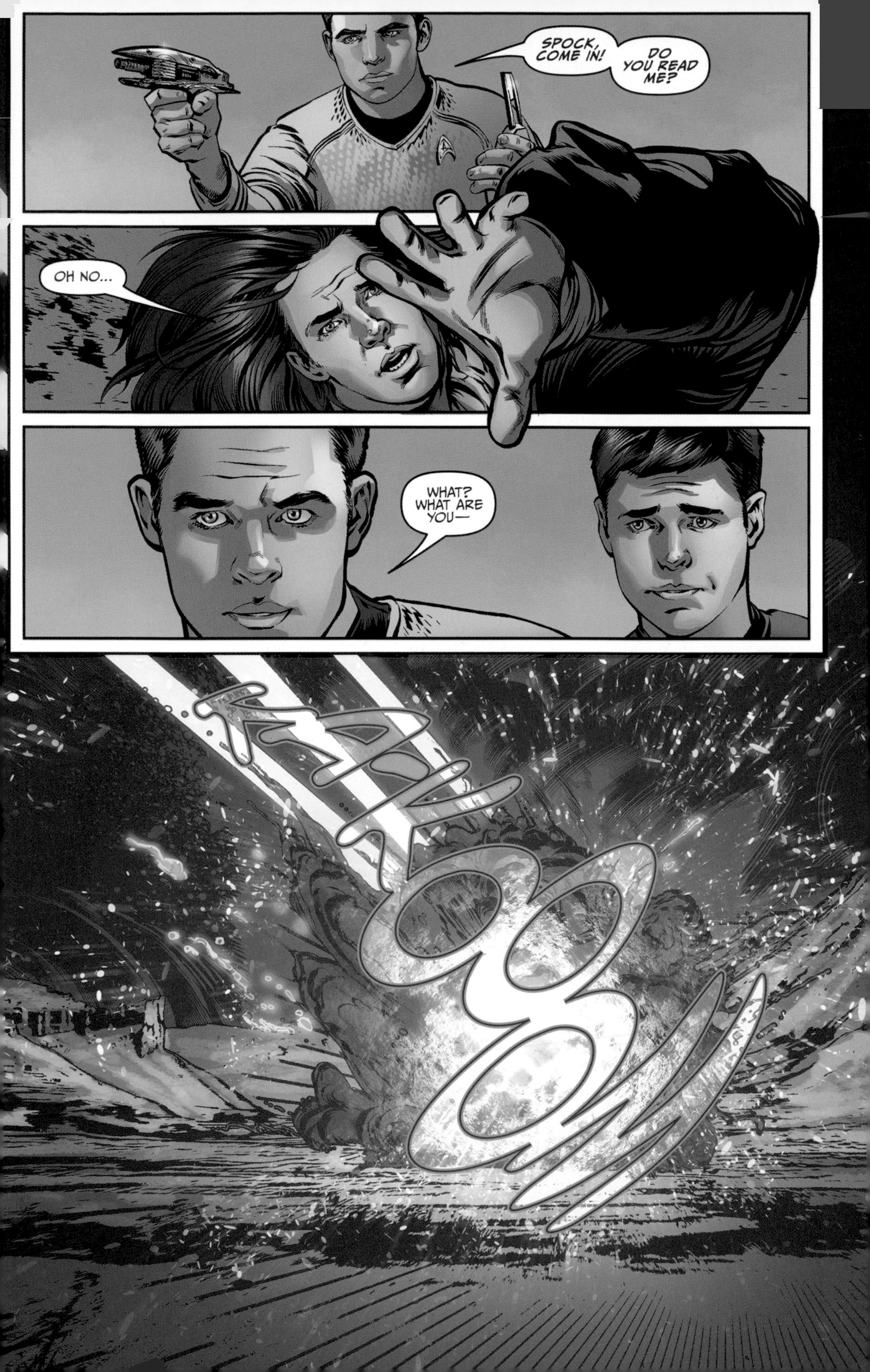
SPOCK, COME IN!
DO YOU READ ME?
OH NO...
WHAT? WHAT ARE YOU—
KABOOM

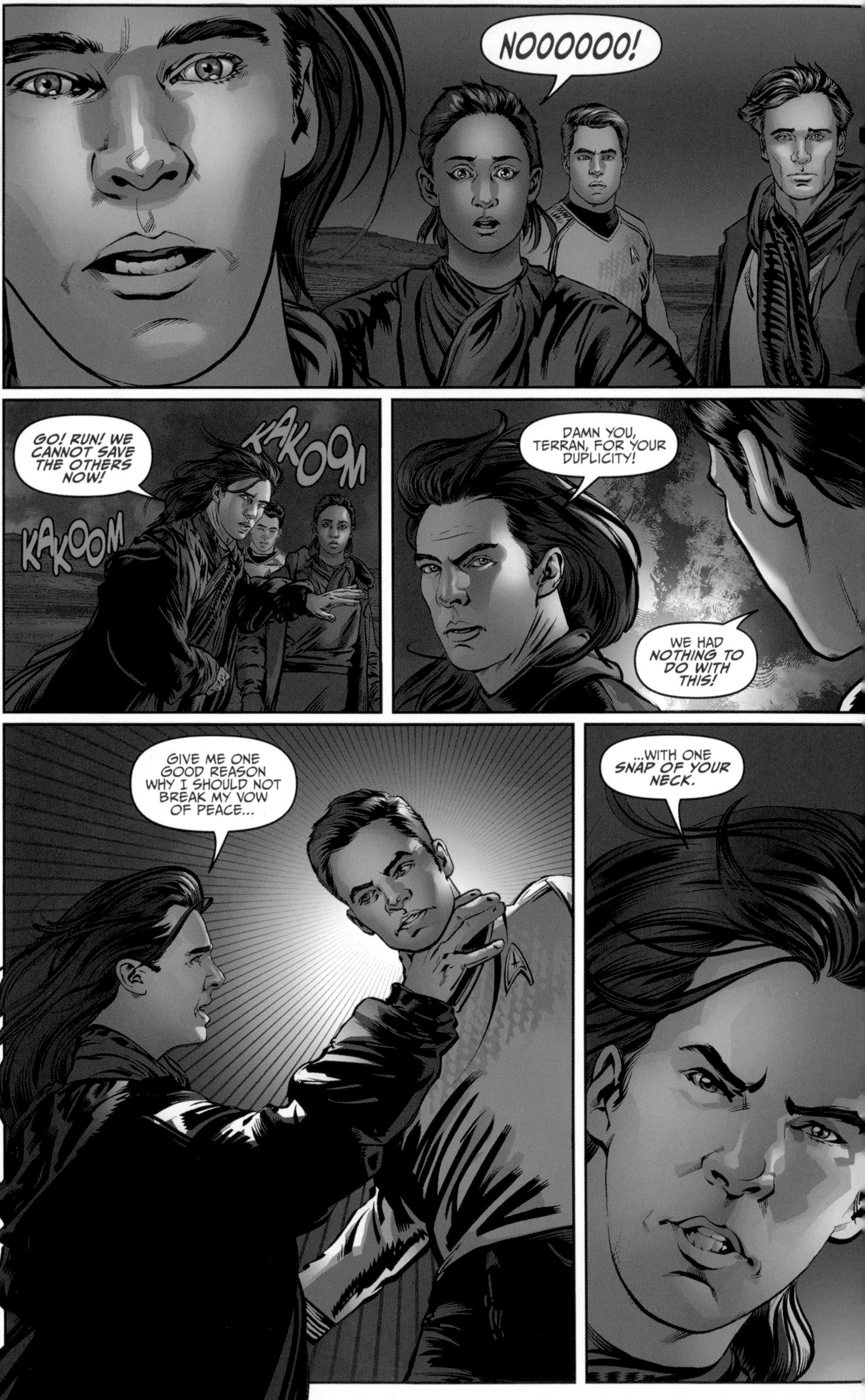
NOOOOOO!
GO! RUN! WE CANNOT SAVE THE OTHERS NOW!
KAKOOM
KAKOOM
DAMN YOU, TERRAN, FOR YOUR DUPLICITY!
WE HAD NOTHING TO DO WITH THIS!
GIVE ME ONE GOOD REASON WHY I SHOULD NOT BREAK MY VOW OF PEACE...
...WITH ONE SNAP OF YOUR NECK.

HUNDREDS OF LIGHT YEARS AWAY.

THE TRADING PLANET *ARRONIA TWO*.

SUCH A *VIOLENT CULTURE* YOU COME FROM.

ASSASSINATING YOUR SUPERIOR OFFICERS IN ORDER TO GAIN RANK?

SOUNDS LIKE BAD *BUSINESS* TO ME.

YOU WOULDN'T UNDERSTAND, MUDD.

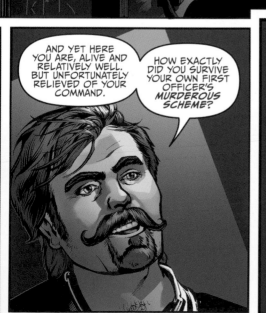

AND YET HERE YOU ARE, ALIVE AND RELATIVELY WELL. BUT UNFORTUNATELY RELIEVED OF YOUR COMMAND.

HOW EXACTLY DID YOU SURVIVE YOUR OWN FIRST OFFICER'S *MURDEROUS SCHEME?*

I HAVE FRIENDS IN LOW PLACES.

THE IMPORTANT THING IS THAT MY FORMER FIRST OFFICER *THINKS* I'M DEAD.

HE'LL LEARN THE TRUTH SOON ENOUGH. AND WHEN HE DOES...

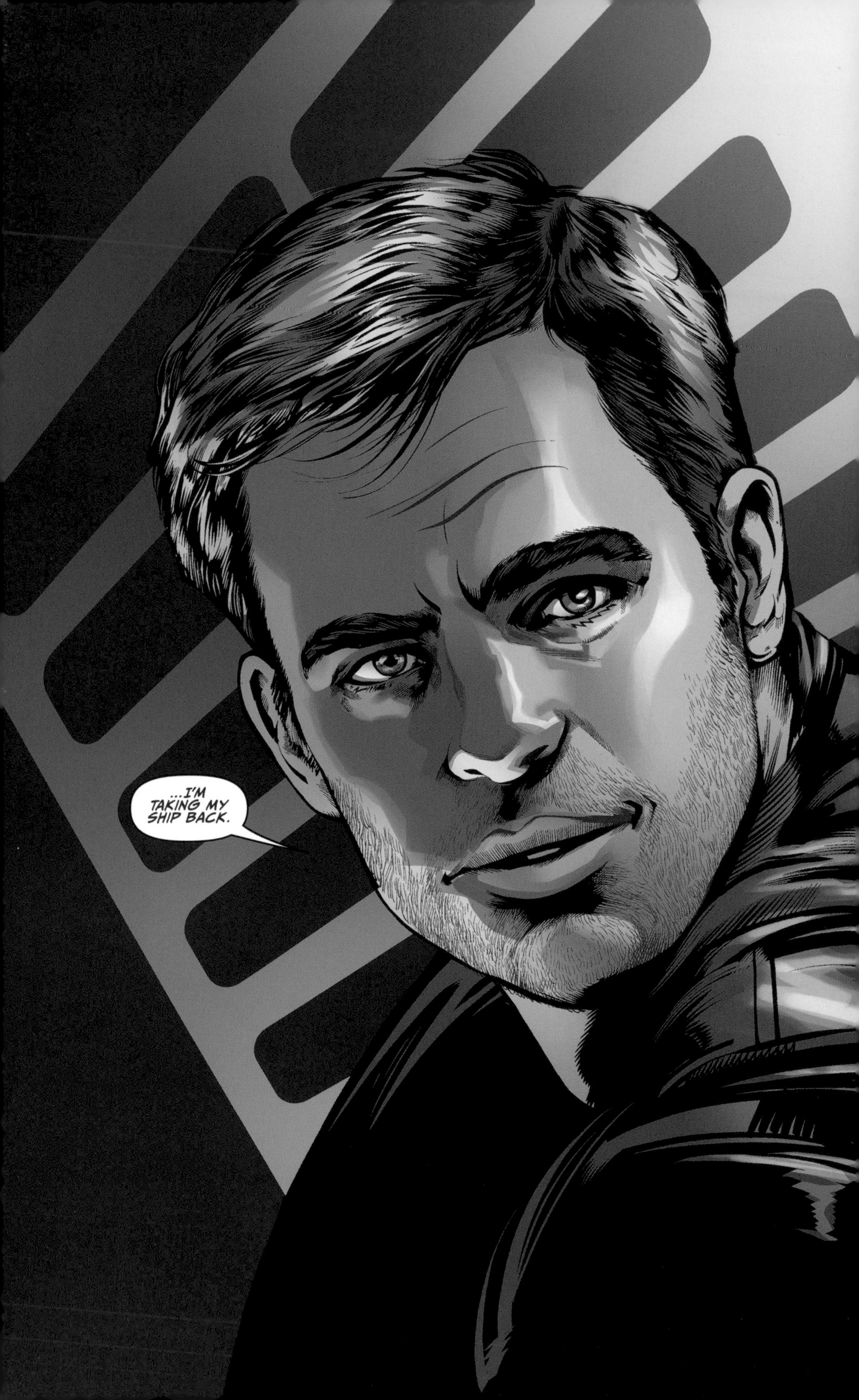
...I'M TAKING MY SHIP BACK.

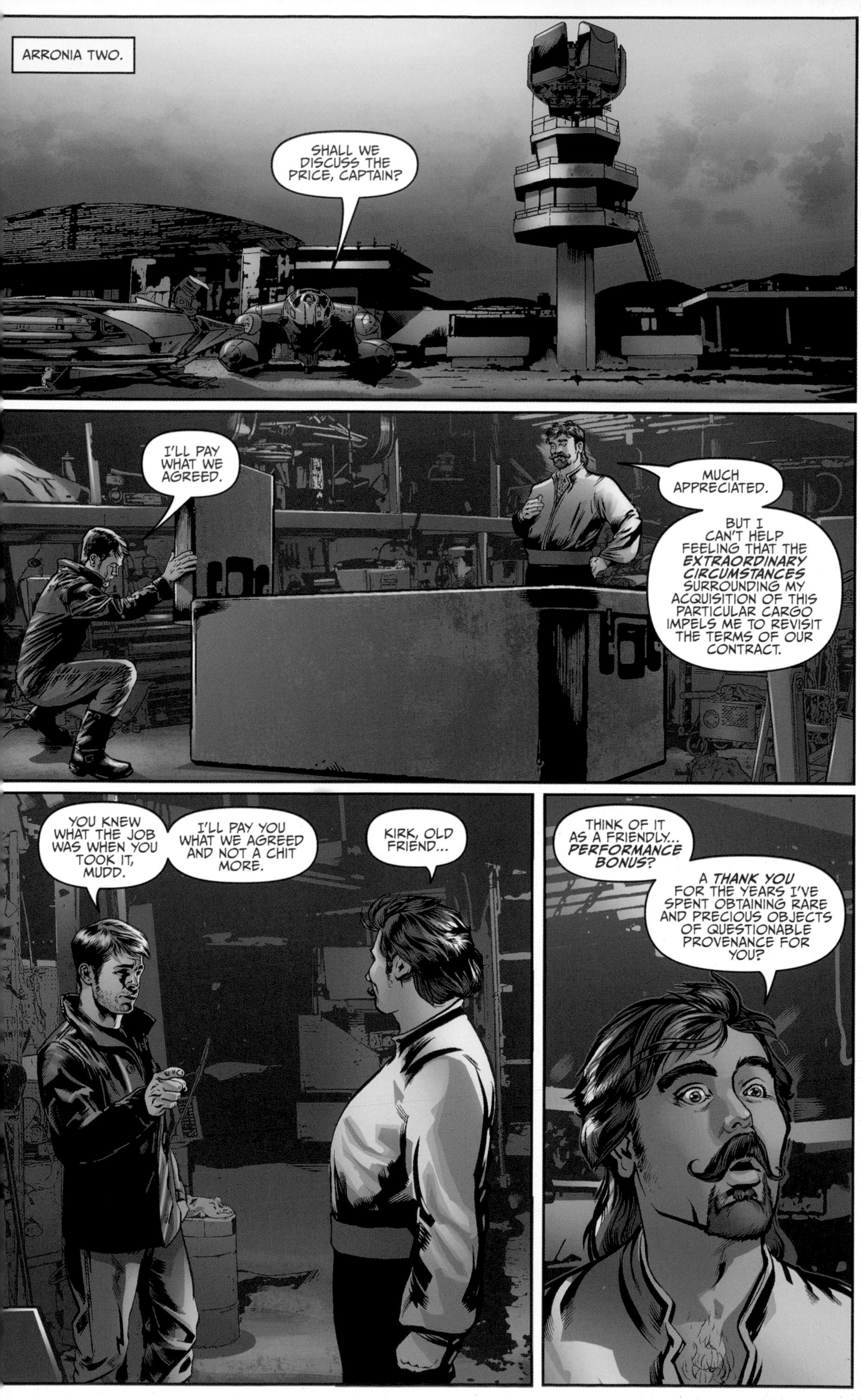
ARRONIA TWO.
SHALL WE DISCUSS THE PRICE, CAPTAIN?
I'LL PAY WHAT WE AGREED.
MUCH APPRECIATED.
BUT I CAN'T HELP FEELING THAT THE *EXTRAORDINARY CIRCUMSTANCES* SURROUNDING MY ACQUISITION OF THIS PARTICULAR CARGO IMPELS ME TO REVISIT THE TERMS OF OUR CONTRACT.
YOU KNEW WHAT THE JOB WAS WHEN YOU TOOK IT, MUDD.
I'LL PAY YOU WHAT WE AGREED AND NOT A CHIT MORE.
KIRK, OLD FRIEND...
THINK OF IT AS A FRIENDLY... *PERFORMANCE BONUS?*
A *THANK YOU* FOR THE YEARS I'VE SPENT OBTAINING RARE AND PRECIOUS OBJECTS OF QUESTIONABLE PROVENANCE FOR YOU?

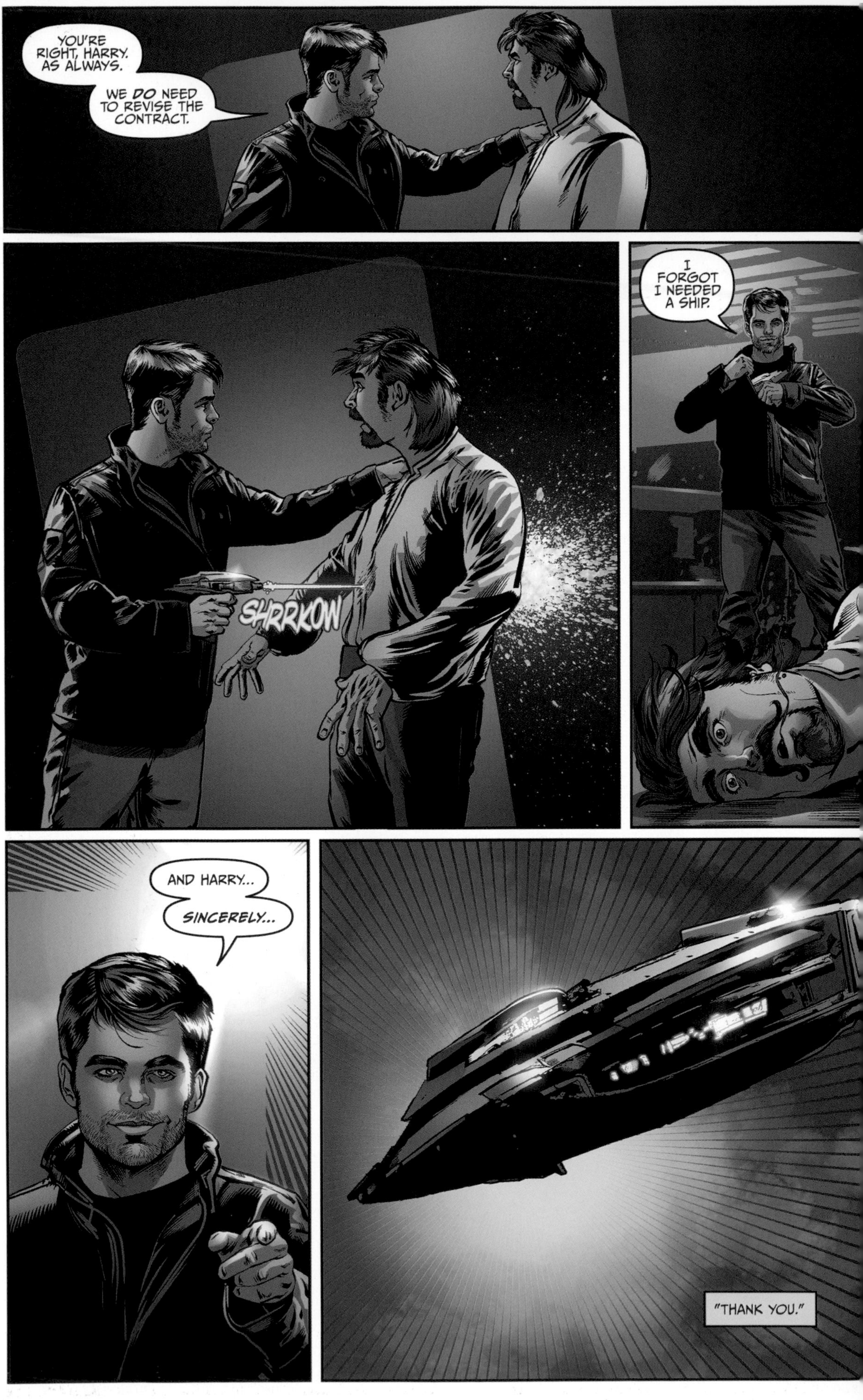
YOU'RE RIGHT, HARRY. AS ALWAYS.
WE DO NEED TO REVISE THE CONTRACT.
SHRRKOW
I FORGOT I NEEDED A SHIP.
AND HARRY...
SINCERELY...
"THANK YOU."

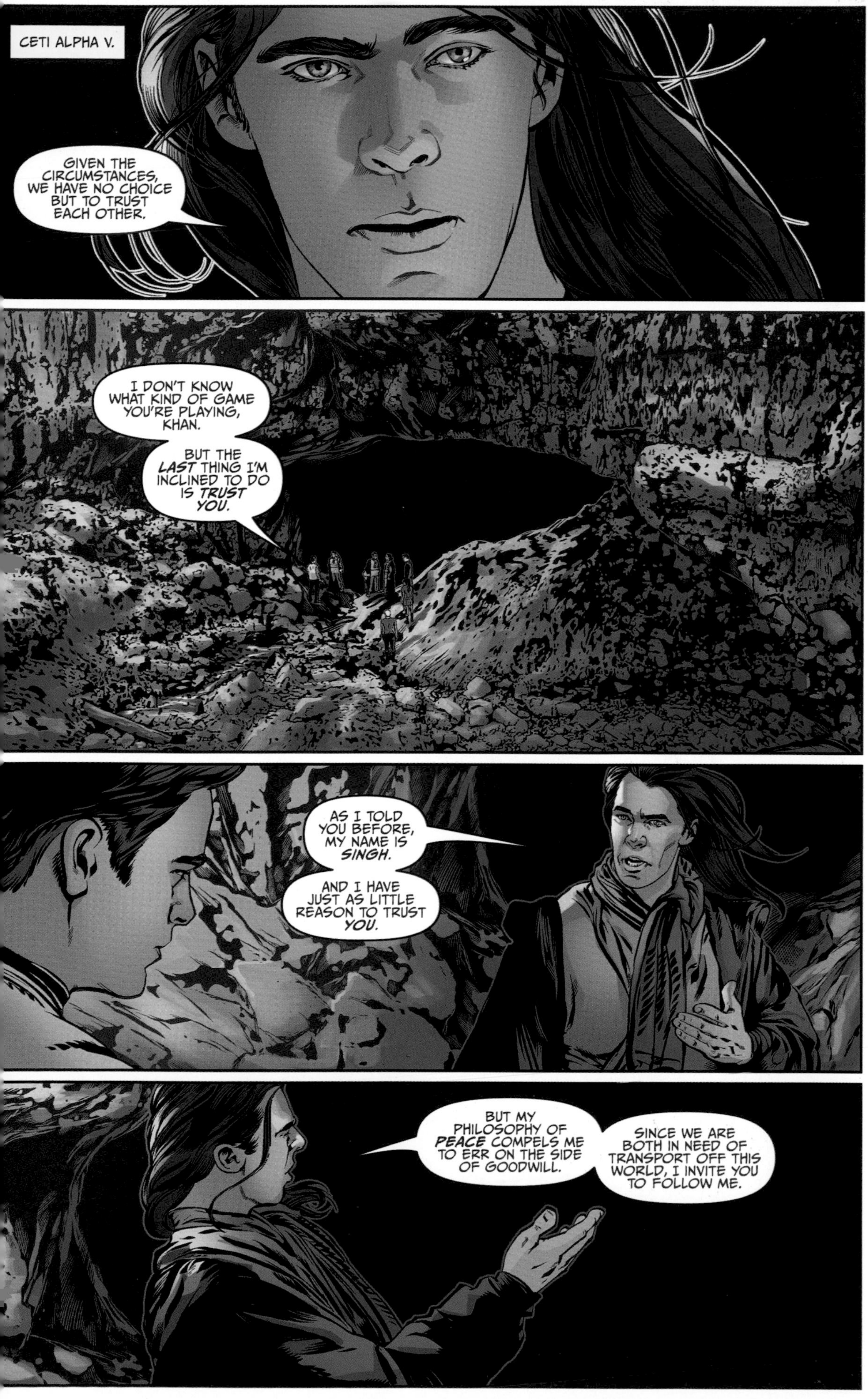
CETI ALPHA V.
GIVEN THE CIRCUMSTANCES, WE HAVE NO CHOICE BUT TO TRUST EACH OTHER.
I DON'T KNOW WHAT KIND OF GAME YOU'RE PLAYING, KHAN.
BUT THE LAST THING I'M INCLINED TO DO IS TRUST YOU.
AS I TOLD YOU BEFORE, MY NAME IS SINGH.
AND I HAVE JUST AS LITTLE REASON TO TRUST YOU.
BUT MY PHILOSOPHY OF PEACE COMPELS ME TO ERR ON THE SIDE OF GOODWILL.
SINCE WE ARE BOTH IN NEED OF TRANSPORT OFF THIS WORLD, I INVITE YOU TO FOLLOW ME.

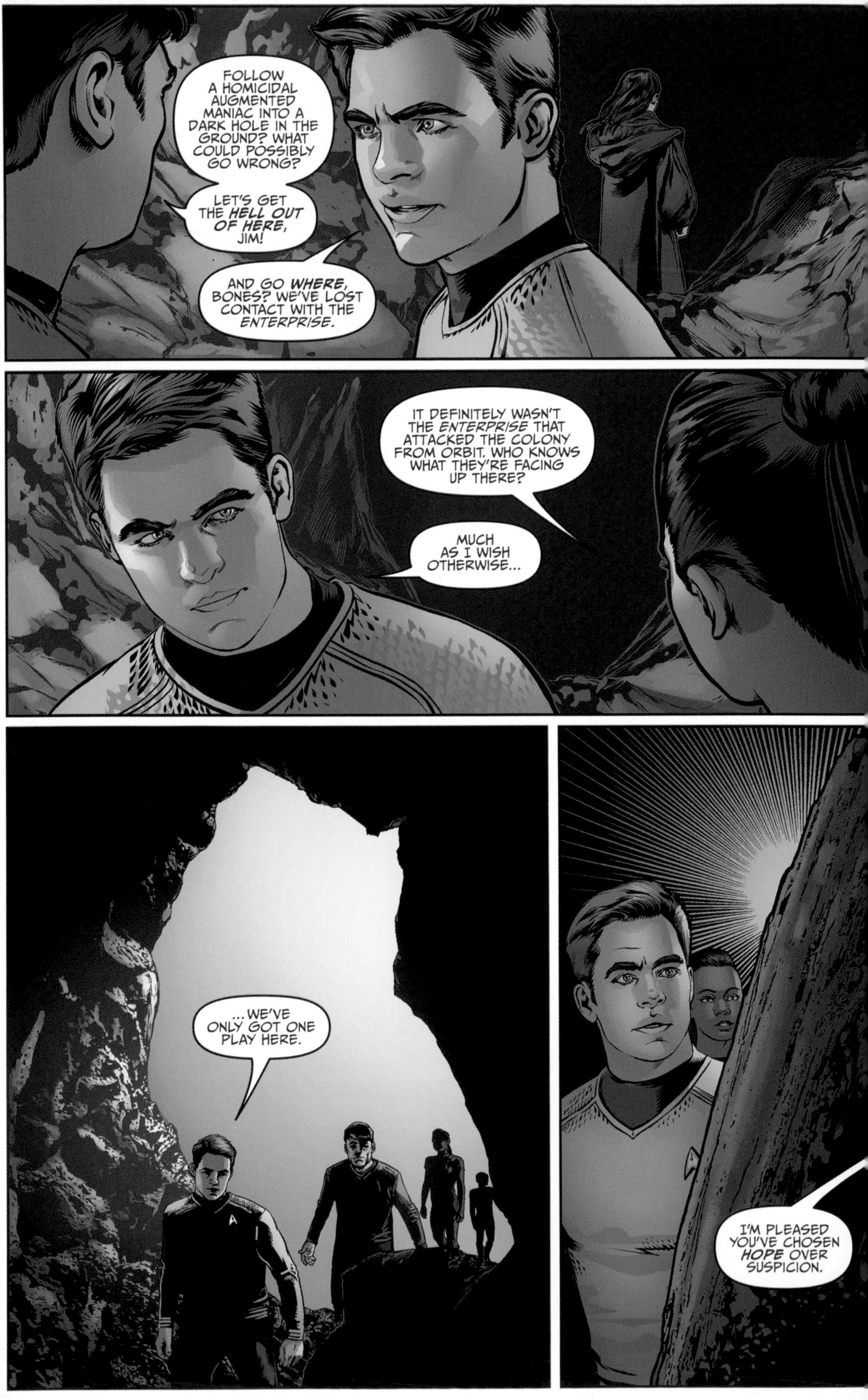
FOLLOW A HOMICIDAL AUGMENTED MANIAC INTO A DARK HOLE IN THE GROUND? WHAT COULD POSSIBLY GO WRONG?
LET'S GET THE HELL OUT OF HERE, JIM!
AND GO WHERE, BONES? WE'VE LOST CONTACT WITH THE ENTERPRISE.
IT DEFINITELY WASN'T THE ENTERPRISE THAT ATTACKED THE COLONY FROM ORBIT. WHO KNOWS WHAT THEY'RE FACING UP THERE?
MUCH AS I WISH OTHERWISE...
...WE'VE ONLY GOT ONE PLAY HERE.
I'M PLEASED YOU'VE CHOSEN HOPE OVER SUSPICION.

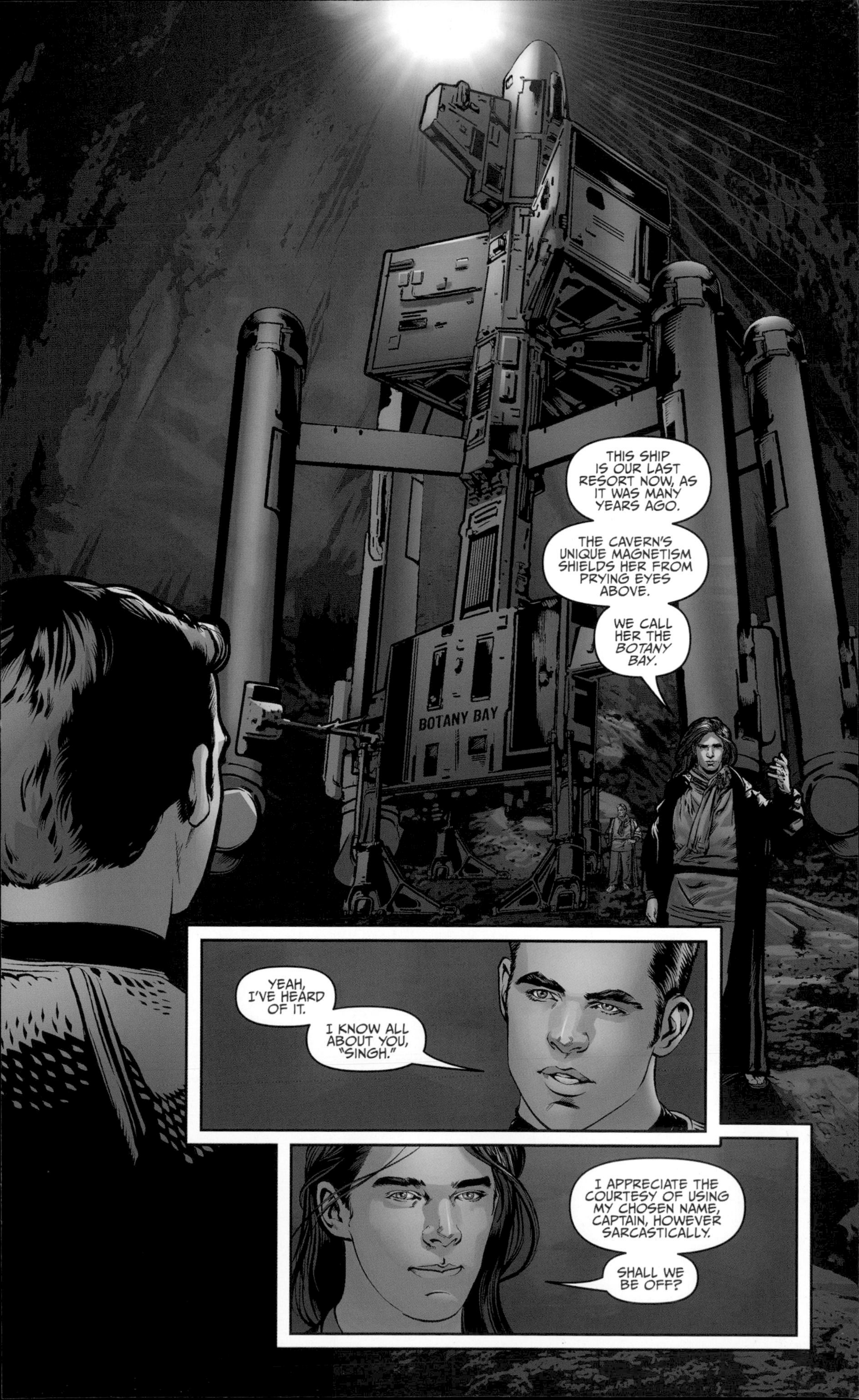
THIS SHIP IS OUR LAST RESORT NOW, AS IT WAS MANY YEARS AGO.
THE CAVERN'S UNIQUE MAGNETISM SHIELDS HER FROM PRYING EYES ABOVE.
WE CALL HER THE *BOTANY BAY*.
BOTANY BAY
YEAH, I'VE HEARD OF IT.
I KNOW ALL ABOUT YOU, "SINGH."
I APPRECIATE THE COURTESY OF USING MY CHOSEN NAME, CAPTAIN, HOWEVER SARCASTICALLY.
SHALL WE BE OFF?

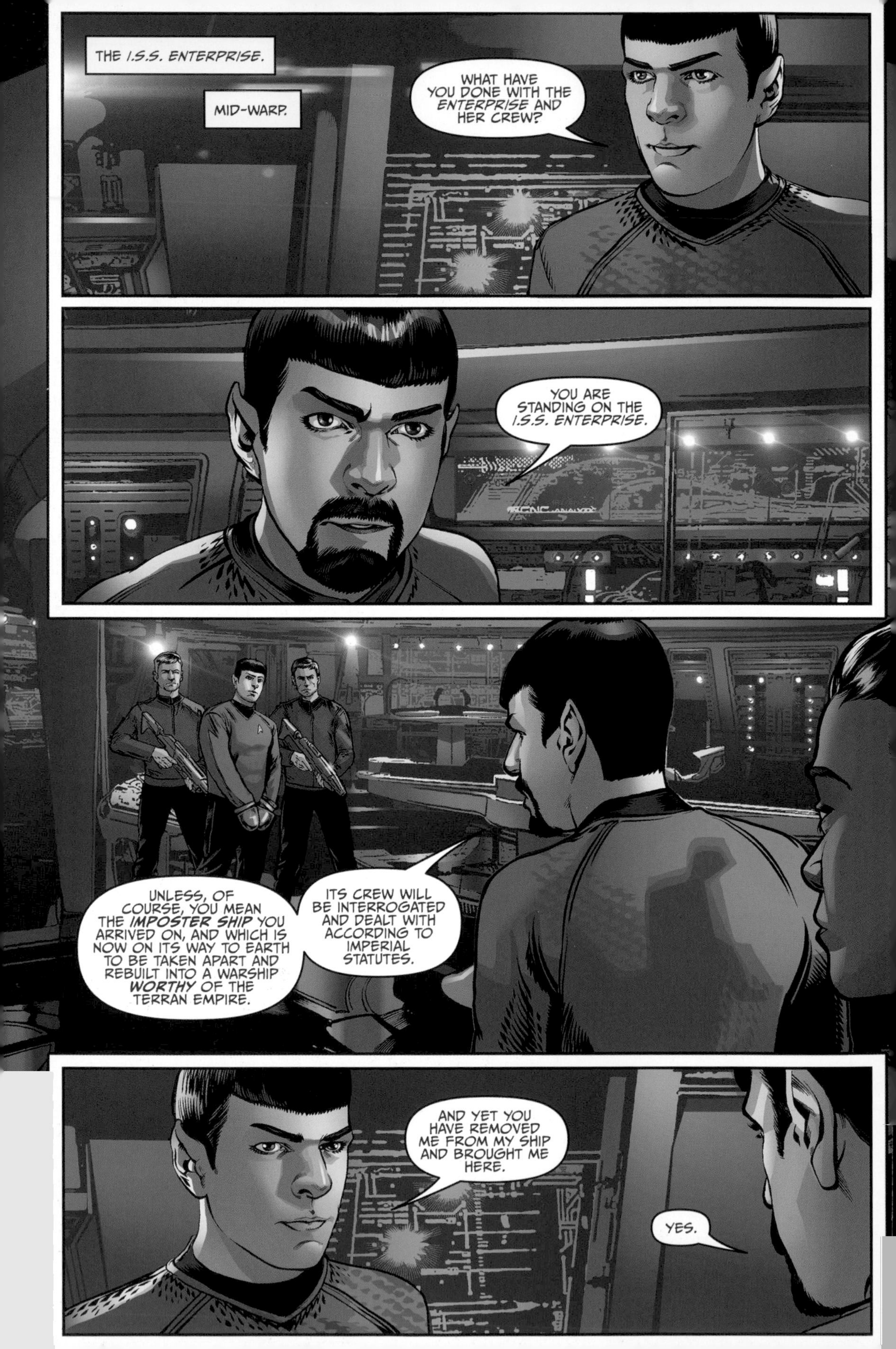
THE I.S.S. ENTERPRISE.
MID-WARP.
WHAT HAVE YOU DONE WITH THE ENTERPRISE AND HER CREW?
YOU ARE STANDING ON THE I.S.S. ENTERPRISE.
UNLESS, OF COURSE, YOU MEAN THE IMPOSTER SHIP YOU ARRIVED ON, AND WHICH IS NOW ON ITS WAY TO EARTH TO BE TAKEN APART AND REBUILT INTO A WARSHIP WORTHY OF THE TERRAN EMPIRE.
ITS CREW WILL BE INTERROGATED AND DEALT WITH ACCORDING TO IMPERIAL STATUTES.
AND YET YOU HAVE REMOVED ME FROM MY SHIP AND BROUGHT ME HERE.
YES.

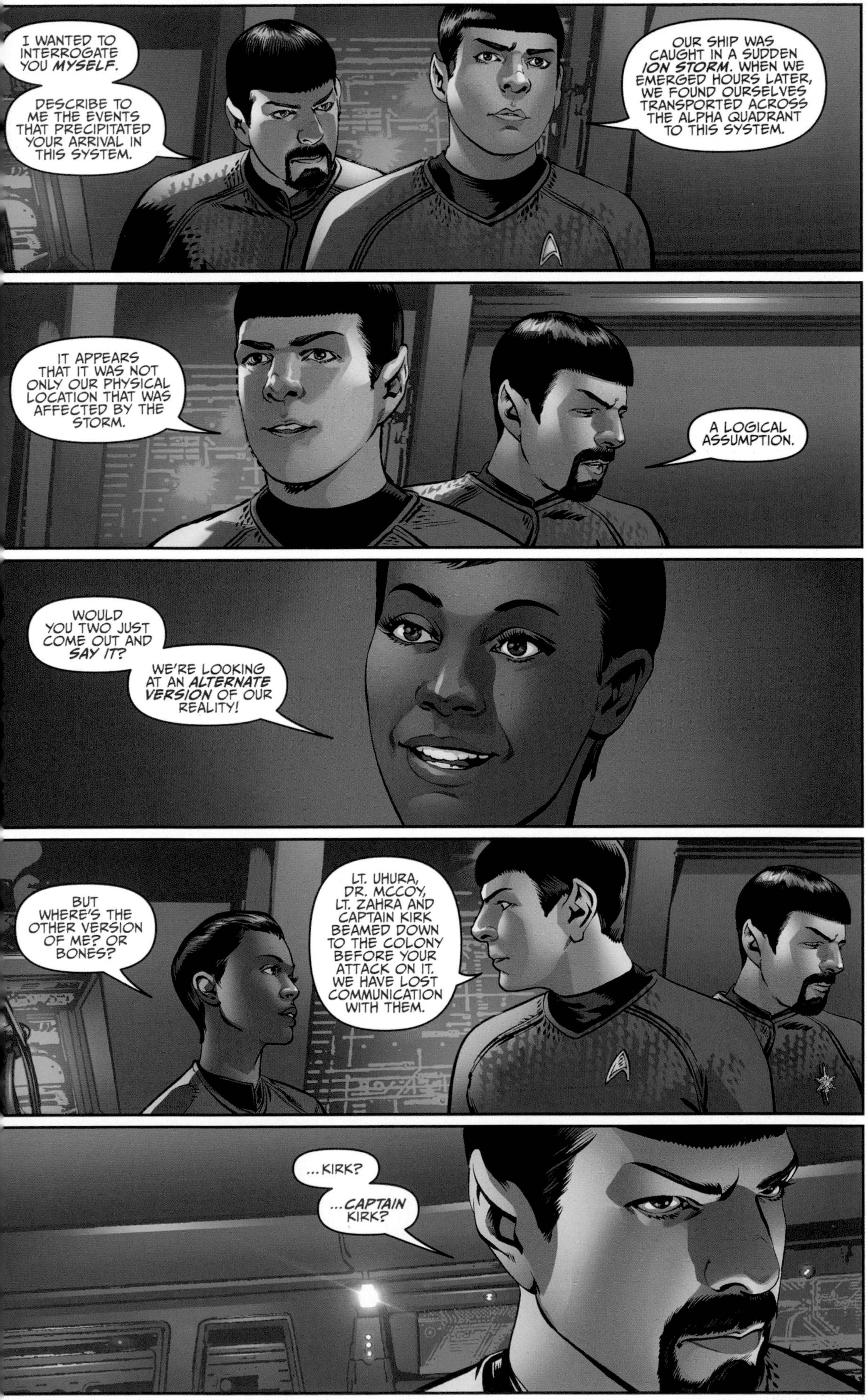
I WANTED TO INTERROGATE YOU *MYSELF*.
DESCRIBE TO ME THE EVENTS THAT PRECIPITATED YOUR ARRIVAL IN THIS SYSTEM.
OUR SHIP WAS CAUGHT IN A SUDDEN *ION STORM*. WHEN WE EMERGED HOURS LATER, WE FOUND OURSELVES TRANSPORTED ACROSS THE ALPHA QUADRANT TO THIS SYSTEM.
IT APPEARS THAT IT WAS NOT ONLY OUR PHYSICAL LOCATION THAT WAS AFFECTED BY THE STORM.
A LOGICAL ASSUMPTION.
WOULD YOU TWO JUST COME OUT AND *SAY IT?*
WE'RE LOOKING AT AN *ALTERNATE VERSION* OF OUR REALITY!
BUT WHERE'S THE OTHER VERSION OF ME? OR BONES?
LT. UHURA, DR. MCCOY, LT. ZAHRA AND CAPTAIN KIRK BEAMED DOWN TO THE COLONY BEFORE YOUR ATTACK ON IT. WE HAVE LOST COMMUNICATION WITH THEM.
...KIRK?
...*CAPTAIN* KIRK?

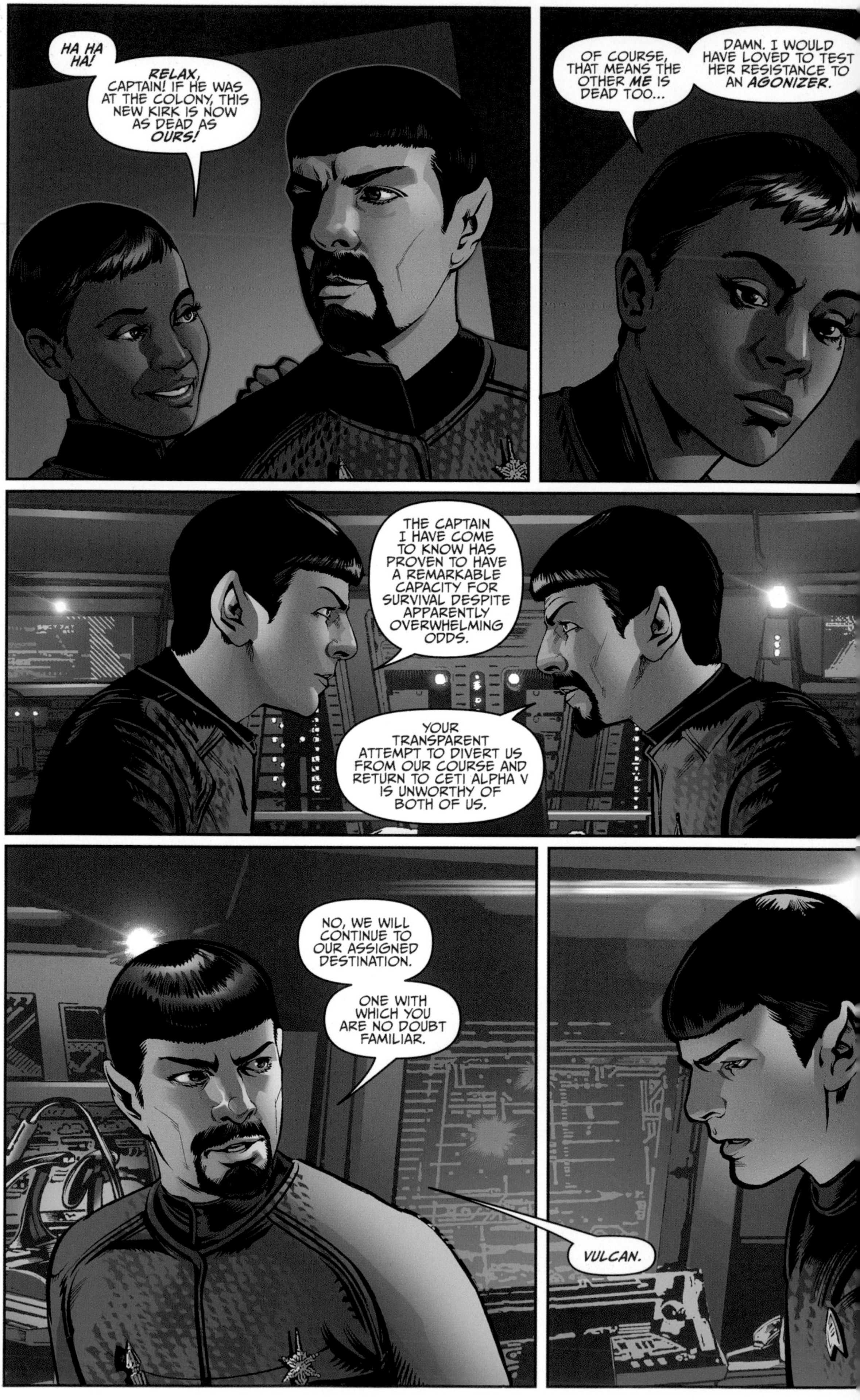

HA HA HA!
RELAX, CAPTAIN! IF HE WAS AT THE COLONY, THIS NEW KIRK IS NOW AS DEAD AS OURS!
OF COURSE, THAT MEANS THE OTHER ME IS DEAD TOO...
DAMN. I WOULD HAVE LOVED TO TEST HER RESISTANCE TO AN AGONIZER.
THE CAPTAIN I HAVE COME TO KNOW HAS PROVEN TO HAVE A REMARKABLE CAPACITY FOR SURVIVAL DESPITE APPARENTLY OVERWHELMING ODDS.
YOUR TRANSPARENT ATTEMPT TO DIVERT US FROM OUR COURSE AND RETURN TO CETI ALPHA V IS UNWORTHY OF BOTH OF US.
NO, WE WILL CONTINUE TO OUR ASSIGNED DESTINATION.
ONE WITH WHICH YOU ARE NO DOUBT FAMILIAR.
VULCAN.

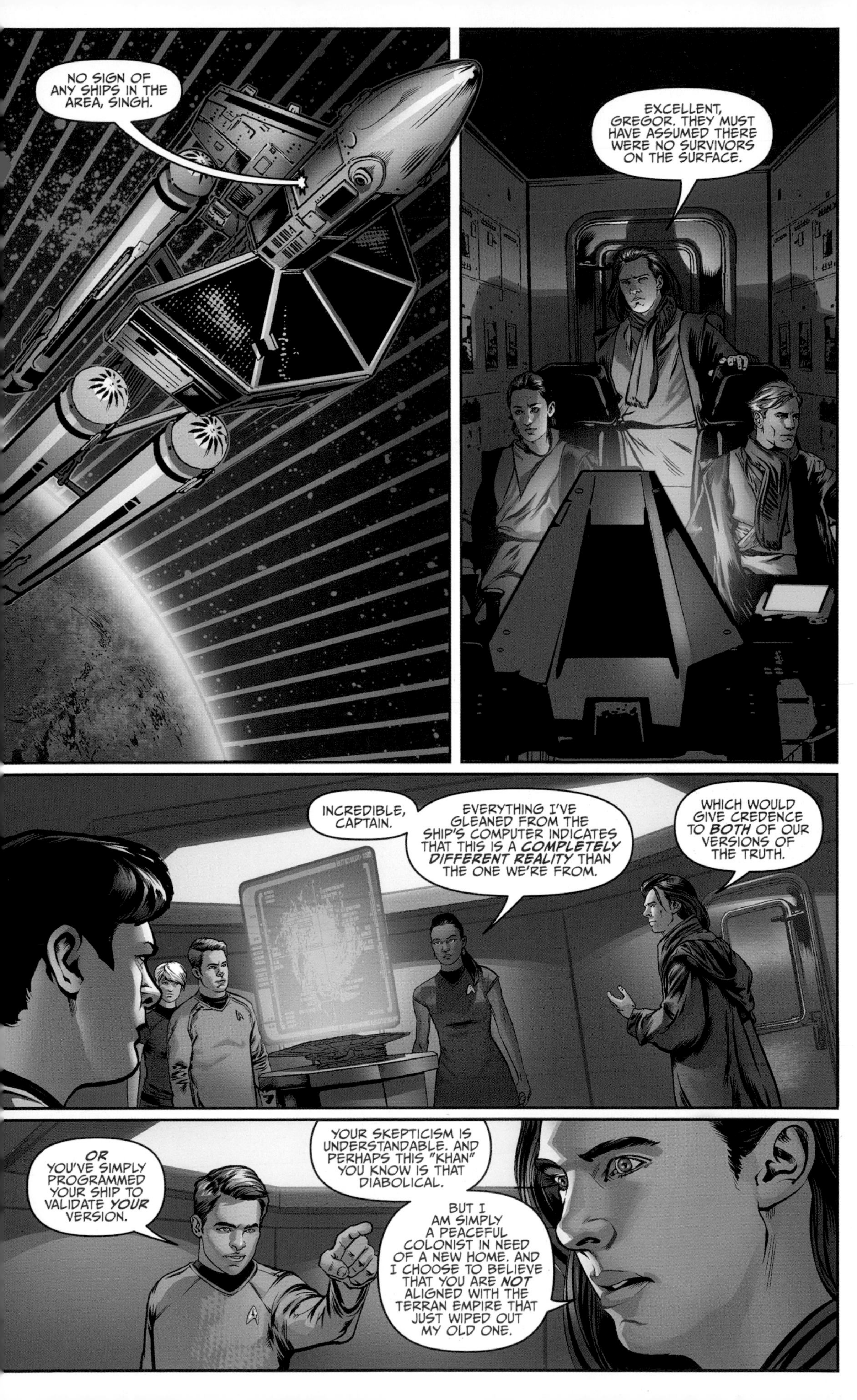
NO SIGN OF ANY SHIPS IN THE AREA, SINGH.
EXCELLENT, GREGOR. THEY MUST HAVE ASSUMED THERE WERE NO SURVIVORS ON THE SURFACE.
INCREDIBLE, CAPTAIN.
EVERYTHING I'VE GLEANED FROM THE SHIP'S COMPUTER INDICATES THAT THIS IS A *COMPLETELY DIFFERENT REALITY* THAN THE ONE WE'RE FROM.
WHICH WOULD GIVE CREDENCE TO *BOTH* OF OUR VERSIONS OF THE TRUTH.
OR YOU'VE SIMPLY PROGRAMMED YOUR SHIP TO VALIDATE *YOUR* VERSION.
YOUR SKEPTICISM IS UNDERSTANDABLE. AND PERHAPS THIS "KHAN" YOU KNOW IS THAT DIABOLICAL.
BUT I AM SIMPLY A PEACEFUL COLONIST IN NEED OF A NEW HOME. AND I CHOOSE TO BELIEVE THAT YOU ARE *NOT* ALIGNED WITH THE TERRAN EMPIRE THAT JUST WIPED OUT MY OLD ONE.

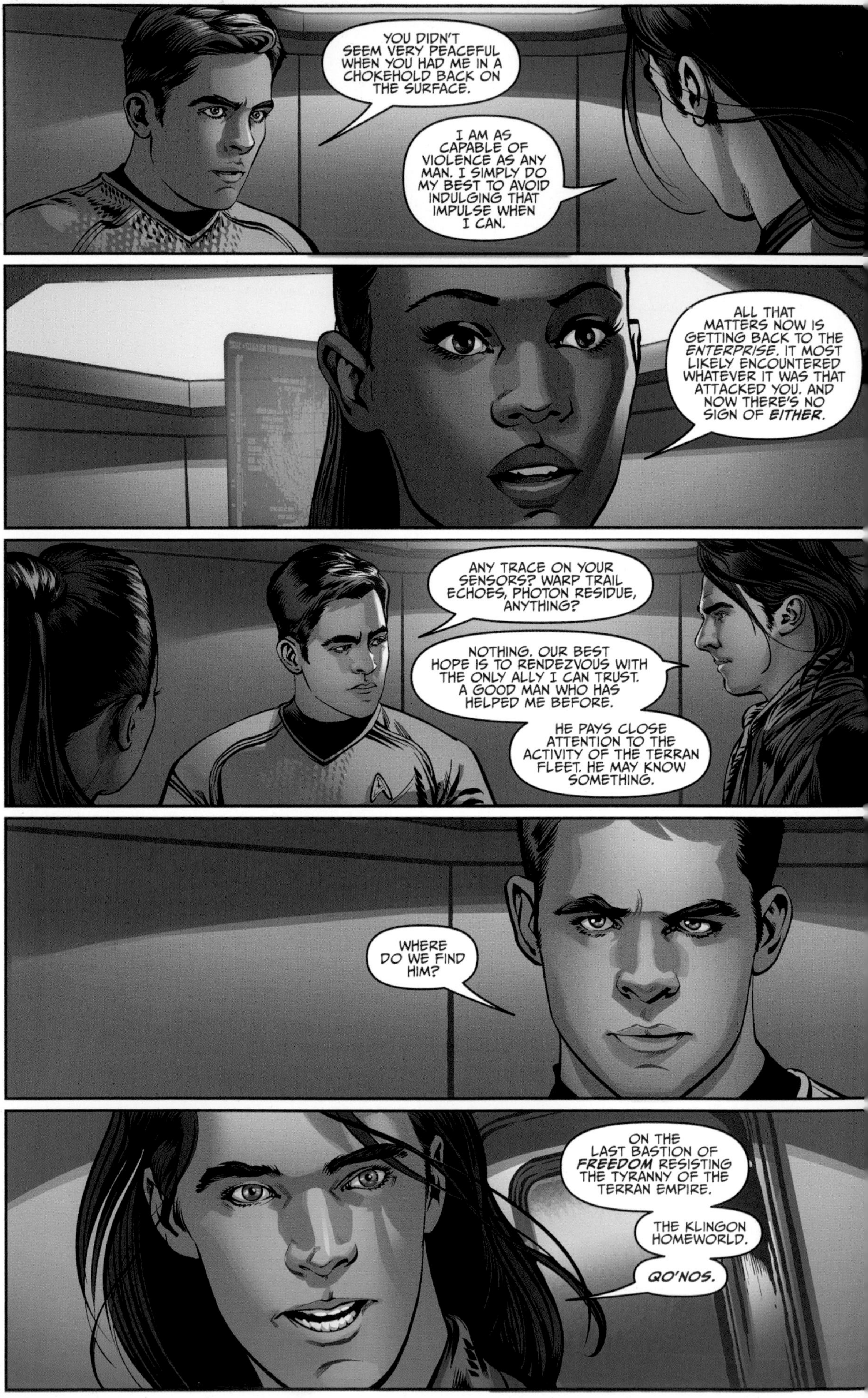
YOU DIDN'T SEEM VERY PEACEFUL WHEN YOU HAD ME IN A CHOKEHOLD BACK ON THE SURFACE.
I AM AS CAPABLE OF VIOLENCE AS ANY MAN. I SIMPLY DO MY BEST TO AVOID INDULGING THAT IMPULSE WHEN I CAN.
ALL THAT MATTERS NOW IS GETTING BACK TO THE *ENTERPRISE*. IT MOST LIKELY ENCOUNTERED WHATEVER IT WAS THAT ATTACKED YOU. AND NOW THERE'S NO SIGN OF ***EITHER***.
ANY TRACE ON YOUR SENSORS? WARP TRAIL ECHOES, PHOTON RESIDUE, ANYTHING?
NOTHING. OUR BEST HOPE IS TO RENDEZVOUS WITH THE ONLY ALLY I CAN TRUST. A GOOD MAN WHO HAS HELPED ME BEFORE.
HE PAYS CLOSE ATTENTION TO THE ACTIVITY OF THE TERRAN FLEET. HE MAY KNOW SOMETHING.
WHERE DO WE FIND HIM?
ON THE LAST BASTION OF ***FREEDOM*** RESISTING THE TYRANNY OF THE TERRAN EMPIRE.
THE KLINGON HOMEWORLD.
QO'NOS.

TIME UNTIL WE REACH EARTH?

I ASKED YOU A *QUESTION,* "SULU."

OR IS THE *ALTERNATE VERSION* OF ME INCAPABLE OF UNDERSTANDING SIMPLE REQUESTS?

WHAT AN *ASS...*

OW!

JAB

I *HEARD* YOU. NINETEEN HOURS.

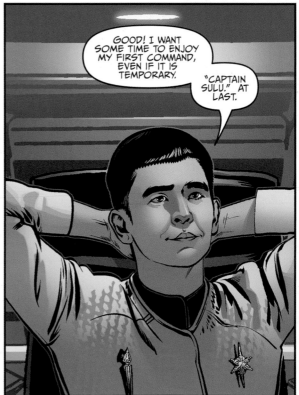

GOOD! I WANT SOME TIME TO ENJOY MY FIRST COMMAND, EVEN IF IT IS TEMPORARY.

"CAPTAIN SULU." AT LAST.

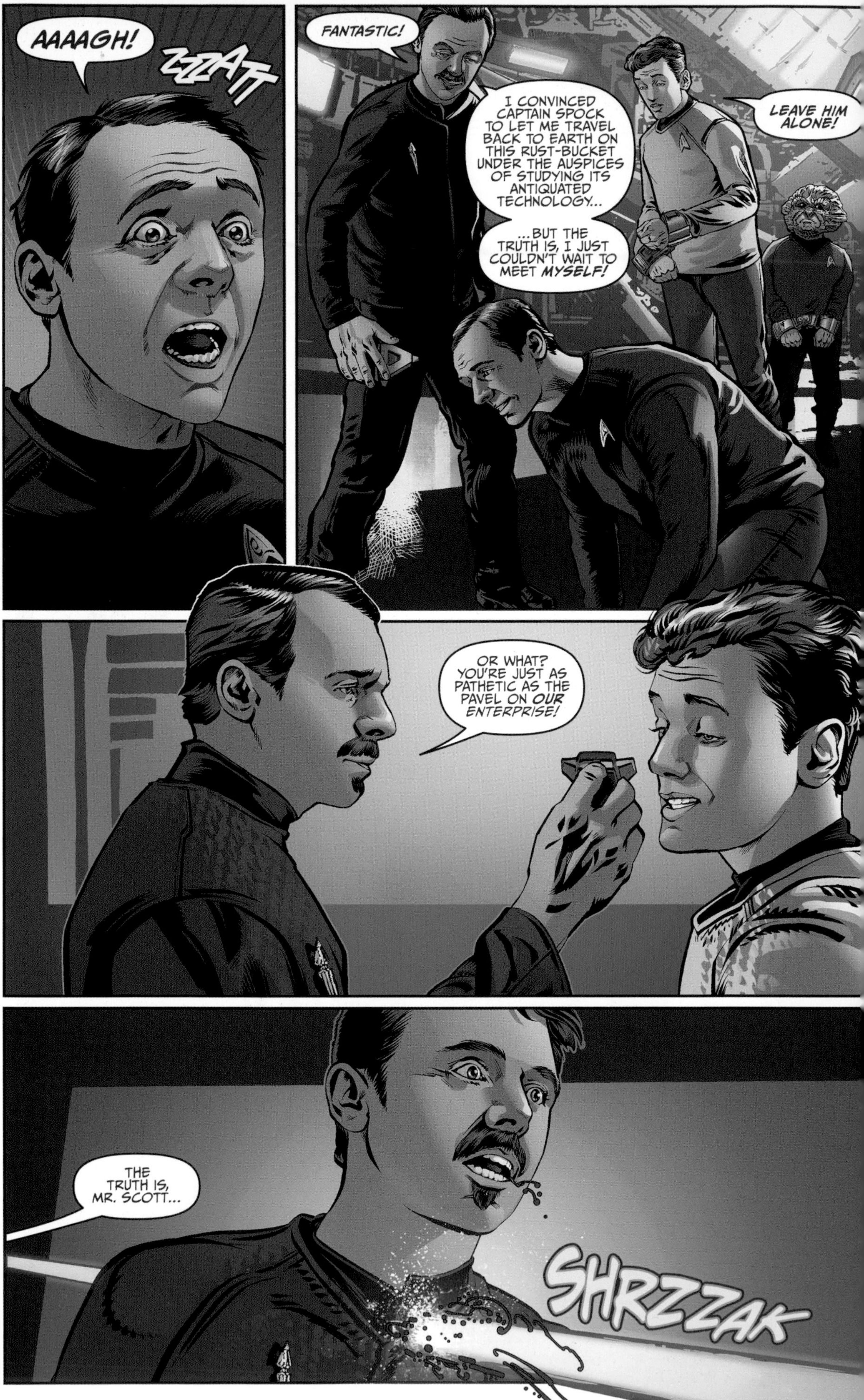
AAAAGH!
ZZZATT
FANTASTIC!
I CONVINCED CAPTAIN SPOCK TO LET ME TRAVEL BACK TO EARTH ON THIS RUST-BUCKET UNDER THE AUSPICES OF STUDYING ITS ANTIQUATED TECHNOLOGY...
...BUT THE TRUTH IS, I JUST COULDN'T WAIT TO MEET *MYSELF!*
LEAVE HIM ALONE!
OR WHAT? YOU'RE JUST AS PATHETIC AS THE PAVEL ON *OUR ENTERPRISE!*
THE TRUTH IS, MR. SCOTT...
SHRZZAK

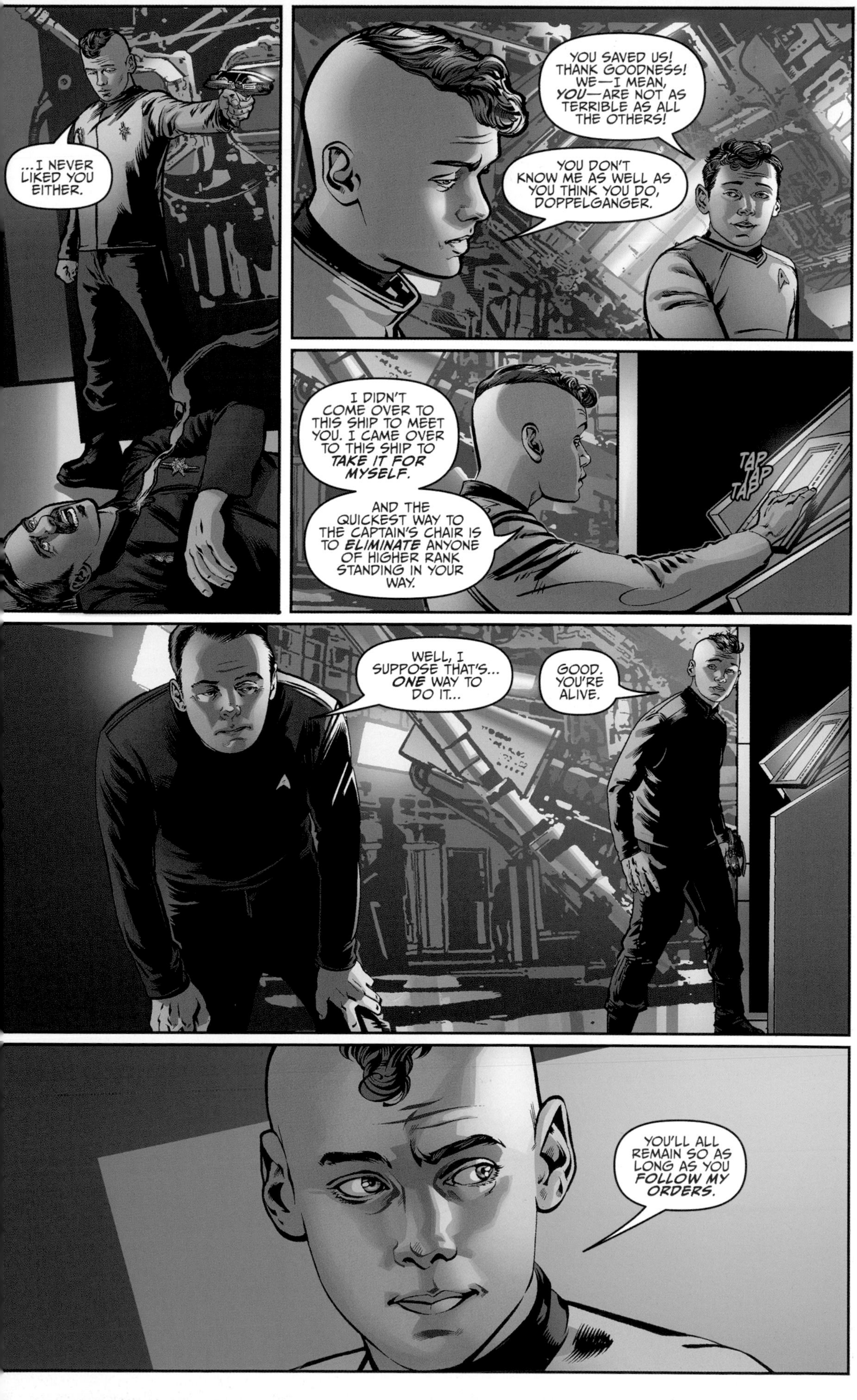
...I NEVER LIKED YOU EITHER.
YOU SAVED US! THANK GOODNESS! WE—I MEAN, YOU—ARE NOT AS TERRIBLE AS ALL THE OTHERS!
YOU DON'T KNOW ME AS WELL AS YOU THINK YOU DO, DOPPELGANGER.
I DIDN'T COME OVER TO THIS SHIP TO MEET YOU. I CAME OVER TO THIS SHIP TO TAKE IT FOR MYSELF.
AND THE QUICKEST WAY TO THE CAPTAIN'S CHAIR IS TO ELIMINATE ANYONE OF HIGHER RANK STANDING IN YOUR WAY.
TAP TAP TAP
WELL, I SUPPOSE THAT'S... ONE WAY TO DO IT...
GOOD. YOU'RE ALIVE.
YOU'LL ALL REMAIN SO AS LONG AS YOU FOLLOW MY ORDERS.

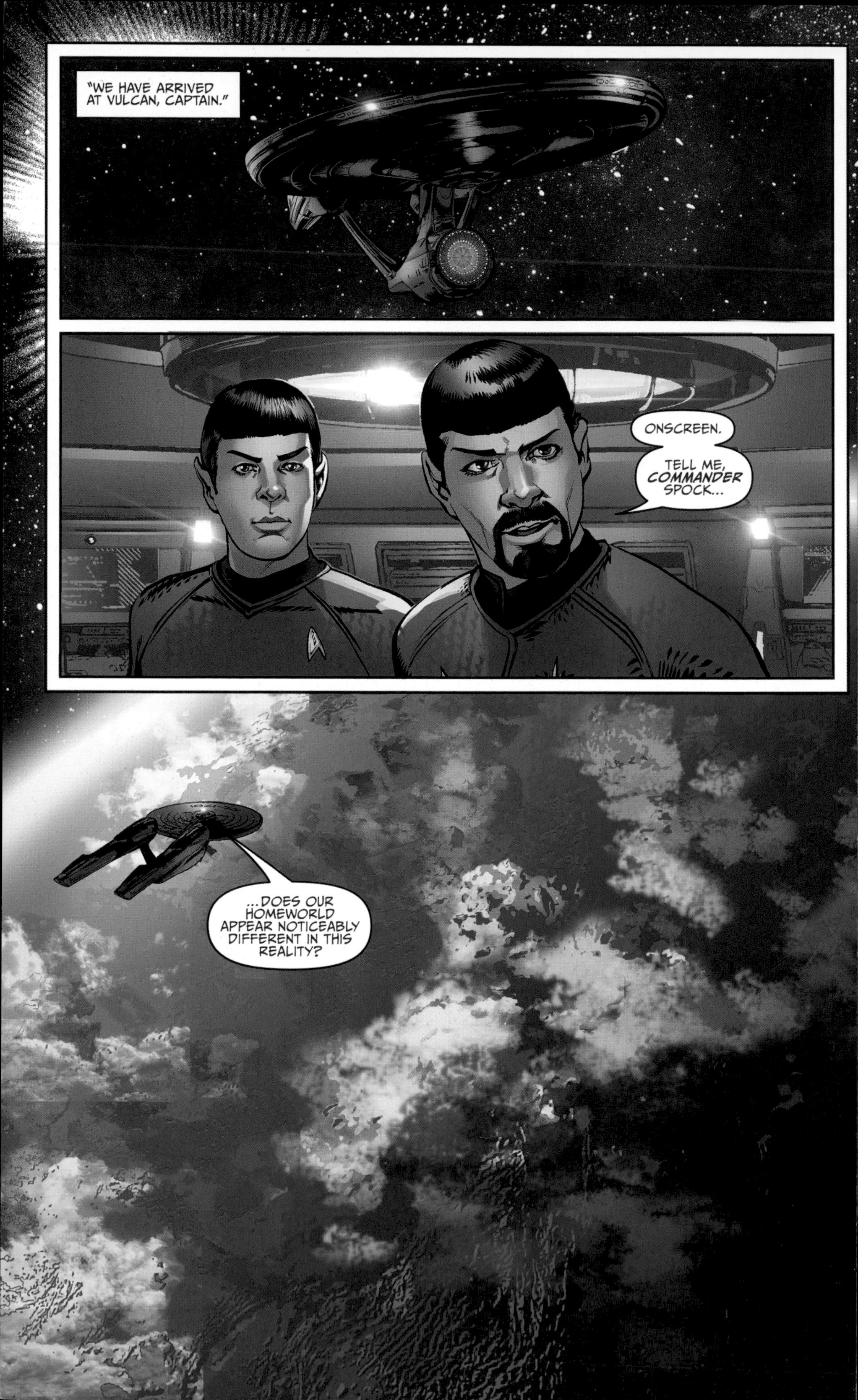
"WE HAVE ARRIVED AT VULCAN, CAPTAIN."
ONSCREEN.
TELL ME, *COMMANDER* SPOCK...
...DOES OUR HOMEWORLD APPEAR NOTICEABLY DIFFERENT IN THIS REALITY?

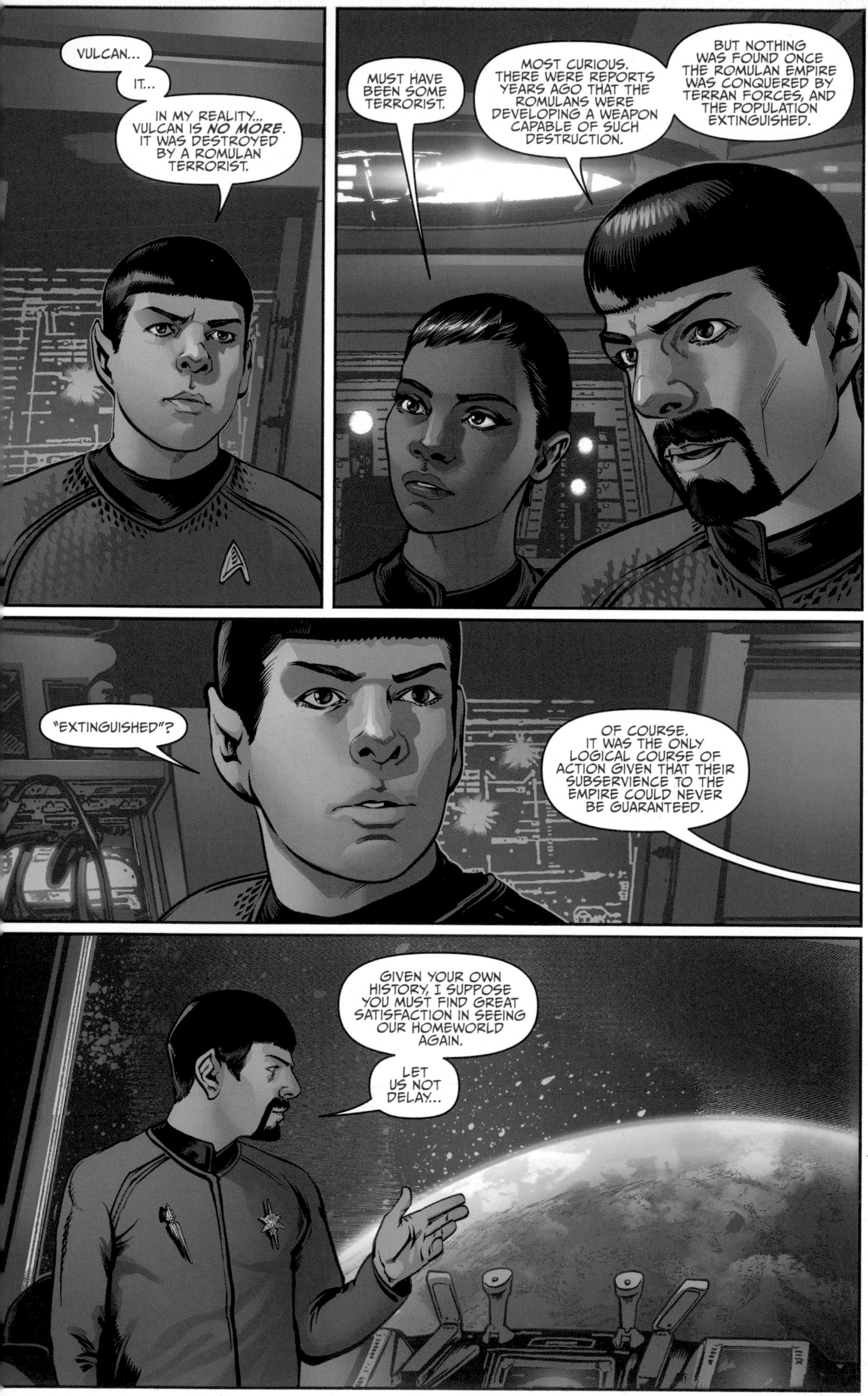
VULCAN...
IT...
IN MY REALITY... VULCAN IS *NO MORE*. IT WAS DESTROYED BY A ROMULAN TERRORIST.
MUST HAVE BEEN SOME TERRORIST.
MOST CURIOUS. THERE WERE REPORTS YEARS AGO THAT THE ROMULANS WERE DEVELOPING A WEAPON CAPABLE OF SUCH DESTRUCTION.
BUT NOTHING WAS FOUND ONCE THE ROMULAN EMPIRE WAS CONQUERED BY TERRAN FORCES, AND THE POPULATION EXTINGUISHED.
"EXTINGUISHED"?
OF COURSE. IT WAS THE ONLY LOGICAL COURSE OF ACTION GIVEN THAT THEIR SUBSERVIENCE TO THE EMPIRE COULD NEVER BE GUARANTEED.
GIVEN YOUR OWN HISTORY, I SUPPOSE YOU MUST FIND GREAT SATISFACTION IN SEEING OUR HOMEWORLD AGAIN.
LET US NOT DELAY...

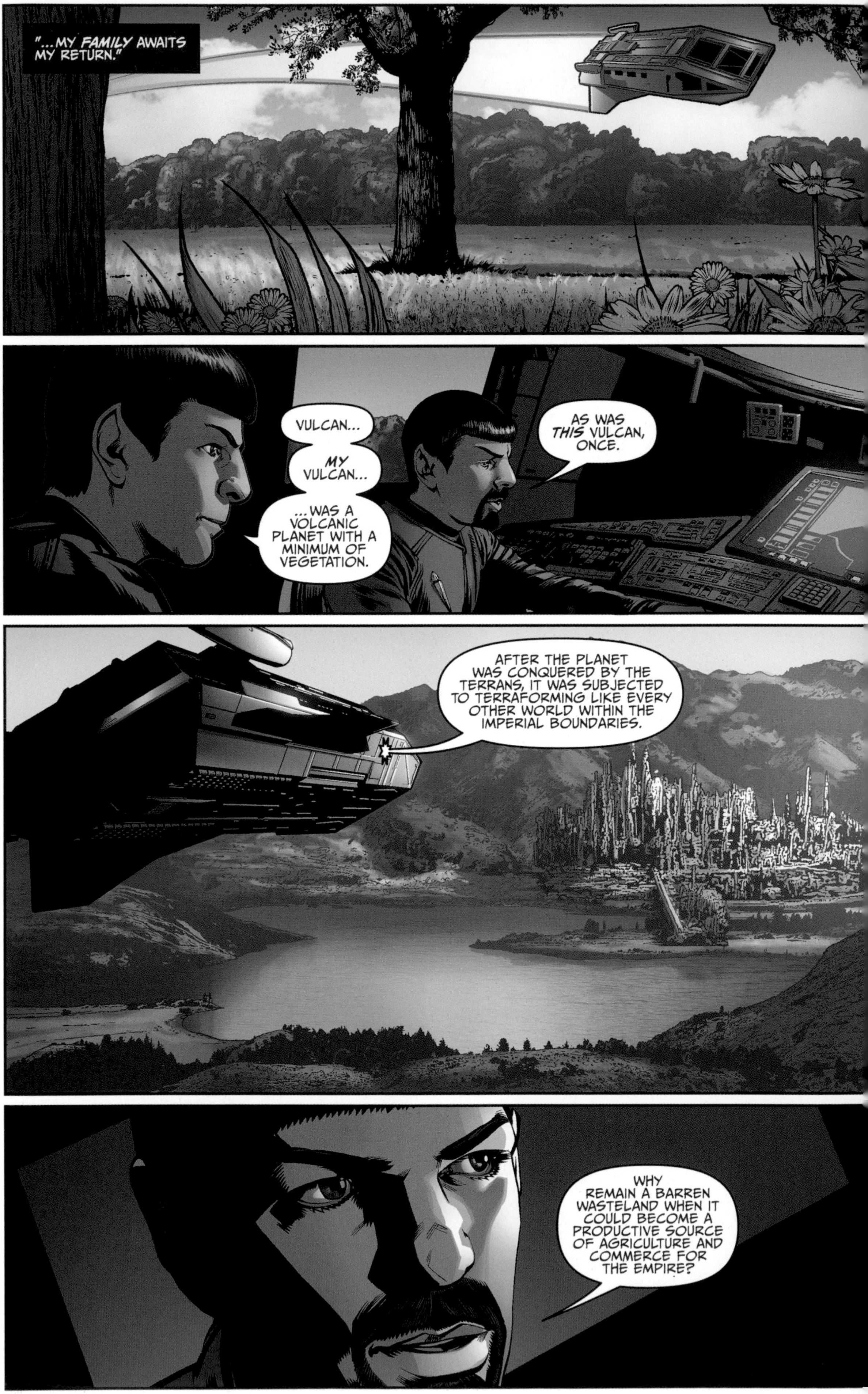
"...MY *FAMILY* AWAITS MY RETURN."
VULCAN...
MY VULCAN...
...WAS A VOLCANIC PLANET WITH A MINIMUM OF VEGETATION.
AS WAS *THIS* VULCAN, ONCE.
AFTER THE PLANET WAS CONQUERED BY THE TERRANS, IT WAS SUBJECTED TO TERRAFORMING LIKE EVERY OTHER WORLD WITHIN THE IMPERIAL BOUNDARIES.
WHY REMAIN A BARREN WASTELAND WHEN IT COULD BECOME A PRODUCTIVE SOURCE OF AGRICULTURE AND COMMERCE FOR THE EMPIRE?

"WHAT IS YOUR PURPOSE IN BRINGING ME HERE?"

"CURIOSITY. BOTH MINE...

"AND MY *FATHER'S*."

YOU TOLD ME YOU WERE BRINGING A MOST UNUSUAL SPECIMEN FOR ME TO EXAMINE, SPOCK.

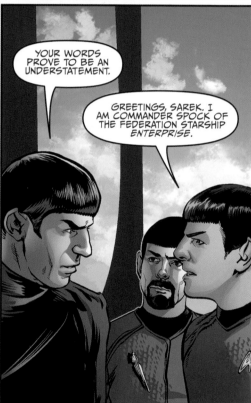

YOUR WORDS PROVE TO BE AN UNDERSTATEMENT.

GREETINGS, SAREK. I AM COMMANDER SPOCK OF THE FEDERATION STARSHIP *ENTERPRISE*.

AM I TO ASSUME THAT, SINCE IN THIS REALITY VULCAN HAS NOT BEEN DESTROYED...

...MY MOTHER IS ALIVE AS WELL?

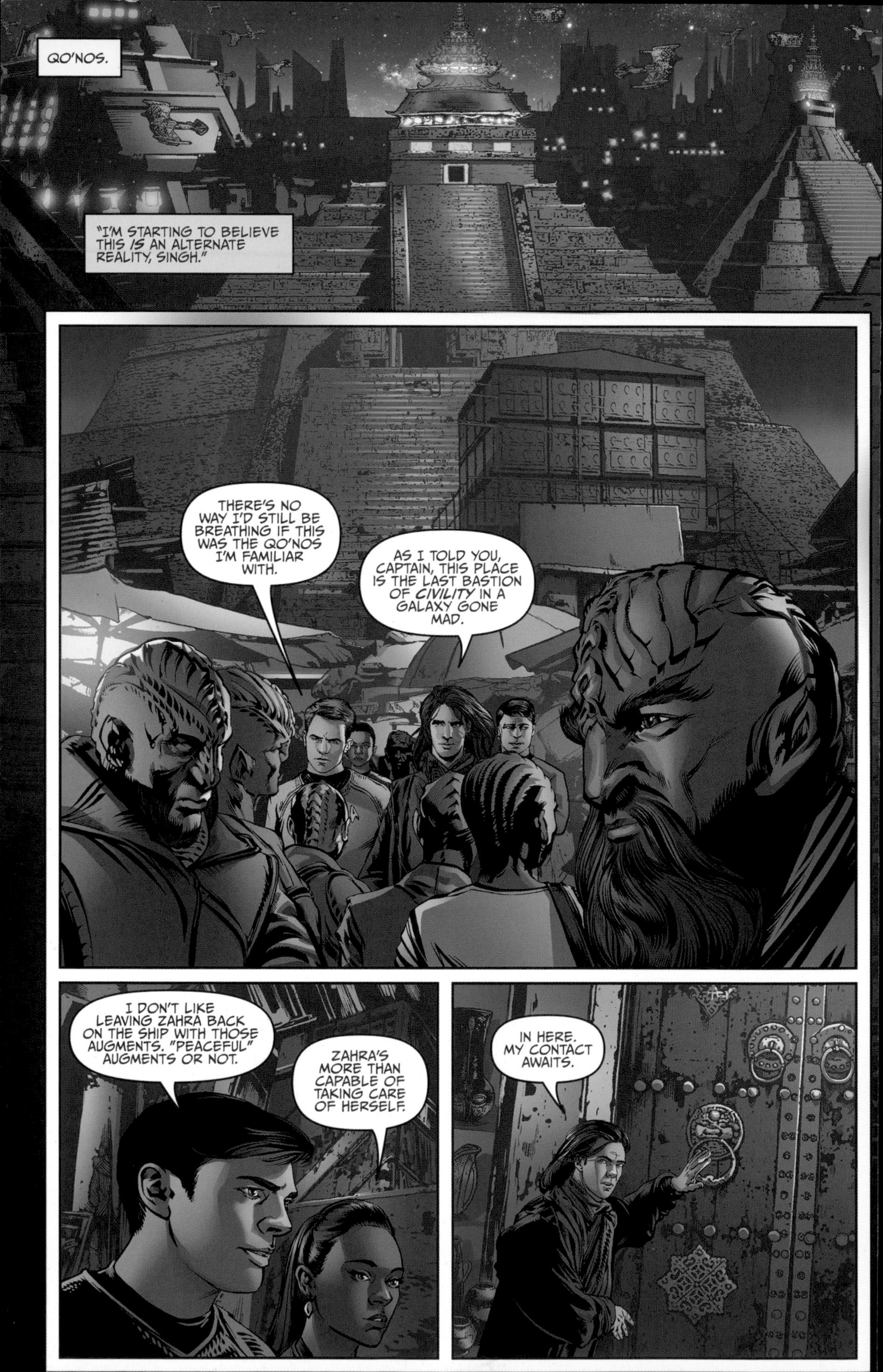
QO'NOS.
"I'M STARTING TO BELIEVE THIS IS AN ALTERNATE REALITY, SINGH."
THERE'S NO WAY I'D STILL BE BREATHING IF THIS WAS THE QO'NOS I'M FAMILIAR WITH.
AS I TOLD YOU, CAPTAIN, THIS PLACE IS THE LAST BASTION OF CIVILITY IN A GALAXY GONE MAD.
I DON'T LIKE LEAVING ZAHRA BACK ON THE SHIP WITH THOSE AUGMENTS. "PEACEFUL" AUGMENTS OR NOT.
ZAHRA'S MORE THAN CAPABLE OF TAKING CARE OF HERSELF.
IN HERE. MY CONTACT AWAITS.

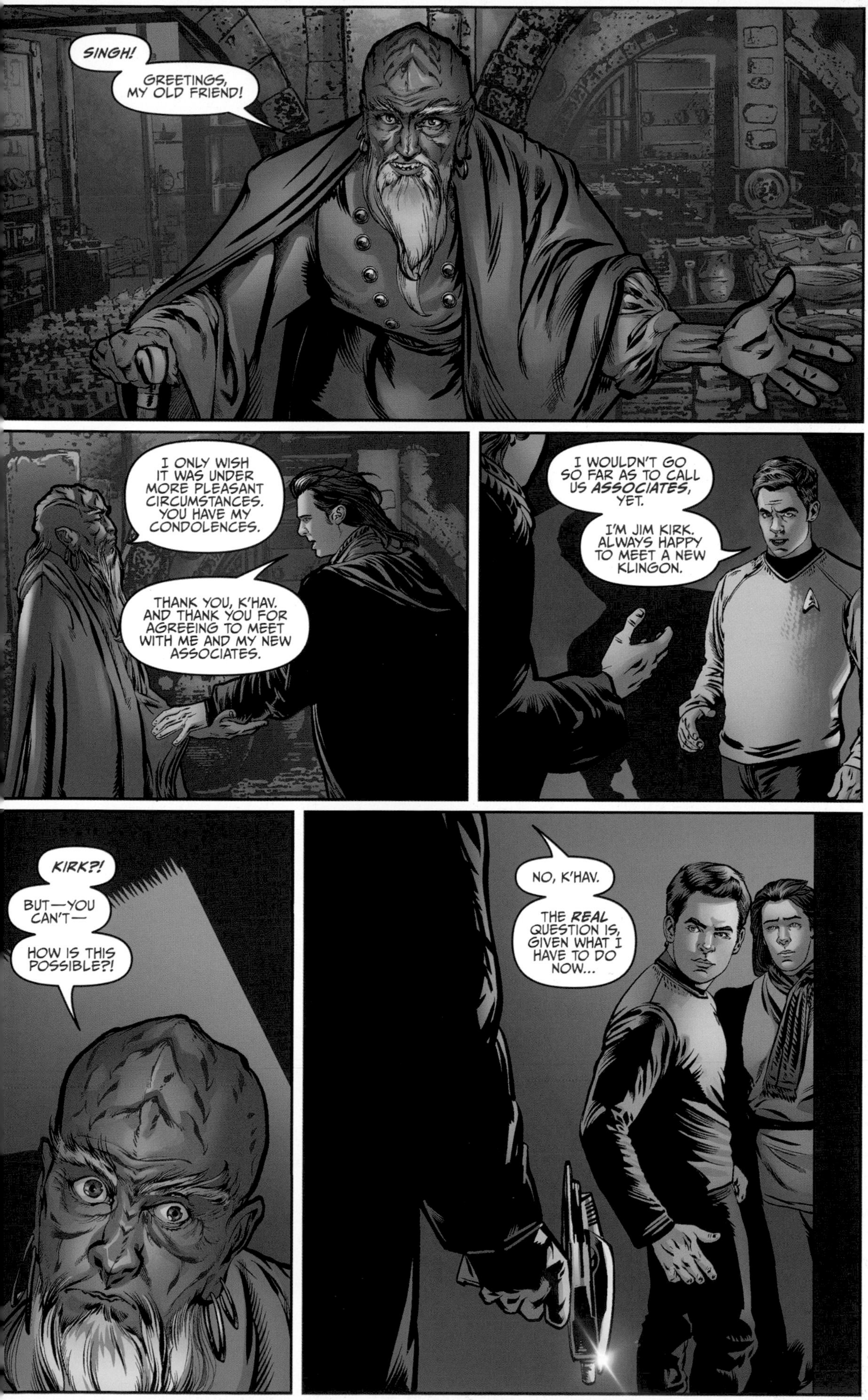
SINGH!
GREETINGS, MY OLD FRIEND!
I ONLY WISH IT WAS UNDER MORE PLEASANT CIRCUMSTANCES. YOU HAVE MY CONDOLENCES.
THANK YOU, K'HAV. AND THANK YOU FOR AGREEING TO MEET WITH ME AND MY NEW ASSOCIATES.
I WOULDN'T GO SO FAR AS TO CALL US *ASSOCIATES*, YET.
I'M JIM KIRK. ALWAYS HAPPY TO MEET A NEW KLINGON.
KIRK?!
BUT—YOU CAN'T—
HOW IS THIS POSSIBLE?!
NO, K'HAV.
THE *REAL* QUESTION IS, GIVEN WHAT I HAVE TO DO NOW...

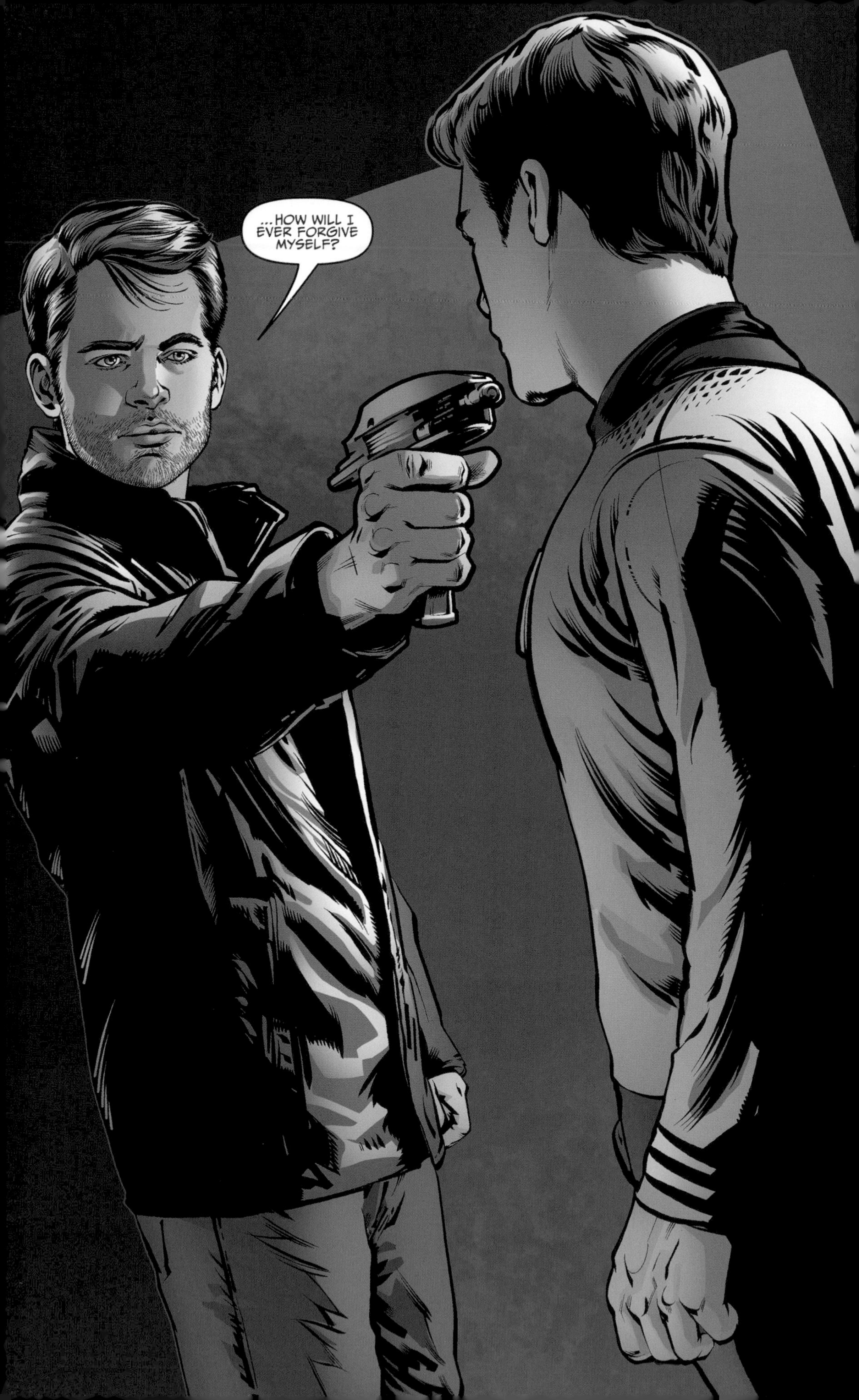
...HOW WILL I EVER FORGIVE MYSELF?

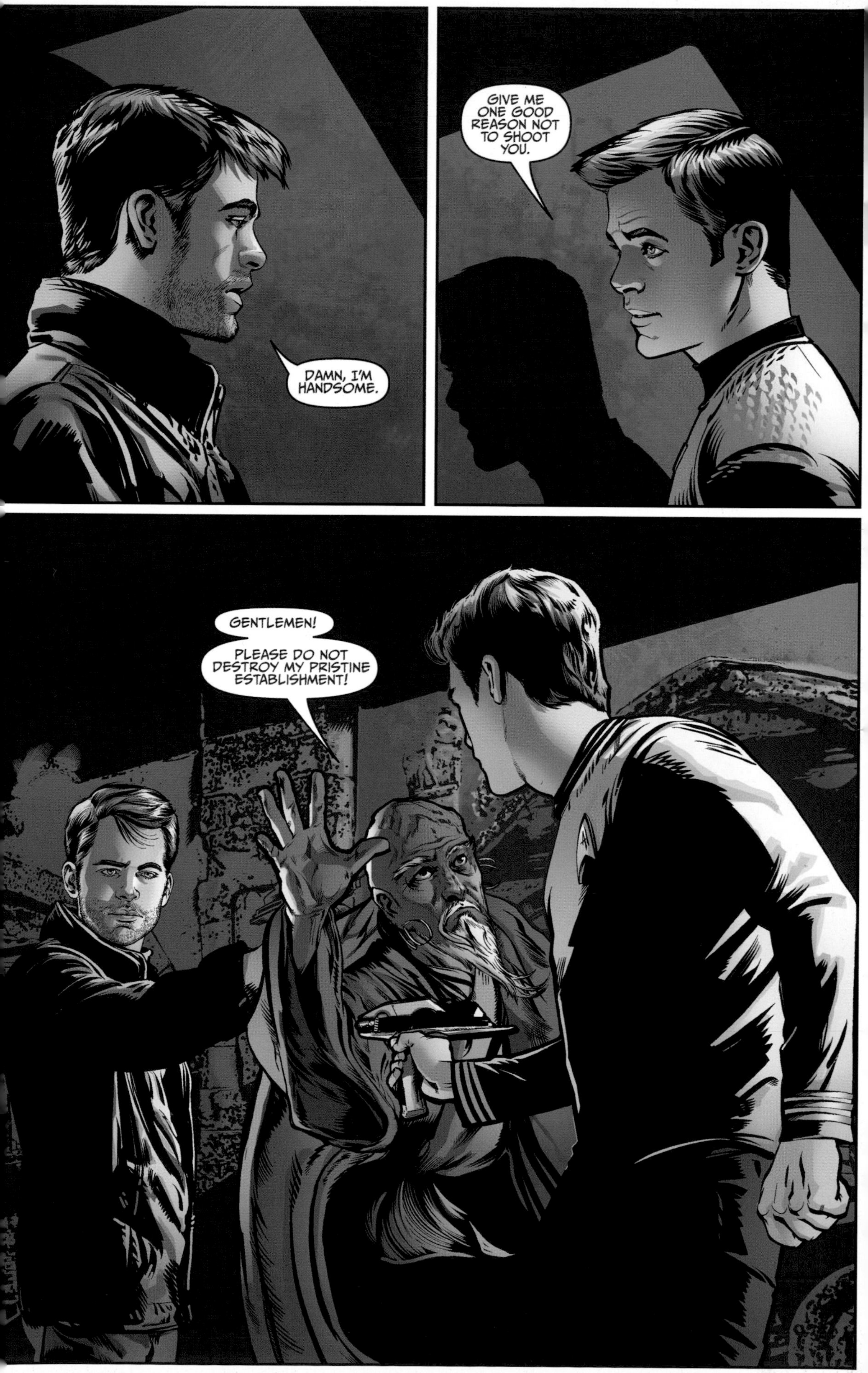
DAMN, I'M HANDSOME.
GIVE ME ONE GOOD REASON NOT TO SHOOT YOU.
GENTLEMEN!
PLEASE DO NOT DESTROY MY PRISTINE ESTABLISHMENT!

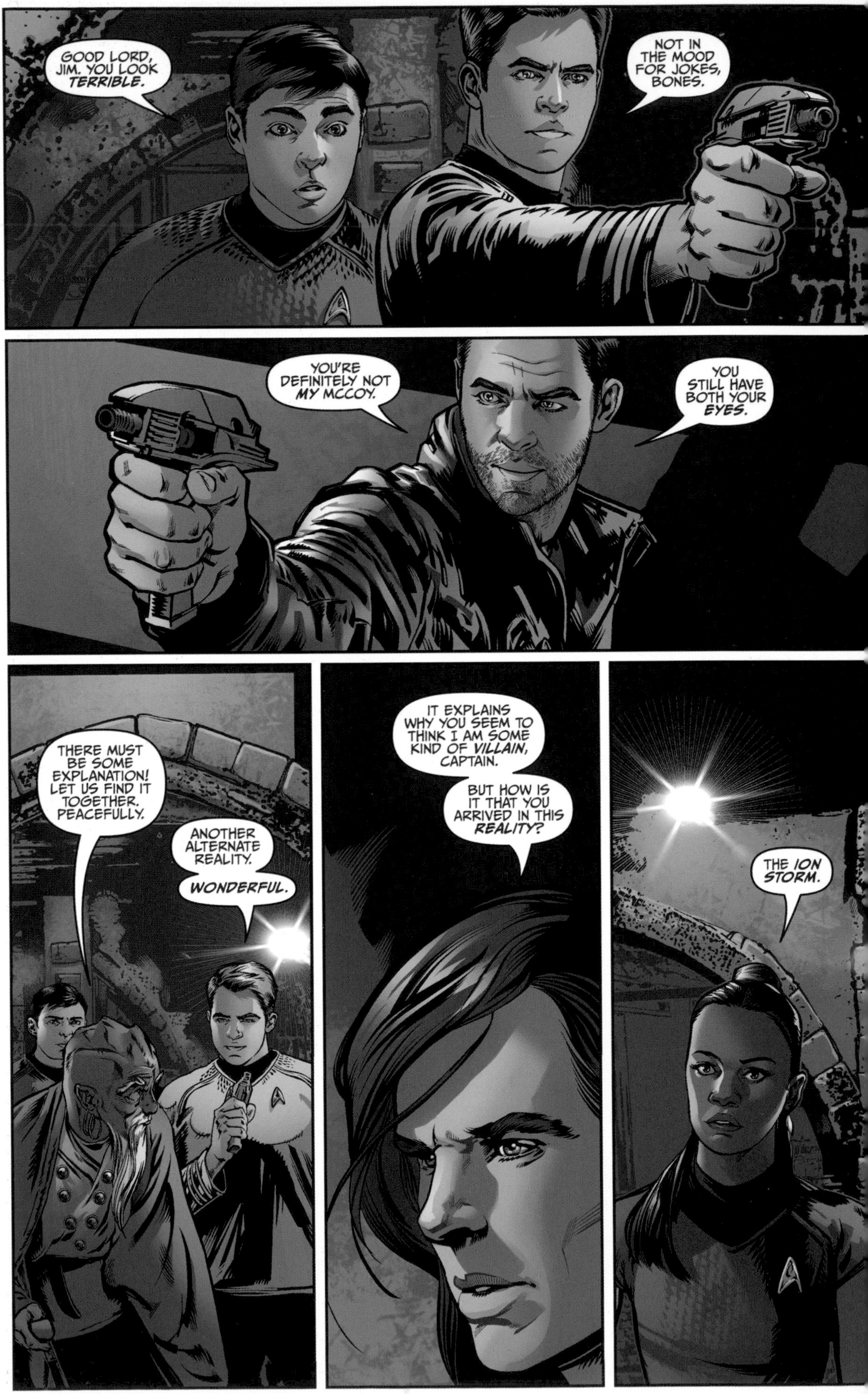
GOOD LORD, JIM. YOU LOOK TERRIBLE.
NOT IN THE MOOD FOR JOKES, BONES.
YOU'RE DEFINITELY NOT MY MCCOY.
YOU STILL HAVE BOTH YOUR EYES.
THERE MUST BE SOME EXPLANATION! LET US FIND IT TOGETHER. PEACEFULLY.
ANOTHER ALTERNATE REALITY.
WONDERFUL.
IT EXPLAINS WHY YOU SEEM TO THINK I AM SOME KIND OF VILLAIN, CAPTAIN.
BUT HOW IS IT THAT YOU ARRIVED IN THIS REALITY?
THE ION STORM.

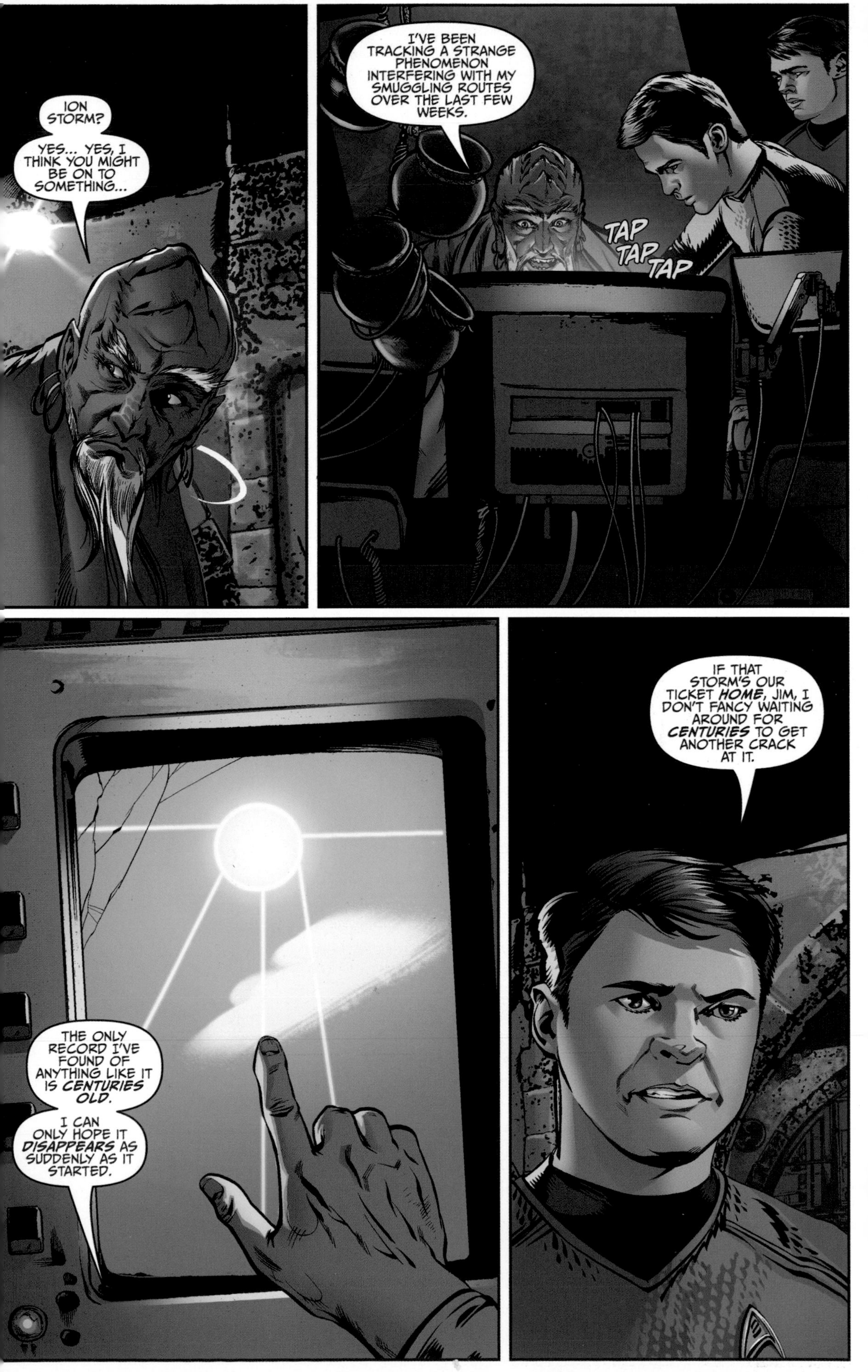
ION STORM?
YES... YES, I THINK YOU MIGHT BE ON TO SOMETHING...
I'VE BEEN TRACKING A STRANGE PHENOMENON INTERFERING WITH MY SMUGGLING ROUTES OVER THE LAST FEW WEEKS.
TAP TAP TAP
THE ONLY RECORD I'VE FOUND OF ANYTHING LIKE IT IS CENTURIES OLD.
I CAN ONLY HOPE IT DISAPPEARS AS SUDDENLY AS IT STARTED.
IF THAT STORM'S OUR TICKET HOME, JIM, I DON'T FANCY WAITING AROUND FOR CENTURIES TO GET ANOTHER CRACK AT IT.

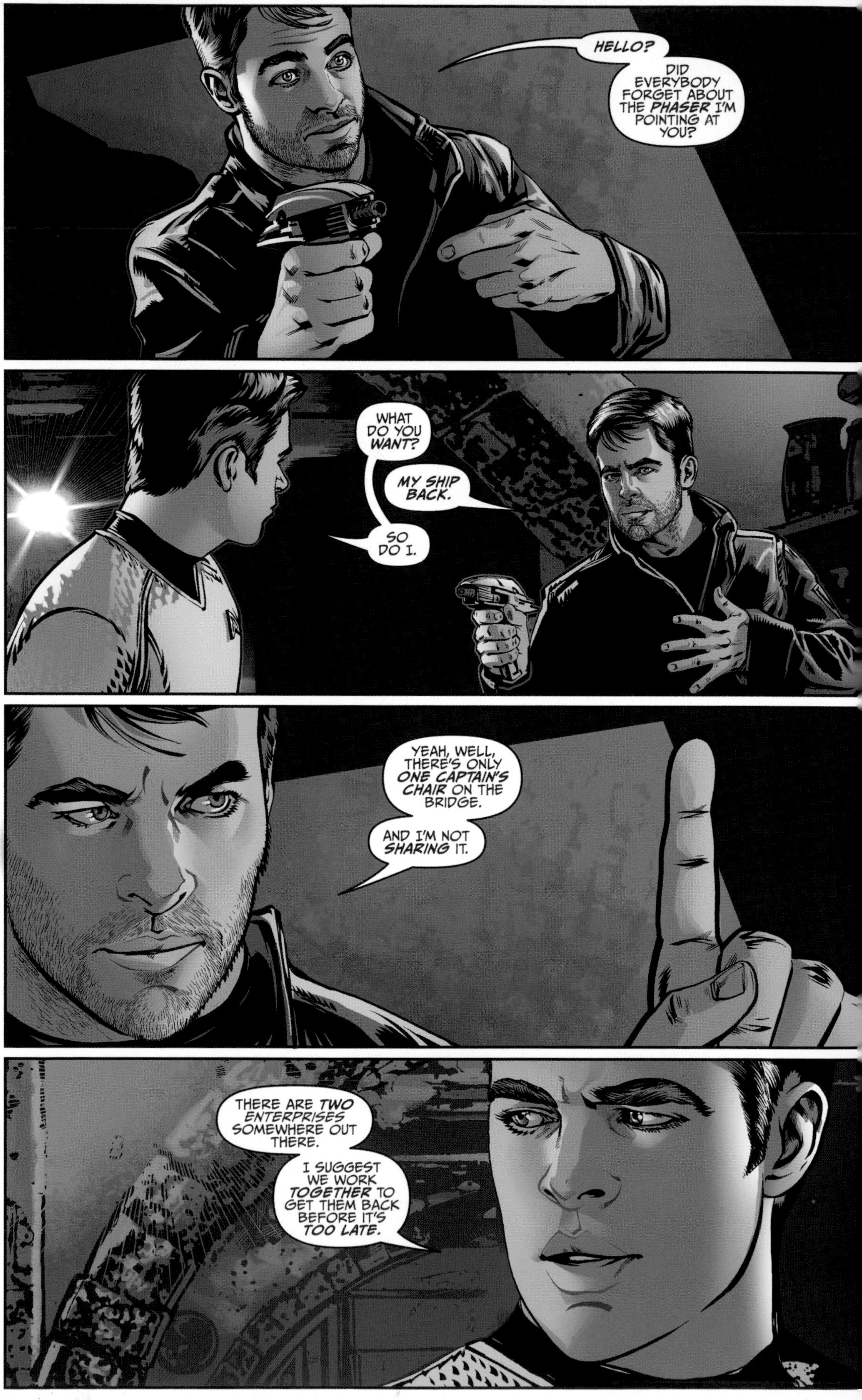
HELLO?
DID EVERYBODY FORGET ABOUT THE PHASER I'M POINTING AT YOU?
WHAT DO YOU WANT?
MY SHIP BACK.
SO DO I.
YEAH, WELL, THERE'S ONLY ONE CAPTAIN'S CHAIR ON THE BRIDGE.
AND I'M NOT SHARING IT.
THERE ARE TWO ENTERPRISES SOMEWHERE OUT THERE.
I SUGGEST WE WORK TOGETHER TO GET THEM BACK BEFORE IT'S TOO LATE.

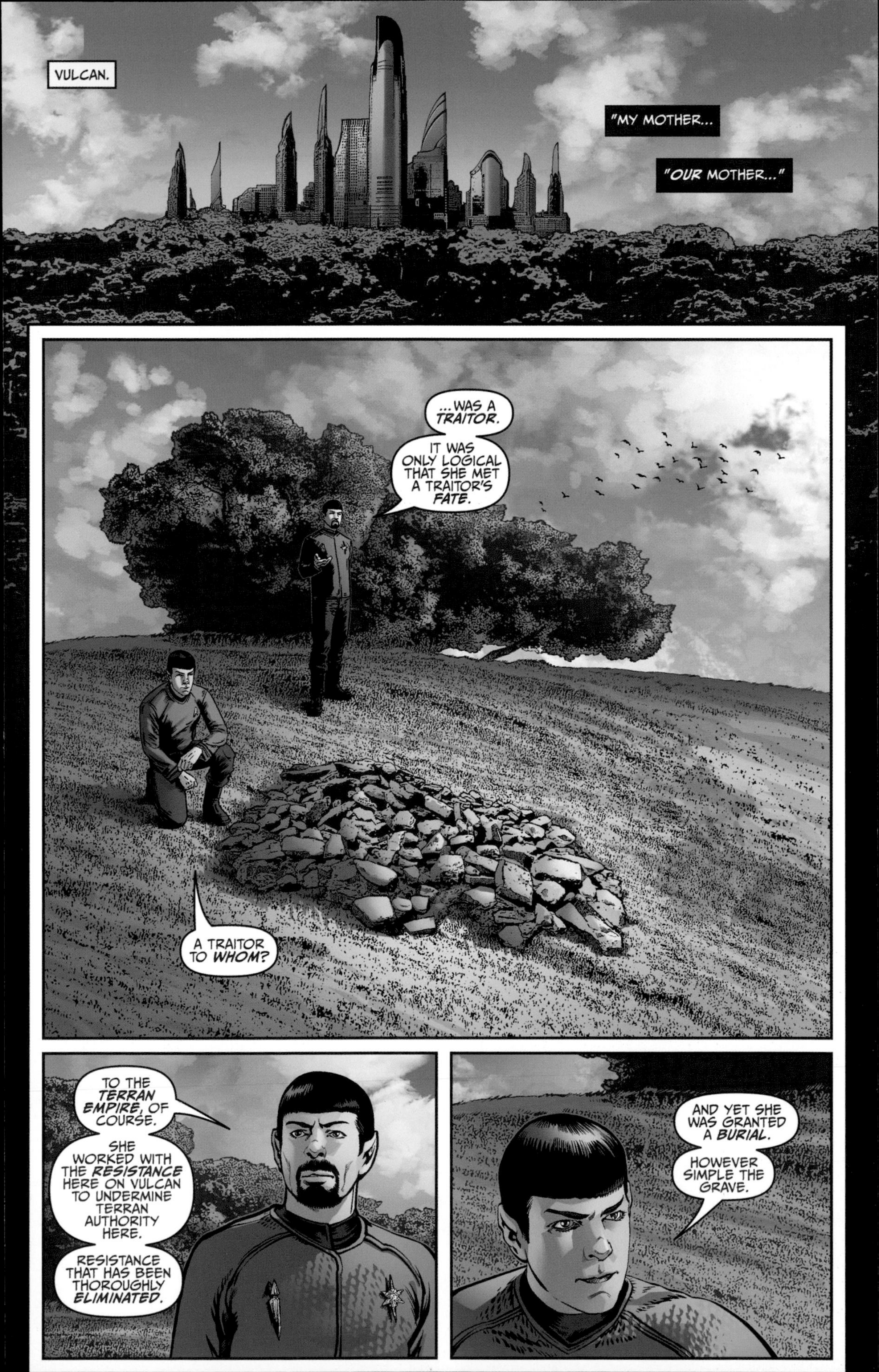
VULCAN.
"MY MOTHER...
"OUR MOTHER..."
...WAS A TRAITOR.
IT WAS ONLY LOGICAL THAT SHE MET A TRAITOR'S FATE.
A TRAITOR TO WHOM?
TO THE TERRAN EMPIRE, OF COURSE.
SHE WORKED WITH THE RESISTANCE HERE ON VULCAN TO UNDERMINE TERRAN AUTHORITY HERE.
RESISTANCE THAT HAS BEEN THOROUGHLY ELIMINATED.
AND YET SHE WAS GRANTED A BURIAL.
HOWEVER SIMPLE THE GRAVE.

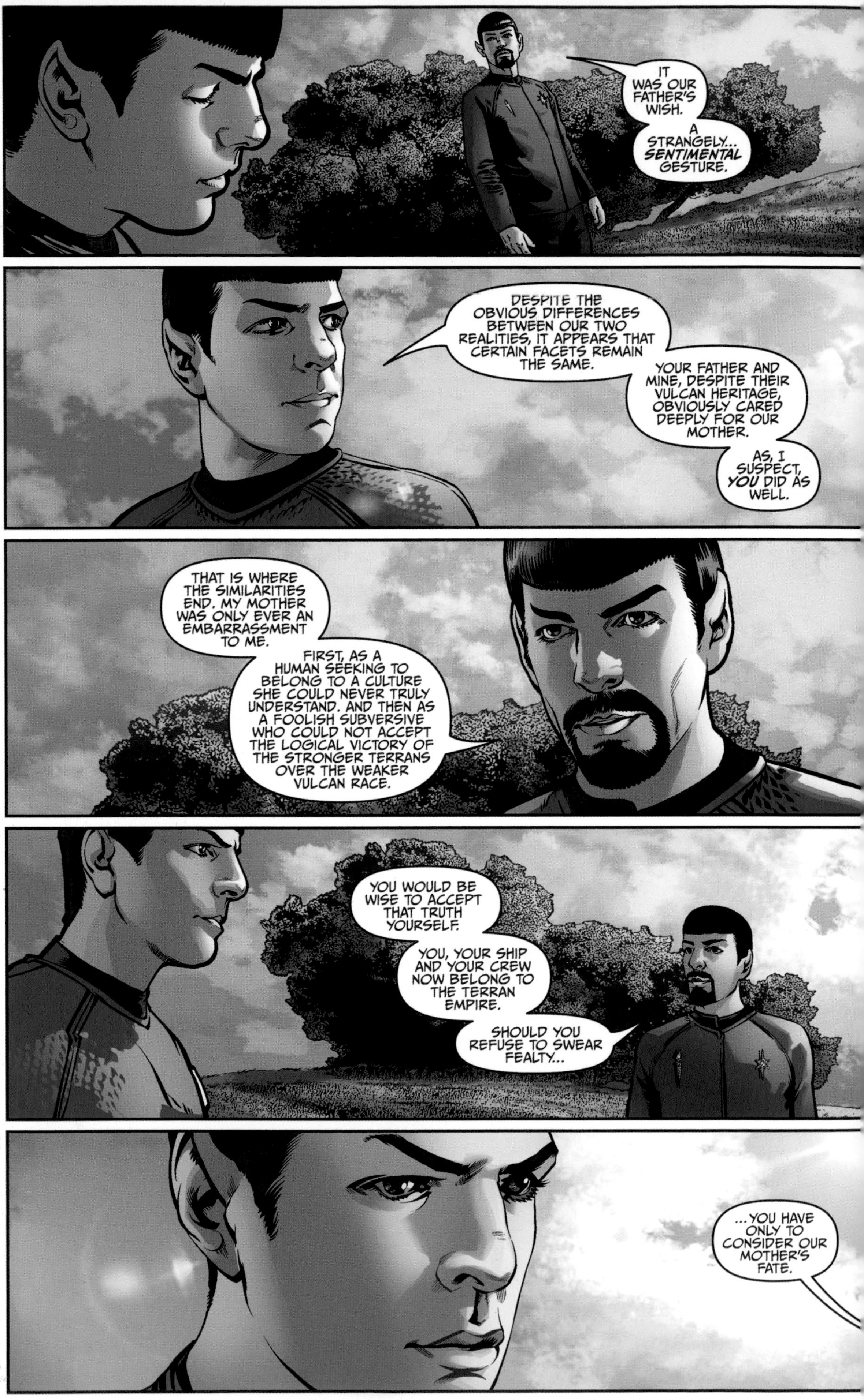
IT WAS OUR FATHER'S WISH.
A STRANGELY... SENTIMENTAL GESTURE.
DESPITE THE OBVIOUS DIFFERENCES BETWEEN OUR TWO REALITIES, IT APPEARS THAT CERTAIN FACETS REMAIN THE SAME.
YOUR FATHER AND MINE, DESPITE THEIR VULCAN HERITAGE, OBVIOUSLY CARED DEEPLY FOR OUR MOTHER.
AS, I SUSPECT, YOU DID AS WELL.
THAT IS WHERE THE SIMILARITIES END. MY MOTHER WAS ONLY EVER AN EMBARRASSMENT TO ME.
FIRST, AS A HUMAN SEEKING TO BELONG TO A CULTURE SHE COULD NEVER TRULY UNDERSTAND. AND THEN AS A FOOLISH SUBVERSIVE WHO COULD NOT ACCEPT THE LOGICAL VICTORY OF THE STRONGER TERRANS OVER THE WEAKER VULCAN RACE.
YOU WOULD BE WISE TO ACCEPT THAT TRUTH YOURSELF.
YOU, YOUR SHIP AND YOUR CREW NOW BELONG TO THE TERRAN EMPIRE.
SHOULD YOU REFUSE TO SWEAR FEALTY...
...YOU HAVE ONLY TO CONSIDER OUR MOTHER'S FATE.

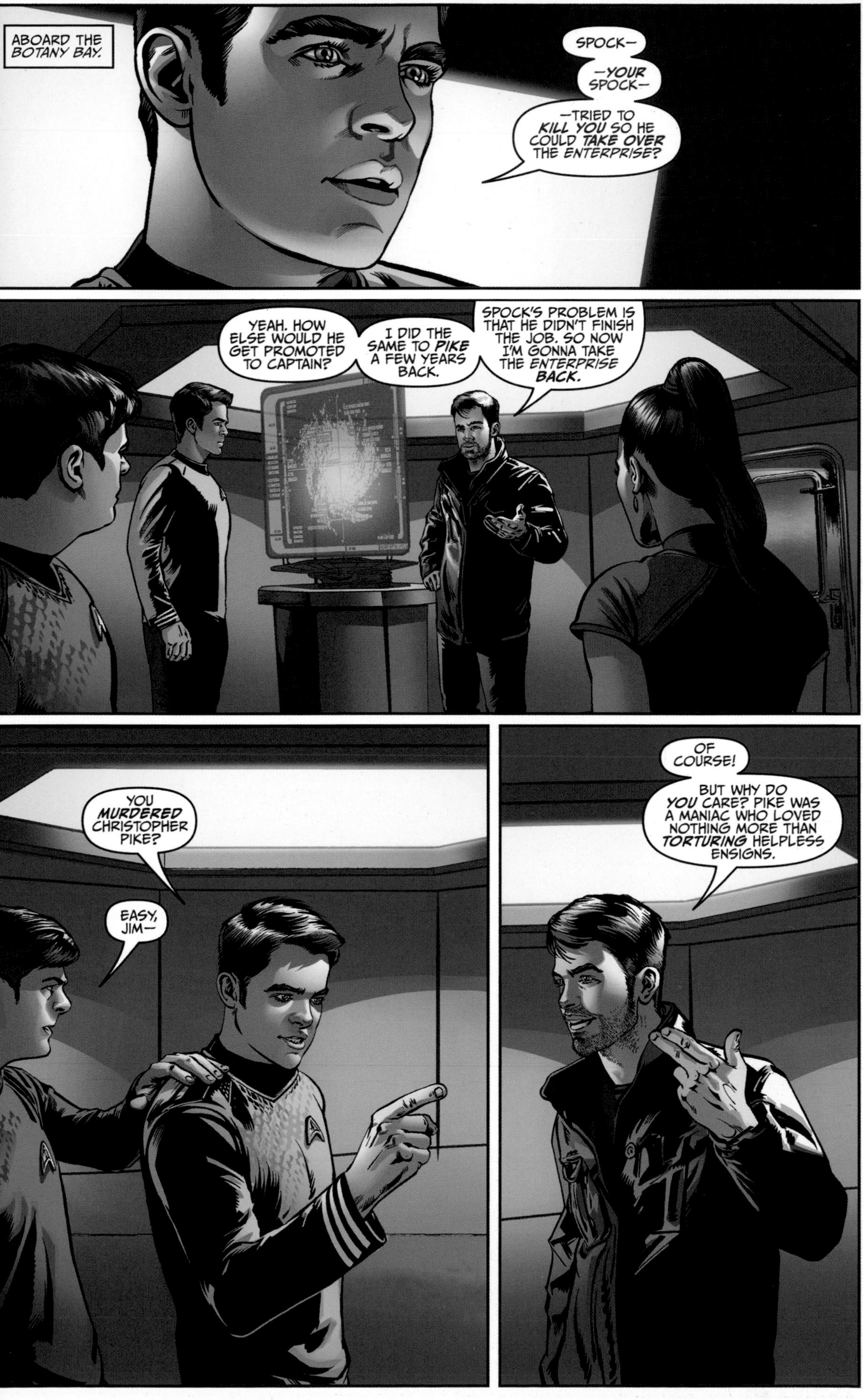
ABOARD THE *BOTANY BAY.*
SPOCK—
—*YOUR* SPOCK—
—TRIED TO ***KILL YOU*** SO HE COULD ***TAKE OVER*** THE *ENTERPRISE*?
YEAH. HOW ELSE WOULD HE GET PROMOTED TO CAPTAIN?
I DID THE SAME TO ***PIKE*** A FEW YEARS BACK.
SPOCK'S PROBLEM IS THAT HE DIDN'T FINISH THE JOB. SO NOW I'M GONNA TAKE THE *ENTERPRISE* ***BACK.***
YOU ***MURDERED*** CHRISTOPHER PIKE?
EASY, JIM—
OF COURSE!
BUT WHY DO ***YOU*** CARE? PIKE WAS A MANIAC WHO LOVED NOTHING MORE THAN ***TORTURING*** HELPLESS ENSIGNS.

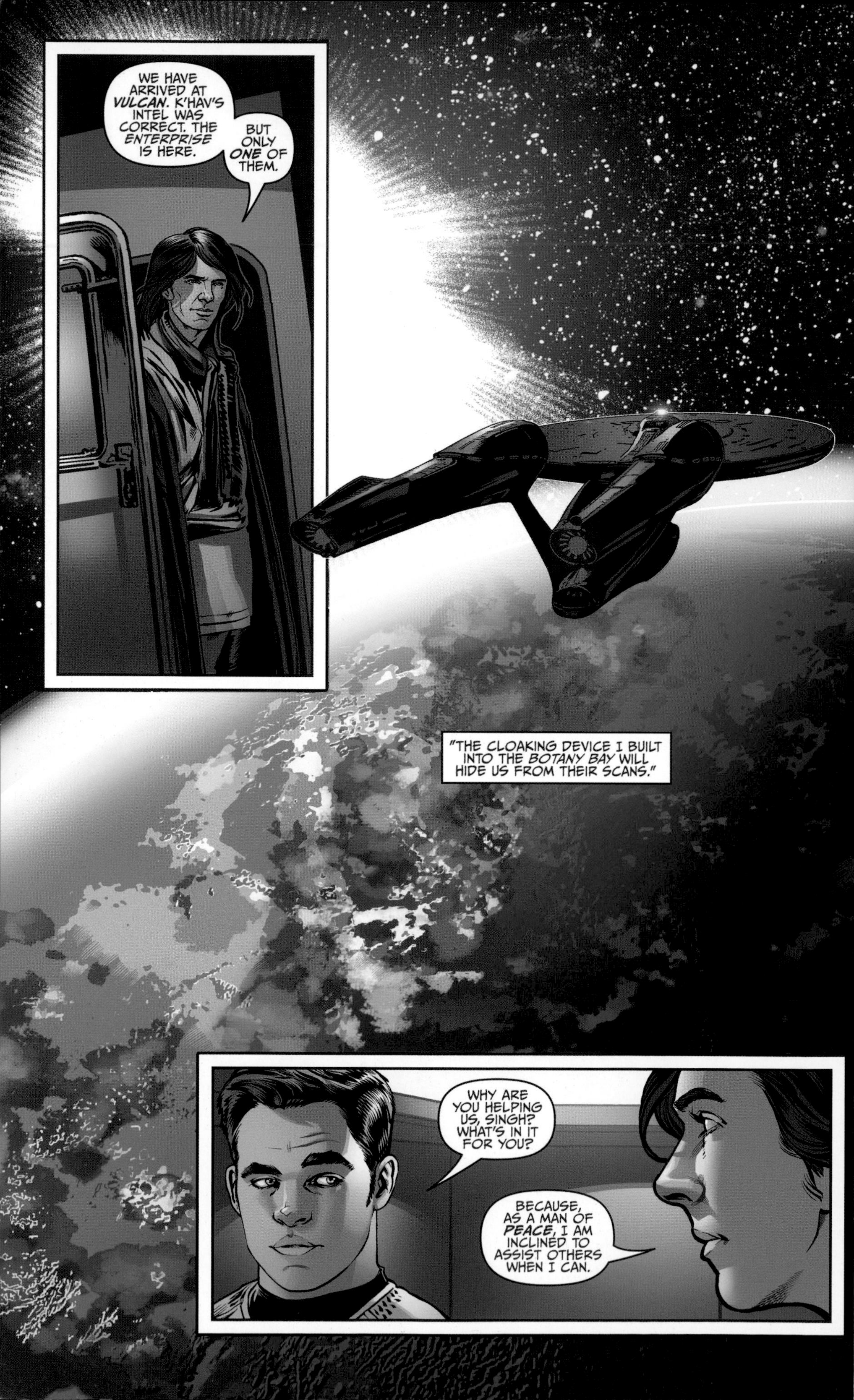
WE HAVE ARRIVED AT VULCAN. K'HAV'S INTEL WAS CORRECT. THE ENTERPRISE IS HERE.
BUT ONLY ONE OF THEM.
"THE CLOAKING DEVICE I BUILT INTO THE BOTANY BAY WILL HIDE US FROM THEIR SCANS."
WHY ARE YOU HELPING US, SINGH? WHAT'S IN IT FOR YOU?
BECAUSE, AS A MAN OF PEACE, I AM INCLINED TO ASSIST OTHERS WHEN I CAN.

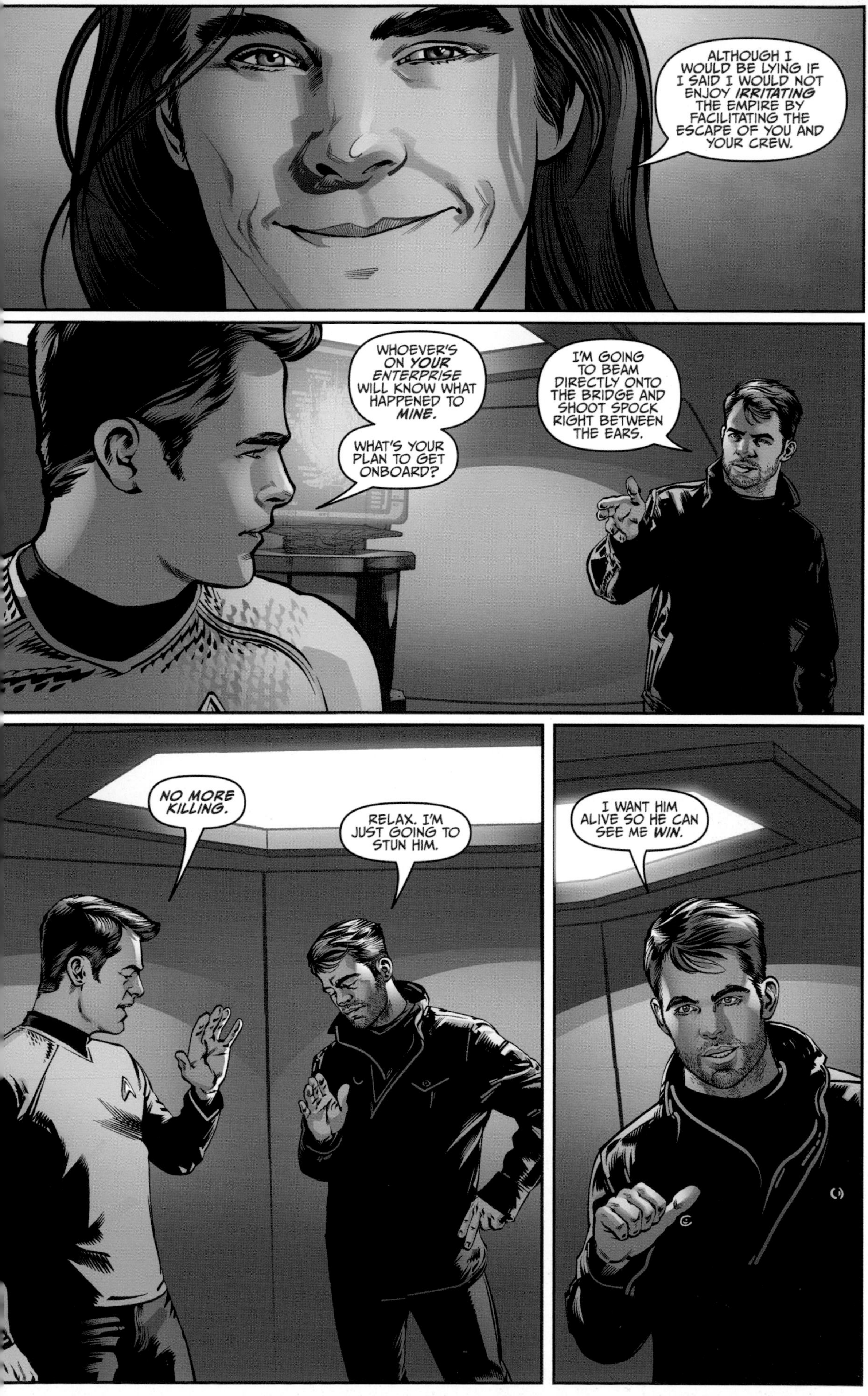
ALTHOUGH I WOULD BE LYING IF I SAID I WOULD NOT ENJOY *IRRITATING* THE EMPIRE BY FACILITATING THE ESCAPE OF YOU AND YOUR CREW.
WHOEVER'S ON *YOUR ENTERPRISE* WILL KNOW WHAT HAPPENED TO *MINE.*
WHAT'S YOUR PLAN TO GET ONBOARD?
I'M GOING TO BEAM DIRECTLY ONTO THE BRIDGE AND SHOOT SPOCK RIGHT BETWEEN THE EARS.
NO MORE KILLING.
RELAX. I'M JUST GOING TO STUN HIM.
I WANT HIM ALIVE SO HE CAN SEE ME *WIN.*

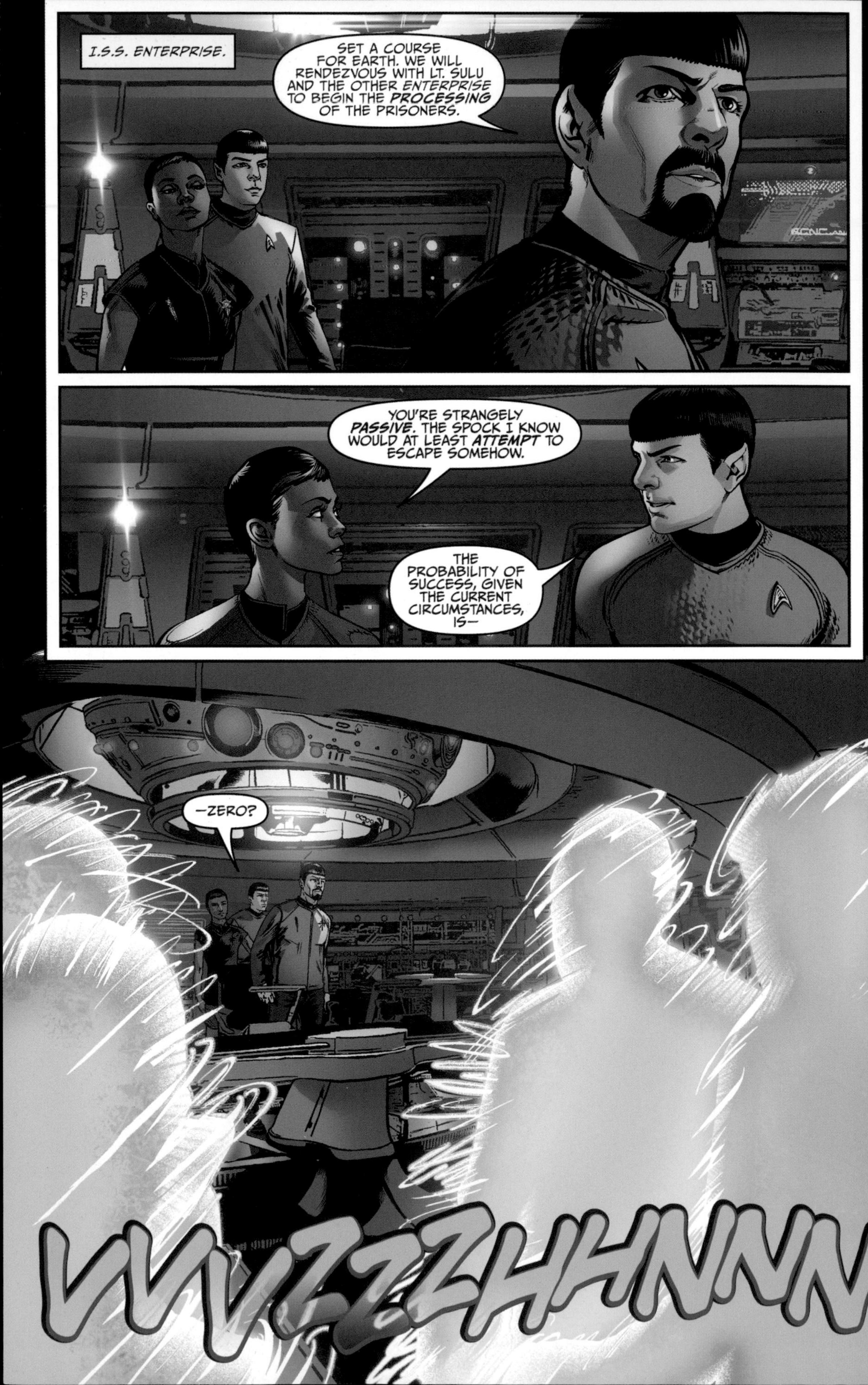
I.S.S. ENTERPRISE.
SET A COURSE FOR EARTH. WE WILL RENDEZVOUS WITH LT. SULU AND THE OTHER ENTERPRISE TO BEGIN THE PROCESSING OF THE PRISONERS.
YOU'RE STRANGELY PASSIVE. THE SPOCK I KNOW WOULD AT LEAST ATTEMPT TO ESCAPE SOMEHOW.
THE PROBABILITY OF SUCCESS, GIVEN THE CURRENT CIRCUMSTANCES, IS—
—ZERO?
VVVZZZHHNNN

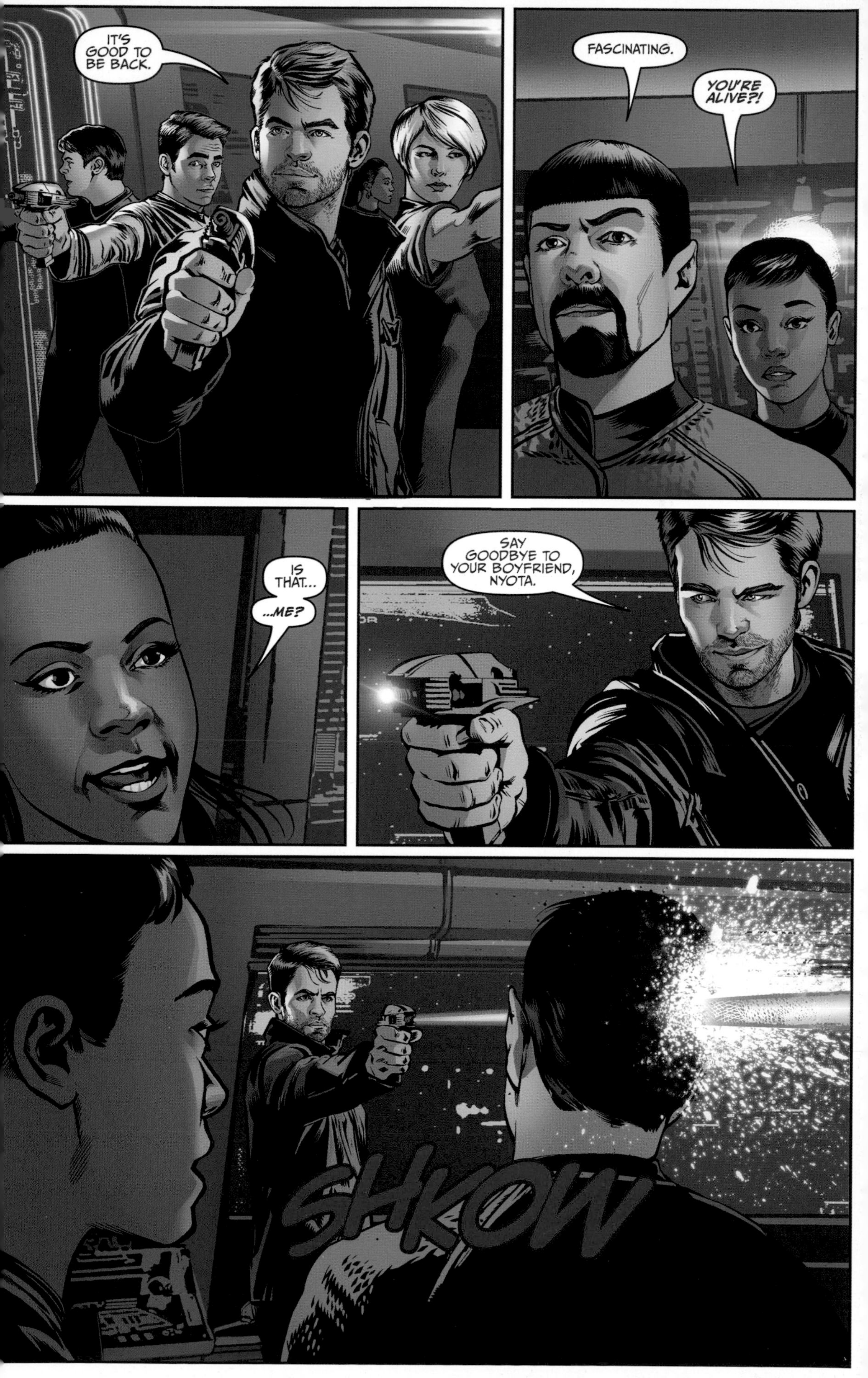
IT'S GOOD TO BE BACK.
FASCINATING.
YOU'RE ALIVE?!
IS THAT...
...ME?
SAY GOODBYE TO YOUR BOYFRIEND, NYOTA.
SHKOW

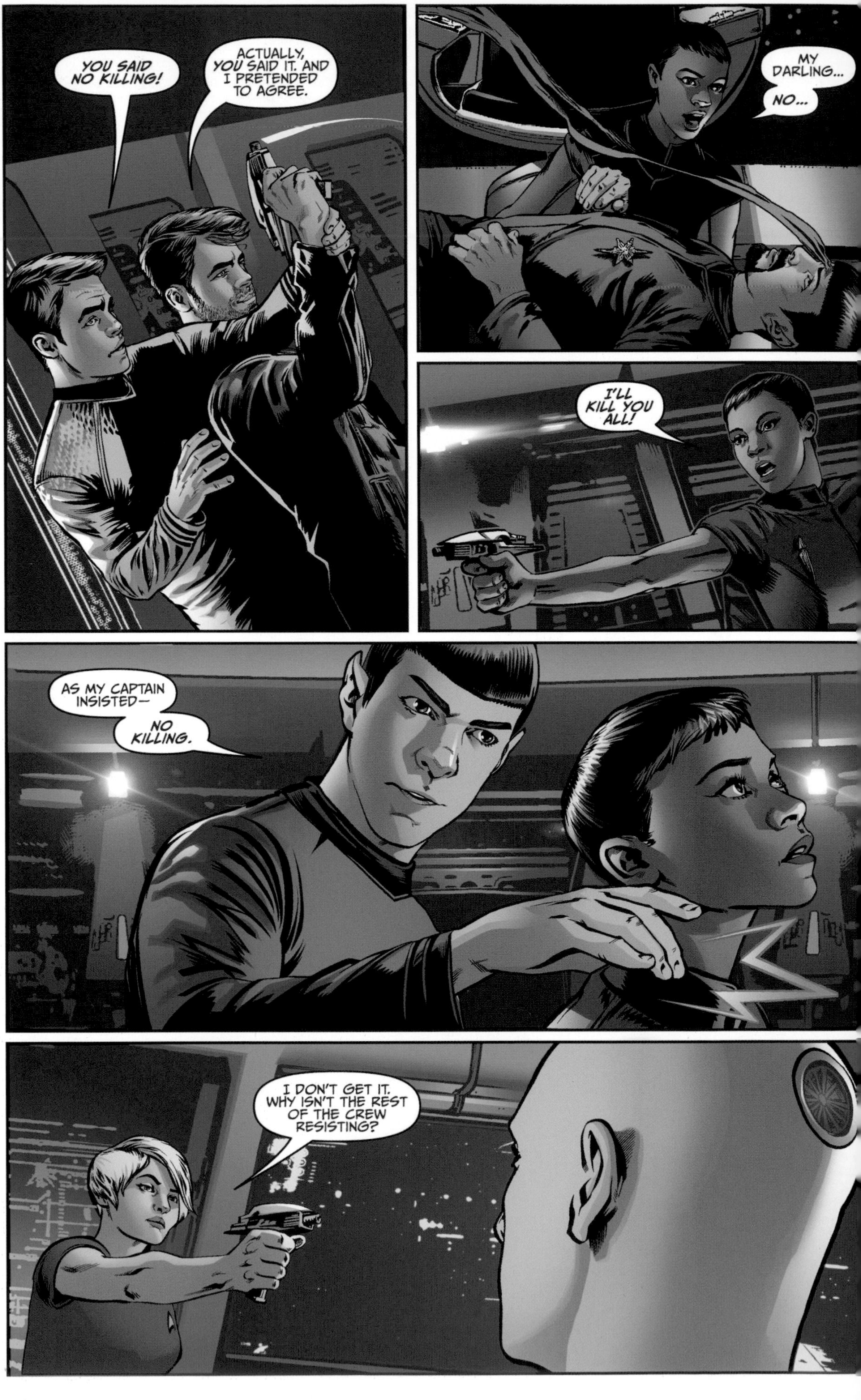
YOU SAID NO KILLING!
ACTUALLY, YOU SAID IT. AND I PRETENDED TO AGREE.
MY DARLING...
NO...
I'LL KILL YOU ALL!
AS MY CAPTAIN INSISTED—
NO KILLING.
I DON'T GET IT. WHY ISN'T THE REST OF THE CREW RESISTING?

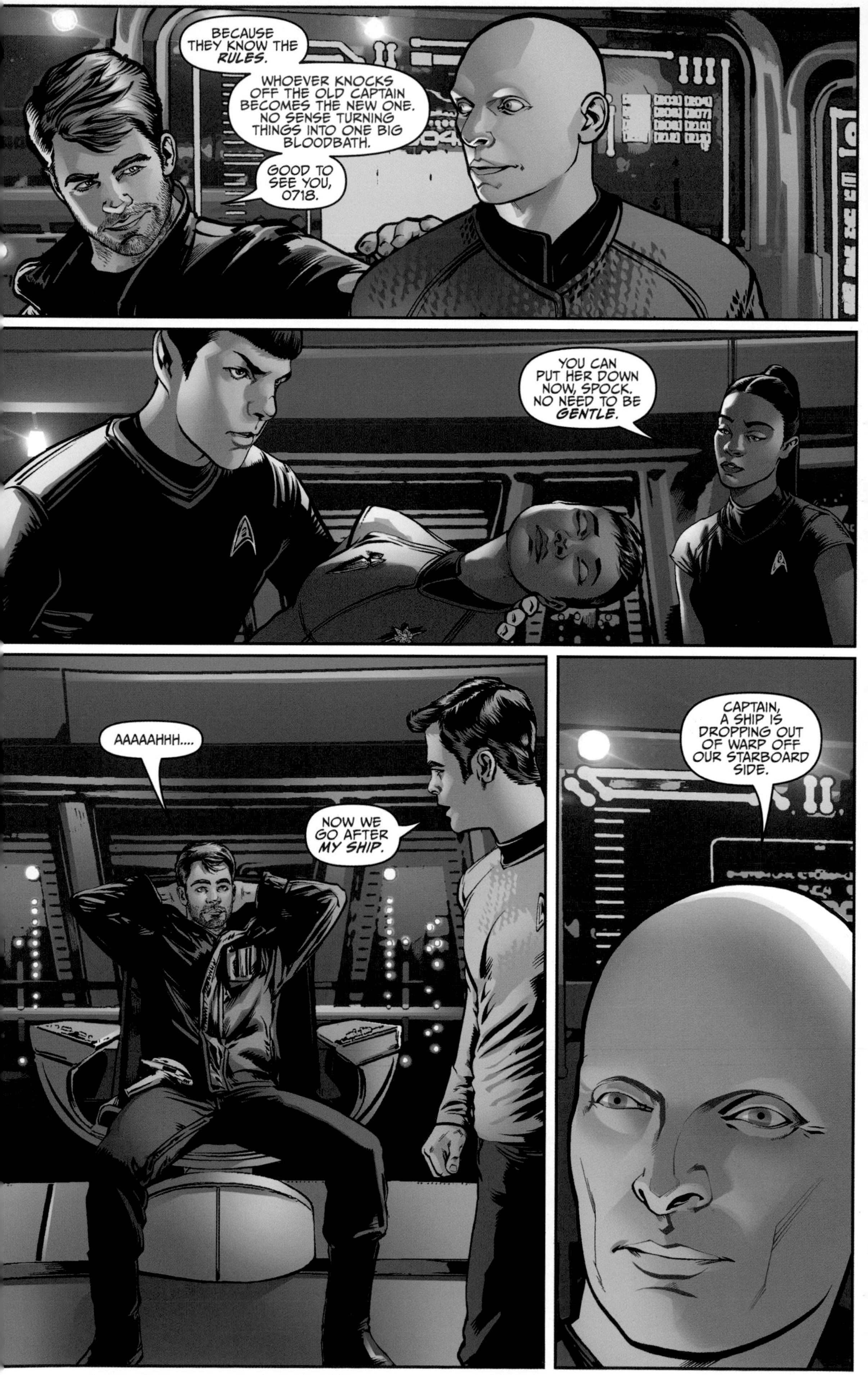
BECAUSE THEY KNOW THE RULES.
WHOEVER KNOCKS OFF THE OLD CAPTAIN BECOMES THE NEW ONE. NO SENSE TURNING THINGS INTO ONE BIG BLOODBATH.
GOOD TO SEE YOU, 0718.
YOU CAN PUT HER DOWN NOW, SPOCK. NO NEED TO BE GENTLE.
AAAAAHHH....
NOW WE GO AFTER MY SHIP.
CAPTAIN, A SHIP IS DROPPING OUT OF WARP OFF OUR STARBOARD SIDE.

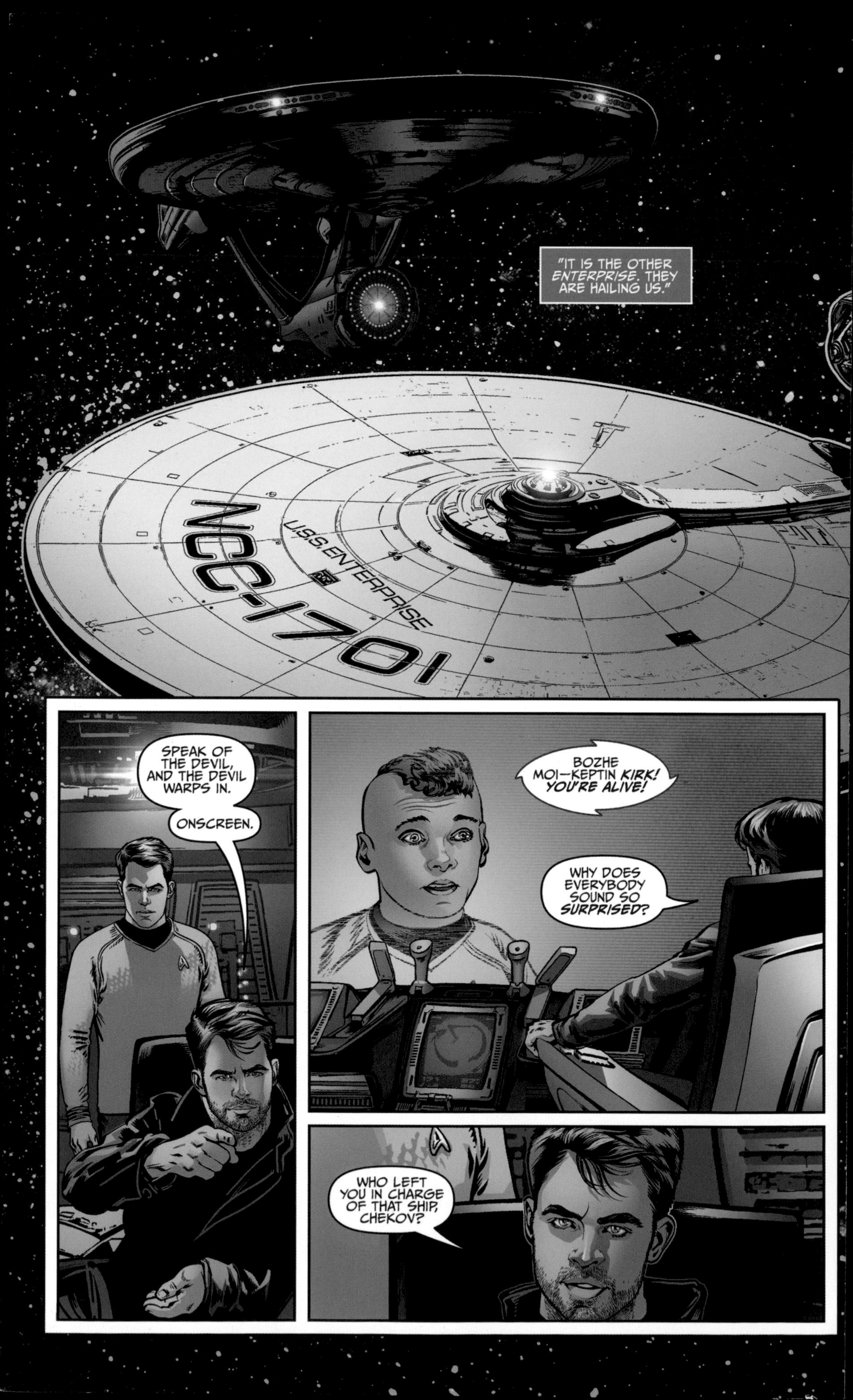
"IT IS THE OTHER ENTERPRISE. THEY ARE HAILING US."
U.S.S. ENTERPRISE
NCC-1701
SPEAK OF THE DEVIL, AND THE DEVIL WARPS IN.
ONSCREEN.
BOZHE MOI—KEPTIN KIRK! YOU'RE ALIVE!
WHY DOES EVERYBODY SOUND SO SURPRISED?
WHO LEFT YOU IN CHARGE OF THAT SHIP, CHEKOV?

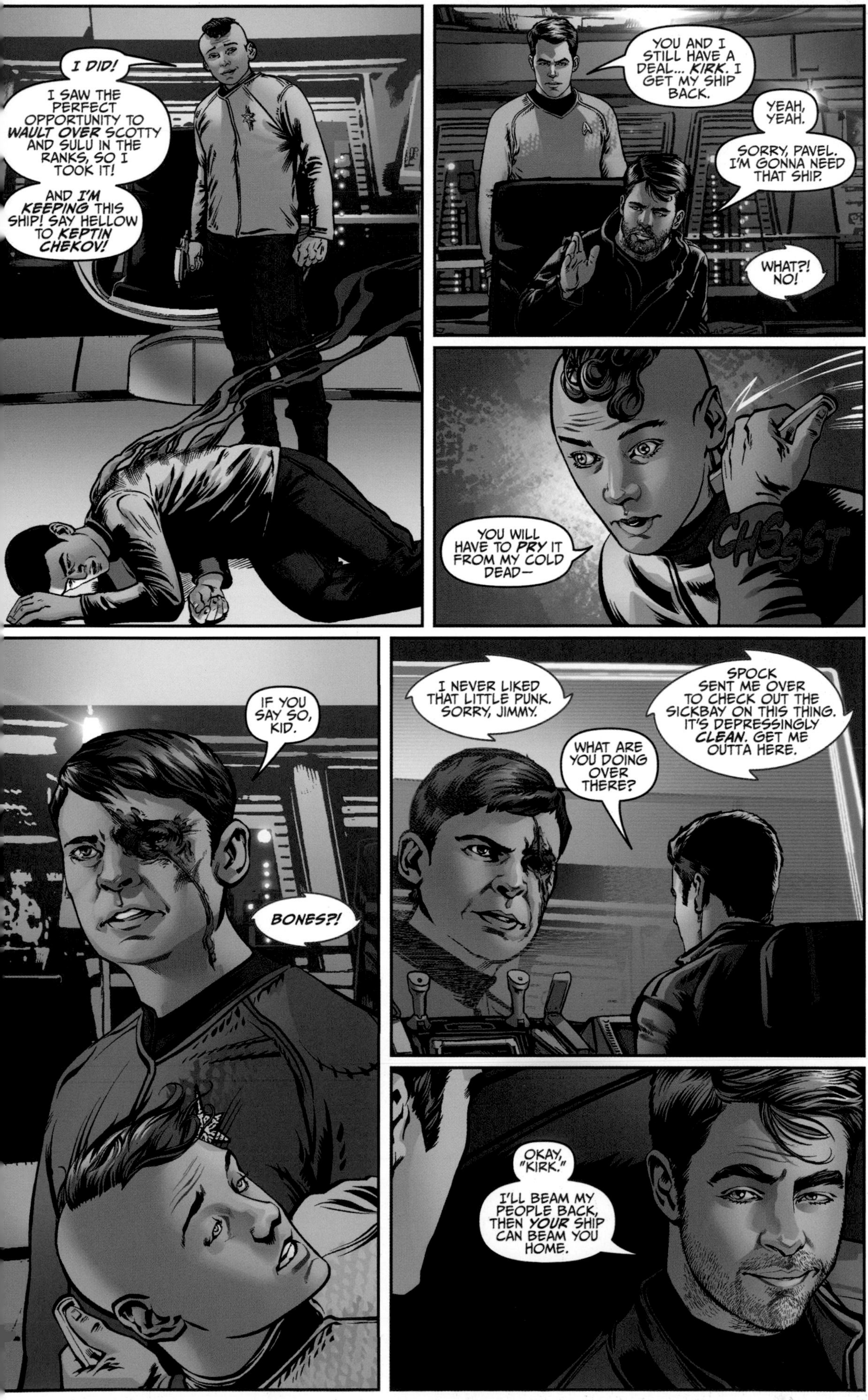
I DID!
I SAW THE PERFECT OPPORTUNITY TO WAULT OVER SCOTTY AND SULU IN THE RANKS, SO I TOOK IT!
AND I'M KEEPING THIS SHIP! SAY HELLOW TO KEPTIN CHEKOV!
YOU AND I STILL HAVE A DEAL... KIRK. I GET MY SHIP BACK.
YEAH, YEAH.
SORRY, PAVEL. I'M GONNA NEED THAT SHIP.
WHAT?! NO!
YOU WILL HAVE TO PRY IT FROM MY COLD DEAD—
CHSSST
IF YOU SAY SO, KID.
BONES?!
I NEVER LIKED THAT LITTLE PUNK. SORRY, JIMMY.
WHAT ARE YOU DOING OVER THERE?
SPOCK SENT ME OVER TO CHECK OUT THE SICKBAY ON THIS THING. IT'S DEPRESSINGLY CLEAN. GET ME OUTTA HERE.
OKAY, "KIRK."
I'LL BEAM MY PEOPLE BACK, THEN YOUR SHIP CAN BEAM YOU HOME.

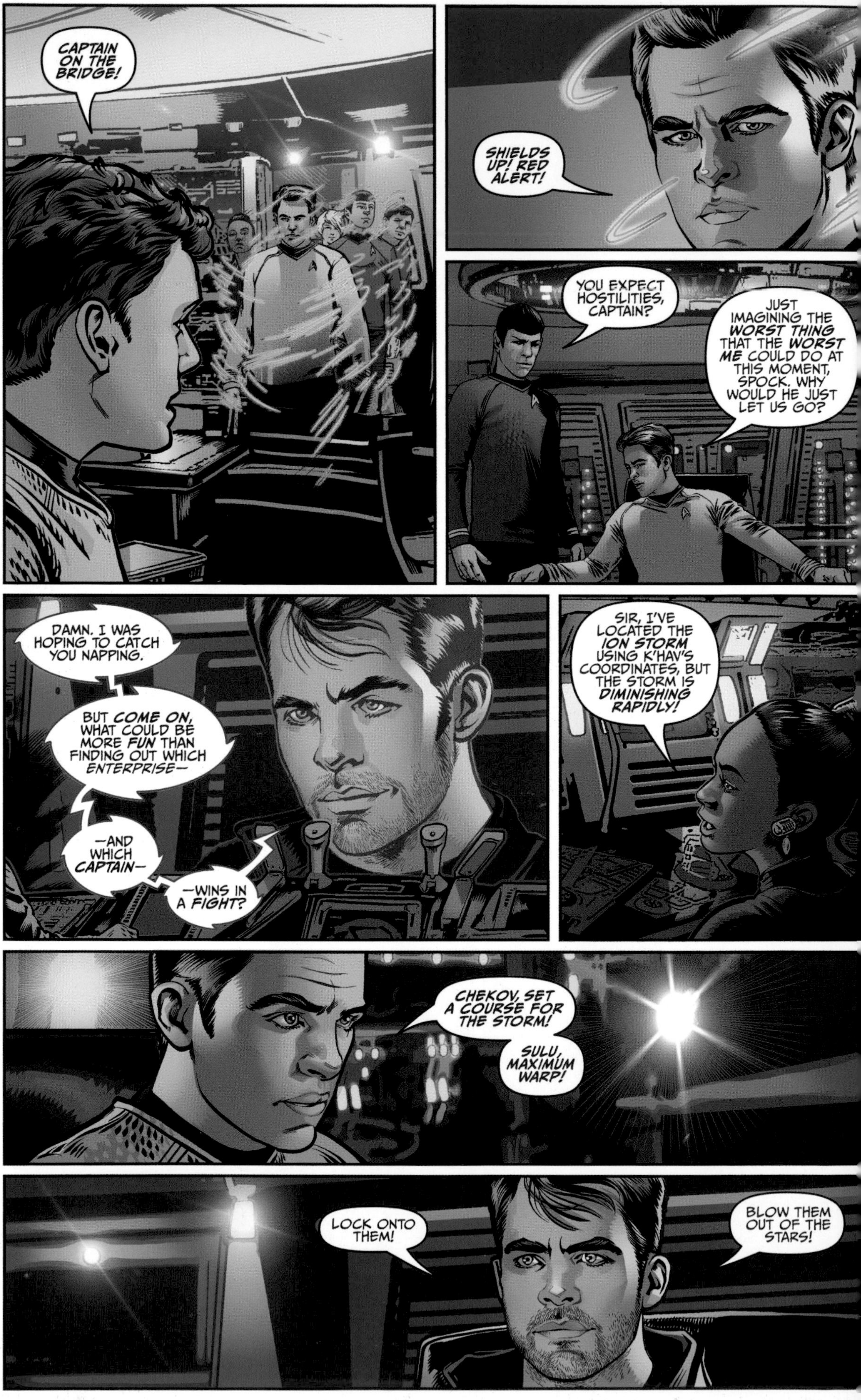
CAPTAIN ON THE BRIDGE!
SHIELDS UP! RED ALERT!
YOU EXPECT HOSTILITIES, CAPTAIN?
JUST IMAGINING THE WORST THING THAT THE WORST ME COULD DO AT THIS MOMENT, SPOCK. WHY WOULD HE JUST LET US GO?
DAMN. I WAS HOPING TO CATCH YOU NAPPING.
BUT COME ON, WHAT COULD BE MORE FUN THAN FINDING OUT WHICH ENTERPRISE—
—AND WHICH CAPTAIN—
—WINS IN A FIGHT?
SIR, I'VE LOCATED THE ION STORM USING K'HAV'S COORDINATES, BUT THE STORM IS DIMINISHING RAPIDLY!
CHEKOV, SET A COURSE FOR THE STORM!
SULU, MAXIMUM WARP!
LOCK ONTO THEM!
BLOW THEM OUT OF THE STARS!

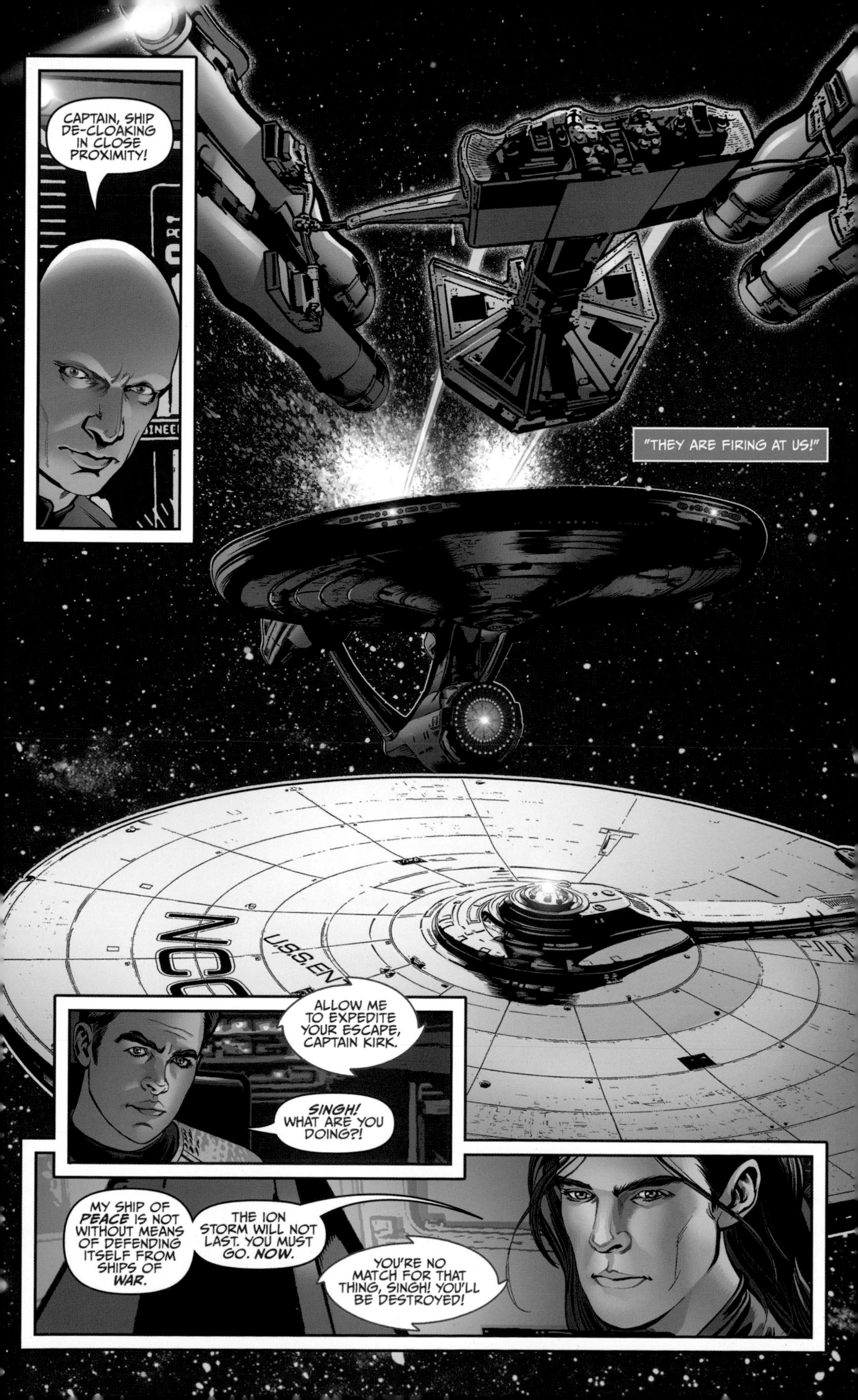
CAPTAIN, SHIP DE-CLOAKING IN CLOSE PROXIMITY!
"THEY ARE FIRING AT US!"
U.S.S. EN
NCC
ALLOW ME TO EXPEDITE YOUR ESCAPE, CAPTAIN KIRK.
SINGH! WHAT ARE YOU DOING?!
MY SHIP OF PEACE IS NOT WITHOUT MEANS OF DEFENDING ITSELF FROM SHIPS OF WAR.
THE ION STORM WILL NOT LAST. YOU MUST GO. NOW.
YOU'RE NO MATCH FOR THAT THING, SINGH! YOU'LL BE DESTROYED!

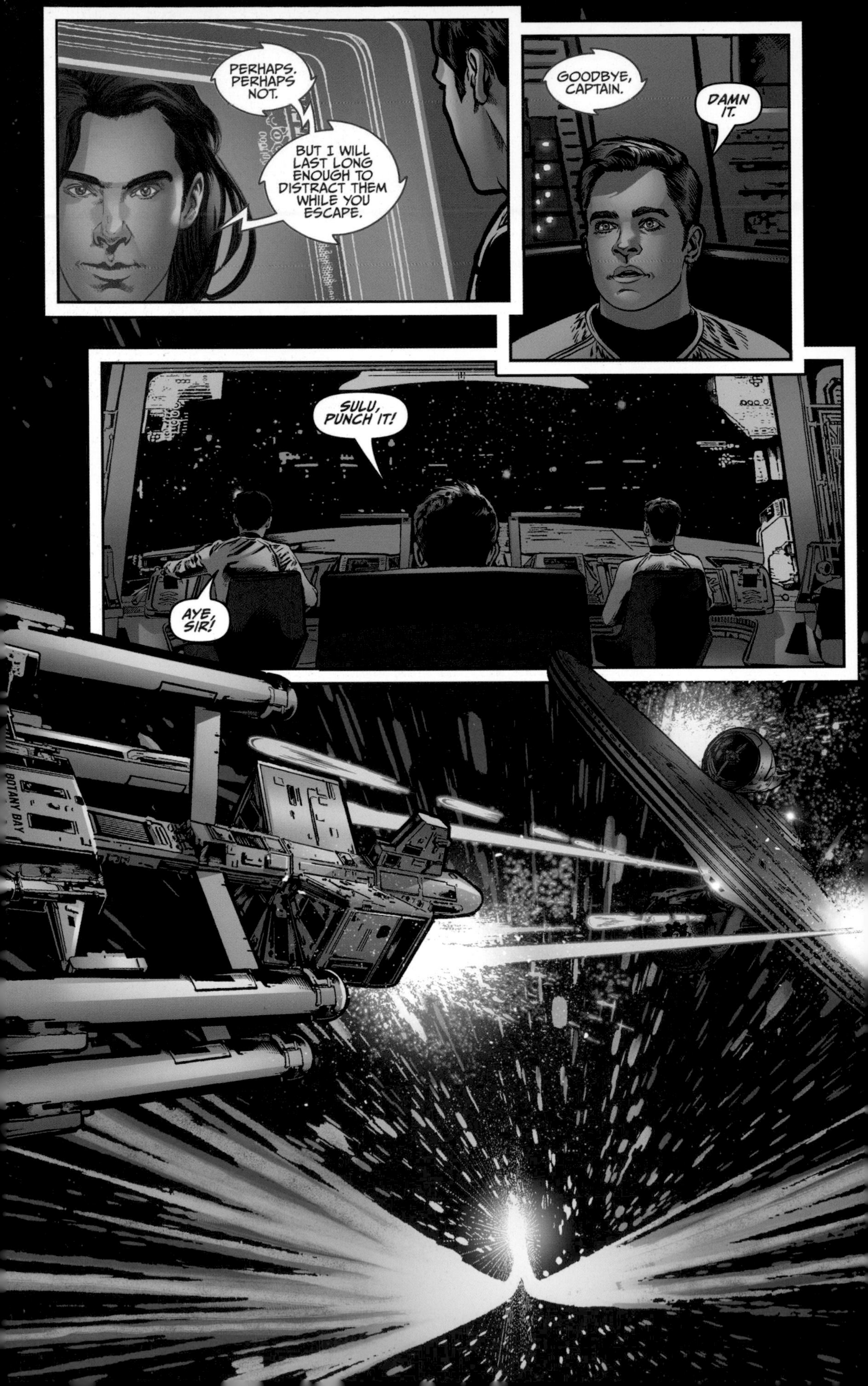
PERHAPS. PERHAPS NOT.
BUT I WILL LAST LONG ENOUGH TO DISTRACT THEM WHILE YOU ESCAPE.
GOODBYE, CAPTAIN.
DAMN IT.
SULU, PUNCH IT!
AYE, SIR!
BOTANY BAY

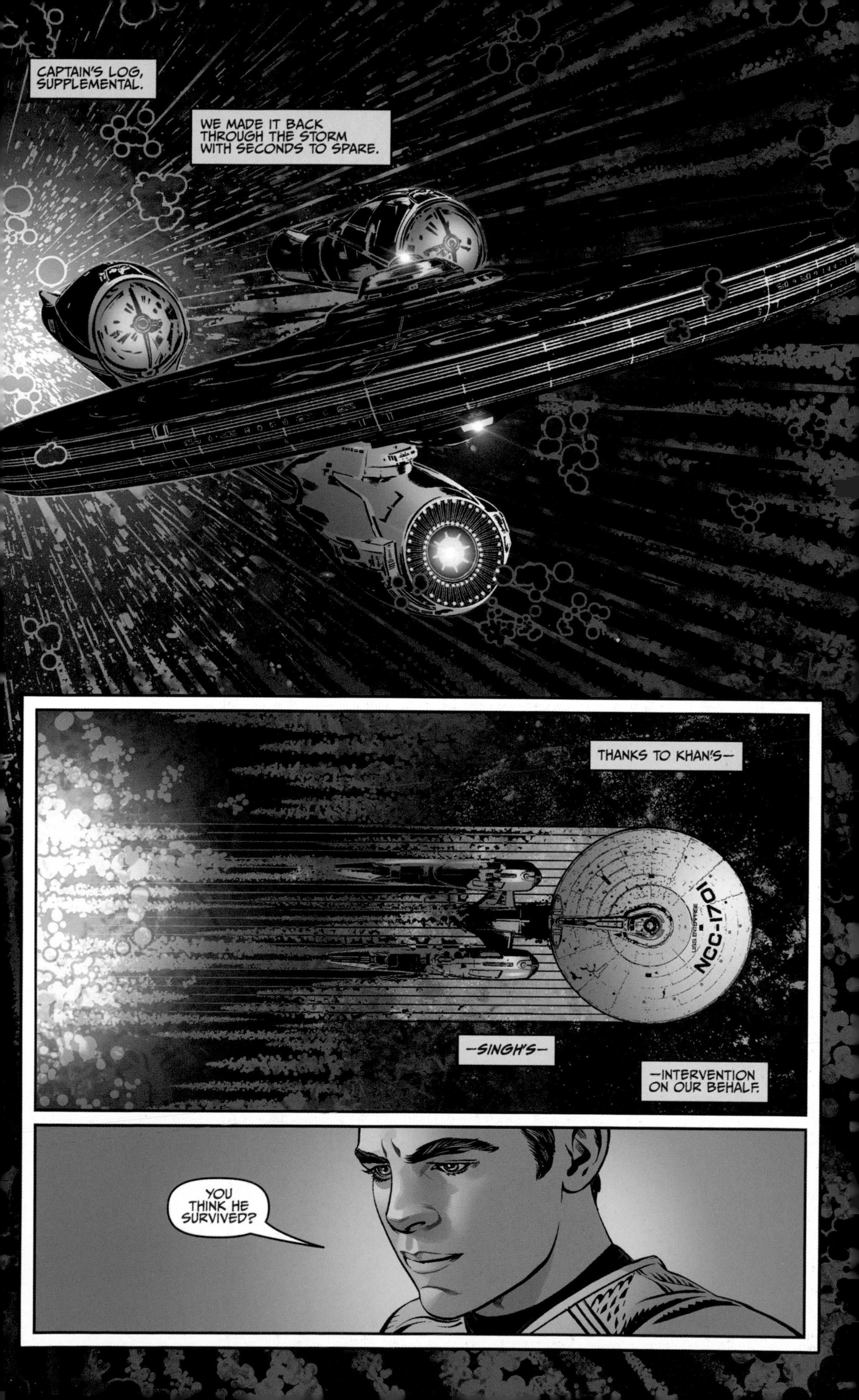
CAPTAIN'S LOG, SUPPLEMENTAL.
WE MADE IT BACK THROUGH THE STORM WITH SECONDS TO SPARE.
THANKS TO KHAN'S—
USS ENTERPRISE
NCC-1701
—SINGH'S—
—INTERVENTION ON OUR BEHALF.
YOU THINK HE SURVIVED?

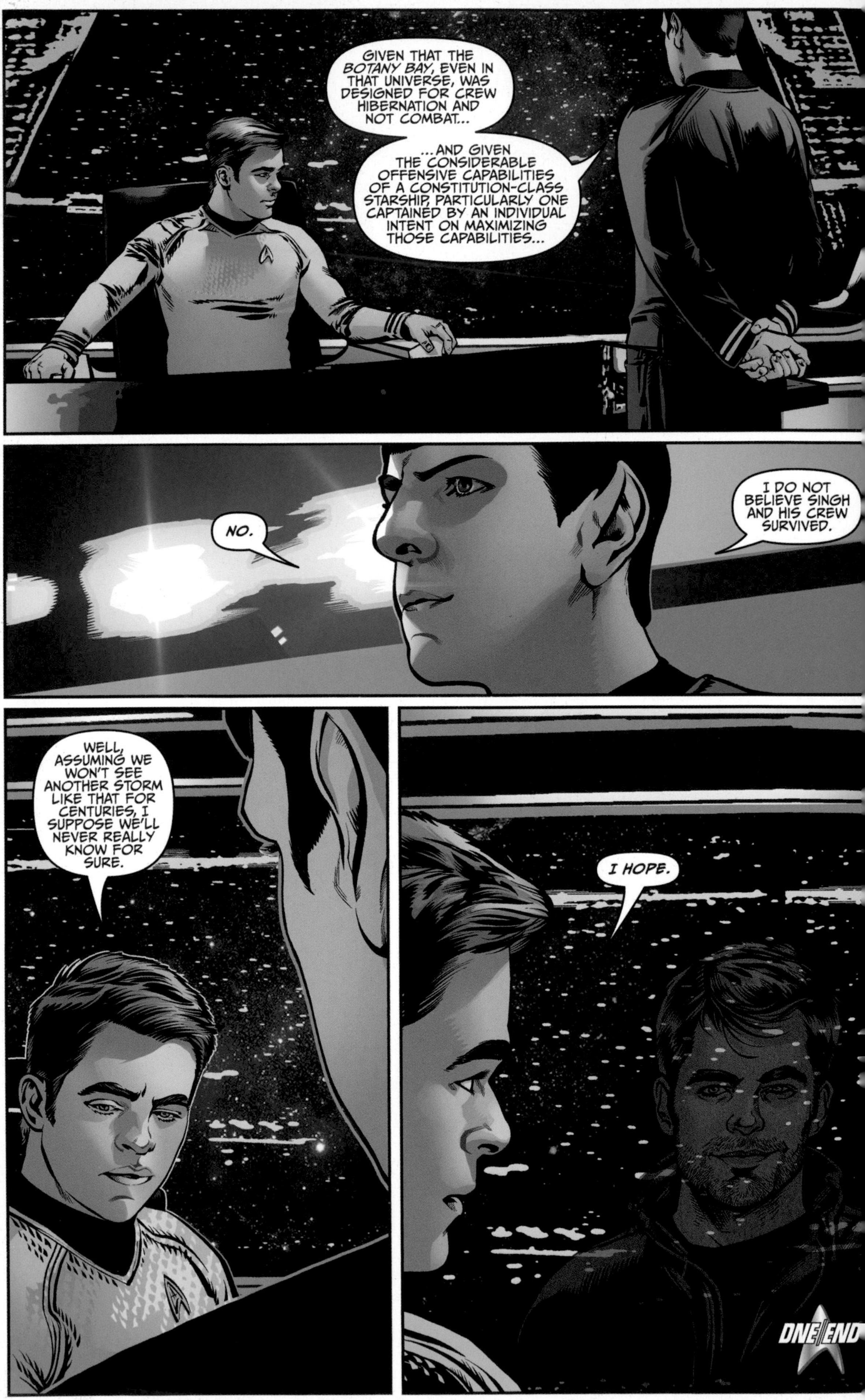
GIVEN THAT THE BOTANY BAY, EVEN IN THAT UNIVERSE, WAS DESIGNED FOR CREW HIBERNATION AND NOT COMBAT...
...AND GIVEN THE CONSIDERABLE OFFENSIVE CAPABILITIES OF A CONSTITUTION-CLASS STARSHIP, PARTICULARLY ONE CAPTAINED BY AN INDIVIDUAL INTENT ON MAXIMIZING THOSE CAPABILITIES...
NO.
I DO NOT BELIEVE SINGH AND HIS CREW SURVIVED.
WELL, ASSUMING WE WON'T SEE ANOTHER STORM LIKE THAT FOR CENTURIES, I SUPPOSE WE'LL NEVER REALLY KNOW FOR SURE.
I HOPE.
ONE END

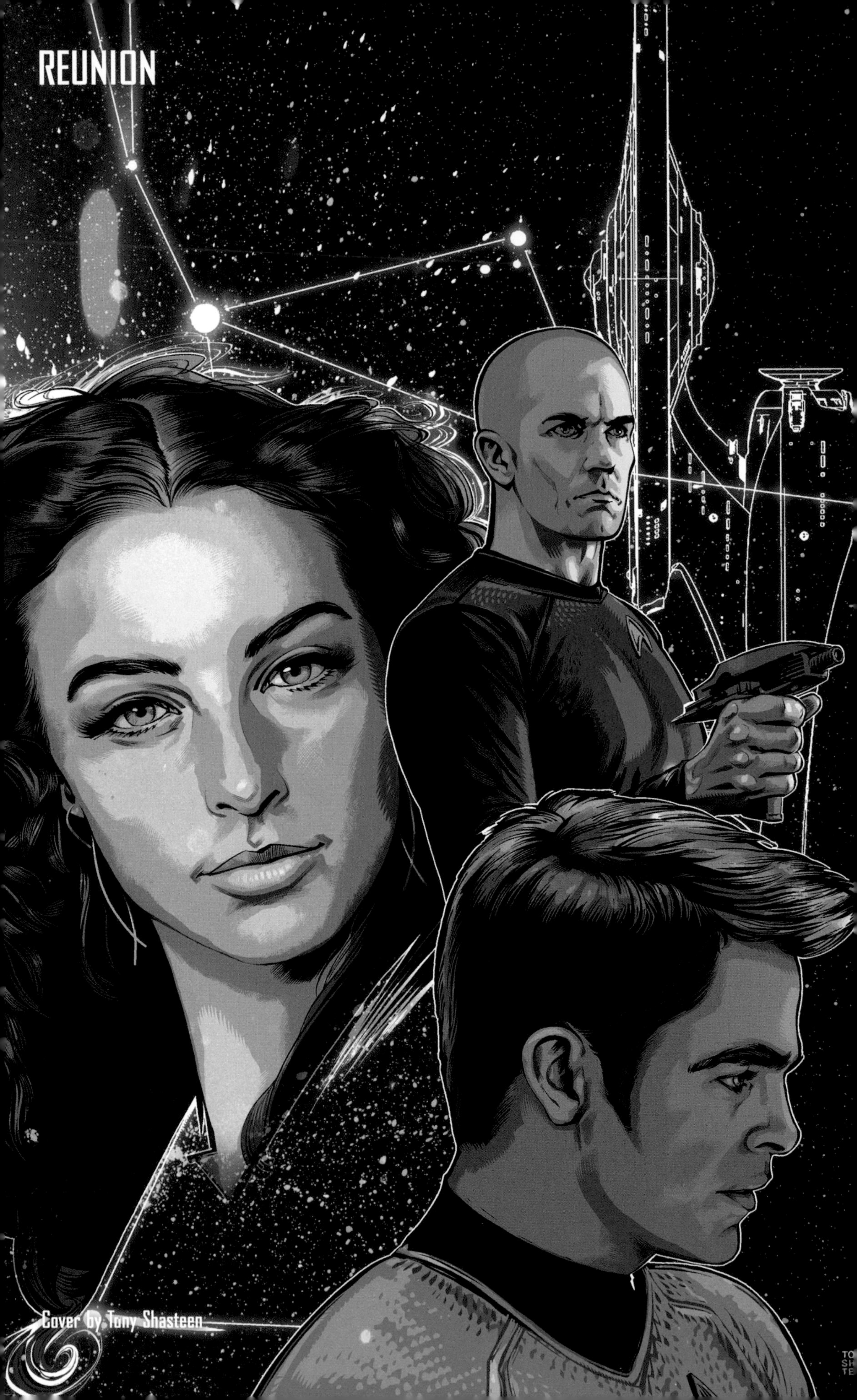
REUNION
Cover by Tony Shasteen

THE ORION CONSTELLATION.

"THESE NEGOTIATIONS HAVE BEEN A PLEASURE.

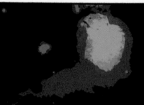

THE ORION HOMESTAR ALNILAM.

"OUR TWO FAMILIES HAVE ESTABLISHED A NEW AND PROFITABLE RELATIONSHIP BETWEEN OUR TWO SPECIES.

VONDEM, THE ORION HOMEWORLD.

"WE HAVE PROVEN WITHOUT A DOUBT THAT PEACE IS MORE PROFITABLE THAN WAR.

THE MAWHRIN AIR-CHIPELAGO IN THE SOUTHERN HEMISPHERE.

"AS A FINAL GESTURE OF GOODWILL, AND IN ACCORDANCE WITH ORION CUSTOM..."

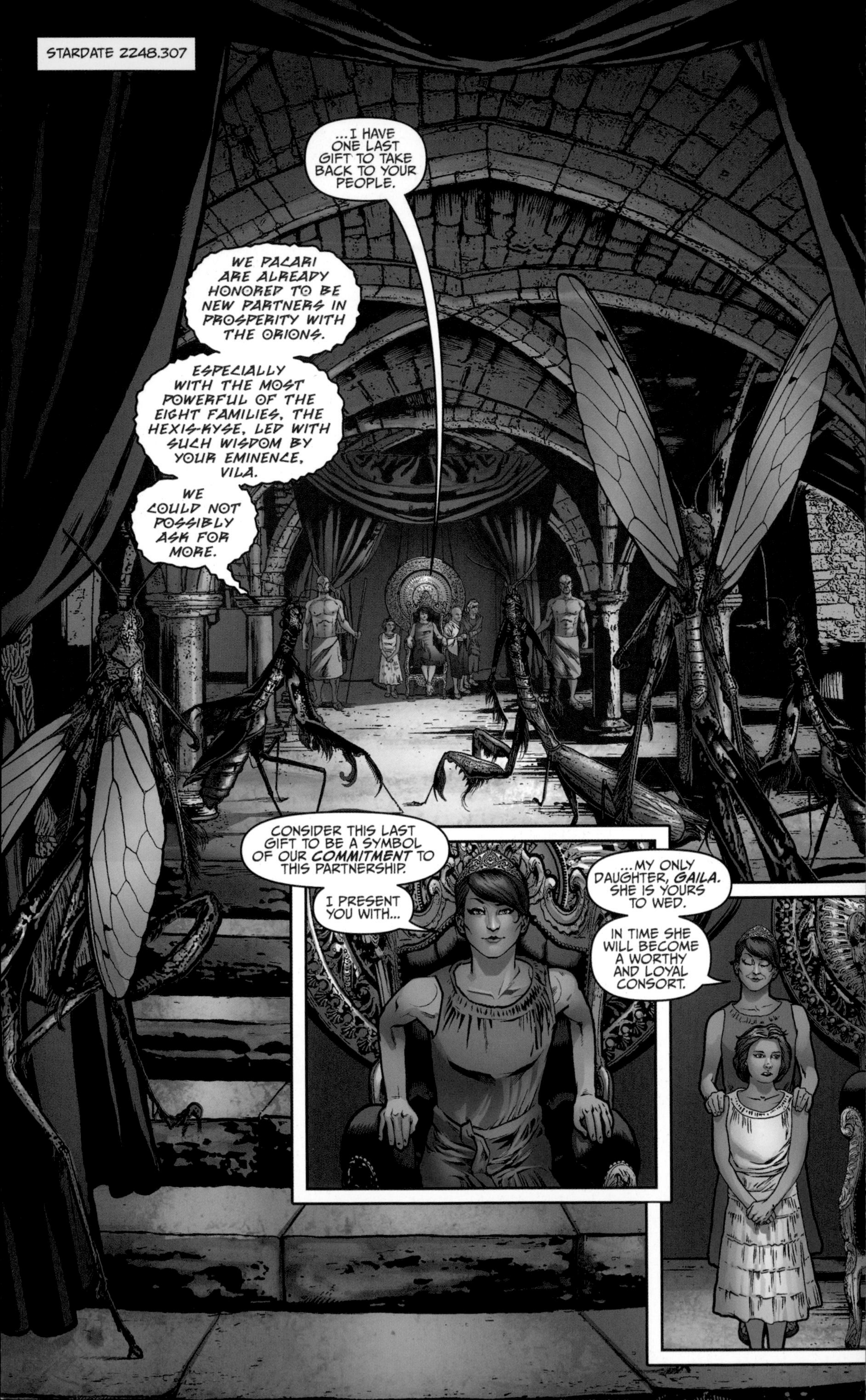
STARDATE 2248.307
WE PACARI ARE ALREADY HONORED TO BE NEW PARTNERS IN PROSPERITY WITH THE ORIONS.
ESPECIALLY WITH THE MOST POWERFUL OF THE EIGHT FAMILIES, THE HEXIS-KYSE, LED WITH SUCH WISDOM BY YOUR EMINENCE, VILA.
WE COULD NOT POSSIBLY ASK FOR MORE.
...I HAVE ONE LAST GIFT TO TAKE BACK TO YOUR PEOPLE.
CONSIDER THIS LAST GIFT TO BE A SYMBOL OF OUR COMMITMENT TO THIS PARTNERSHIP.
I PRESENT YOU WITH...
...MY ONLY DAUGHTER, GAILA. SHE IS YOURS TO WED.
IN TIME SHE WILL BECOME A WORTHY AND LOYAL CONSORT.

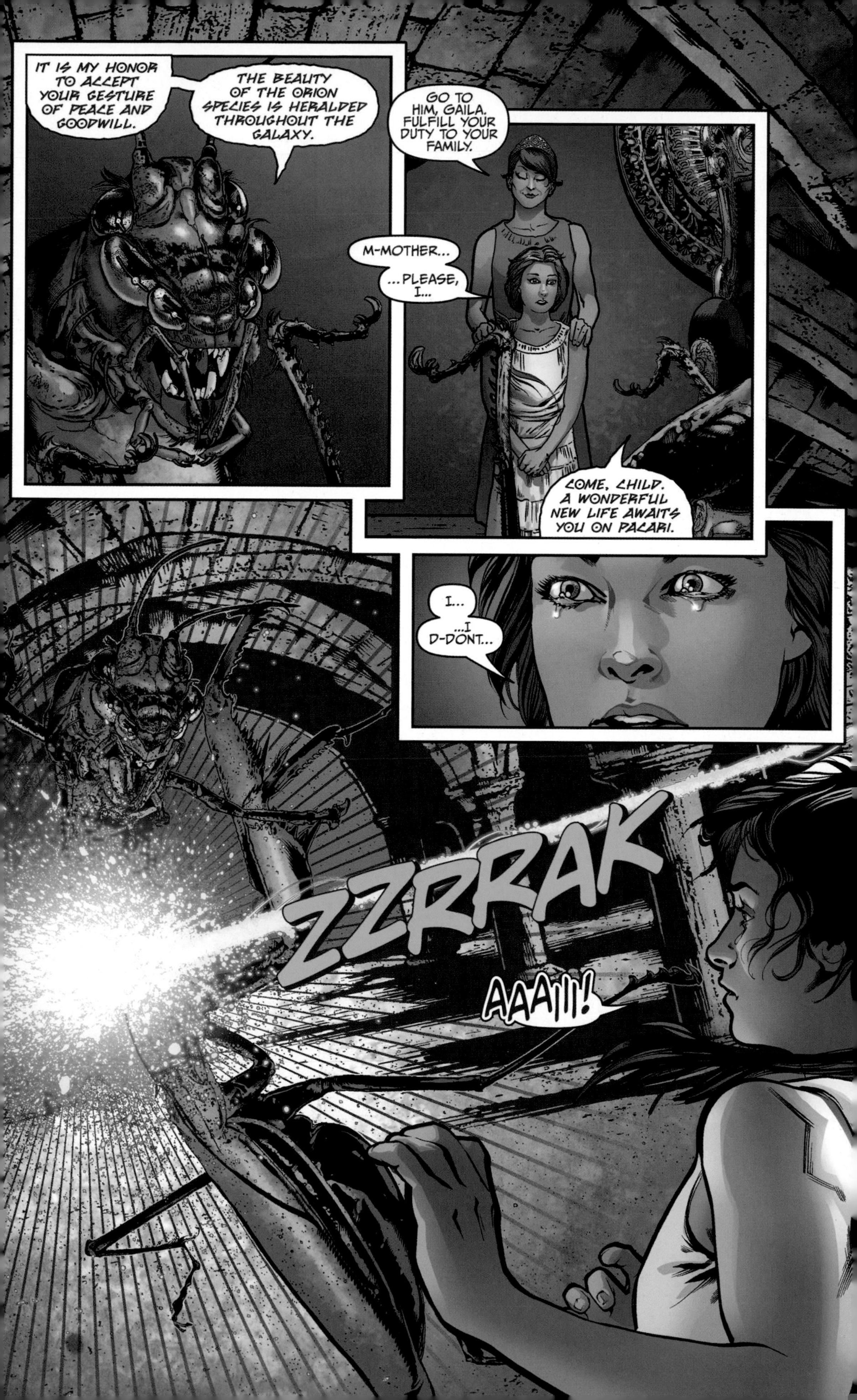
IT IS MY HONOR TO ACCEPT YOUR GESTURE OF PEACE AND GOODWILL.
THE BEAUTY OF THE ORION SPECIES IS HERALDED THROUGHOUT THE GALAXY.
GO TO HIM, GAILA. FULFILL YOUR DUTY TO YOUR FAMILY.
M-MOTHER...
...PLEASE, I...
COME, CHILD. A WONDERFUL NEW LIFE AWAITS YOU ON PACARI.
I...
...I D-DONT...
ZZRRAK
AAAIIII!

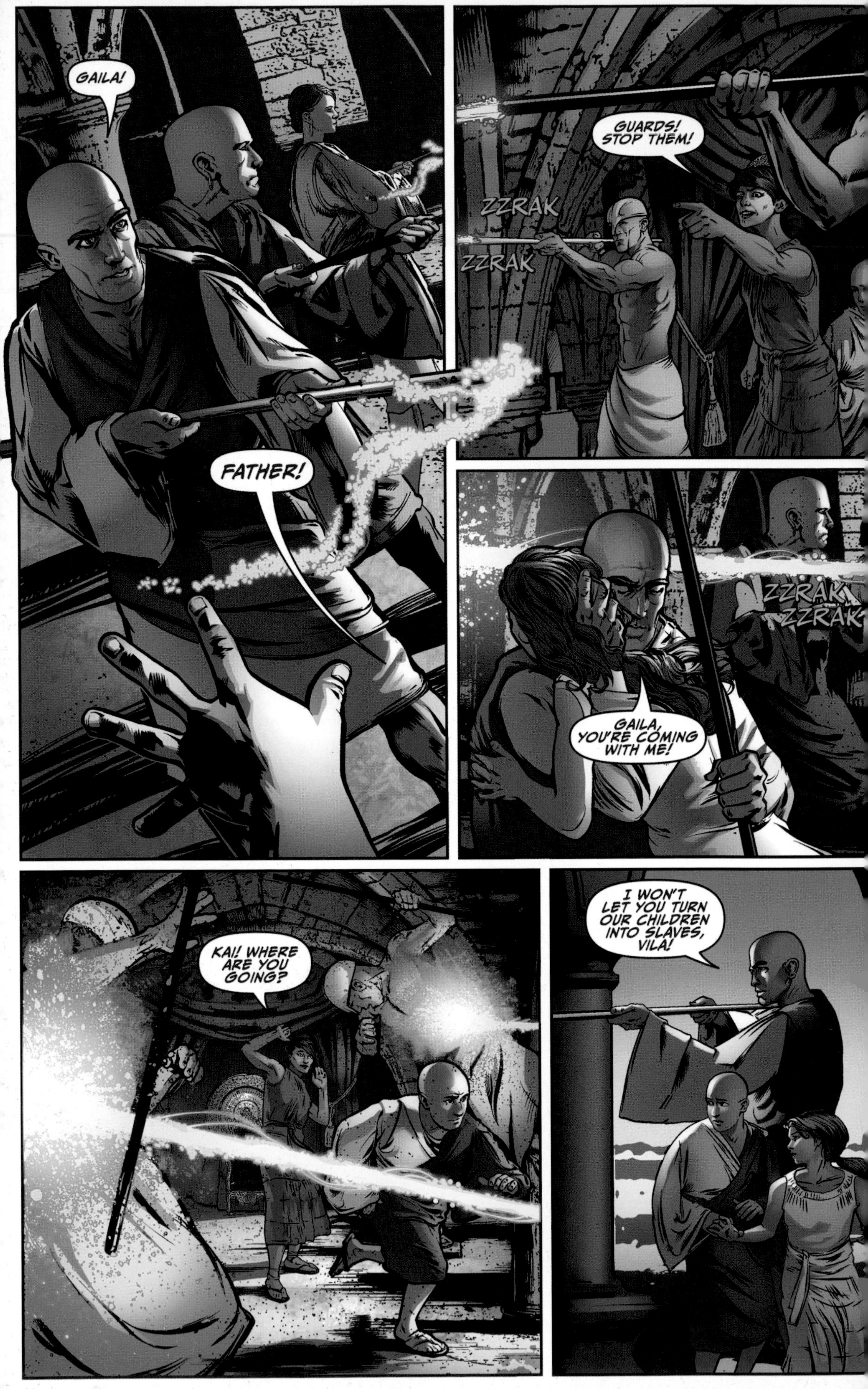
GAILA!
FATHER!
GUARDS! STOP THEM!
ZZRAK
ZZRAK
ZZRAK
ZZRAK
GAILA, YOU'RE COMING WITH ME!
KAI! WHERE ARE YOU GOING?
I WON'T LET YOU TURN OUR CHILDREN INTO SLAVES, VILA!

YOU THINK I'LL LET YOU HAVE THEM, KAZEK?!

I'LL HAVE YOUR HEAD FOR THIS!

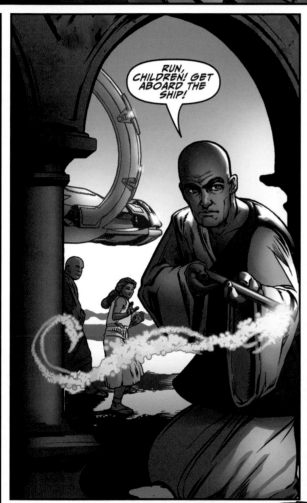

RUN, CHILDREN! GET ABOARD THE SHIP!

SHRAAK

SHRAAK

NO MATTER WHERE YOU RUN TO, DEAR HUSBAND...

"NO MATTER HOW FAR..."

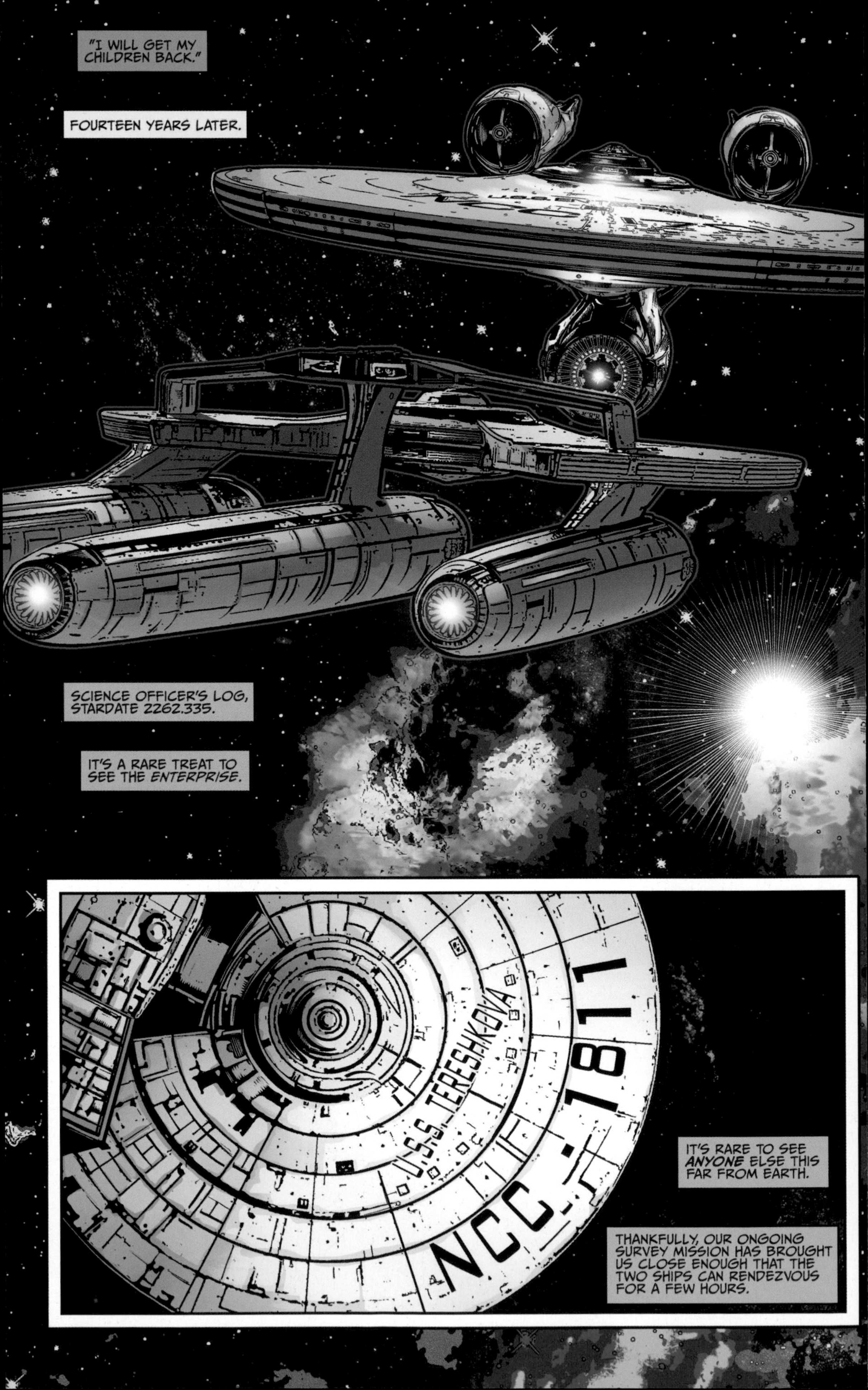
"I WILL GET MY CHILDREN BACK."
FOURTEEN YEARS LATER.
SCIENCE OFFICER'S LOG, STARDATE 2262.335.
IT'S A RARE TREAT TO SEE THE *ENTERPRISE*.
U.S.S. TERESHKOVA
NCC-1811
IT'S RARE TO SEE *ANYONE* ELSE THIS FAR FROM EARTH.
THANKFULLY, OUR ONGOING SURVEY MISSION HAS BROUGHT US CLOSE ENOUGH THAT THE TWO SHIPS CAN RENDEZVOUS FOR A FEW HOURS.

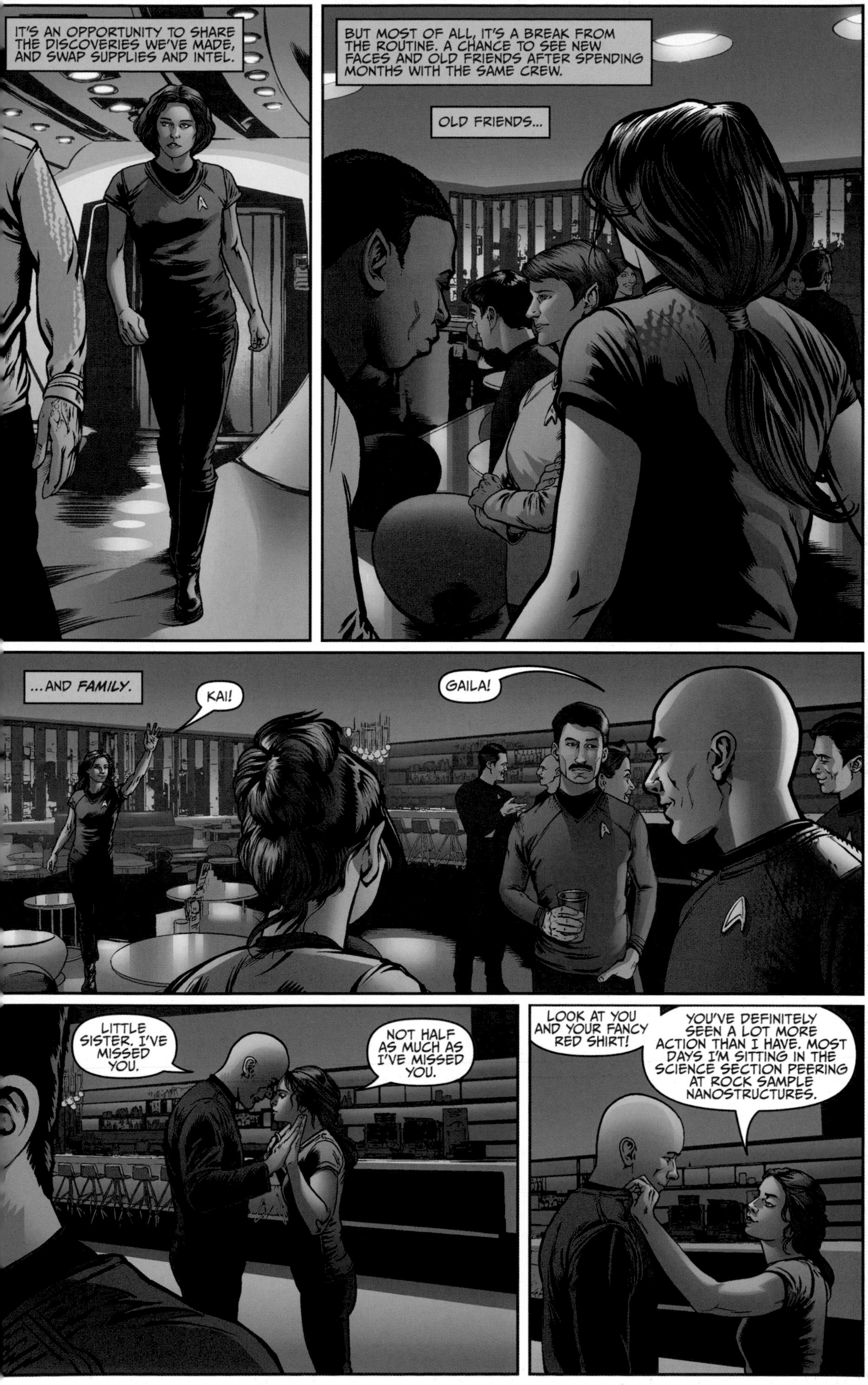
IT'S AN OPPORTUNITY TO SHARE THE DISCOVERIES WE'VE MADE, AND SWAP SUPPLIES AND INTEL.
BUT MOST OF ALL, IT'S A BREAK FROM THE ROUTINE. A CHANCE TO SEE NEW FACES AND OLD FRIENDS AFTER SPENDING MONTHS WITH THE SAME CREW.
OLD FRIENDS...
...AND *FAMILY*.
KAI!
GAILA!
LITTLE SISTER. I'VE MISSED YOU.
NOT HALF AS MUCH AS I'VE MISSED YOU.
LOOK AT YOU AND YOUR FANCY RED SHIRT!
YOU'VE DEFINITELY SEEN A LOT MORE ACTION THAN I HAVE. MOST DAYS I'M SITTING IN THE SCIENCE SECTION PEERING AT ROCK SAMPLE NANOSTRUCTURES.

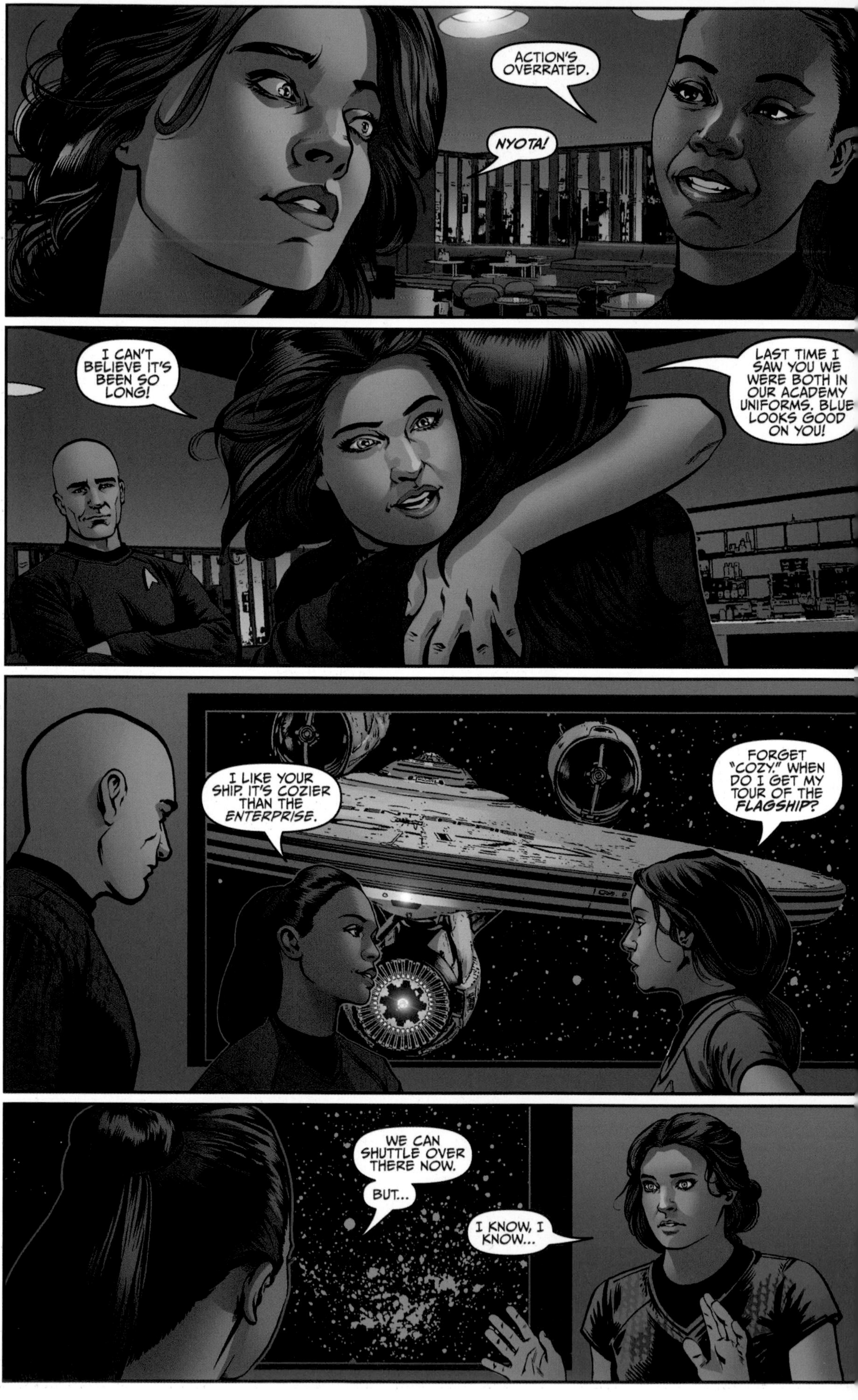
ACTION'S OVERRATED.
NYOTA!
I CAN'T BELIEVE IT'S BEEN SO LONG!
LAST TIME I SAW YOU WE WERE BOTH IN OUR ACADEMY UNIFORMS. BLUE LOOKS GOOD ON YOU!
I LIKE YOUR SHIP. IT'S COZIER THAN THE *ENTERPRISE*.
FORGET "COZY." WHEN DO I GET MY TOUR OF THE ***FLAGSHIP?***
WE CAN SHUTTLE OVER THERE NOW.
BUT...
I KNOW, I KNOW...

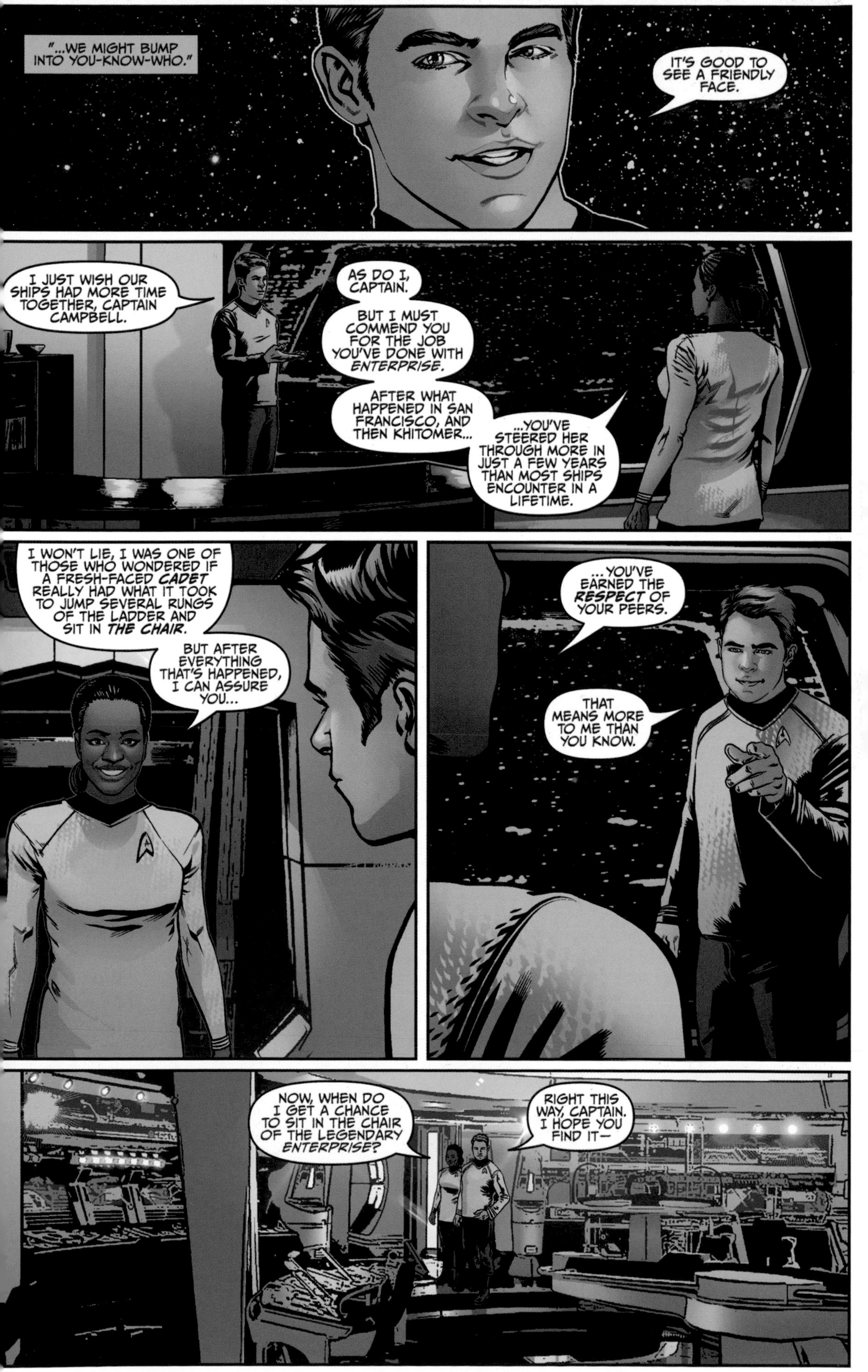
"...WE MIGHT BUMP INTO YOU-KNOW-WHO."
IT'S GOOD TO SEE A FRIENDLY FACE.
I JUST WISH OUR SHIPS HAD MORE TIME TOGETHER, CAPTAIN CAMPBELL.
AS DO I, CAPTAIN.
BUT I MUST COMMEND YOU FOR THE JOB YOU'VE DONE WITH *ENTERPRISE*.
AFTER WHAT HAPPENED IN SAN FRANCISCO, AND THEN KHITOMER...
...YOU'VE STEERED HER THROUGH MORE IN JUST A FEW YEARS THAN MOST SHIPS ENCOUNTER IN A LIFETIME.
I WON'T LIE, I WAS ONE OF THOSE WHO WONDERED IF A FRESH-FACED ***CADET*** REALLY HAD WHAT IT TOOK TO JUMP SEVERAL RUNGS OF THE LADDER AND SIT IN ***THE CHAIR***.
BUT AFTER EVERYTHING THAT'S HAPPENED, I CAN ASSURE YOU...
...YOU'VE EARNED THE ***RESPECT*** OF YOUR PEERS.
THAT MEANS MORE TO ME THAN YOU KNOW.
NOW, WHEN DO I GET A CHANCE TO SIT IN THE CHAIR OF THE LEGENDARY *ENTERPRISE*?
RIGHT THIS WAY, CAPTAIN. I HOPE YOU FIND IT—

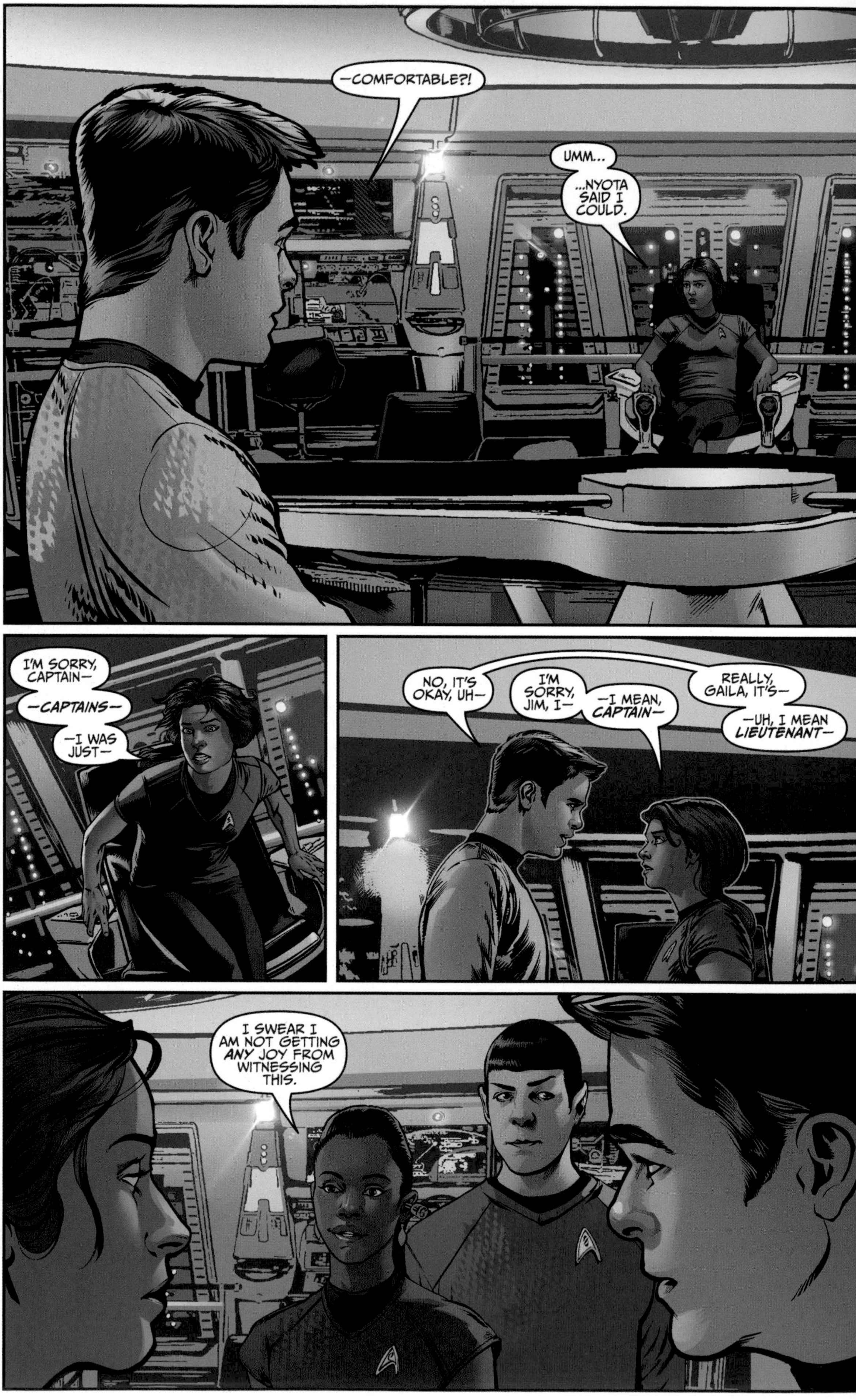
—COMFORTABLE?!
UMM...
...NYOTA SAID I COULD.
I'M SORRY, CAPTAIN—
—*CAPTAINS*—
—I WAS JUST—
NO, IT'S OKAY, UH—
I'M SORRY, JIM, I—
—I MEAN, *CAPTAIN*—
REALLY, GAILA, IT'S—
—UH, I MEAN *LIEUTENANT*—
I SWEAR I AM NOT GETTING *ANY* JOY FROM WITNESSING THIS.

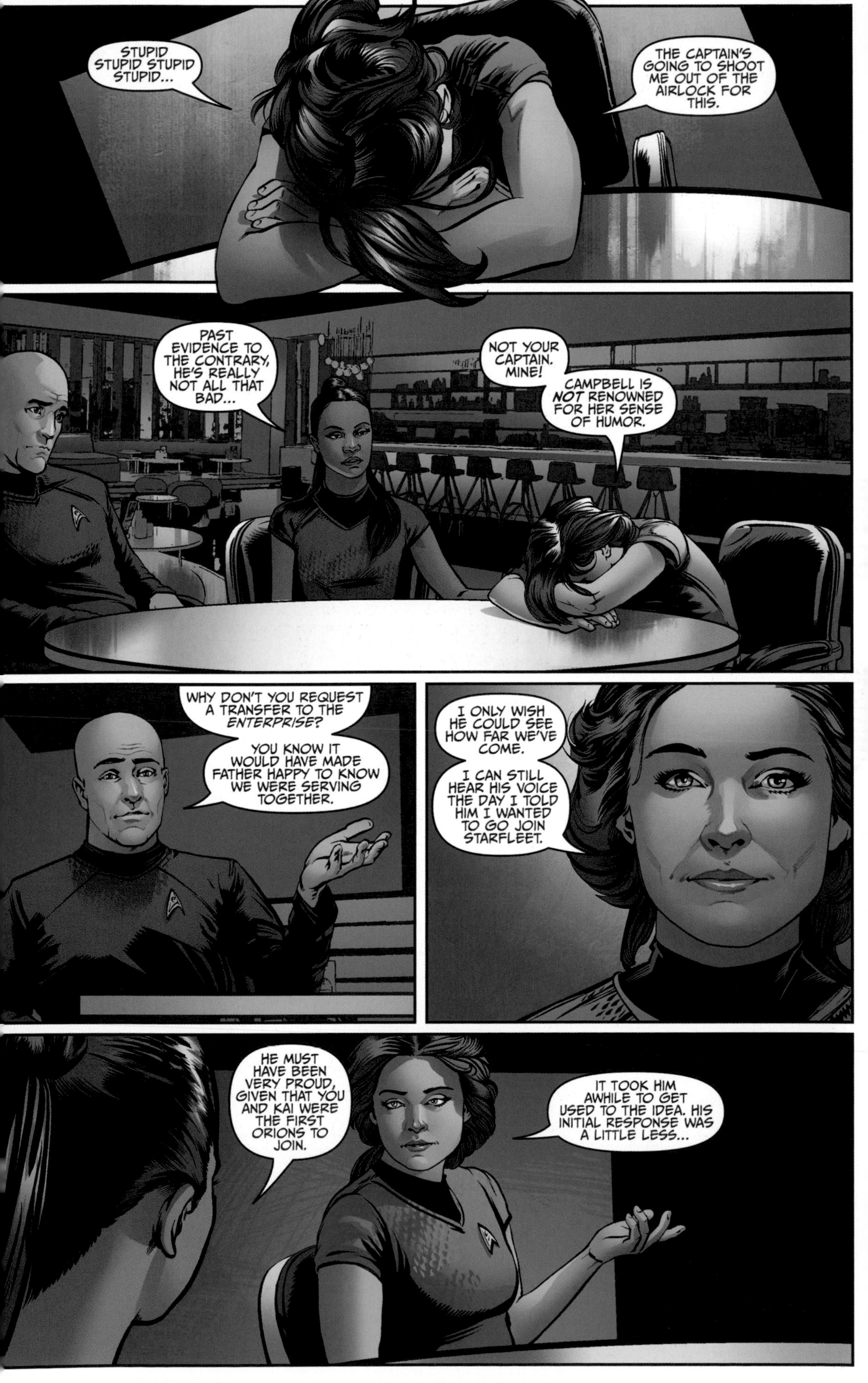
STUPID STUPID STUPID STUPID...
THE CAPTAIN'S GOING TO SHOOT ME OUT OF THE AIRLOCK FOR THIS.
PAST EVIDENCE TO THE CONTRARY, HE'S REALLY NOT ALL THAT BAD...
NOT YOUR CAPTAIN. MINE!
CAMPBELL IS NOT RENOWNED FOR HER SENSE OF HUMOR.
WHY DON'T YOU REQUEST A TRANSFER TO THE ENTERPRISE?
YOU KNOW IT WOULD HAVE MADE FATHER HAPPY TO KNOW WE WERE SERVING TOGETHER.
I ONLY WISH HE COULD SEE HOW FAR WE'VE COME.
I CAN STILL HEAR HIS VOICE THE DAY I TOLD HIM I WANTED TO GO JOIN STARFLEET.
HE MUST HAVE BEEN VERY PROUD, GIVEN THAT YOU AND KAI WERE THE FIRST ORIONS TO JOIN.
IT TOOK HIM AWHILE TO GET USED TO THE IDEA. HIS INITIAL RESPONSE WAS A LITTLE LESS...

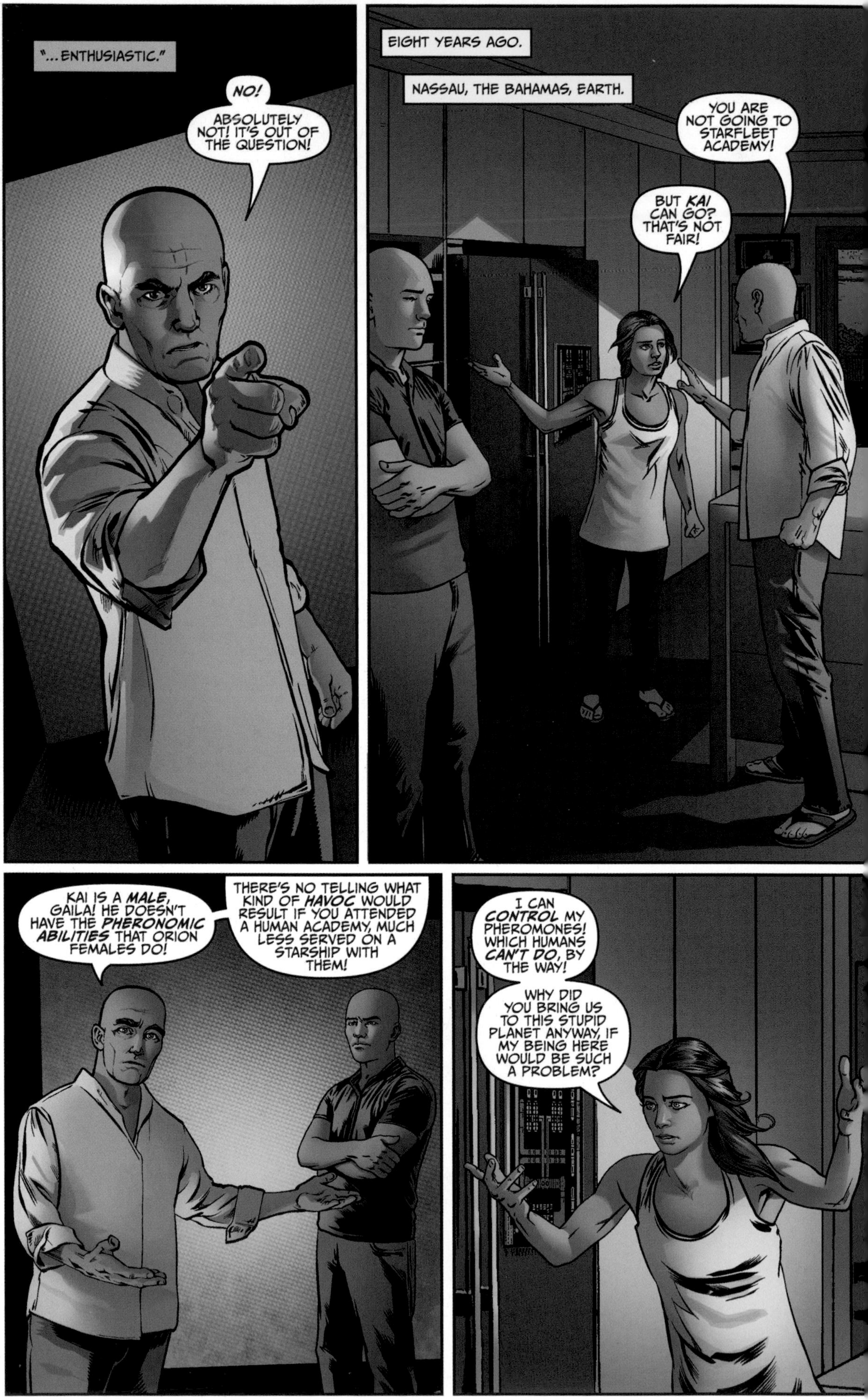
"...ENTHUSIASTIC."
NO! ABSOLUTELY NOT! IT'S OUT OF THE QUESTION!
EIGHT YEARS AGO.
NASSAU, THE BAHAMAS, EARTH.
YOU ARE NOT GOING TO STARFLEET ACADEMY!
BUT KAI CAN GO? THAT'S NOT FAIR!
KAI IS A MALE, GAILA! HE DOESN'T HAVE THE PHERONOMIC ABILITIES THAT ORION FEMALES DO!
THERE'S NO TELLING WHAT KIND OF HAVOC WOULD RESULT IF YOU ATTENDED A HUMAN ACADEMY, MUCH LESS SERVED ON A STARSHIP WITH THEM!
I CAN CONTROL MY PHEROMONES! WHICH HUMANS CAN'T DO, BY THE WAY!
WHY DID YOU BRING US TO THIS STUPID PLANET ANYWAY, IF MY BEING HERE WOULD BE SUCH A PROBLEM?

YOU KNOW WHY, GAILA. THE FEDERATION OFFERED US *REFUGE* AFTER OUR ESCAPE FROM ORION.

YOUR MOTHER COULD NOT RISK FOLLOWING US WITHOUT VIOLATING THE TRUCE BETWEEN THE FEDERATION AND THE *EIGHT FAMILIES*.

IT HAS BEEN A PRIVILEGE TO CALL EARTH HOME. I HAVE DONE EVERYTHING IN MY POWER TO KEEP YOU SAFE.

EVEN RAISING YOU HERE, IN THE ISLANDS. A SMALL REMEMBRANCE OF THE HOME WE LEFT BEHIND.

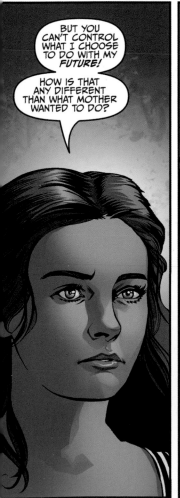

BUT YOU CAN'T CONTROL WHAT I CHOOSE TO DO WITH MY *FUTURE!*

HOW IS THAT ANY DIFFERENT THAN WHAT MOTHER WANTED TO DO?

GAILA'S RIGHT, FATHER. I KNOW YOU WANT TO PROTECT US, BUT YOU CAN'T DO IT FOREVER.

AND IF GAILA CANNOT ATTEND THE ACADEMY...

...NEITHER WILL I.

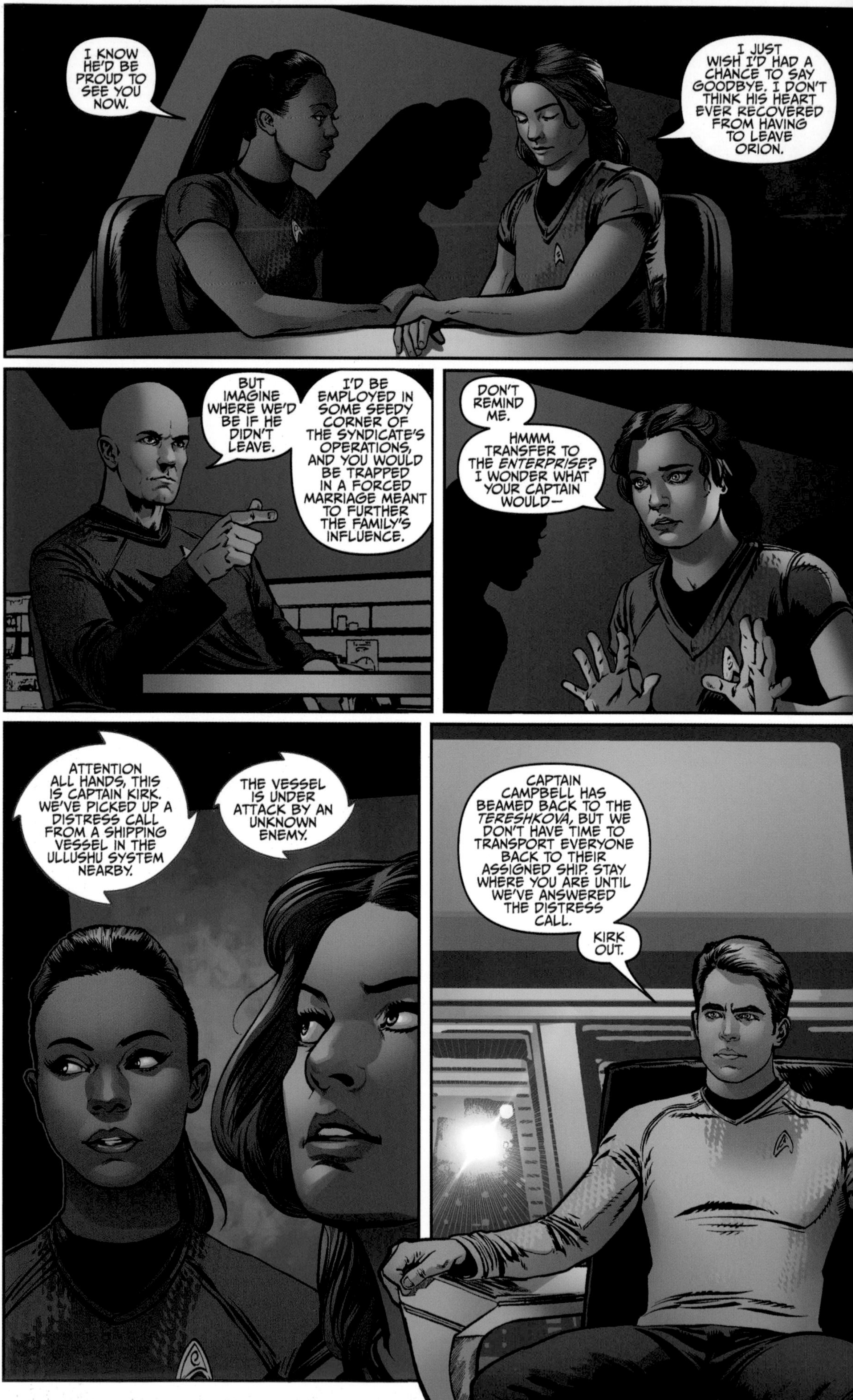
I KNOW HE'D BE PROUD TO SEE YOU NOW.
I JUST WISH I'D HAD A CHANCE TO SAY GOODBYE. I DON'T THINK HIS HEART EVER RECOVERED FROM HAVING TO LEAVE ORION.
BUT IMAGINE WHERE WE'D BE IF HE DIDN'T LEAVE.
I'D BE EMPLOYED IN SOME SEEDY CORNER OF THE SYNDICATE'S OPERATIONS, AND YOU WOULD BE TRAPPED IN A FORCED MARRIAGE MEANT TO FURTHER THE FAMILY'S INFLUENCE.
DON'T REMIND ME.
HMMM. TRANSFER TO THE *ENTERPRISE*? I WONDER WHAT YOUR CAPTAIN WOULD—
ATTENTION ALL HANDS, THIS IS CAPTAIN KIRK. WE'VE PICKED UP A DISTRESS CALL FROM A SHIPPING VESSEL IN THE ULLUSHU SYSTEM NEARBY.
THE VESSEL IS UNDER ATTACK BY AN UNKNOWN ENEMY.
CAPTAIN CAMPBELL HAS BEAMED BACK TO THE *TERESHKOVA*, BUT WE DON'T HAVE TIME TO TRANSPORT EVERYONE BACK TO THEIR ASSIGNED SHIP. STAY WHERE YOU ARE UNTIL WE'VE ANSWERED THE DISTRESS CALL.
KIRK OUT.

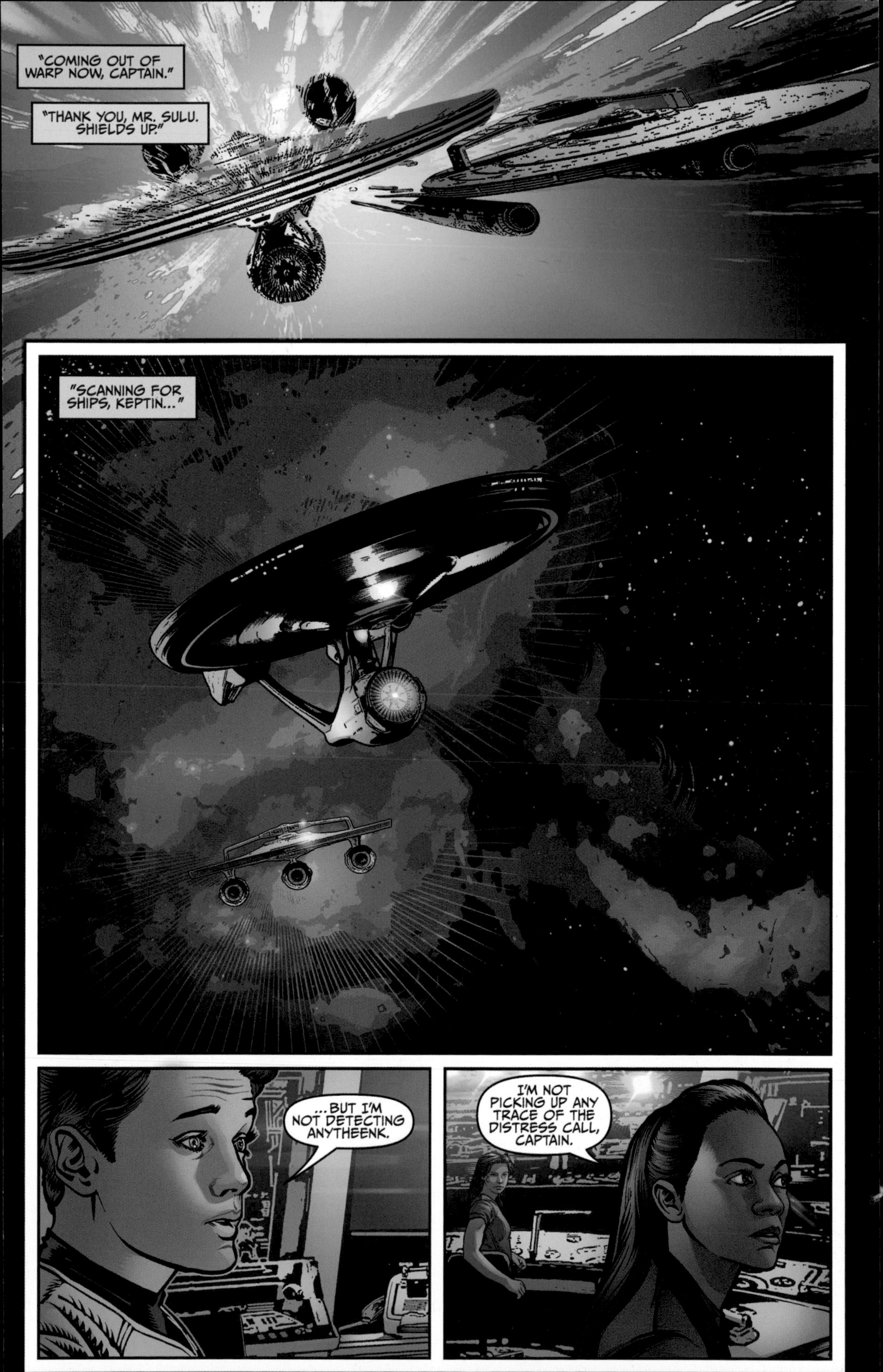
"COMING OUT OF WARP NOW, CAPTAIN."
"THANK YOU, MR. SULU. SHIELDS UP."
"SCANNING FOR SHIPS, KEPTIN..."
...BUT I'M NOT DETECTING ANYTHEENK.
I'M NOT PICKING UP ANY TRACE OF THE DISTRESS CALL, CAPTAIN.

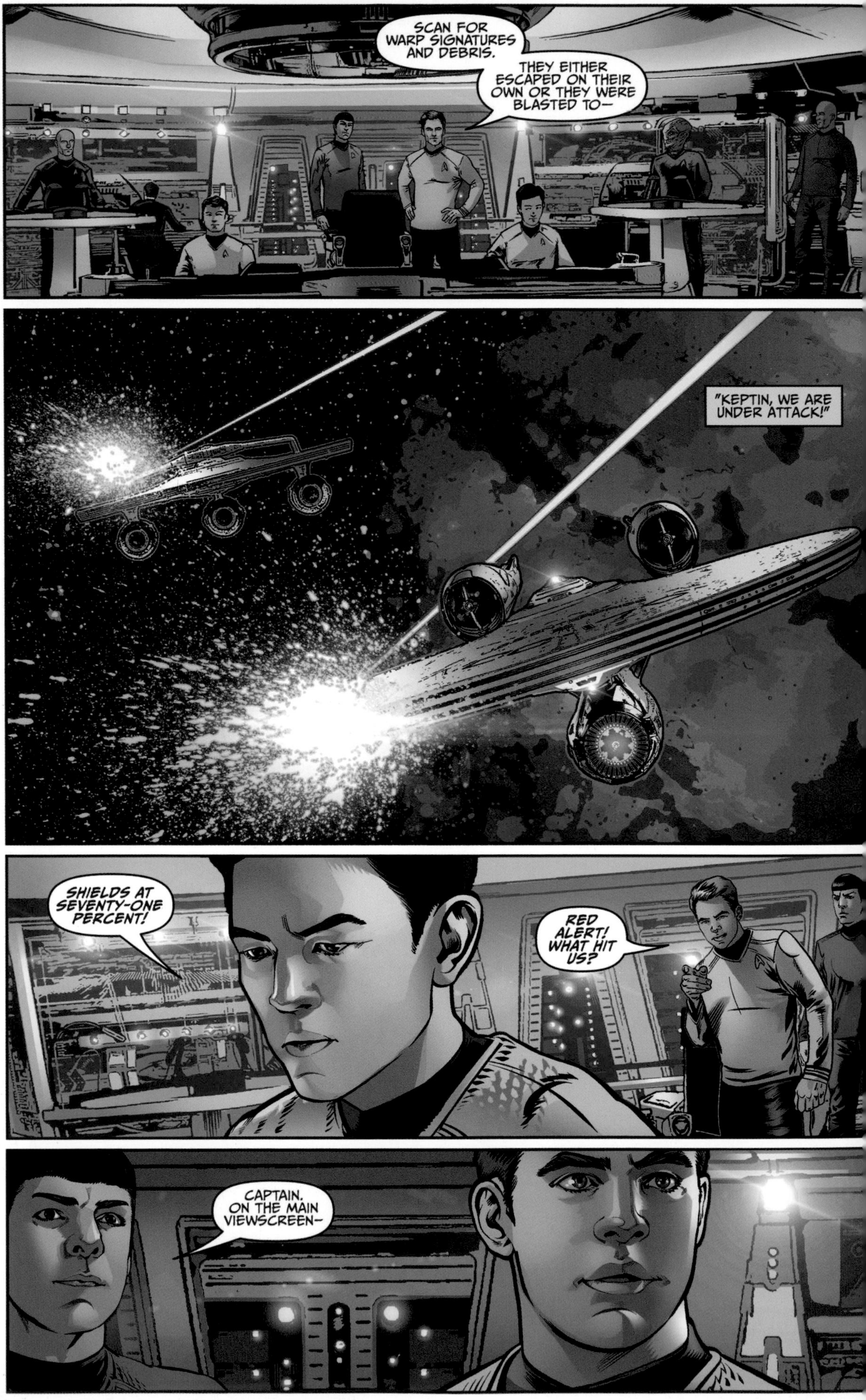
SCAN FOR WARP SIGNATURES AND DEBRIS.
THEY EITHER ESCAPED ON THEIR OWN OR THEY WERE BLASTED TO—
"KEPTIN, WE ARE UNDER ATTACK!"
SHIELDS AT SEVENTY-ONE PERCENT!
RED ALERT! WHAT HIT US?
CAPTAIN. ON THE MAIN VIEWSCREEN—

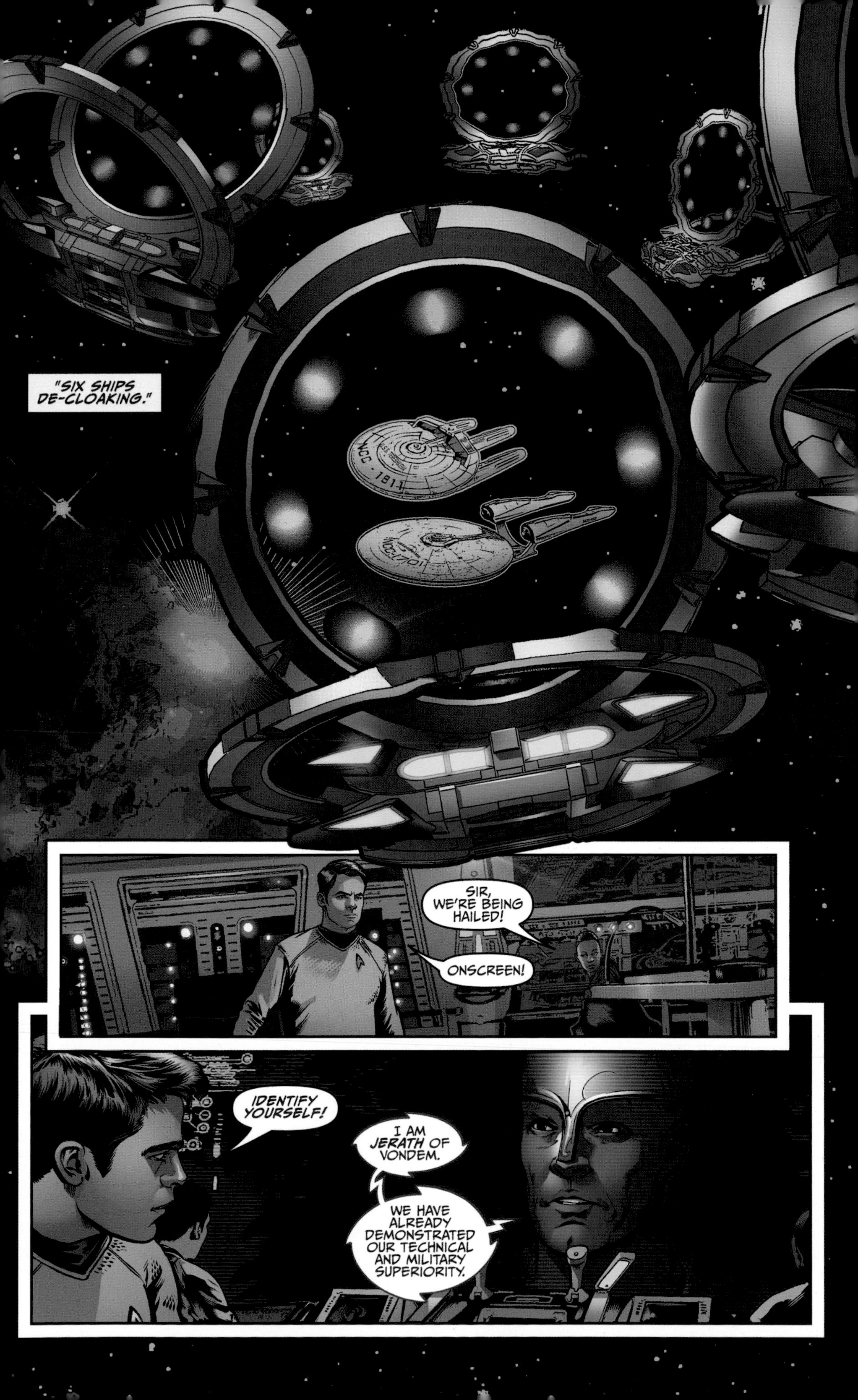
"SIX SHIPS DE-CLOAKING."
NCC-1811
NCC-1701
SIR, WE'RE BEING HAILED!
ONSCREEN!
IDENTIFY YOURSELF!
I AM JERATH OF VONDEM.
WE HAVE ALREADY DEMONSTRATED OUR TECHNICAL AND MILITARY SUPERIORITY.

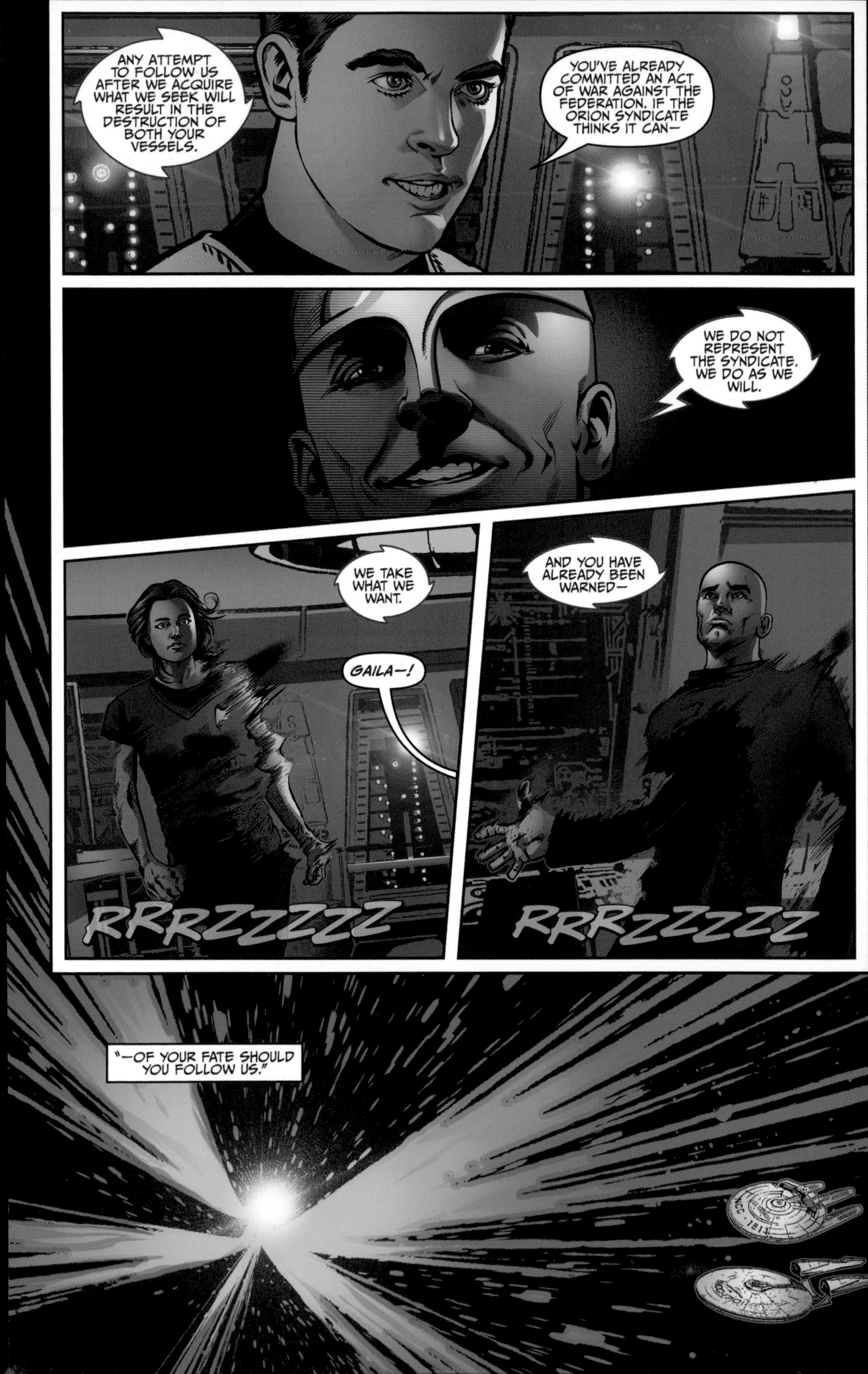
ANY ATTEMPT TO FOLLOW US AFTER WE ACQUIRE WHAT WE SEEK WILL RESULT IN THE DESTRUCTION OF BOTH YOUR VESSELS.
YOU'VE ALREADY COMMITTED AN ACT OF WAR AGAINST THE FEDERATION. IF THE ORION SYNDICATE THINKS IT CAN—
WE DO NOT REPRESENT THE SYNDICATE. WE DO AS WE WILL.
WE TAKE WHAT WE WANT.
GAILA—!
RRRZZZZZZ
AND YOU HAVE ALREADY BEEN WARNED—
RRRZZZZZZ
"—OF YOUR FATE SHOULD YOU FOLLOW US."

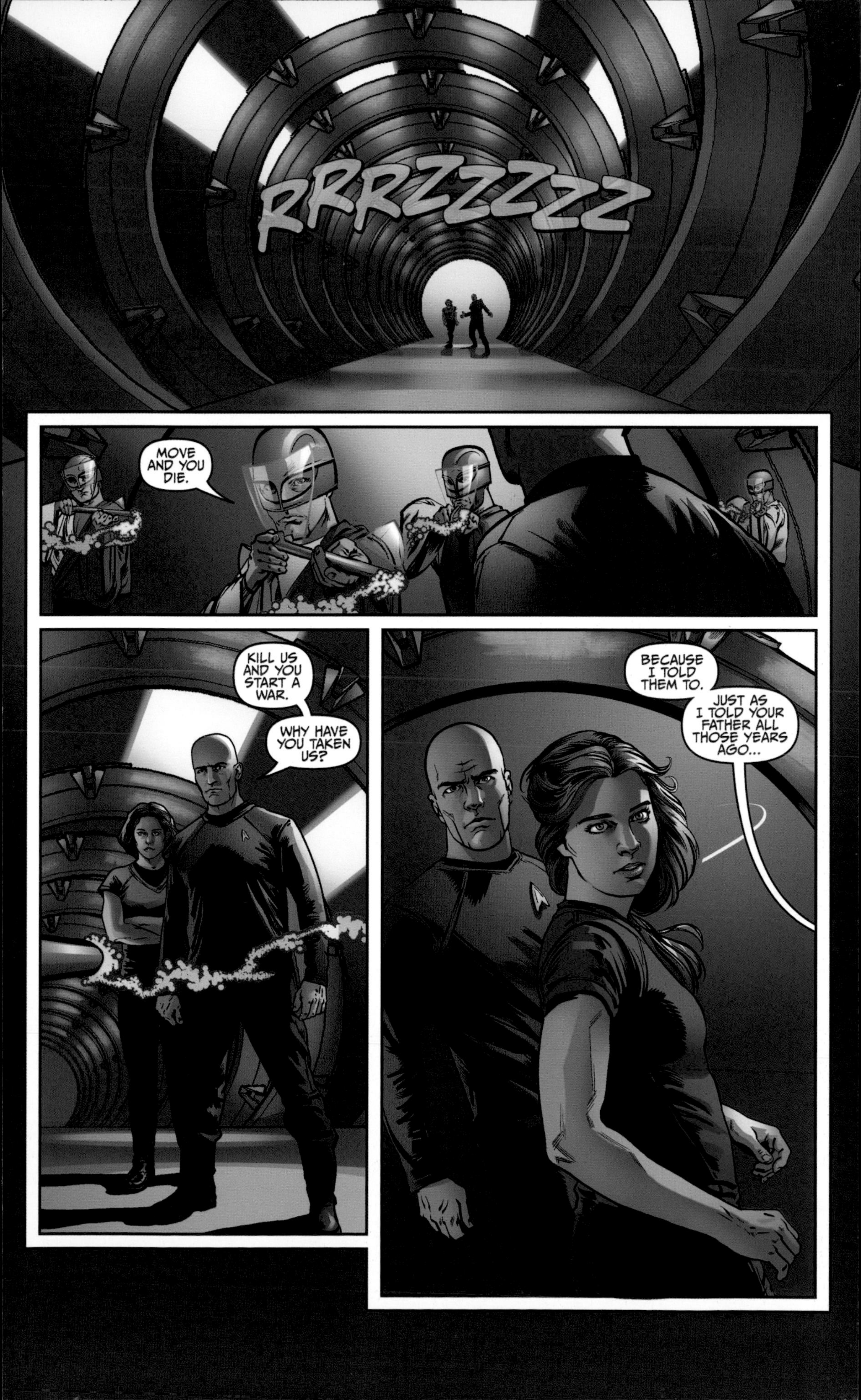
RRRZZZZZ
MOVE AND YOU DIE.
KILL US AND YOU START A WAR.
WHY HAVE YOU TAKEN US?
BECAUSE I TOLD THEM TO.
JUST AS I TOLD YOUR FATHER ALL THOSE YEARS AGO...

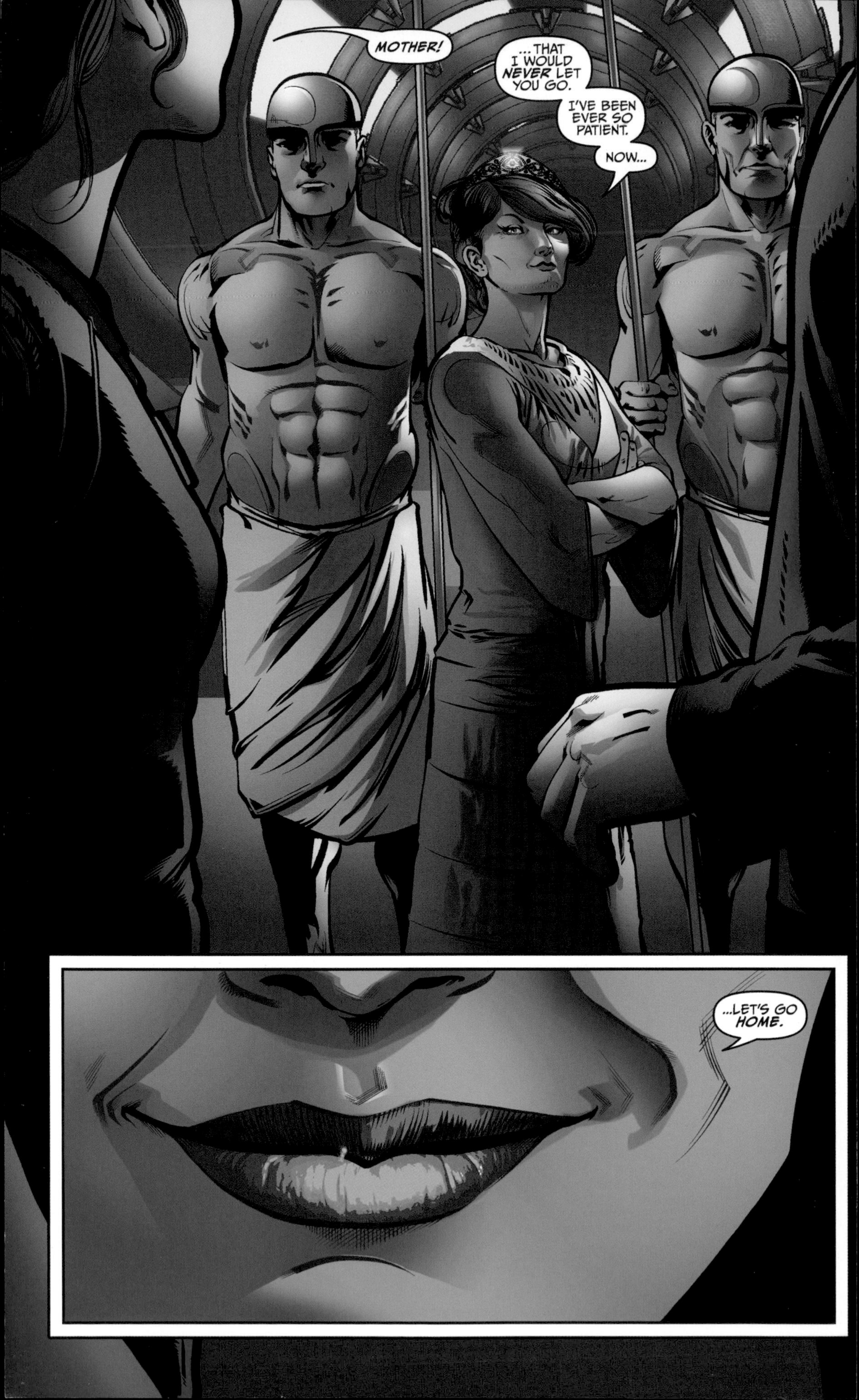
MOTHER!
...THAT I WOULD NEVER LET YOU GO.
I'VE BEEN EVER SO PATIENT.
NOW...
...LET'S GO HOME.

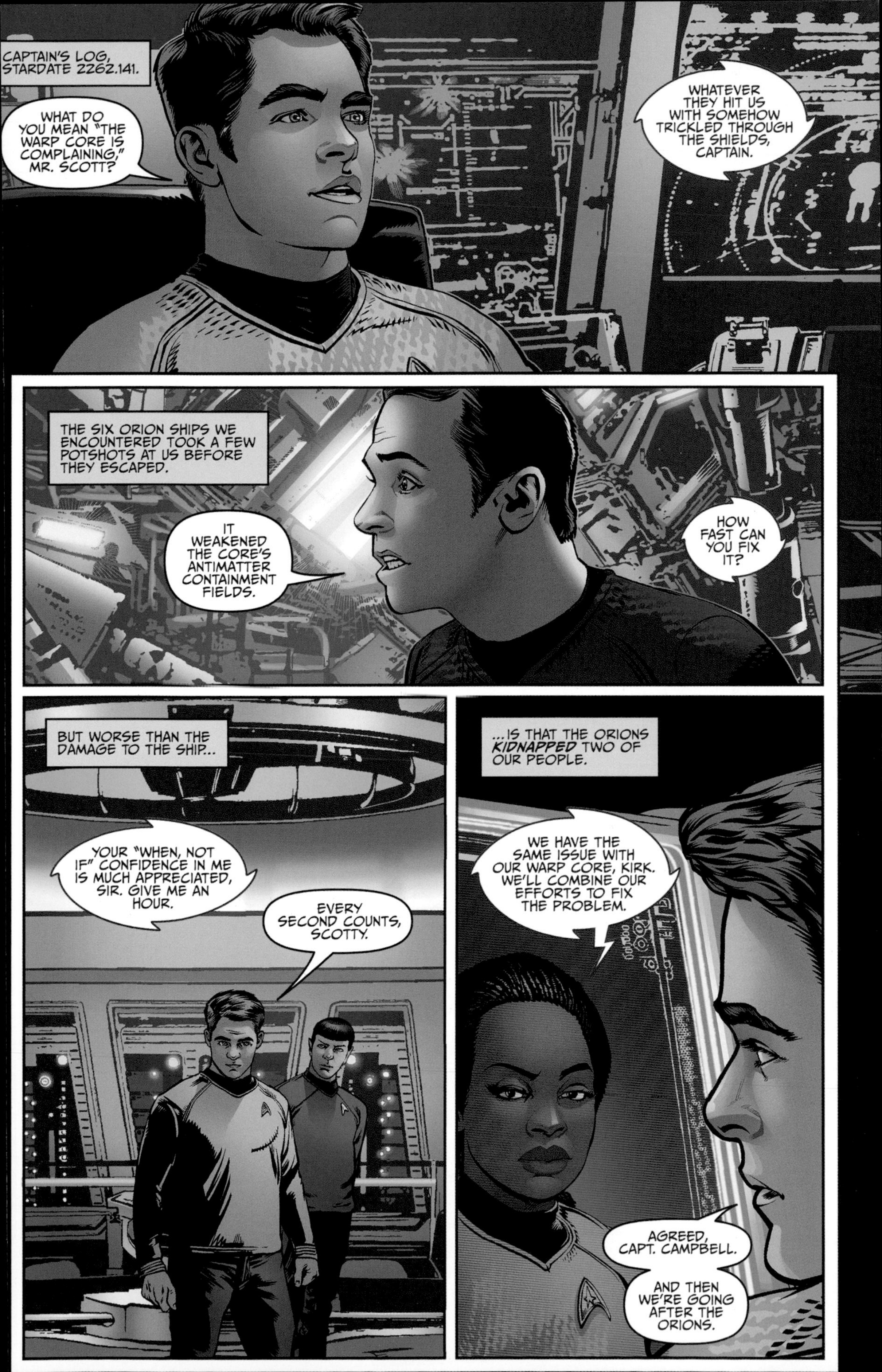
CAPTAIN'S LOG, STARDATE 2262.141.
WHAT DO YOU MEAN "THE WARP CORE IS COMPLAINING," MR. SCOTT?
WHATEVER THEY HIT US WITH SOMEHOW TRICKLED THROUGH THE SHIELDS, CAPTAIN.
THE SIX ORION SHIPS WE ENCOUNTERED TOOK A FEW POTSHOTS AT US BEFORE THEY ESCAPED.
IT WEAKENED THE CORE'S ANTIMATTER CONTAINMENT FIELDS.
HOW FAST CAN YOU FIX IT?
BUT WORSE THAN THE DAMAGE TO THE SHIP...
YOUR "WHEN, NOT IF" CONFIDENCE IN ME IS MUCH APPRECIATED, SIR. GIVE ME AN HOUR.
EVERY SECOND COUNTS, SCOTTY.
...IS THAT THE ORIONS *KIDNAPPED* TWO OF OUR PEOPLE.
WE HAVE THE SAME ISSUE WITH OUR WARP CORE, KIRK. WE'LL COMBINE OUR EFFORTS TO FIX THE PROBLEM.
AGREED, CAPT. CAMPBELL.
AND THEN WE'RE GOING AFTER THE ORIONS.

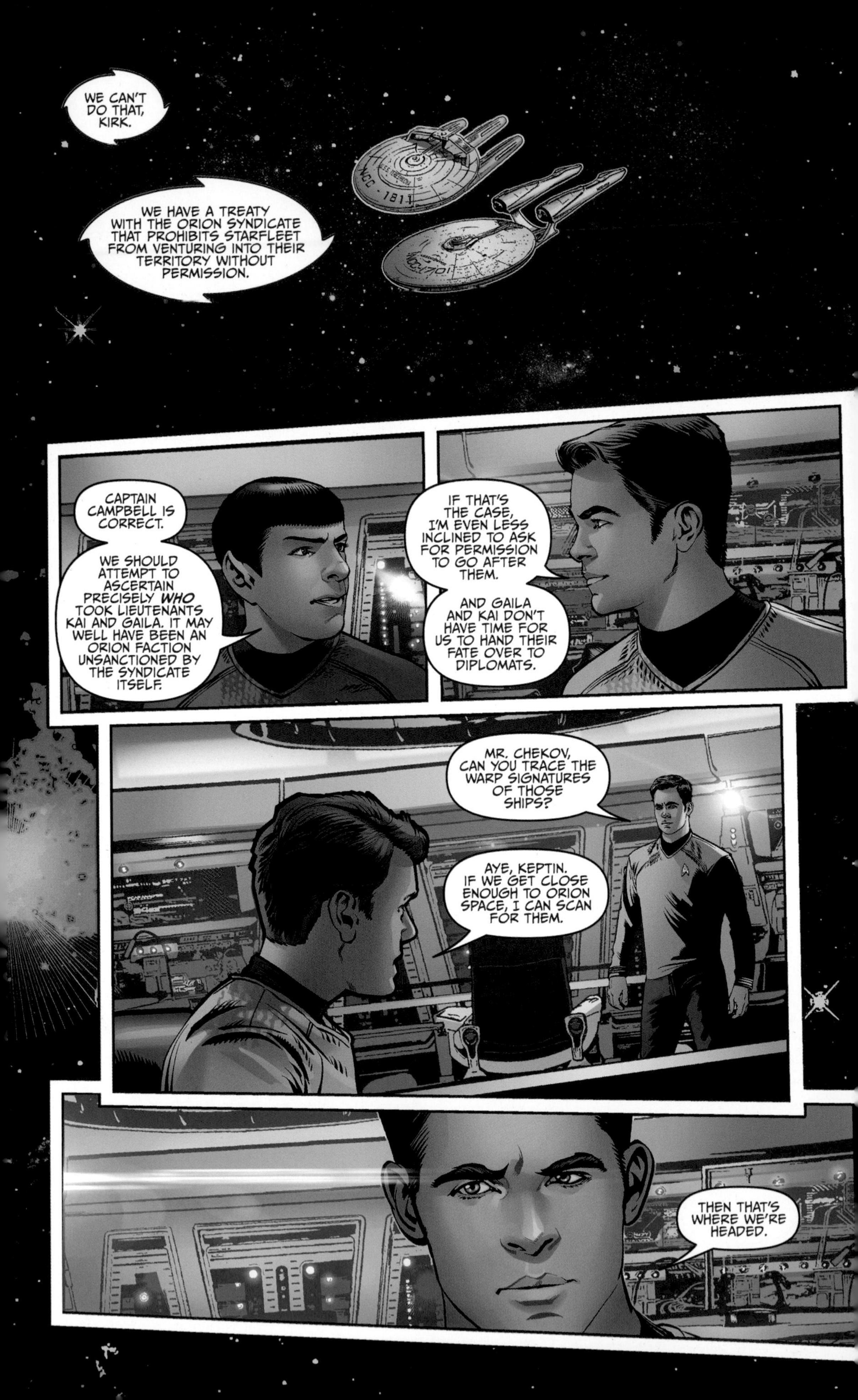

WE CAN'T DO THAT, KIRK.
WE HAVE A TREATY WITH THE ORION SYNDICATE THAT PROHIBITS STARFLEET FROM VENTURING INTO THEIR TERRITORY WITHOUT PERMISSION.
CAPTAIN CAMPBELL IS CORRECT.
WE SHOULD ATTEMPT TO ASCERTAIN PRECISELY *WHO* TOOK LIEUTENANTS KAI AND GAILA. IT MAY WELL HAVE BEEN AN ORION FACTION UNSANCTIONED BY THE SYNDICATE ITSELF.
IF THAT'S THE CASE, I'M EVEN LESS INCLINED TO ASK FOR PERMISSION TO GO AFTER THEM.
AND GAILA AND KAI DON'T HAVE TIME FOR US TO HAND THEIR FATE OVER TO DIPLOMATS.
MR. CHEKOV, CAN YOU TRACE THE WARP SIGNATURES OF THOSE SHIPS?
AYE, KEPTIN. IF WE GET CLOSE ENOUGH TO ORION SPACE, I CAN SCAN FOR THEM.
THEN THAT'S WHERE WE'RE HEADED.

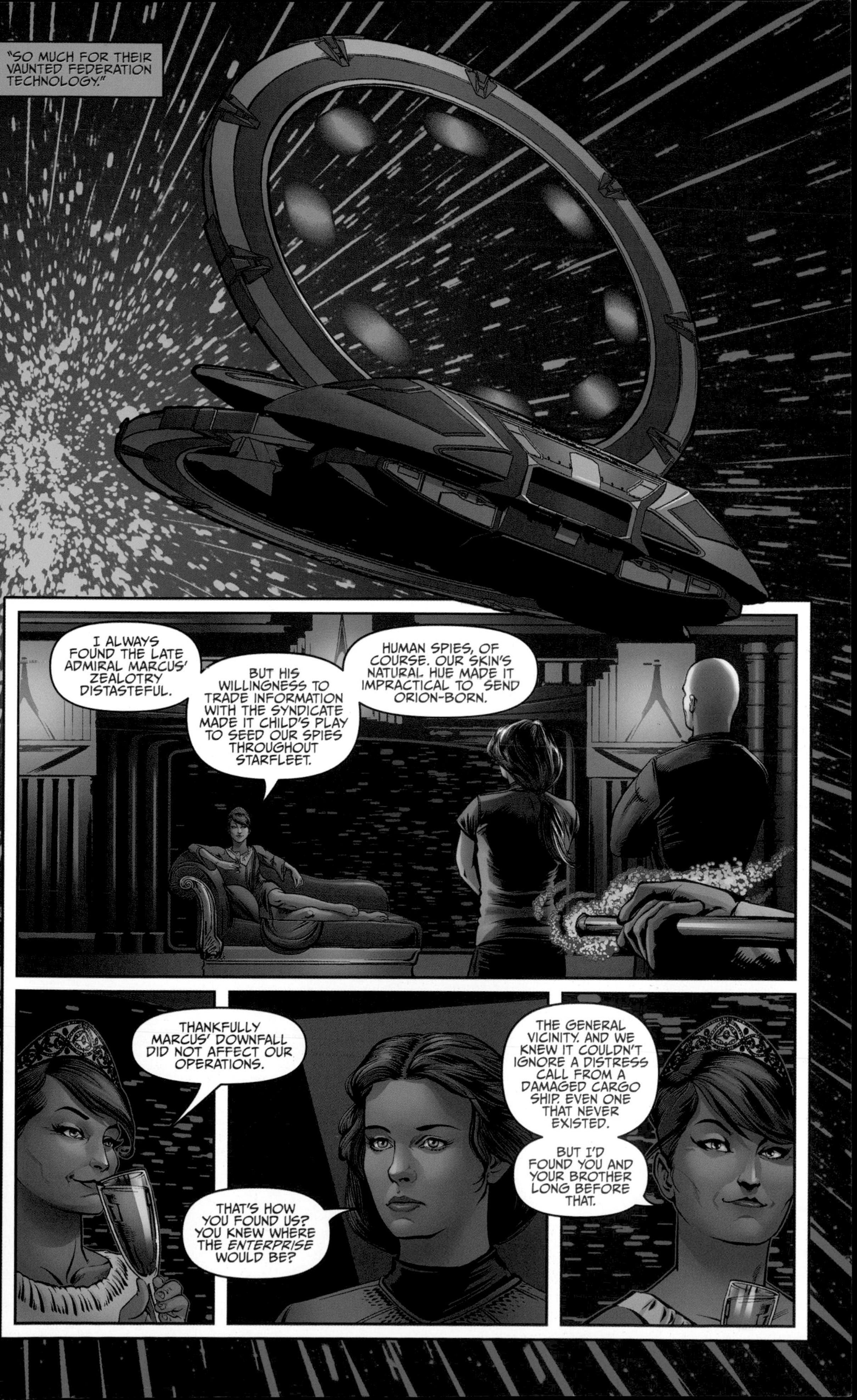
"SO MUCH FOR THEIR VAUNTED FEDERATION TECHNOLOGY."
I ALWAYS FOUND THE LATE ADMIRAL MARCUS' ZEALOTRY DISTASTEFUL.
BUT HIS WILLINGNESS TO TRADE INFORMATION WITH THE SYNDICATE MADE IT CHILD'S PLAY TO SEED OUR SPIES THROUGHOUT STARFLEET.
HUMAN SPIES, OF COURSE. OUR SKIN'S NATURAL HUE MADE IT IMPRACTICAL TO SEND ORION-BORN.
THANKFULLY MARCUS' DOWNFALL DID NOT AFFECT OUR OPERATIONS.
THAT'S HOW YOU FOUND US? YOU KNEW WHERE THE ENTERPRISE WOULD BE?
THE GENERAL VICINITY. AND WE KNEW IT COULDN'T IGNORE A DISTRESS CALL FROM A DAMAGED CARGO SHIP. EVEN ONE THAT NEVER EXISTED.
BUT I'D FOUND YOU AND YOUR BROTHER LONG BEFORE THAT.

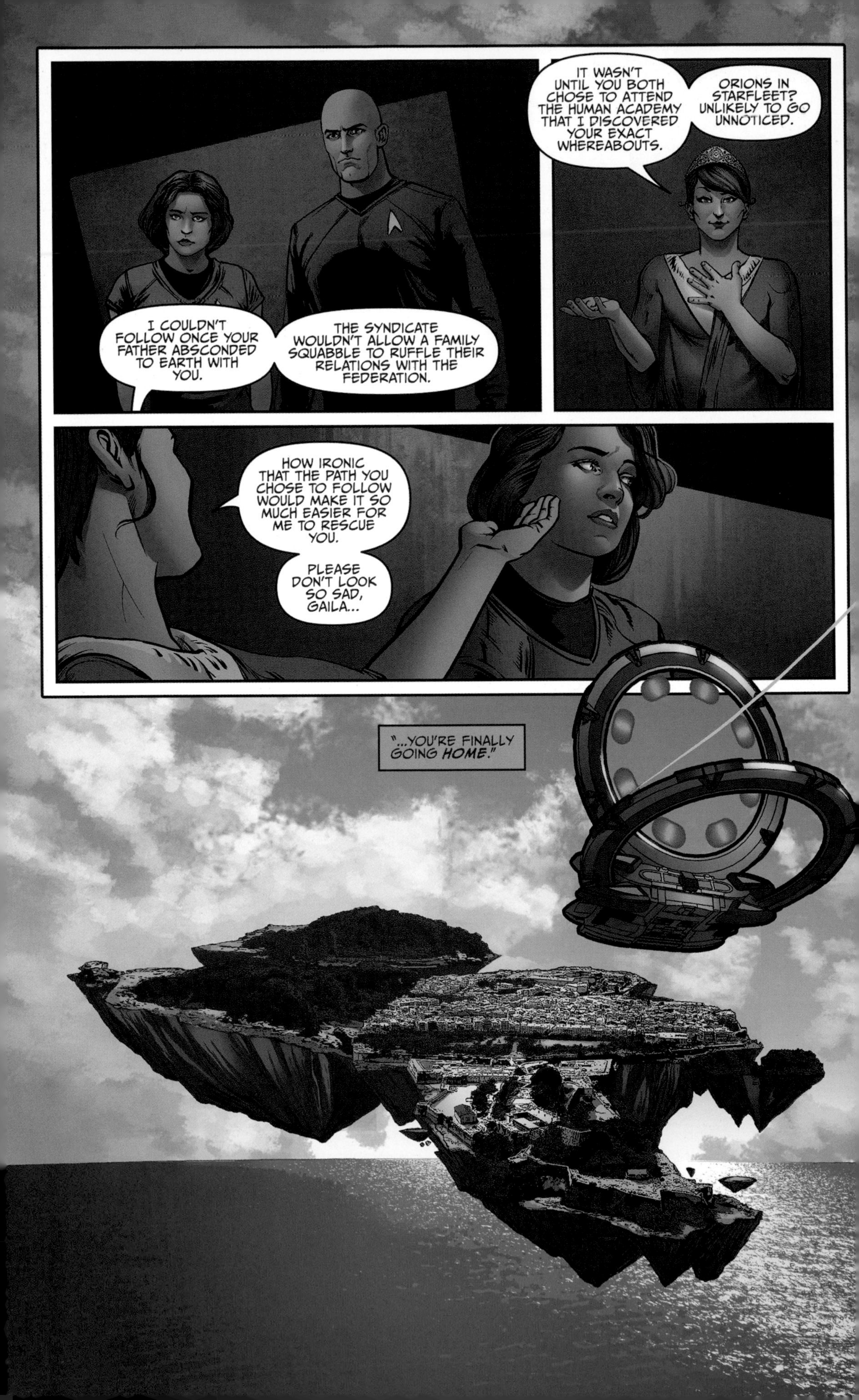
I COULDN'T FOLLOW ONCE YOUR FATHER ABSCONDED TO EARTH WITH YOU.
THE SYNDICATE WOULDN'T ALLOW A FAMILY SQUABBLE TO RUFFLE THEIR RELATIONS WITH THE FEDERATION.
IT WASN'T UNTIL YOU BOTH CHOSE TO ATTEND THE HUMAN ACADEMY THAT I DISCOVERED YOUR EXACT WHEREABOUTS.
ORIONS IN STARFLEET? UNLIKELY TO GO UNNOTICED.
HOW IRONIC THAT THE PATH YOU CHOSE TO FOLLOW WOULD MAKE IT SO MUCH EASIER FOR ME TO RESCUE YOU.
PLEASE DON'T LOOK SO SAD, GAILA...
"...YOU'RE FINALLY GOING *HOME*."

CAPTAIN'S LOG, SUPPLEMENTAL.

FIVE DAYS. I'LL NEVER FORGIVE MYSELF!

REPAIRS TOOK MUCH LONGER THAN ANTICIPATED. BUT WE'VE GOT OUR SPEED BACK.

I KNOW YOU DID THE BEST YOU COULD, SCOTTY.

ALL THAT MATTERS IS WHAT WE DO *NEXT*.

I DON'T AGREE WITH YOUR COURSE OF ACTION, KIRK. AND THE ORIONS WON'T BE HAPPY. BUT I'M NOT GOING TO STOP YOU.

I APPRECIATE THAT, CAPTAIN. I KNOW YOU HAVE TO REPORT BACK TO STARFLEET ON MY DECISION.

PLEASE MAKE SURE TO NOTE THAT MY FIRST OFFICER AGREES WITH YOU.

AND TRY TO LOOK ON THE BRIGHT SIDE.

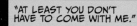

"AT LEAST YOU DON'T HAVE TO COME WITH ME."

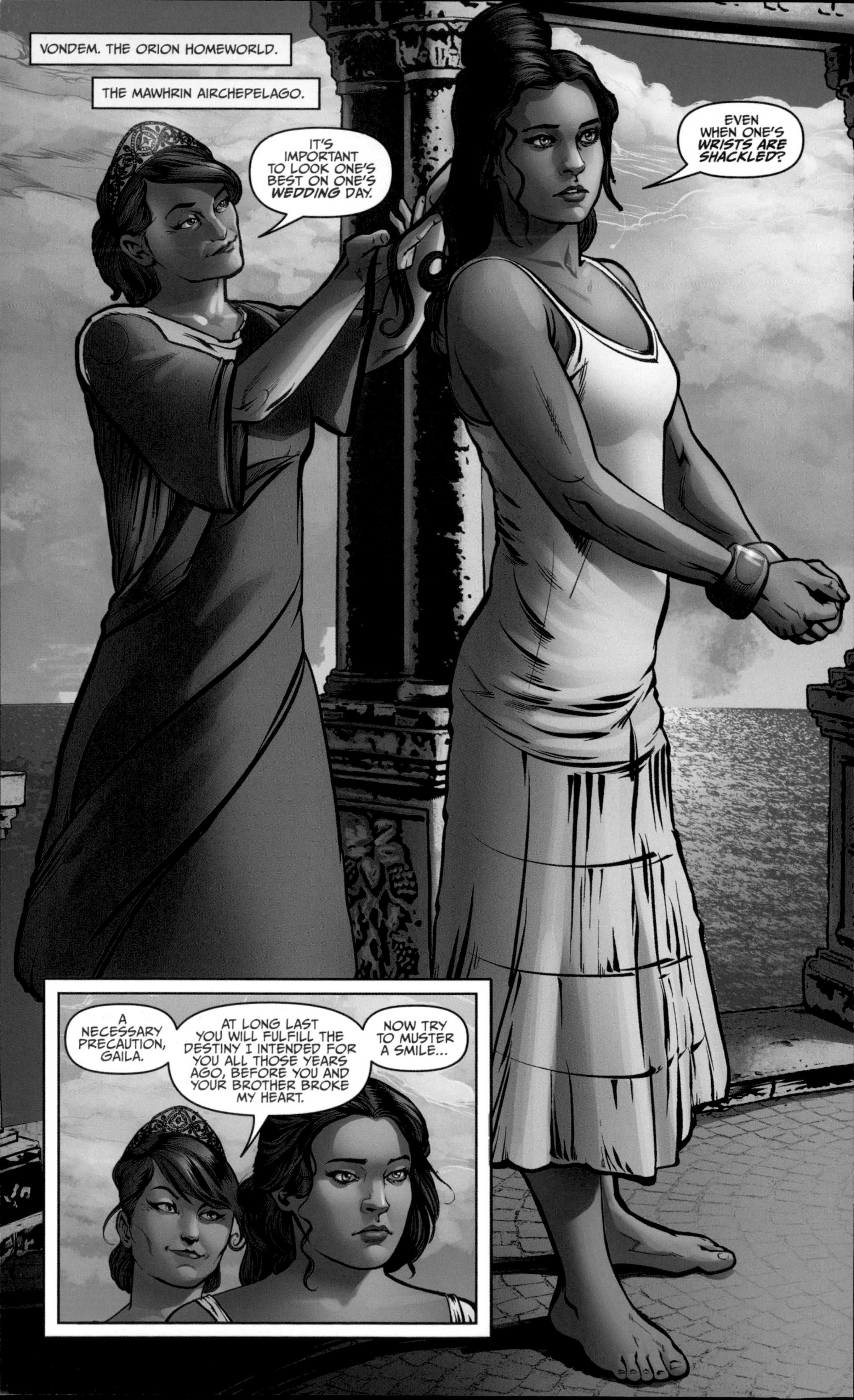
VONDEM. THE ORION HOMEWORLD.
THE MAWHRIN AIRCHEPELAGO.
IT'S IMPORTANT TO LOOK ONE'S BEST ON ONE'S WEDDING DAY.
EVEN WHEN ONE'S WRISTS ARE SHACKLED?
A NECESSARY PRECAUTION, GAILA.
AT LONG LAST YOU WILL FULFILL THE DESTINY I INTENDED FOR YOU ALL THOSE YEARS AGO, BEFORE YOU AND YOUR BROTHER BROKE MY HEART.
NOW TRY TO MUSTER A SMILE...

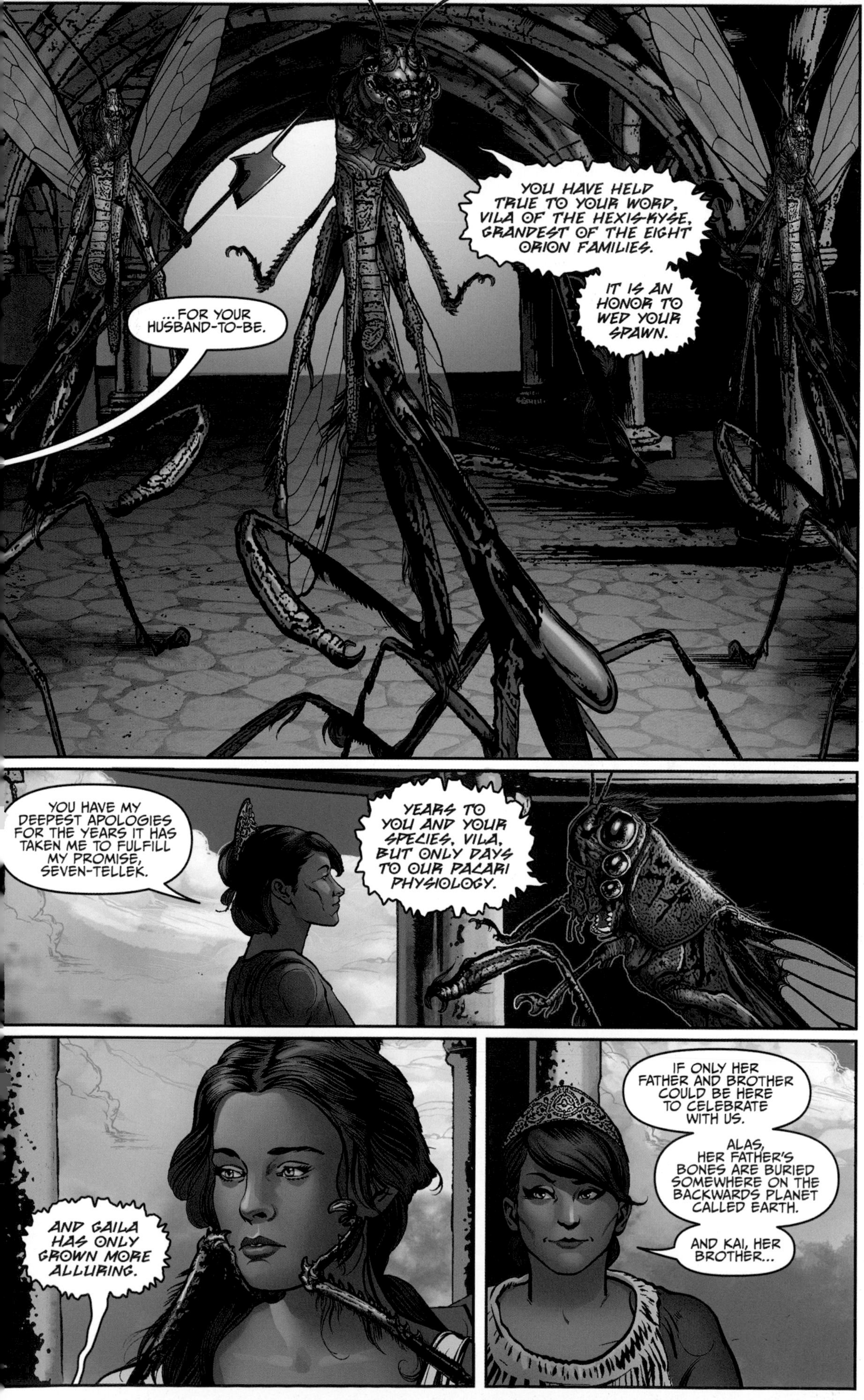
YOU HAVE HELD TRUE TO YOUR WORD, VILA OF THE HEXIS-KYSE, GRANDEST OF THE EIGHT ORION FAMILIES.
IT IS AN HONOR TO WED YOUR SPAWN.
...FOR YOUR HUSBAND-TO-BE.
YOU HAVE MY DEEPEST APOLOGIES FOR THE YEARS IT HAS TAKEN ME TO FULFILL MY PROMISE, SEVEN-TELLEK.
YEARS TO YOU AND YOUR SPECIES, VILA, BUT ONLY DAYS TO OUR PACARI PHYSIOLOGY.
AND GAILA HAS ONLY GROWN MORE ALLURING.
IF ONLY HER FATHER AND BROTHER COULD BE HERE TO CELEBRATE WITH US.
ALAS, HER FATHER'S BONES ARE BURIED SOMEWHERE ON THE BACKWARDS PLANET CALLED EARTH.
AND KAI, HER BROTHER...

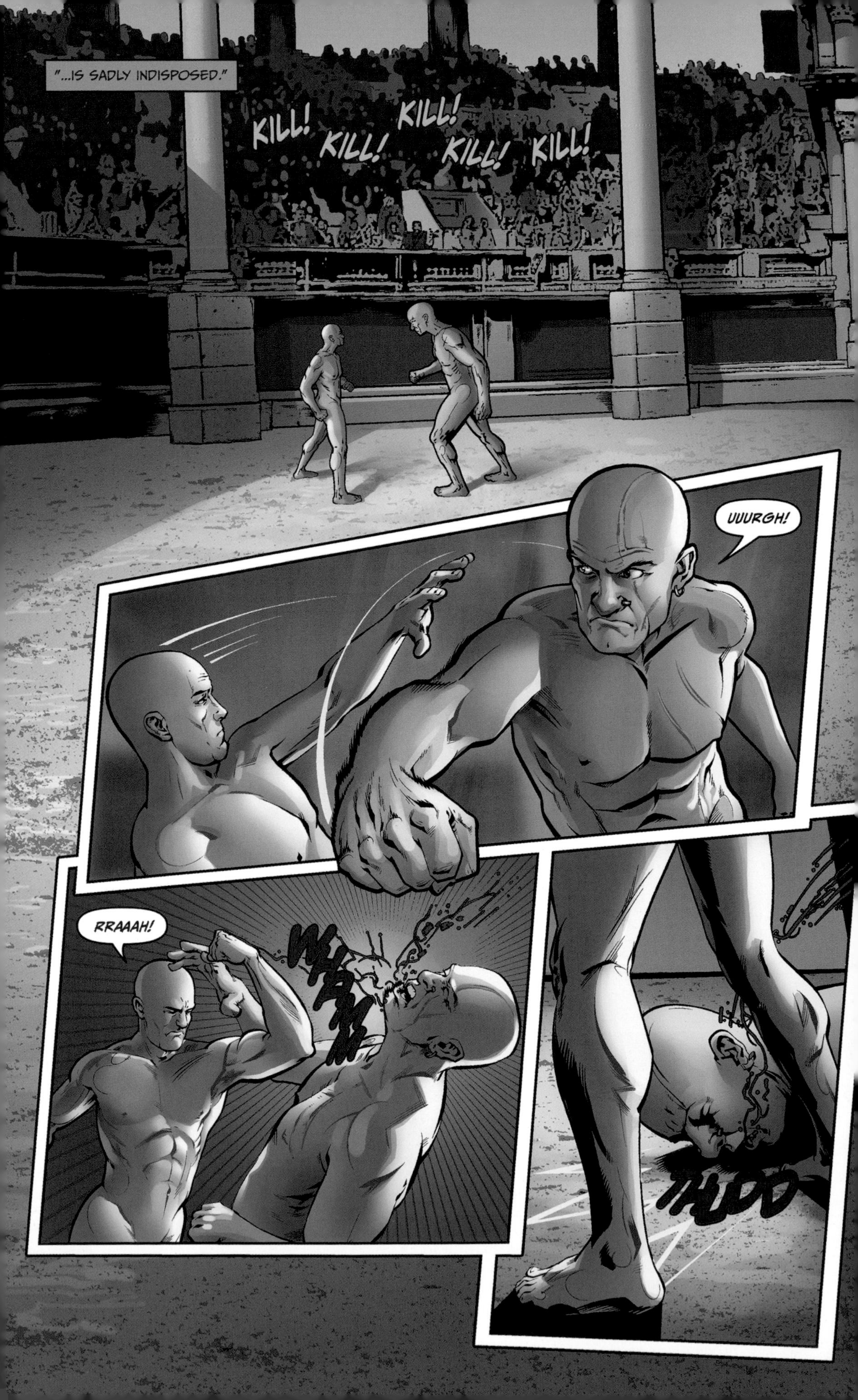
"...IS SADLY INDISPOSED."
KILL!
KILL!
KILL!
KILL!
KILL!
UUURGH!
RRAAAH!
THUD

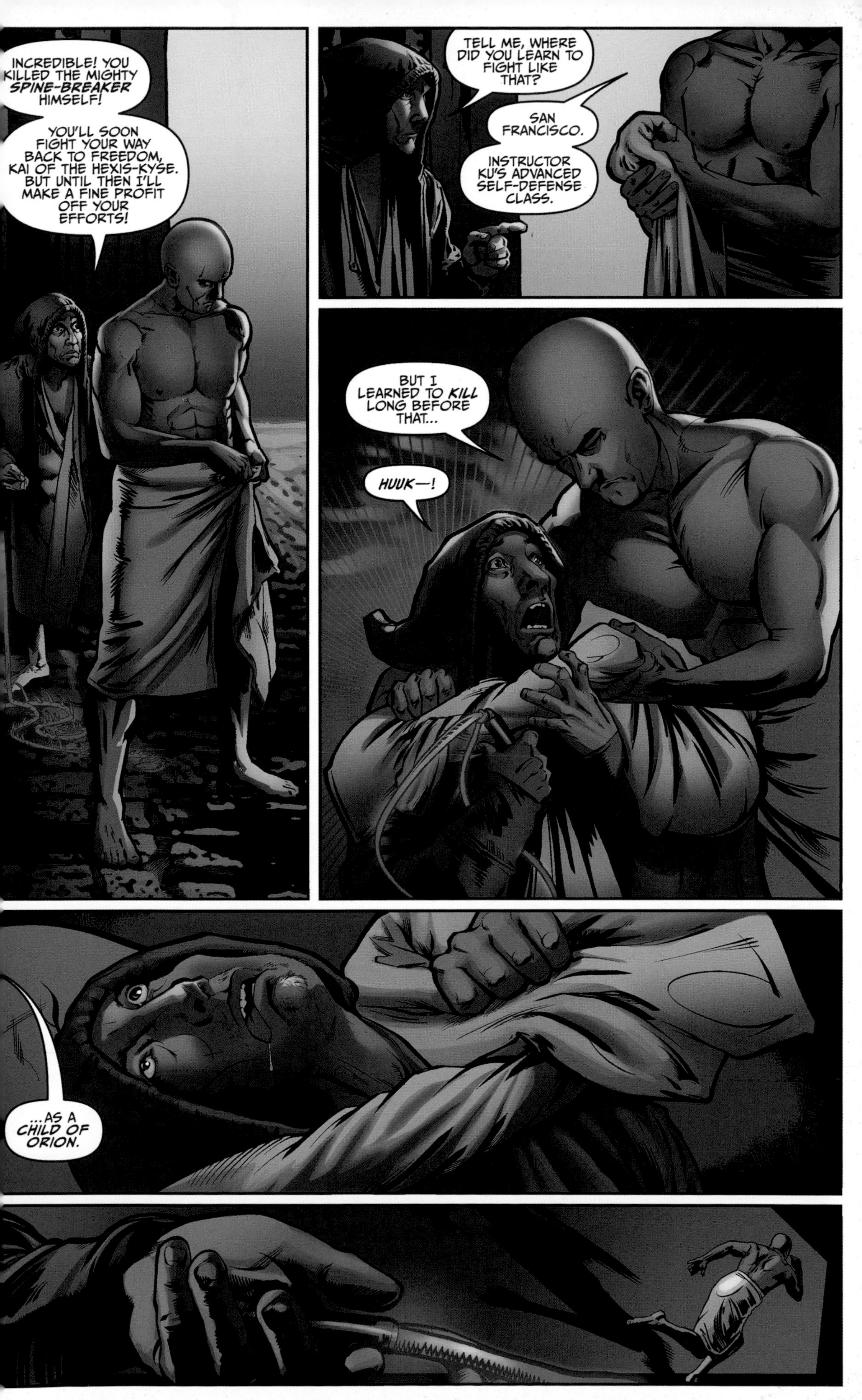
INCREDIBLE! YOU KILLED THE MIGHTY SPINE-BREAKER HIMSELF!
YOU'LL SOON FIGHT YOUR WAY BACK TO FREEDOM, KAI OF THE HEXIS-KYSE. BUT UNTIL THEN I'LL MAKE A FINE PROFIT OFF YOUR EFFORTS!
TELL ME, WHERE DID YOU LEARN TO FIGHT LIKE THAT?
SAN FRANCISCO.
INSTRUCTOR KU'S ADVANCED SELF-DEFENSE CLASS.
BUT I LEARNED TO KILL LONG BEFORE THAT...
HUUK—!
...AS A CHILD OF ORION.

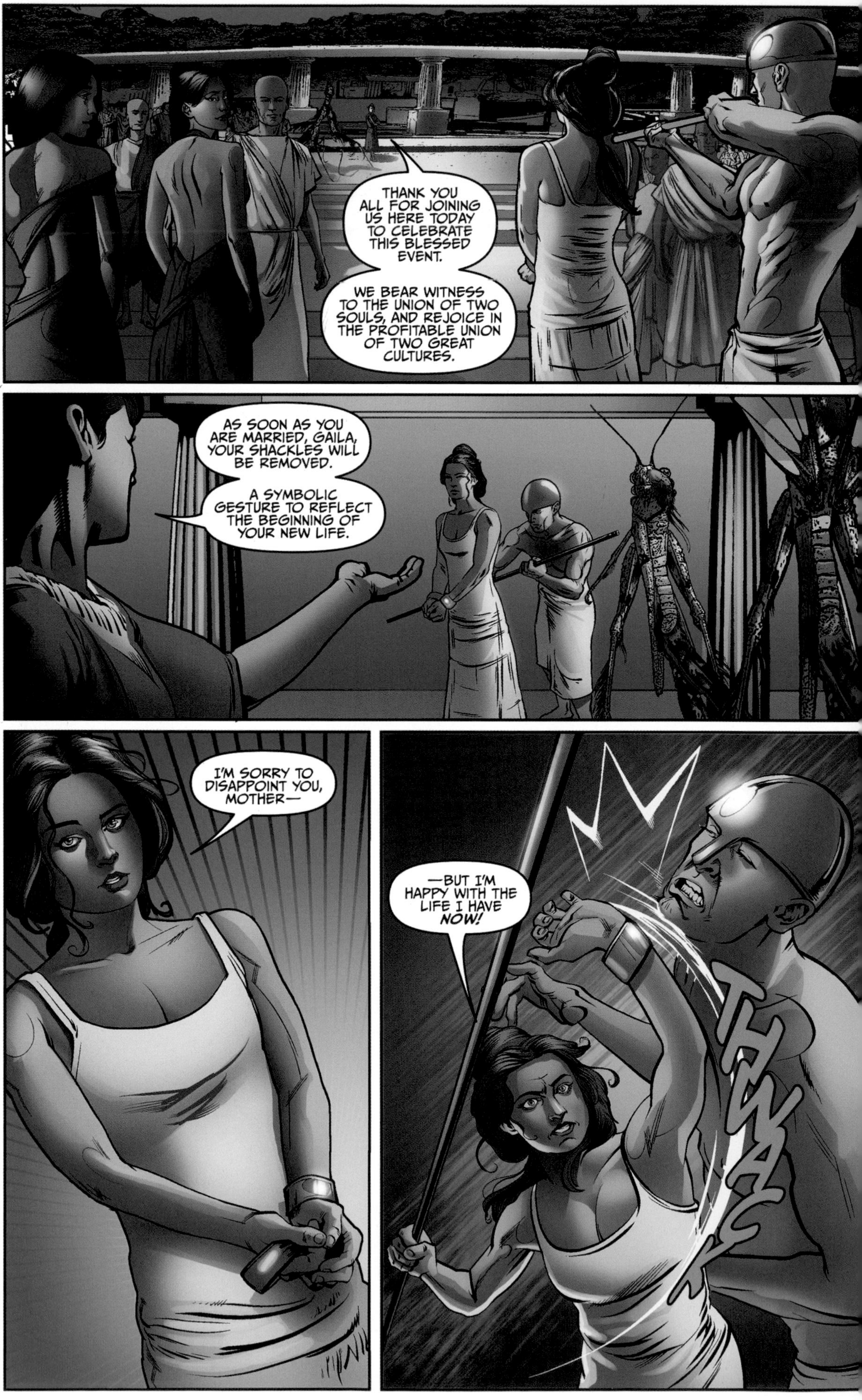
THANK YOU ALL FOR JOINING US HERE TODAY TO CELEBRATE THIS BLESSED EVENT.
WE BEAR WITNESS TO THE UNION OF TWO SOULS, AND REJOICE IN THE PROFITABLE UNION OF TWO GREAT CULTURES.
AS SOON AS YOU ARE MARRIED, GAILA, YOUR SHACKLES WILL BE REMOVED.
A SYMBOLIC GESTURE TO REFLECT THE BEGINNING OF YOUR NEW LIFE.
I'M SORRY TO DISAPPOINT YOU, MOTHER—
—BUT I'M HAPPY WITH THE LIFE I HAVE *NOW!*
THWACK

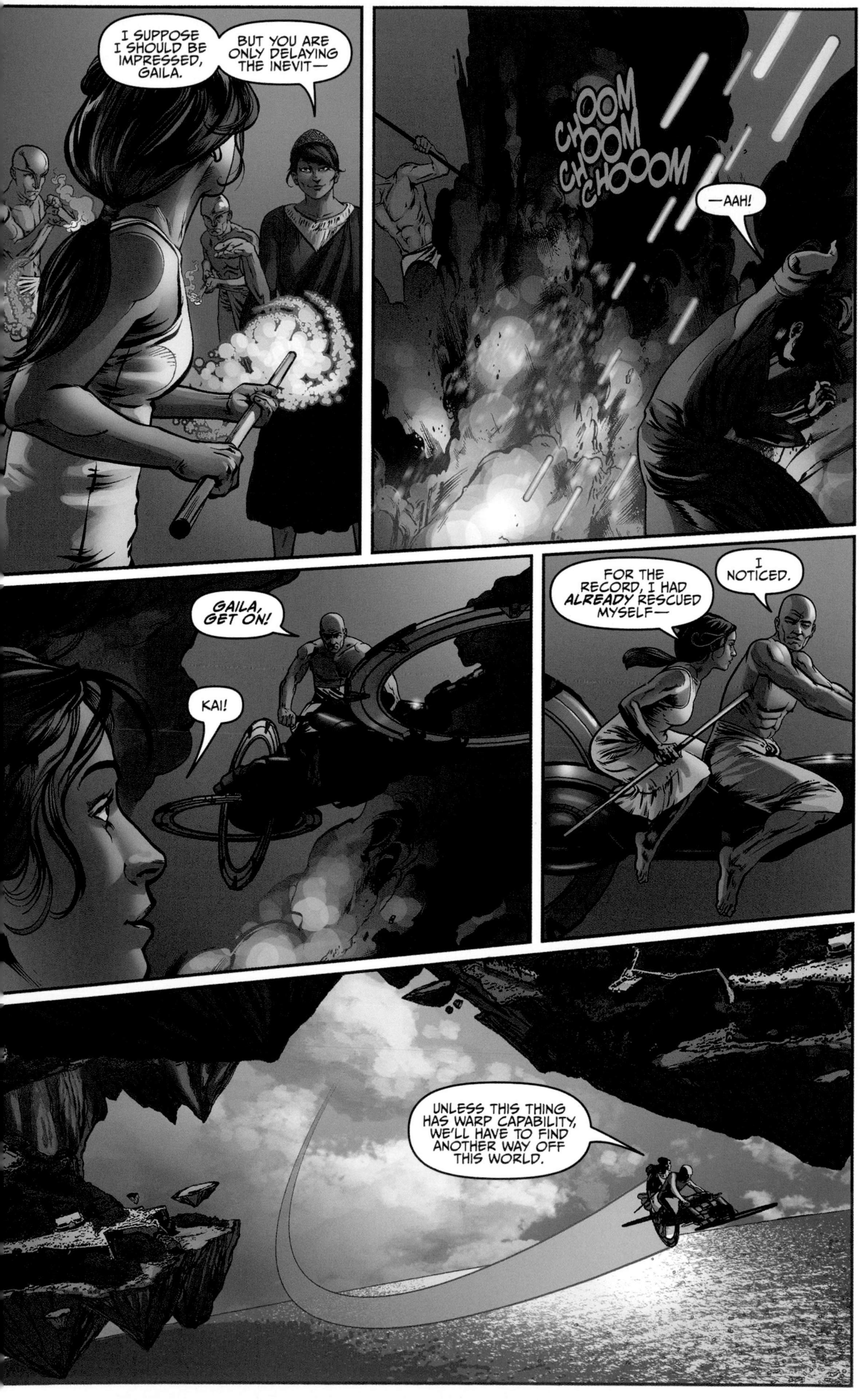
I SUPPOSE I SHOULD BE IMPRESSED, GAILA.
BUT YOU ARE ONLY DELAYING THE INEVIT—
CHOOM
CHOOM
CHOOOM
—AAH!
GAILA, GET ON!
KAI!
FOR THE RECORD, I HAD ***ALREADY*** RESCUED MYSELF—
I NOTICED.
UNLESS THIS THING HAS WARP CAPABILITY, WE'LL HAVE TO FIND ANOTHER WAY OFF THIS WORLD.

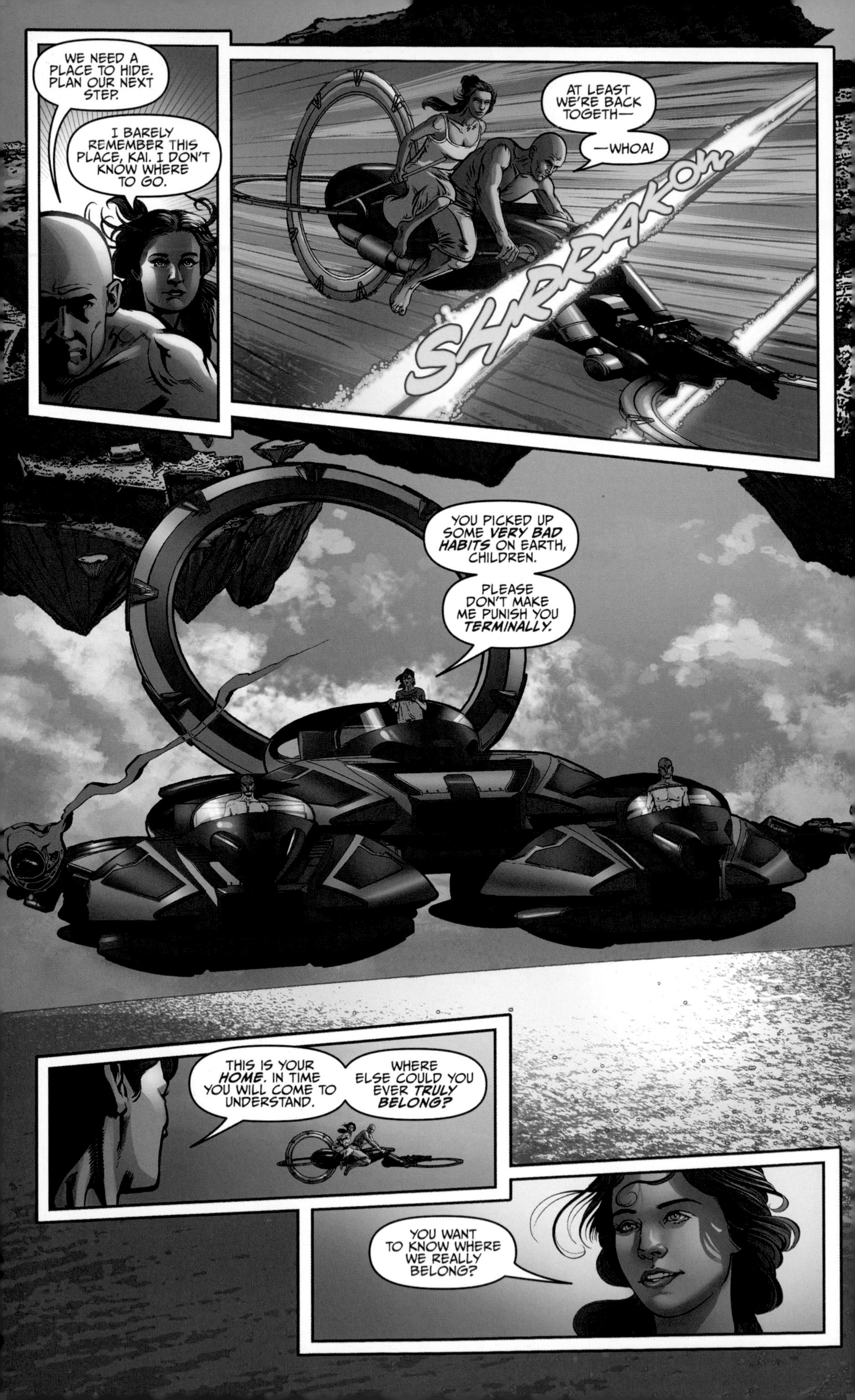
WE NEED A PLACE TO HIDE. PLAN OUR NEXT STEP.
I BARELY REMEMBER THIS PLACE, KAI. I DON'T KNOW WHERE TO GO.
AT LEAST WE'RE BACK TOGETH—
—WHOA!
SHRRAKOW
YOU PICKED UP SOME VERY BAD HABITS ON EARTH, CHILDREN.
PLEASE DON'T MAKE ME PUNISH YOU TERMINALLY.
THIS IS YOUR HOME. IN TIME YOU WILL COME TO UNDERSTAND.
WHERE ELSE COULD YOU EVER TRULY BELONG?
YOU WANT TO KNOW WHERE WE REALLY BELONG?

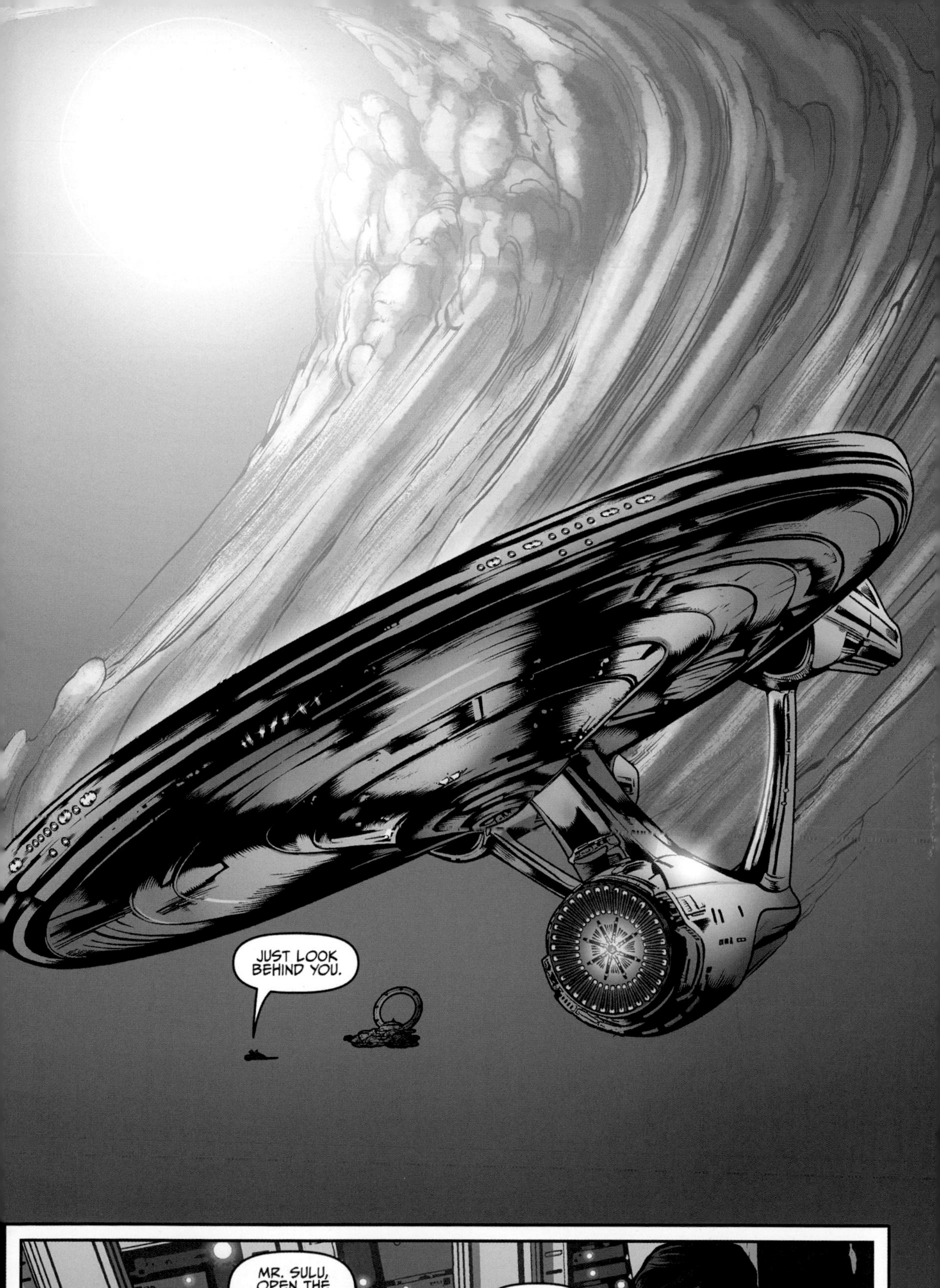
JUST LOOK BEHIND YOU.

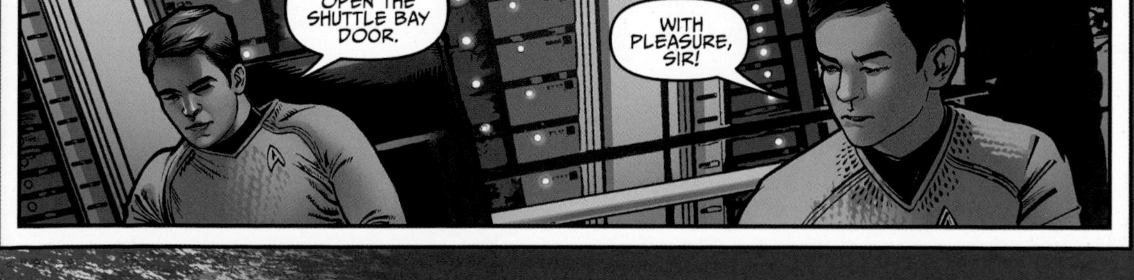
MR. SULU, OPEN THE SHUTTLE BAY DOOR.
WITH PLEASURE, SIR!

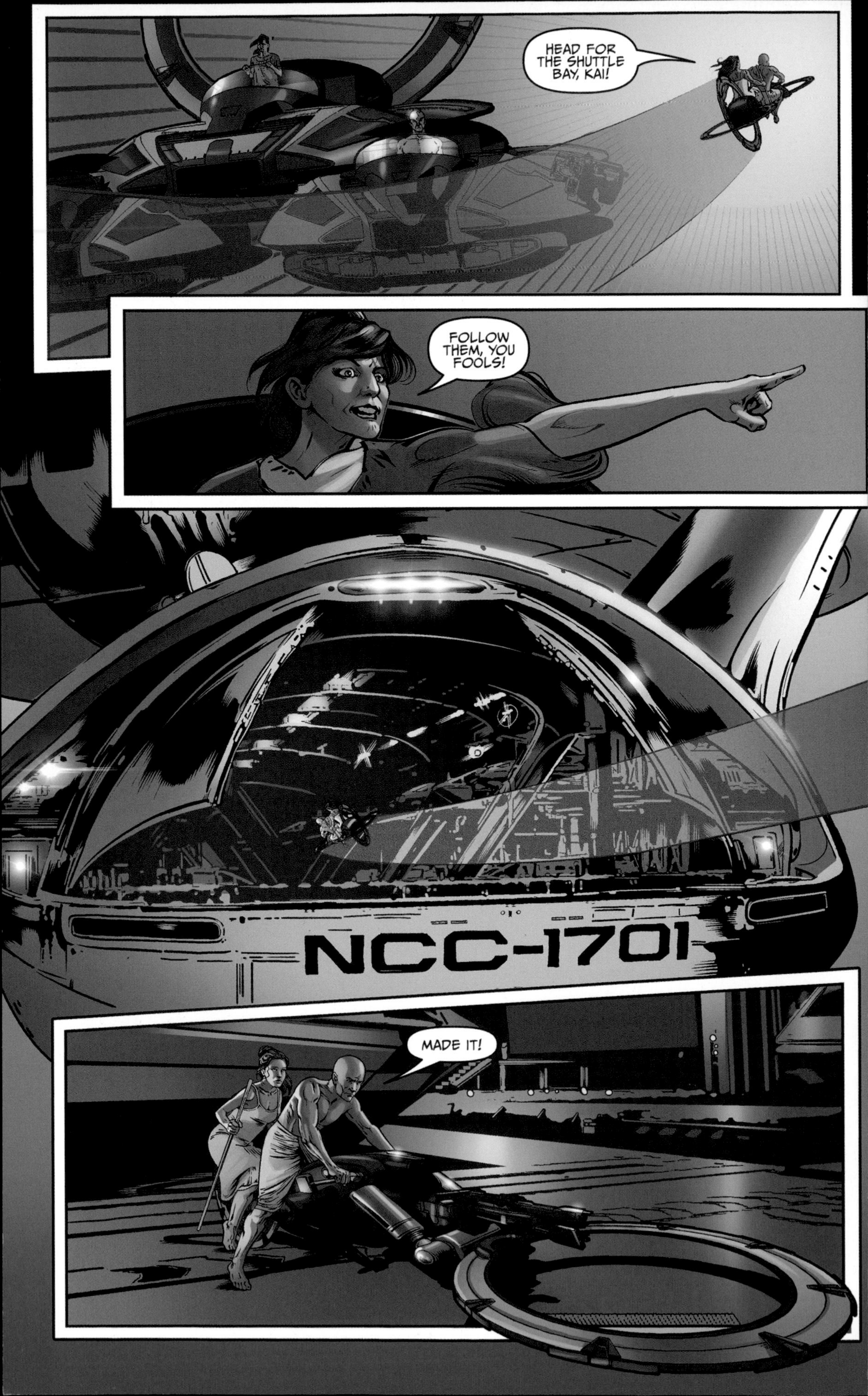
HEAD FOR THE SHUTTLE BAY, KAI!
FOLLOW THEM, YOU FOOLS!
NCC-1701
MADE IT!

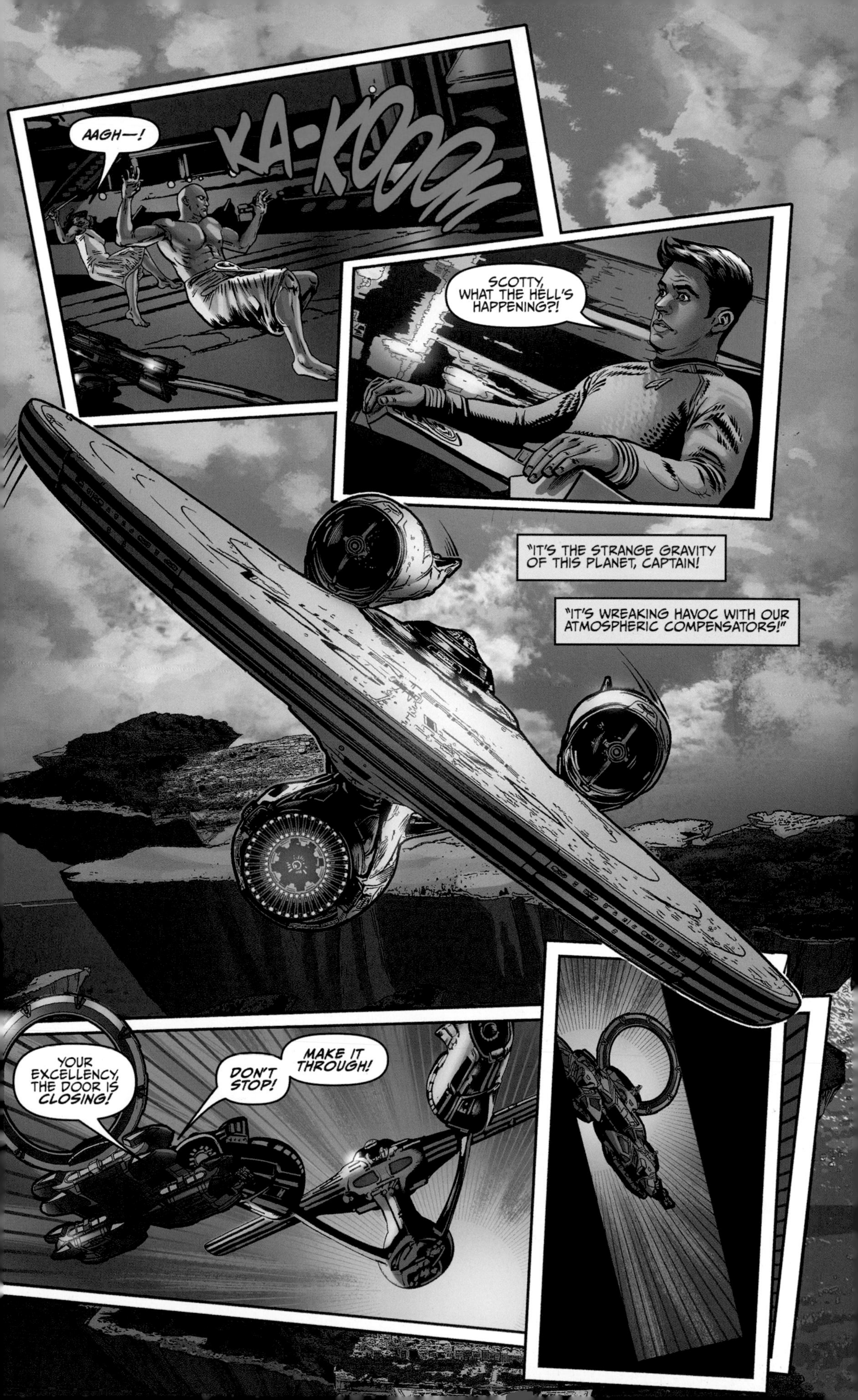
AAGH—!
KA-KOOOM
SCOTTY, WHAT THE HELL'S HAPPENING?!
"IT'S THE STRANGE GRAVITY OF THIS PLANET, CAPTAIN!
"IT'S WREAKING HAVOC WITH OUR ATMOSPHERIC COMPENSATORS!"
YOUR EXCELLENCY, THE DOOR IS CLOSING!
DON'T STOP!
MAKE IT THROUGH!

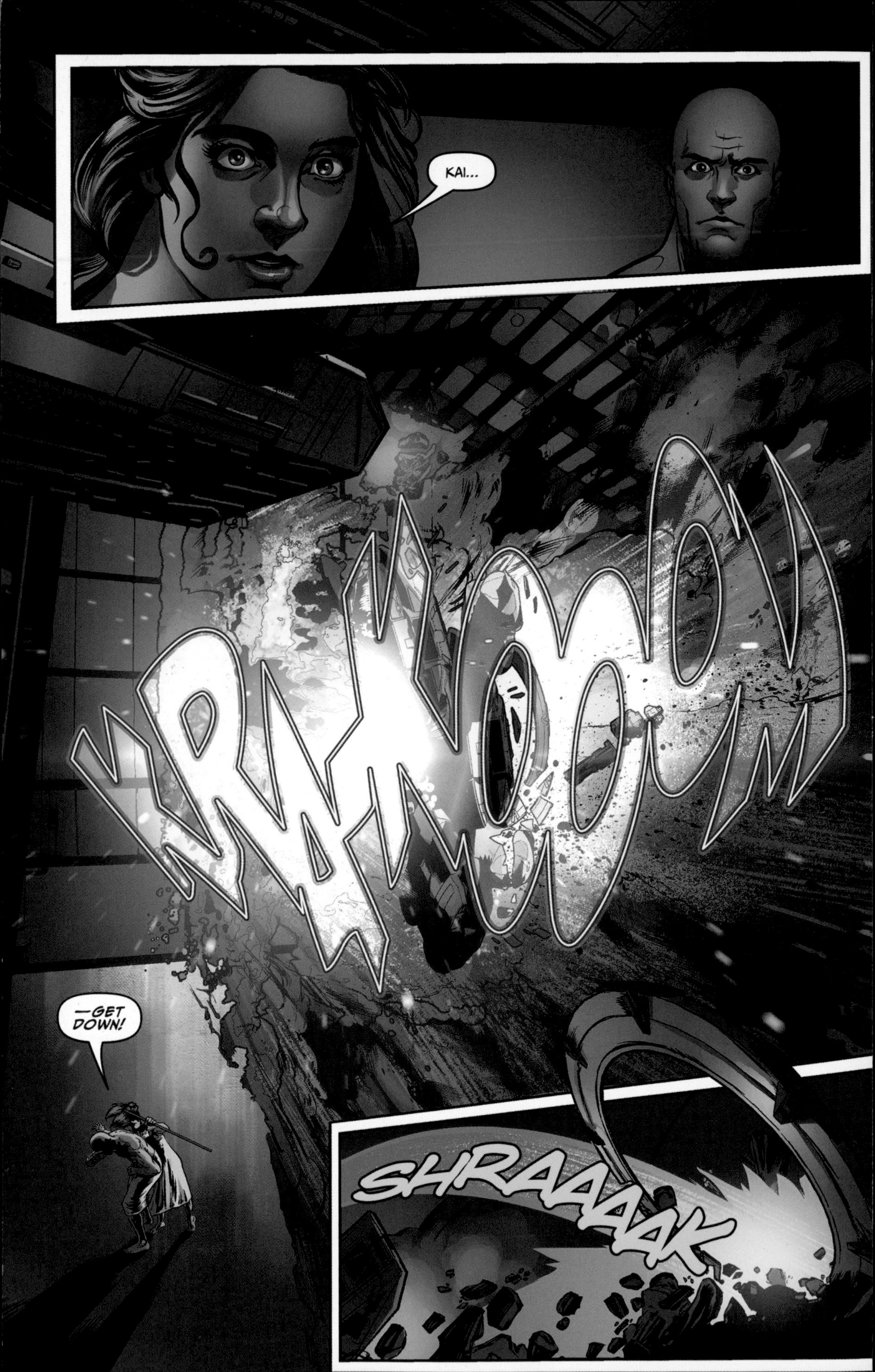
KAI...
BRAKOOOOM
—GET DOWN!
SHRAAAAK

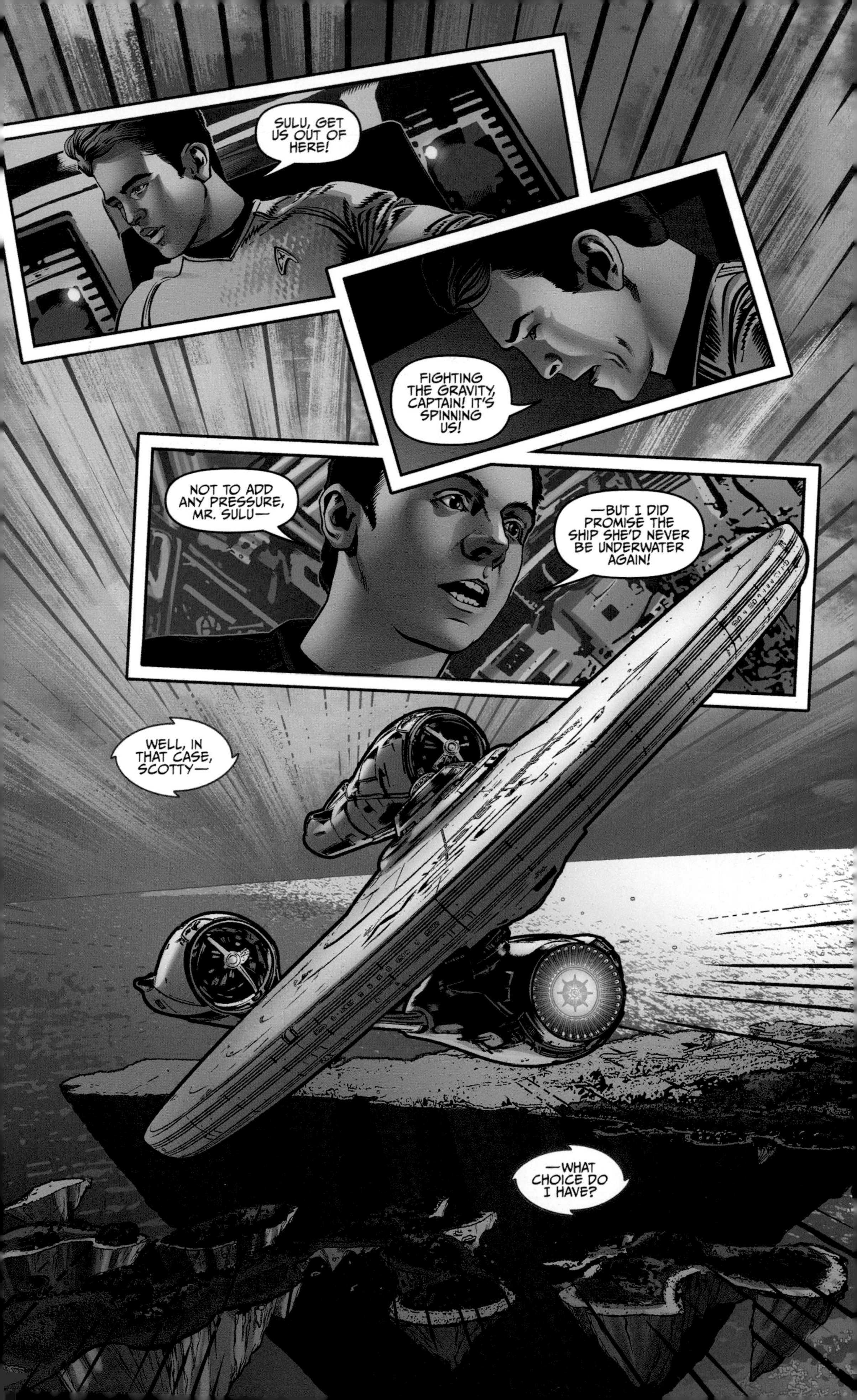
SULU, GET US OUT OF HERE!
FIGHTING THE GRAVITY, CAPTAIN! IT'S SPINNING US!
NOT TO ADD ANY PRESSURE, MR. SULU—
—BUT I DID PROMISE THE SHIP SHE'D NEVER BE UNDERWATER AGAIN!
WELL, IN THAT CASE, SCOTTY—
—WHAT CHOICE DO I HAVE?

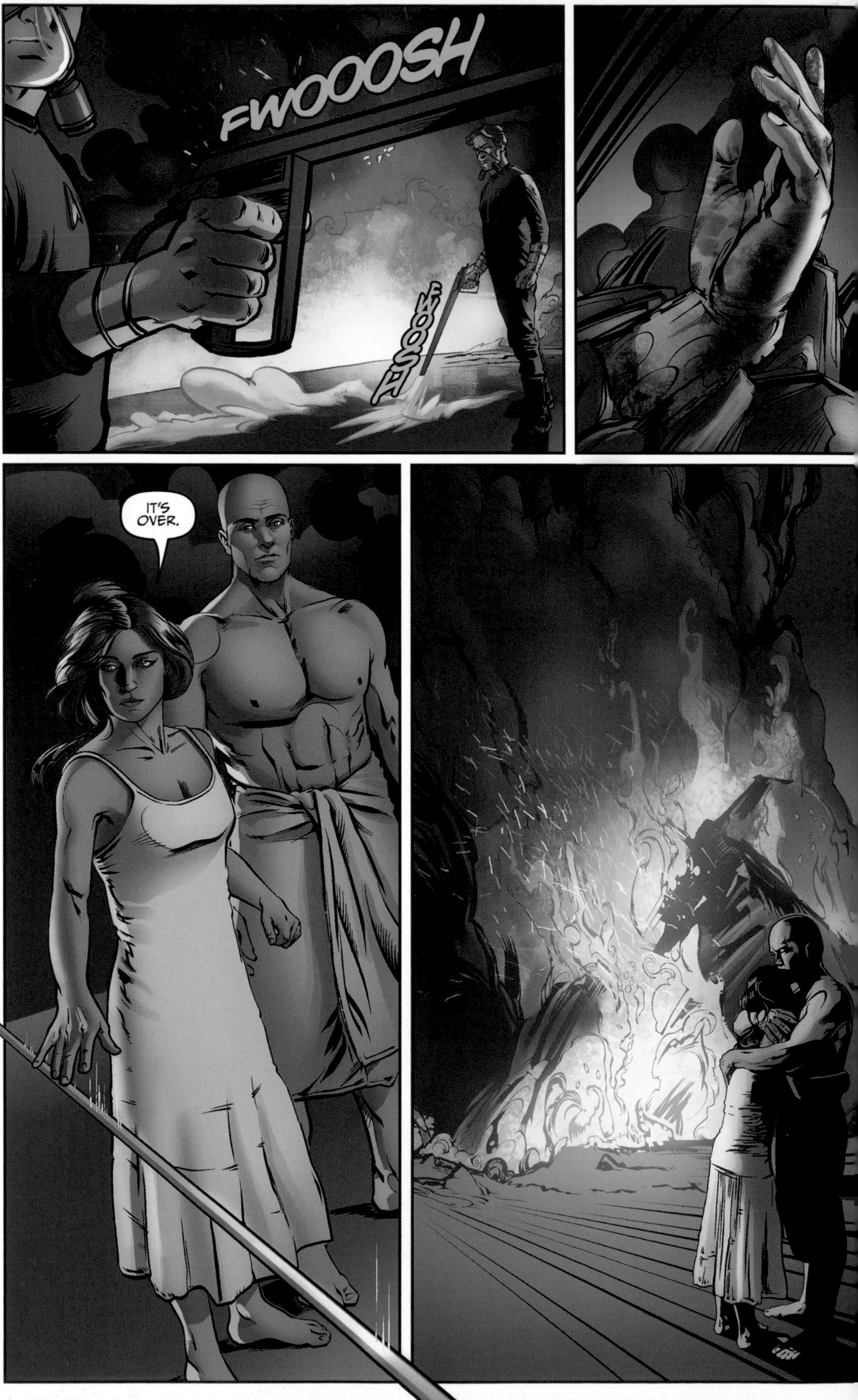
FWOOOSH
FWOOSH
IT'S OVER.

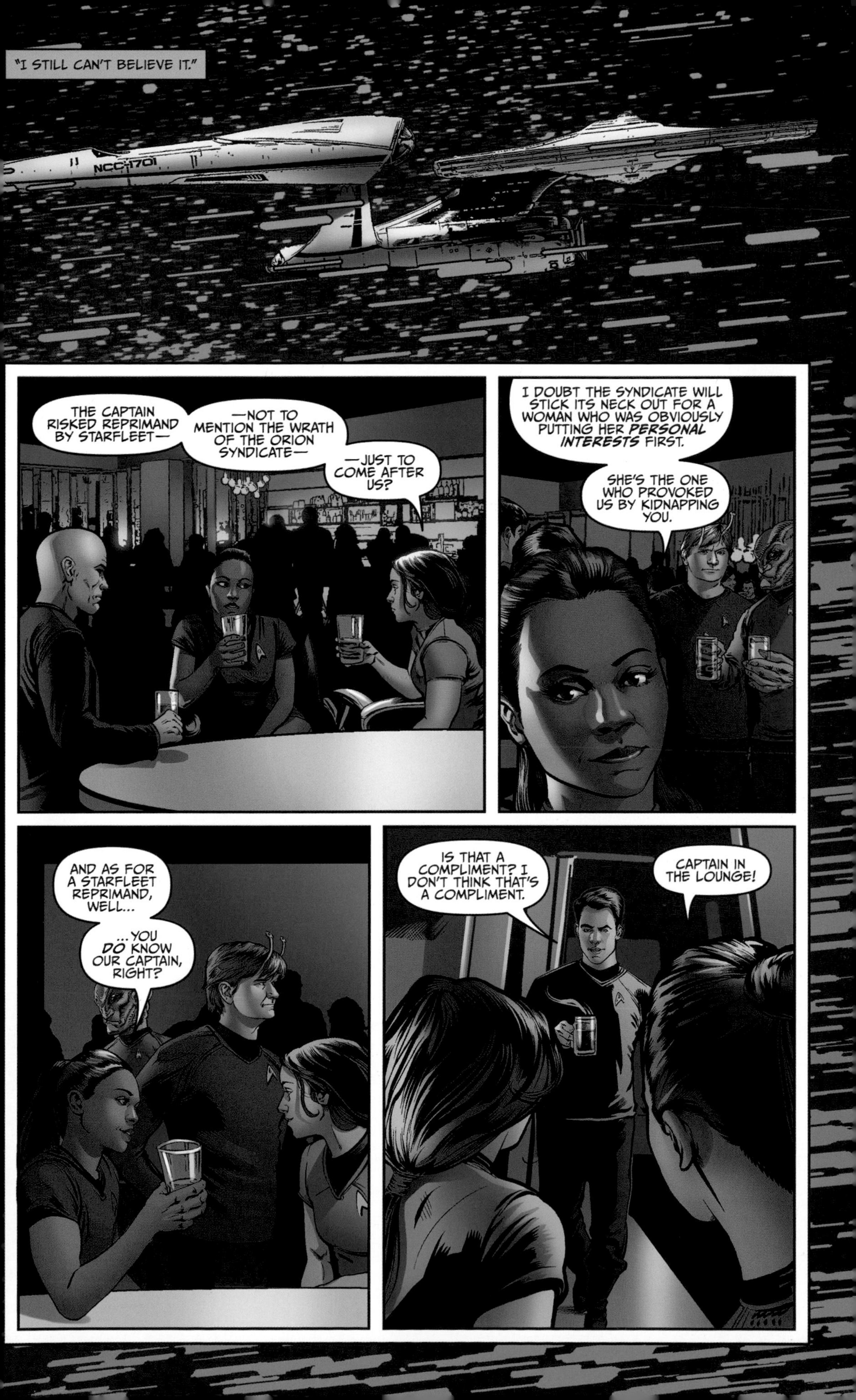
"I STILL CAN'T BELIEVE IT."
NCC-1701
THE CAPTAIN RISKED REPRIMAND BY STARFLEET—
—NOT TO MENTION THE WRATH OF THE ORION SYNDICATE—
—JUST TO COME AFTER US?
I DOUBT THE SYNDICATE WILL STICK ITS NECK OUT FOR A WOMAN WHO WAS OBVIOUSLY PUTTING HER PERSONAL INTERESTS FIRST.
SHE'S THE ONE WHO PROVOKED US BY KIDNAPPING YOU.
AND AS FOR A STARFLEET REPRIMAND, WELL...
...YOU DO KNOW OUR CAPTAIN, RIGHT?
IS THAT A COMPLIMENT? I DON'T THINK THAT'S A COMPLIMENT.
CAPTAIN IN THE LOUNGE!

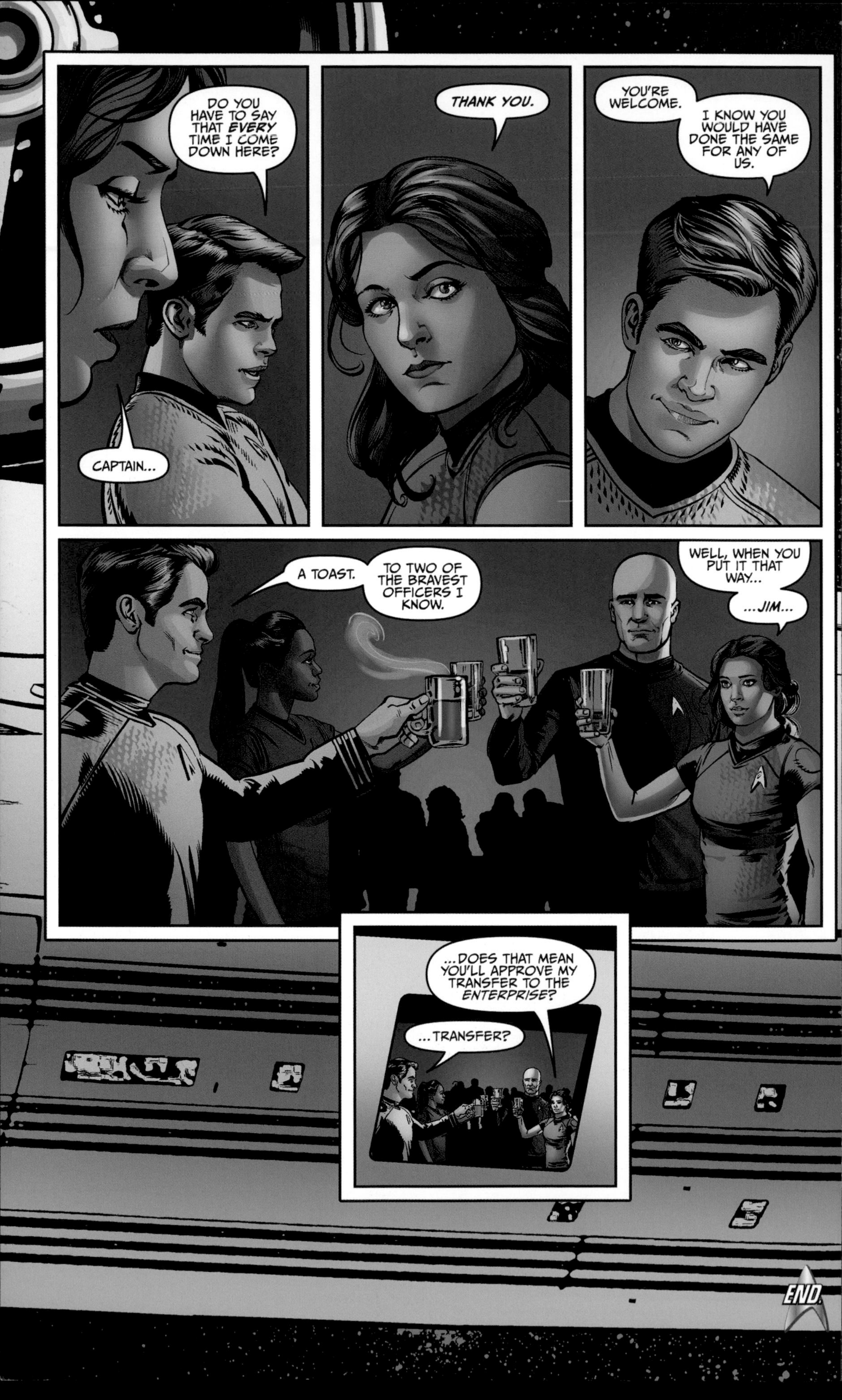

DO YOU HAVE TO SAY THAT EVERY TIME I COME DOWN HERE?
CAPTAIN...
THANK YOU.
YOU'RE WELCOME.
I KNOW YOU WOULD HAVE DONE THE SAME FOR ANY OF US.
A TOAST.
TO TWO OF THE BRAVEST OFFICERS I KNOW.
WELL, WHEN YOU PUT IT THAT WAY...
...JIM...
...DOES THAT MEAN YOU'LL APPROVE MY TRANSFER TO THE ENTERPRISE?
...TRANSFER?
END.

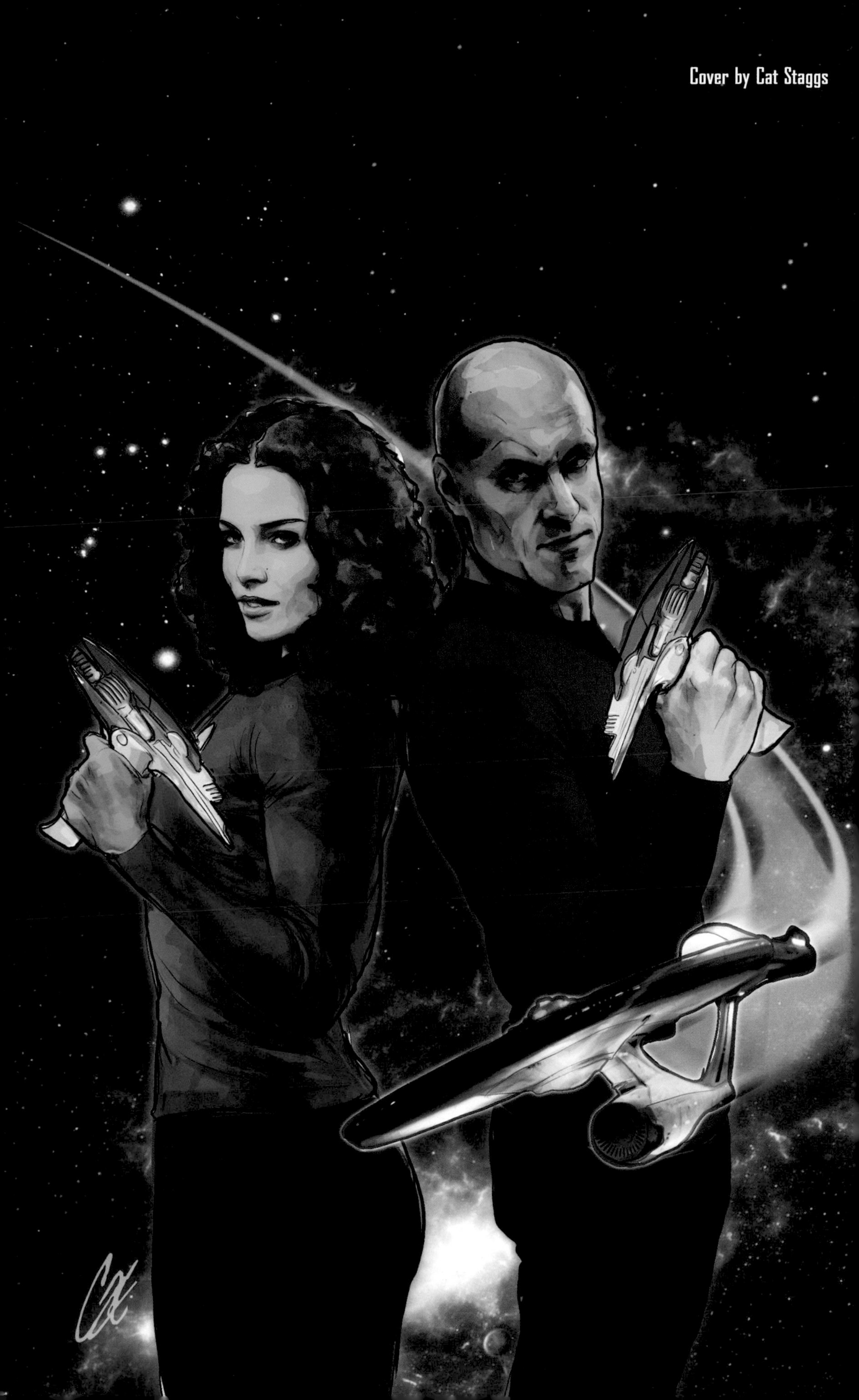

Cover by Cat Staggs

Cover by Tony Shasteen

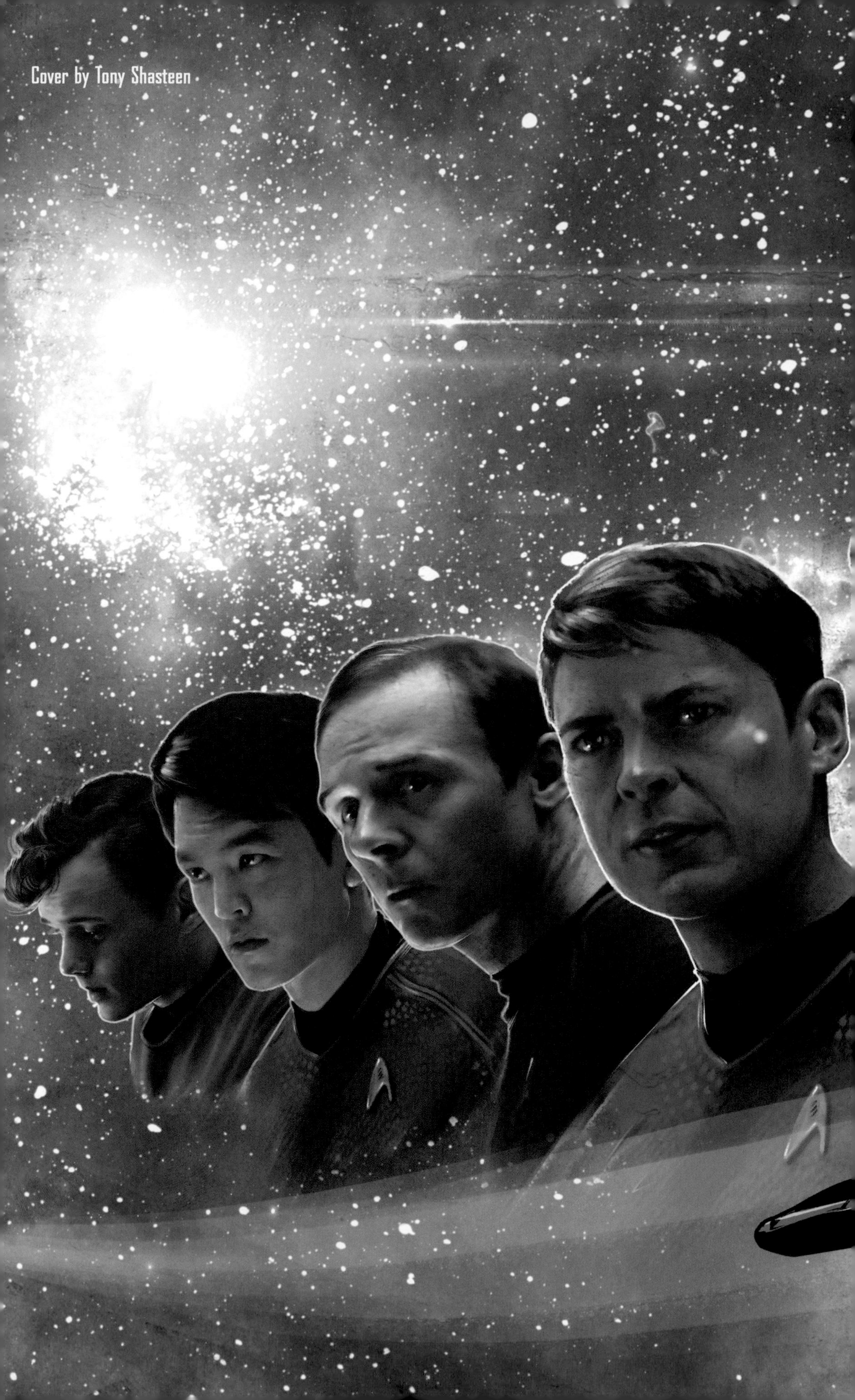

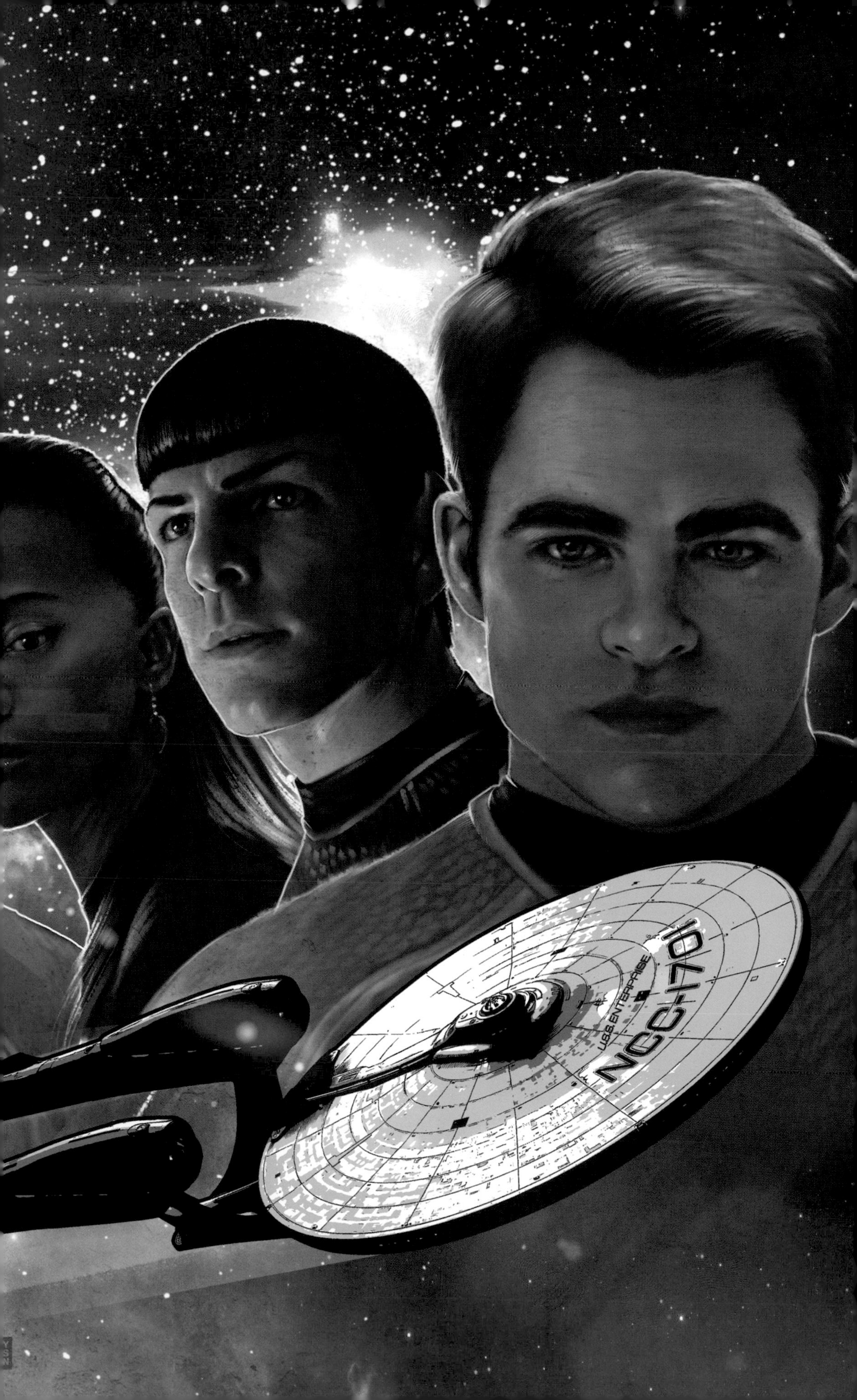
U.S.S. ENTERPRISE
NCC-1701

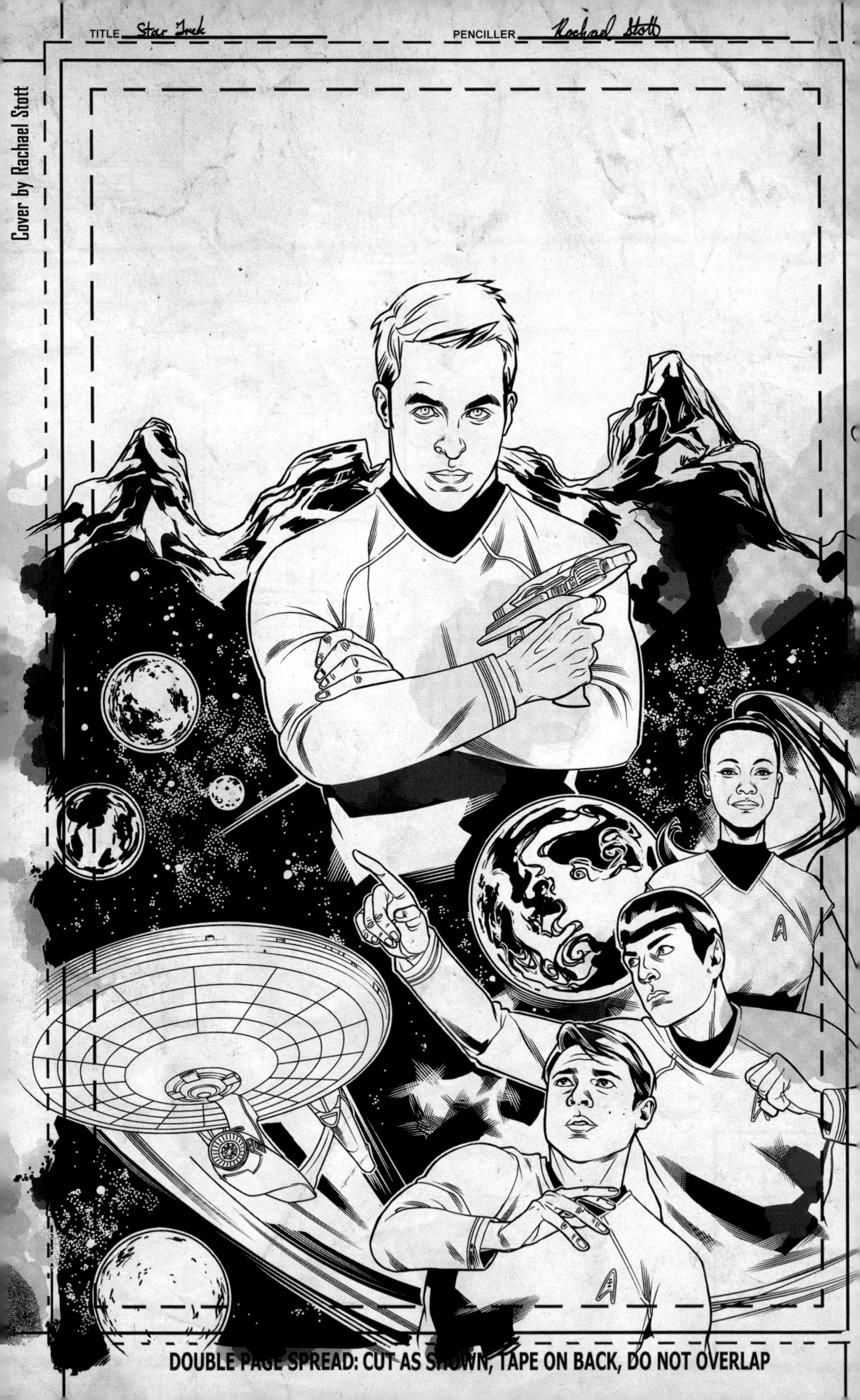
TITLE Star Trek
PENCILLER Rachael Stott
Cover by Rachael Stott
DOUBLE PAGE SPREAD: CUT AS SHOWN, TAPE ON BACK, DO NOT OVERLAP

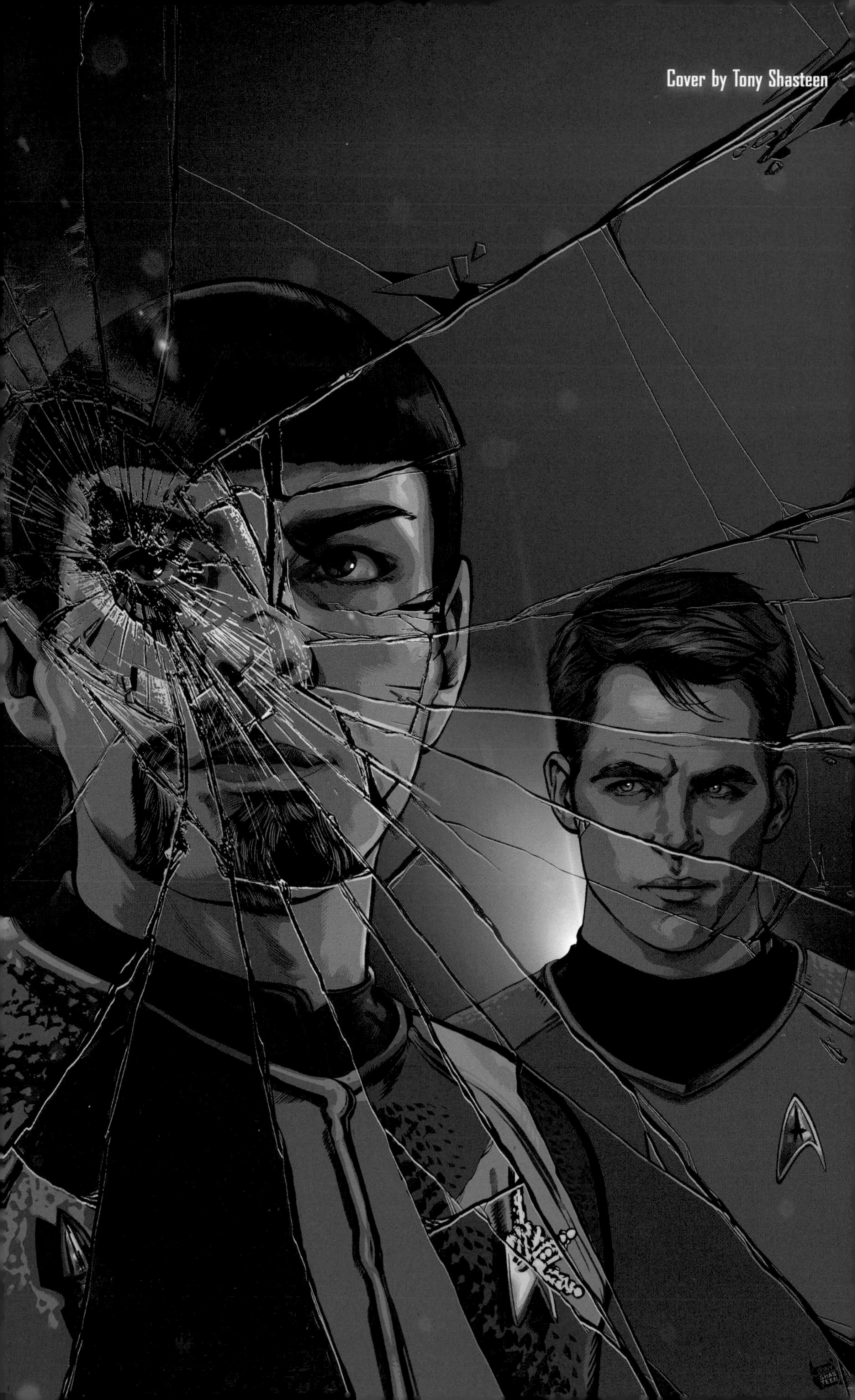

Cover by Tony Shasteen

Cover by Lorelei Bunjes

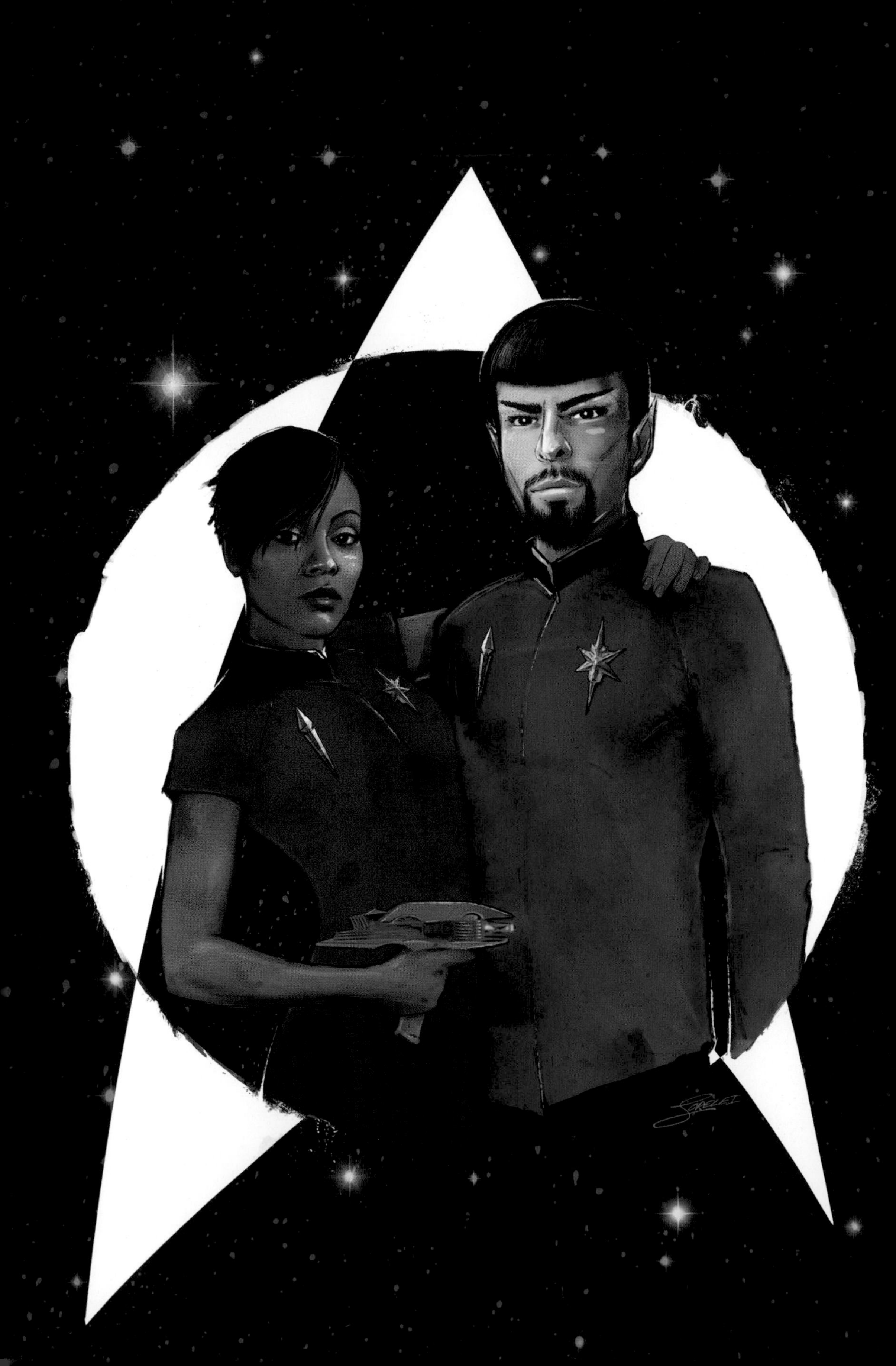

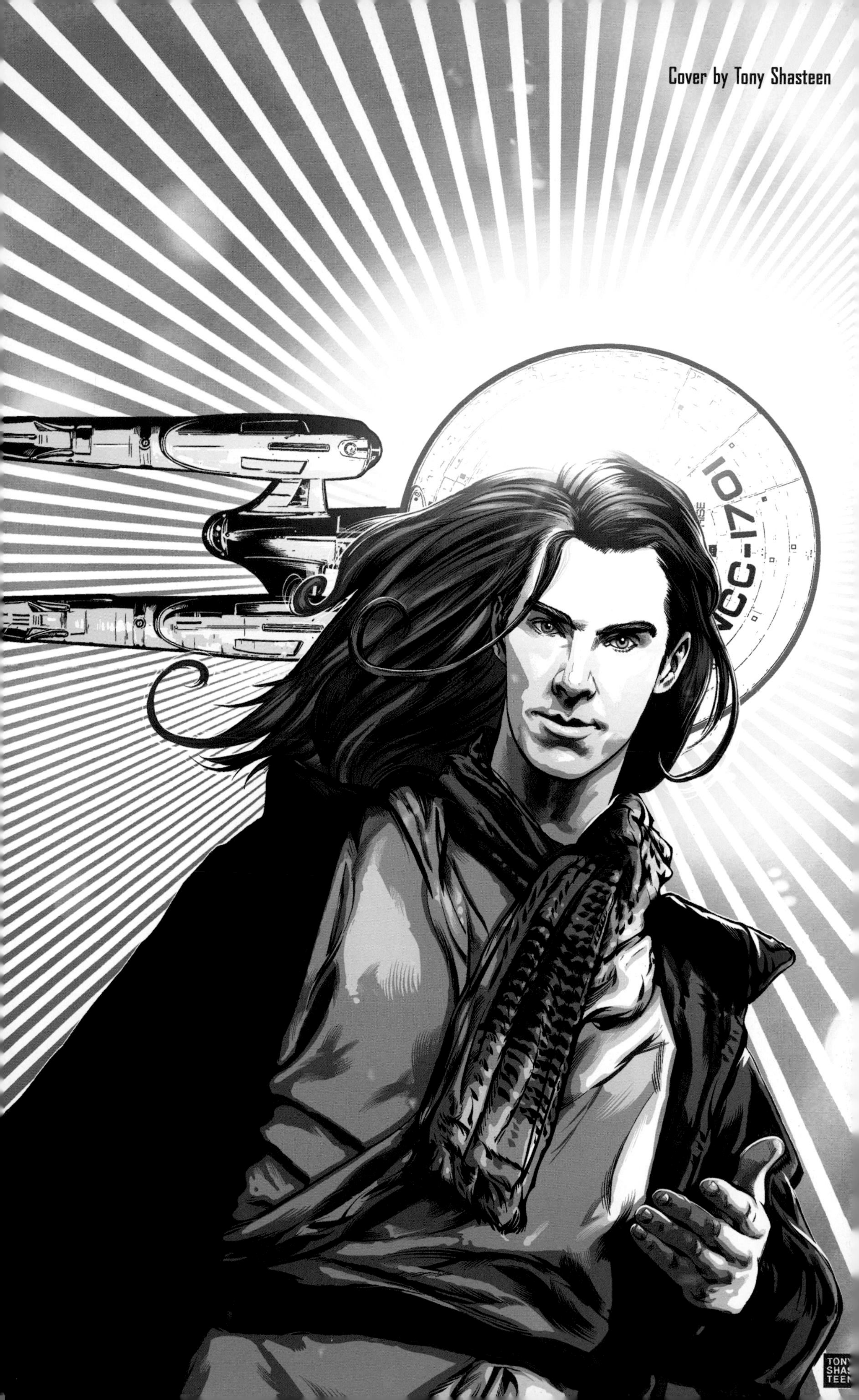
NCC-1701

Cover by Tony Shasteen

Cover by Dan Parent

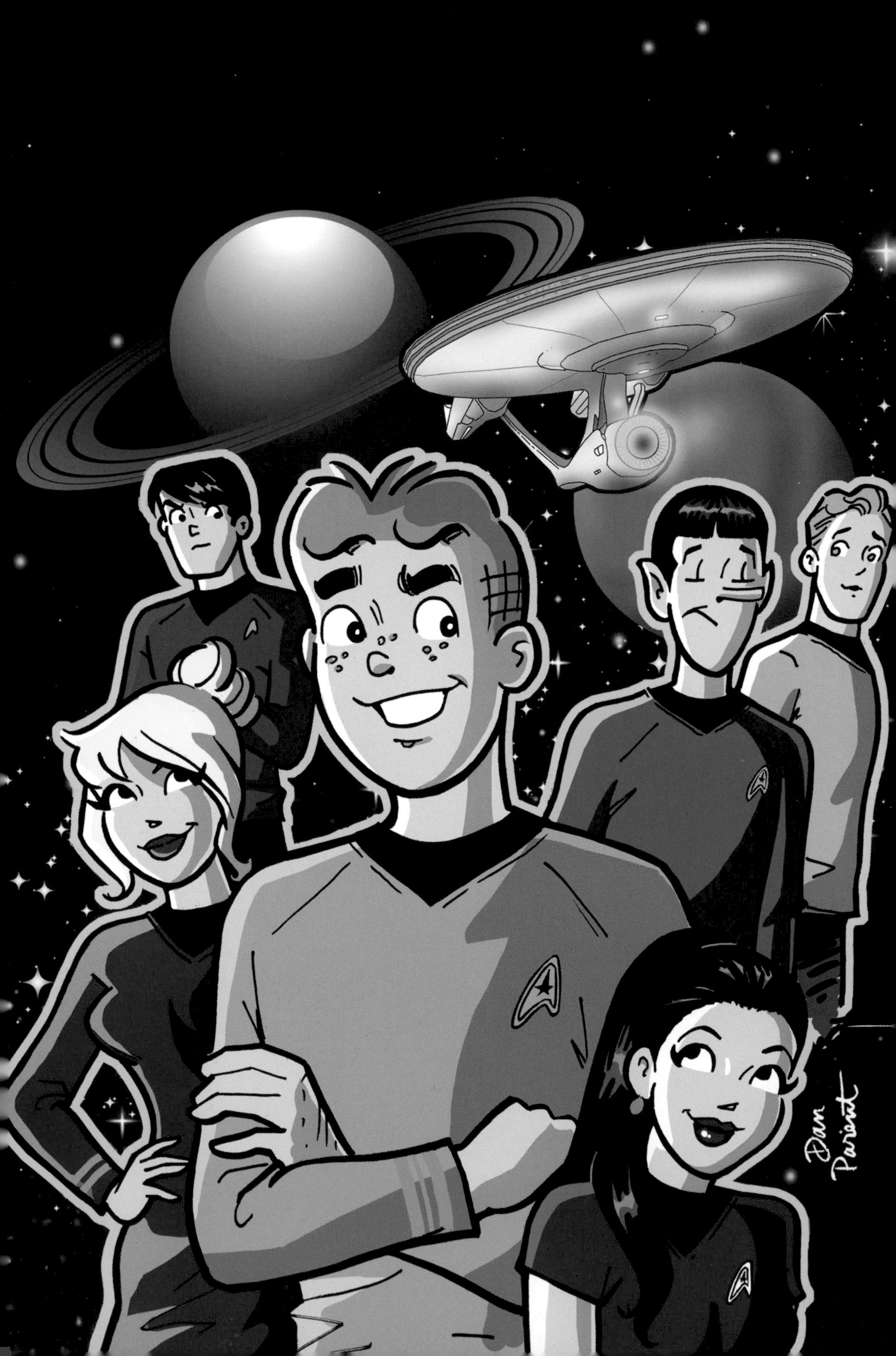
Dan Parent

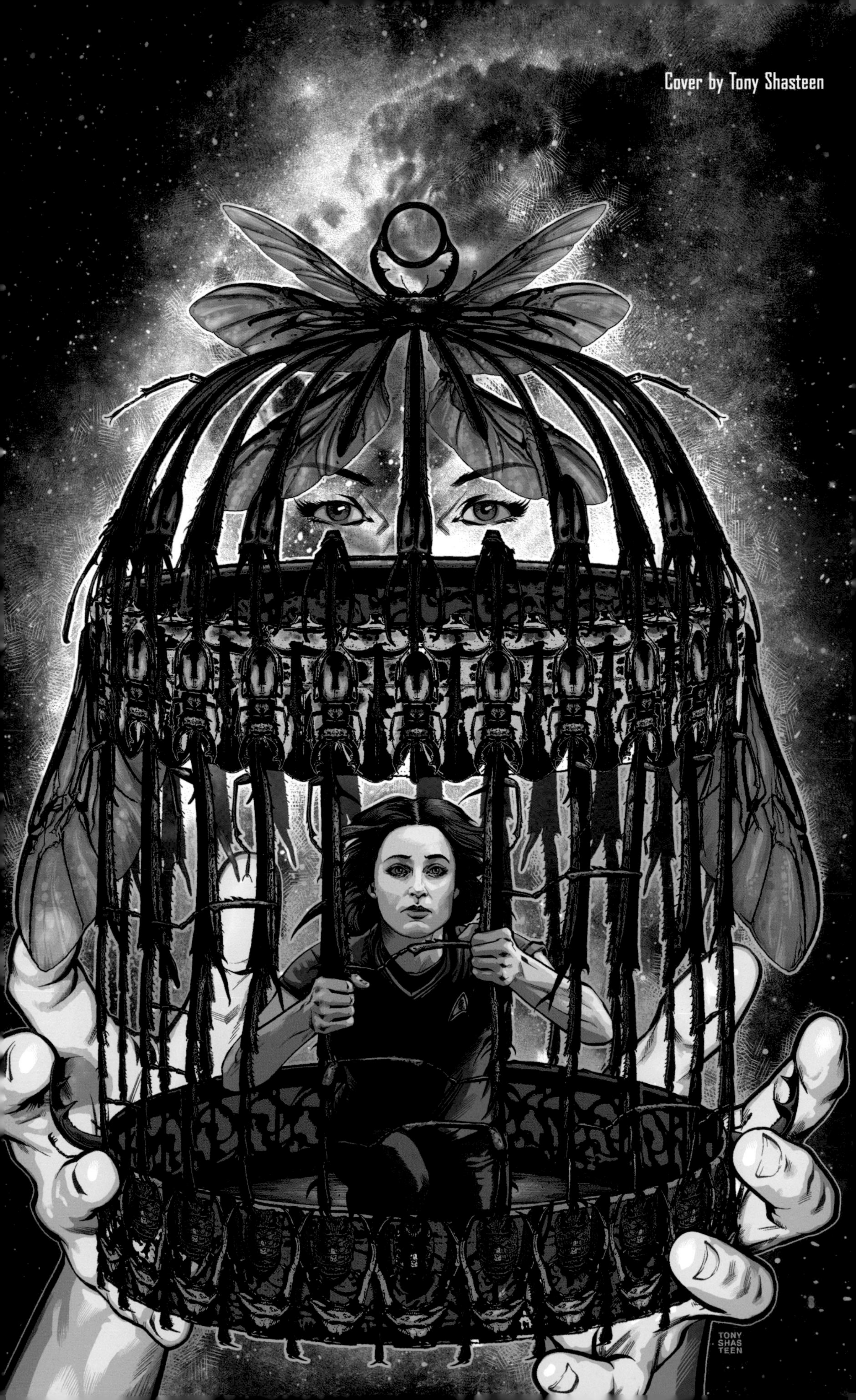
TONY
SHAS
TEEN
Cover by Tony Shasteen

Cover by Derek Charm

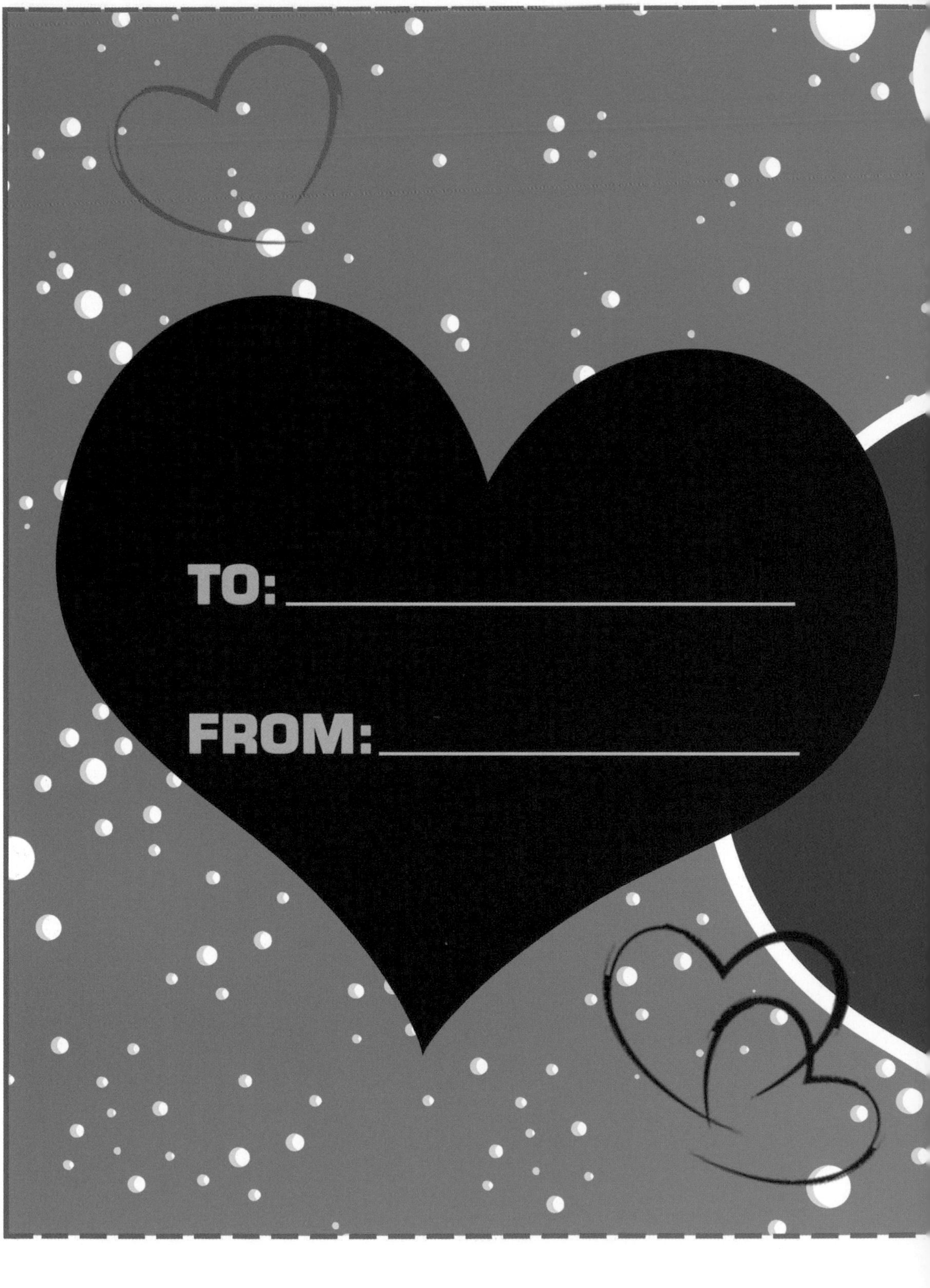
TO:
FROM:

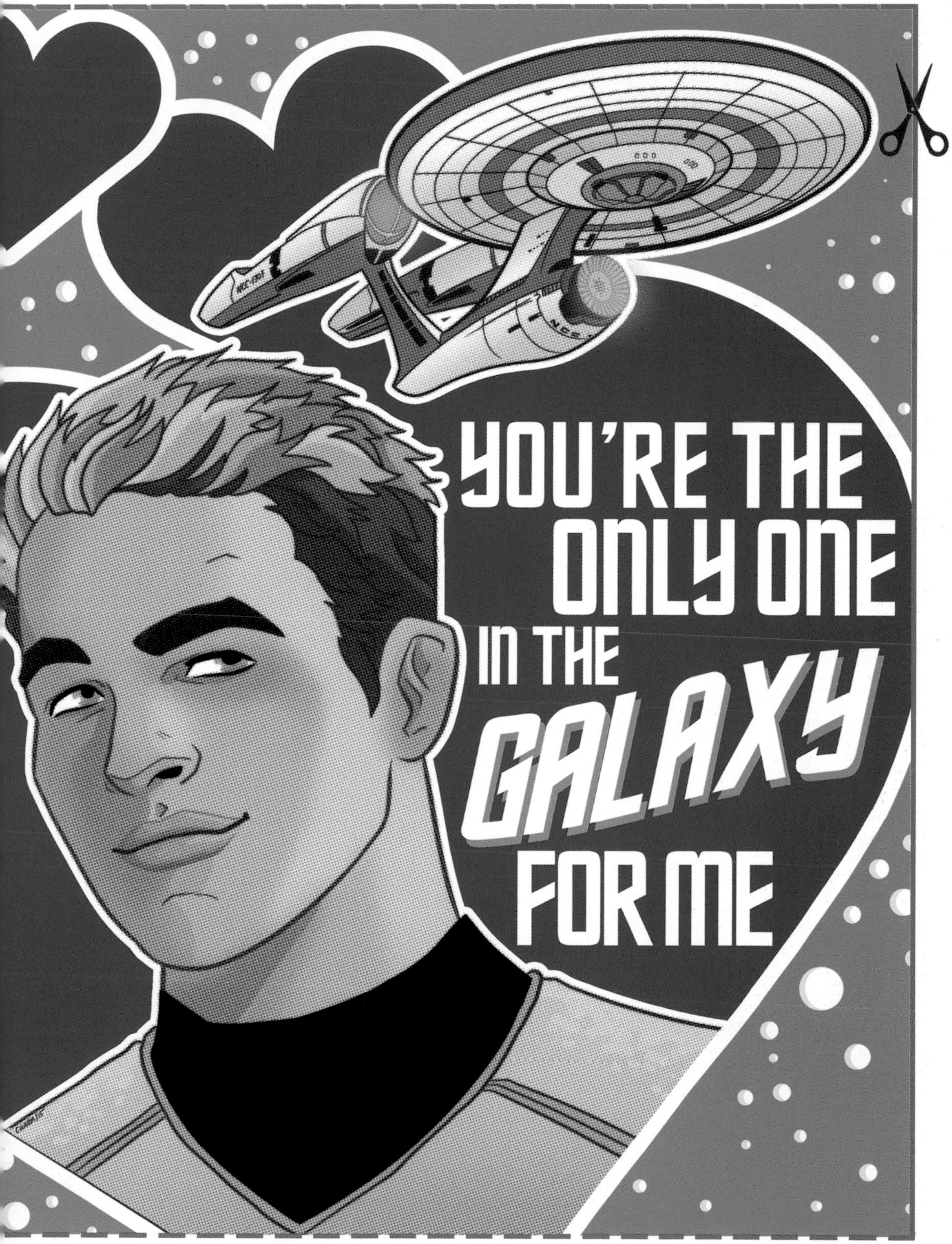
YOU'RE THE
ONLY ONE
IN THE
GALAXY
FOR ME

STAR TREK®

THE MISSION CONTINUES

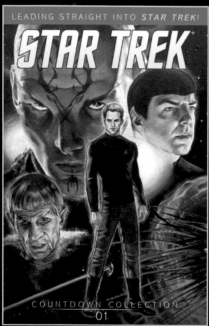

LEADING STRAIGHT INTO STAR TREK!
STAR TREK
COUNTDOWN COLLECTION
01

STAR TREK: COUNTDOWN COLLECTION, VOL. 1
ISBN: 978-1-63140-632-4

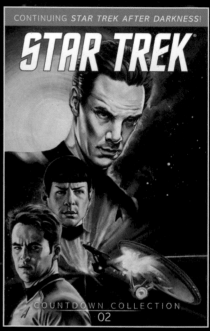

CONTINUING STAR TREK AFTER DARKNESS!
STAR TREK
COUNTDOWN COLLECTION
02

STAR TREK: COUNTDOWN COLLECTION, VOL. 2
ISBN: 978-1-63140-633-1

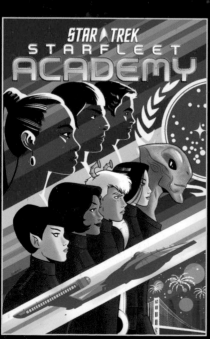

STAR TREK
STARFLEET
ACADEMY

STAR TREK: STARFLEET ACADEMY
ISBN: 978-1-63140-663-8

STAR TREK

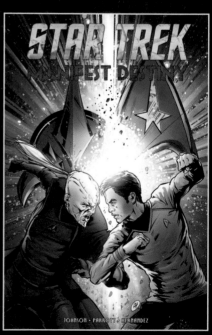

STAR TREK: MANIFEST DESTINY
ISBN: 978-1-63140-634-8